ADVANCE PRAISE FOR ROWENA CHERRY AND *FORCED MATE*!

"A fantastically original page-turner!"
—Susan Grant, *New York Times* bestselling author

Forced Mate is "an intriguing story that has lingered in my memory."
—Kathleen Nance, bestselling author of *Day of Fire*

"Wow! What a book!"
—The Best Reviews

"*Forced Mate* is a terrific science fiction tale."
—Harriet Klausner

"*Forced Mate* absolutely ROCKS!"
—EscapeToRomance

"You will laugh until it hurts."
—The Romance Studio

"This is fantasy on a mega-scale."
—A Romance Review

"*Forced Mate* is one of the best science fiction romances I've read all year."
—romancejunkies.com

"Highly recommended. *Forced Mate* is something any fan of futuristic romance will enjoy."
—MyShelf.com

A BATTLE FOR HER HEART

"She's a fighting Saurian Knight." He put a slight emphasis on "fighting" and smiled self-deprecatingly. "Getting her into bed is more work than turning a Gravity-class war-star."

"Are you telling me that she fought you? You?"

"My Imperial Machismo forbids me to confirm or deny something so damaging to my reputation," Tarrant-Arragon replied with a mocking twist of his lips. "I will admit, she doesn't know what she's up against. I'm conducting an experiment to see whether I can get a virtuous girl to love me—not the next Emperor, but me—for my sweet nature and sense of humor."

His half-sheathed-weapon smile became a sudden chuckle.

"My fierce little Saurian would probably try to castrate me if she knew who I am. She cheerfully toasts my impotence."

Madam Tarra knew the toast to which he referred. "How very provocative of you to choose one of the Saurian Dragon's Knights for your carnal experiments," she replied.

"I didn't take her because she's a Knight." He threw back his head, half closed his eyes, and tapped his upper lip with two fingers. No doubt the wicked boy was deciding how much of the truth to tell her. "Ah...I think I've fallen in love."

FORCED MATE

ROWENA CHERRY

LOVE SPELL NEW YORK CITY

LOVE SPELL®

November 2004

Published by

Dorchester Publishing Co., Inc.
200 Madison Avenue
New York, NY 10016

ISBN 0-505-52601-8

The name "Love Spell" and its logo are trademarks of Dorchester Publishing Co., Inc.

Printed in the United States of America.

Visit us on the web at www.dorchesterpub.com.

ACKNOWLEDGMENTS

I'd like to thank Sensei Sally Eaton and Sensei Lyn Ross, formerly of the Warrior Training Center (Clawson), who choreographed my fight scenes; Dr. James Kryvicky for his advice about violence and the human body, though I took liberties with alien anatomy; the deliberately anonymous Bloomfield Township Police sharpshooter; all the long-distance friends who have encouraged and supported me; and Kyla, my daughter, who for the first seven years of her delightful existence has informed my pregnancy and childhood-backstory scenes.

Thank you all!

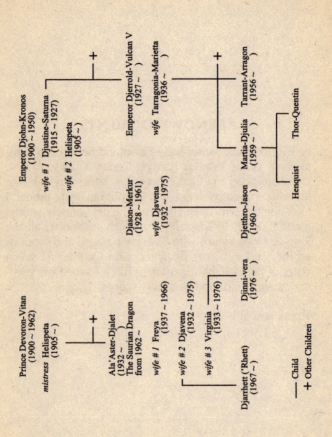

Emperor Djohn-Kronos
(1900 ~ 1950)

wife #1 Djustine-Saturna
(1915 ~ 1927)

wife #2 Helispeta
(1905 ~)

Djason-Merkur
(1928 ~ 1961)

wife Djavena
(1932 ~ 1975)

Emperor Djerrold-Vulcan V
(1927 ~)

wife Tarragonia-Marietta
(1936 ~)

Djetthro-Jason
(1960 ~)

Martia-Djulia
(1959 ~)

Tarrant-Arragon
(1956 ~)

Henquist   Thor-Quentin

Prince Devoron-Vitan
(1900 ~ 1962)

mistress Helispeta
(1905 ~)

Ala'Aster-Djalet
(1932 ~)
The Saurian Dragon
from 1962 ~

wife #1 Freya
(1937 ~ 1966)

wife #2 Djavena
(1932 ~ 1975)

wife #3 Virginia
(1933 ~ 1976)

Djinni-vera
(1976 ~)

Djarrhett ('Rhett)
(1967 ~)

— Child
+ Other Children

FORCED MATE

Prologue

The Cambridge Road, England. Earth date 1994

"The more powerful he is, the more terrible he'll be . . . in bed, and as a husband. Especially if he enjoys his 'god's Right' all over the galaxy. Grandmama, after all the dreadful stories you've told me about the god-Emperors of Tigron—"

"By all the Lechers of Antiquity!" Tarrant-Arragon swore. Impossible that the unseen mate of his dreams had been caught on tape speculating that he was a brute and a bore in bed. Impossible that she could be talking about anyone else.

"My dear, your qualms would be forgivable if you were being forced to marry the wicked Prince Tarrant-Arragon," a regally venomous voice sizzled from his car's speakers.

"Stop the tape," Tarrant-Arragon ordered.

"Sorry about that, Your Highness." The human driver silenced the stereo system, while maintaining the stretch limousine's speed on the deserted, dark motorway. "As we backward Earthlings say, eavesdroppers seldom overhear praise of themselves."

His reluctant mate's opinion of his sexual prowess would be the talk of his Star Forces. As would his reaction. As the next god-Emperor of Tigron, he'd be expected to say something depraved.

"I don't usually take any notice of virginal fears," he drawled for the two Tigrons sharing the car, although he spoke in English. "However, I may improve my chances of a happy mating if I pay attention to hers. I wonder which 'dreadful stories' she's heard."

It was reprehensible of him to encourage lewd speculation, but the more the Tigrons obsessed about his sexual notoriety, the less attention they'd pay to the spy tape, and the older woman's very peculiar turn of phrase.

"Happy mating? Is that important to you, Sir?"

Sarcasm. Tarrant-Arragon raised an eyebrow. Presumably the driver had no idea how dangerous it was to annoy a Great Djinn.

"Mating is. A god-Emperor's heir does not concern himself with his mate's happiness." The girl belonged by "god's Right" and by necessity to the last legitimate Great Djinn. Himself. To admit that he wanted her happy would be out of keeping with his very nasty reputation.

"I suppose that's why we're taking her to a certain romantic hot-spot."

The driver had all but called him a liar to his face. No one had ever dared question his motives or his veracity. This human insolence was . . . fascinating.

"Whatever it takes," Tarrant-Arragon conceded, amused. "I've staked the fate of an Empire on my success with her. As long as she is fertile, I have no objection to making her happy."

"Big of you, Sir. But you're quite right not to want to hear any more. It only gets worse." Tarrant-Arragon saw an assessing flicker of the driver's light blue eyes in the rearview mirror.

What was on the rest of the tape that the driver didn't want him to hear? Protocol be damned, he wanted to know the worst.

"*We* wouldn't miss it for ten worlds' tribute." Tarrant-

Arragon deployed the Royal Pronoun. "Rewind. Play it from where my girl alleges that I'm, ah, terrible in bed."

Machinery whirred. The girl restated her ill-informed fears. Hers was a voice of contradictions, an exotic siren's breath from the lips of a nineteen-year-old, an English upper-class accent with a nervous crack in it when she mentioned "bed," "husband," and "god's Right." She had good reason to be nervous if she publicly attacked his royal sexual prerogatives.

Tarrant-Arragon never discussed his infamous Right to deflower any virgin he wanted—or the fact that he had never exerted it.

He certainly had no intention of explaining himself to a judgmental human who was a very temporary member of the abduction party. No matter what else was on the tape.

As for the Tigrons, if they heard something they shouldn't, they could be managed. The Storm-Master was loyal; the physician understood the dynastic necessity of taking what might be the last fertile Djinn female in existence anywhere.

According to his spies on Earth, this girl was the daughter of a rogue Djinn—reportedly assassinated—and a clairvoyant Englishwoman who had died in childbed. With such a mate, he might not only save the Great Djinn from extinction, but also restore lost psychic power to the Imperial bloodline.

Having spies on Earth was illegal. Crossing the Earth Exclusion Zone to come after her was a violation of Communicating Worlds' treaties. If abducting her meant war, so be it. Psychic or not, if she were truly his half-Djinn second cousin, it was worth any risk to have her. If.

She was almost too perfect. He hadn't crossed galaxies to carry off a feminine impostor, or to saunter into an attractively baited trap set by his great enemy the Saurian Dragon.

The minutiae hadn't seemed important until now.

"One moment, driver. How did we obtain this tape?"

"Sheer luck, Sir. We couldn't get a tap on her phone. Not without the local authorities' help, and they'd take a dim view of our activities if they knew you aliens from outer space existed . . ."

While the driver discoursed in a fragmented and round-about style in keeping with the state of British roads, Tarrant-Arragon turned on the reading lights, picked up a file that he'd tossed onto the seat beside him, and extracted surveillance photographs of his quarry.

This time, he studied them closely. Could one tell from a photograph whether a girl was more or less than she seemed?

In the first, his spies had captured her on film swerving through Cambridge's crenellated cloisters on a man's bicycle, a navy and white striped Homerton College scarf across her face, wearing camouflage fatigues and high heels.

In the next, she fought with a rapier, face mesh-masked, her body padded and buttoned-up, her long, long legs sheathed in skintight, sword-fighting white. Again, she wore heels. Why? Her opponent was light-worlder lean, of similar height. Human.

In the third, she practiced martial arts, her loose white garments fastened with a knotted black belt, a shapely foot—bare for once—nanoseconds from a man's throat. Her hair was tied back but visible. It was red-brown. A full-Djinn would have black or silver hair. But she was half-human.

Alone. Fighting human males for fun. No sign that his enemy's Knights watched over her. These photographs told him nothing except that the girl had an idiosyncratic sense of style and unfeminine tendencies.

"We couldn't break in to plant a bug," the driver was saying. "Her locks are unpickable—"

"I forbade the use of obvious force. I didn't want her fore-warned." Tarrant-Arragon smiled ruefully into the driver's mirror. "But it seems she is expecting me anyway. So?"

"So we got lucky. She gets up to paint in the dead of night. Oil paints stink. I'd say that's why she opens her window. There you go. Two midnights ago, the window is open. Your spy's spying. Her phone rings. It's a transatlantic call from her grandmother. The little miss is painting like a demon is after her—"

One is, Tarrant-Arragon mused.

"So she uses the speakerphone. Bingo! Both are recordable."

"She paints? Do we know what?" Tarrant-Arragon loved detail for its own sake and as a mark of his agents' competence. Now his interest was more than academic.

"Self-portraits in sexy, historical/mythical settings, Sir. We got lucky there, too. She took her artwork to a psychology seminar. Photos in the purple file, on the booze cabinet. Light good enough for you, Sir?"

"My eyes are ten times better in the dark than yours are, human." *To say nothing of my other senses.*

"How very sharklike of you, Sir!"

Ignoring the questionable compliment, Tarrant-Arragon reached forward, took the file, and sat back using the smoke-gray carpeted transmission hump as a footstool. His first impression was of a pale female trying to interest a big male in a game of outdoor chess, despite a gathering storm, and despite the obviously lecherous intentions of her open-robed hero.

Defying the dark forces from behind two ranks of waist-high white chessmen, she stood tall, straight-backed, slender, and full-breasted, with her undjinnlike hair billowing across a high forehead.

What he could see of her face was hauntingly beautiful with large, dark eyes, high, cat-delicate cheekbones, a straight, narrow nose, and a suspicion of a stubborn chin. Hard to believe that this was the girl he'd seen in the black-and-white newspaper photograph that his spies had sent to Tigron.

"*Self*-portraits, you say?"

"Perhaps she isn't photogenic," the driver suggested.

"Perhaps." Feeling perverse and predatory, Tarrant-Arragon examined the self-portrait for further reasons to distrust the girl. A title caught his eye.

Forced Mate? Not a very attractive title, but appropriate under the circumstances. Too slack damned appropriate.

Tarrant-Arragon assumed his Chess Grand Master pose, eyes narrowed, two long fingers tapping his upper lip.

Forced Mate had a chess meaning. Thanks to his chess rival, Jason, he knew that it was the name a human, Pandolfini, had given to the endgame where the board is reduced to the two Kings, each racing to make a pawn his Queen.

A reference to a royal rival? Carnality!

"If you were being forced to marry the wicked *Prince* Tarrant-Arragon.*"* The incongruous emphasis of the taped voice replayed in his mind. Should he read something sinister into the way Grandmama's voice shook with hate when she pronounced his name?

What if the recorded conversation had been about a suitor other than himself? Who the Carnality could the girl have spoken about in such terms if not himself? Impossible that an unknown Djinn prince—and potential usurper—might exist! He was the last of his kind.

Or was he?

Tarrant-Arragon glared jealously at the male in his mate's self-portrait. Face in shadow. Broad shoulders, dark hairy chest. The muscular build of a heavy-worlder, the gravity-defying height of a Prince of Tigron. Robes like those he would have worn if he weren't disguised as a modern English gentleman. Black robes. The black reserved exclusively throughout the Tigron Empire for Tarrant-Arragon.

"Great swirling nebulae, she's 'Seen' me. She *is* psychic!" He traced a finger over the image of the bride he'd come to take by stealth if possible, by force if necessary. "Physically, at least, I appear to be your ideal mate. And—one way or another—you are mine!"

Reflected in dark, bulletproof, tinted windows, Tarrant-Arragon's habitual sneer twisted into his first genuine smile in a long time. He felt ridiculously happy.

"Marry Tarrant-Arragon? Never!" the girl's taped voice declared.

Given that she was psychic, and assuming that she had no idea she was being recorded, her vehemence about not marrying him could perhaps be explained away if she had been humoring her malevolent grandmother, the exiled Empress Helispeta of Tigron.

"My honor as a Saurian Knight would require me to fall on my

sword if the Tiger Prince came courting. . . . As if he would."

No time to savor the irony. The ramifications of her Knighthood should be made clear to the too-talkative driver.

"Driver, she is a Saurian Knight. Do you comprehend what that means?"

"Saurians. The *other* cosmic superpower. Self-appointed intergalactic peacekeepers. Bit of a cross between our UN, our NATO and the Freemasons, Sir. Full of their own virtue, your enemies, and too democratic for their own good."

Although he suspected that the driver had rehearsed this partisan little speech, Tarrant-Arragon was amused.

"Near enough, but not quite what I meant."

"No, Sir. I expect you meant to say that it's not natural for a young lady to be a Knight, Sir."

"Quite so. I find it incredible that the Saurian Knight's leader—the so-called Dragon—would allow a girl to be a member of his inner circle. Not just a girl, but a girl-Djinn. He must know her identity."

Tarrant-Arragon thrust one hand into a special, deep pocket and toyed with the three Rings of Power that identified him as the most feared ruler ever to dominate the Tigron Empire. He considered the matter.

"Of course he does. My great enemy is no fool. We must assume there's a connection. Whether she knows it or not, she may be a 'poisoned pawn.' A chess term. Meaning that my enemy may have deliberately exposed her to me, hoping that I will take her and thereby come to harm.

"You see, driver, the Saurian Knights are sworn to thwart and defy me, or die in the attempt. If she is a Knight, she has taken the same deadly vow.

"Since I mean to mate with her, she is honor-bound to kill herself before I can, ah, touch her, or else she will attempt to kill me . . . if she knows whose bed she's in. Which is why she must not find out who I am."

Part One
Earth

Chapter One

Number 14, Rock Road, Cambridge. March 30, 1994

So you think Tarrant-Arragon is a brute and a bore in bed? Tarrant-Arragon seethed as he watched his quarry emerge from her dark, Victorian redbrick row house. *I'm glad that at least one pleasant surprise awaits you, my erratic little psychic.*

She seemed unaware of her peril. Beyond belief that one so precious should be so unguarded! No weapons. No nervous glances his way before she knelt to unchain a bicycle from the cat-spray bitter hedge that sheltered the cold-loving leafy plants in her front garden.

Now! He advanced. She couldn't escape. One way or another, he had her. He had only to remember the Saurian Knights' archaic code words of greeting, a "secret" toast, and their Freemasonic handshake . . . and she'd come quietly.

" 'Your indulgence,' Djinni-vera." He mispronounced her name as if he didn't know that the *D* in the Dj-prefix was silent in Djinn names. As if he didn't have two royal Djinn names himself. He mind-shielded the thought.

"It's Djinni. J-I-N-N-Y." She misspelled her name without

looking up, still feigning nonchalance. And she was feigning. Standing over her now, he could hear her rapid heartbeat and see her breath erupting in quick white puffs on the cold air.

So she wanted to play cat-and-mouse over her identity, did she? With a Tiger Prince of Tigron? Not by the quiver of a nostril did he let on how much of an advantage his seven highly developed senses gave him in the game.

"Djinni-vera literally means True-Djinn, doesn't it?" he purred at her, all pretended innocence and sheathed claws.

"You know the meaning, but not the pronunciation?"

"If you were an impostor, you might have let it pass. The Saurian Dragon told me all about you, Djinni. I know who and what you are. . . ." He counted her steadying heartbeats as his lie registered. "Did your father take leave of his senses, first impregnating an Earthling, which is illegal, then advertising your identity with a Djinn name? Djinni-vera is a name guaranteed to attract trouble."

"And here you are, I suppose. Trouble personified." Still kneeling, she flashed an impudent smile up at him.

It was his first clear sight of her face. She was far lovelier than her self-portraits, but, unlike the dark-eyed girl in her paintings, she had silver-streaked amethyst eyes. Eyes like a fast-world's dawn. He wanted to catch her mischievous face in his hands and stare.

"You might think so." He smiled back and gestured out of habit, giving her permission to rise.

That she might think of a bicycle chain as a weapon hadn't occurred to him until she put it aside and extended her right hand. Otherwise, she did not move.

The girl was trying a power play! In order to take her hand, he'd have to go down on one knee. He never knelt.

"You have the advantage of me, sir."

"Damned right I do." He knew that she had asked his name in the archaic manner of the Saurians. He deemed it an unnecessary risk to borrow a Saurian Knight's reptilian code name at random. To distract her, he pretended to take her literally. "Because I'm bigger, stronger, and more experienced."

"You mean I'm not qualified to take on our enemy, Tarrant-Arragon?" Her indignant eyes flashed silver and purple daggers.

"Are you? Come questing with me and you may have to, ah, take him on," he teased, unable to resist playing with fire. *If he doesn't take you first.*

Color flooded her face, as if she'd had the same thought.

"You're blushing." His delighted remark seemed to disconcert her even more, so he pressed this new advantage shamelessly. "From the movies we pirate off Earth's satellites, I know of two causes—social embarrassment or sexual arousal. Which is it?"

"Annoyance," she said, and looked away.

Tarrant-Arragon knew evasion when he saw it. Perhaps she did find him sexually interesting? The possibility made him draw in his breath. Chill early-morning air prickled in his nostrils, and a sudden eddy of faint fragrances made him stiffen.

The girls who came to Court didn't blush. Nor did they come so sweetly unperfumed. And when Tigron virgins knelt, it was to kiss his thighs and ring hand in proper, grateful submission. This girl crouched like a small tigress, prepared to slash his legs open.

He fought a strong urge to pounce on her.

Hard-damn, he hadn't expected to react like this. Like a throbbing boy. However, it was possible that he'd come upon her, his first and only female Djinn, at or near her most dangerous—fertile—time. Even if Djinni wasn't Djinn enough to be rut-rageous, she was the only girl he'd ever approached who was by no means a sure thing. He'd every reason to be excited.

Mind-shield! he reminded himself. Far more than the Imperial Machismo was at stake if Djinni read his intentions and took a dislike to them. Which she would if she knew who he was.

"Are you trying to flirt with me, sir?" She glared.

"No," he lied, while mentally undressing her.

Why would she want to cover the supple promise of her back with a dust-drab sleeveless jacket worn over combat fatigues? Only a trained military eye, such as his own, could discern the femininity beneath all that camouflage.

With all the hardware—zippers, snaps, ring-clips—taking her in his arms would be like cuddling a heavy-terrain trooper's knapsack. But he was damned well going to cuddle her as much and as long as he wanted.

"The high heels, are they practical?" Tarrant-Arragon inquired. He was fascinated. He'd never seen such ridiculous heels, or such light-worlder-long legs. Add perfect, high breasts like hers to the equation, and how did she keep her balance?

"No, but I like them. And most of our Cambridge campus wolves only lust after women shorter and sillier than themselves. Do you plan to shake hands, sir?"

He'd been stalling. She wasn't going to let him get away with it. Her hand was still held out—on a level with his aching groin—and he knew that she expected the Saurian Knights' secret handshake. He gave her a crooked smile.

"I've never been comfortable about the handshake." The prisoner who had taught him how to impersonate a Saurian Knight had been terrified. Were his fingers meant to tremble? "There's something unmasculine about males tickling each other's wrists."

"Are you sensitive about your masculinity?"

By the Lechers! The kitten had claws, too. What had he said to give her such a splendid idea? Recalling what he'd heard about her terror of sexually aggressive males, he hesitated, and then remembered something else. Tarrant-Arragon gambled.

"How did you guess? Are you reading my mind?"

"I most certainly am not!" She looked up at his mouth, not into his eyes. "If you knew how disturbing the thoughts of lustful males can be, not that I mean to suggest that you're—oh, dear! Besides, it'd be dishonorable to deliberately read the mind of anyone other than a proven enemy."

Her refusal to meet his eyes confirmed that she'd tried to read his mind. Now she was flustered. Tarrant-Arragon knew why. He excelled at psychological warfare. "Your sense of honor is a grave handicap." *And you are hopelessly outclassed, my dear.*

"My sense of honor defines me as a Saurian Knight."

"I know." Tarrant-Arragon grinned and hoped his expression was beguiling. He ought to have practiced smiling. However, even if he got the handshake wrong, he'd still have a firm grip on her. Squatting in front of her, he took her hand in a double clasp.

A chemical flare rocketed to his loins. Great bursts of sunfire! He wanted to taste her, to wrap his arms around her and thrust his tongue into her mouth. He wanted to have her, right there in her flower bed.

"Sir! You forget yourself," Djinni gasped as his hands seized hers and powerful sexual images filled her mind.

How dare he! He'd made no attempt to think about anything other than sex from the moment he'd swaggered uninvited into her front garden and stood over her. In fact, he showed none of the diplomatic charm and sexual political correctness she'd expect of one of the Saurian Dragon's most trusted Knights.

"I want you," he blurted out in a strangled sort of snarl.

"To . . . ?" Djinni prompted, heart racing. Cool tactics that wilted the ardor of Cambridge's overgrown, ball-playing "Blues" hadn't worked on him. Her only recourse was to call his bluff. She was as good as a nineteen-year-old could be, but her experience in crossing verbal swords was limited, and she'd be a fool to think she was a match for this smoothly dangerous male.

"To—? Ah, 'I want you to welcome me,'" he resumed the time-honored greeting.

He'd said that the Saurian Dragon had told him all about her. He'd used the correct code words. She'd have to give him the benefit of the doubt over the handshake, since she could hardly admit that she hadn't recognized it because she'd been distracted by what was on his mind.

"Welcome me," he repeated. "Remember, you are honor-bound to 'receive me and accommodate my desires.' Must I invoke your vow 'to help a brother Knight in need'? Then I invoke it."

"You're right. I ought to offer you something to drink—"

The third and final proof of his Saurian identity should be the toasts, but she was reluctant to ask him into her house. If he was as deep in her father's confidence as he seemed to be, he might also know her fiancé, J-J. That could be a problem.

J-J was not just a ferociously jealous Great Djinn—always looking for rivals—but also the future god-Emperor of Tigron once Tarrant-Arragon was overthrown.

She shuddered to think of the trouble she'd be in if a friend of J-J's saw her sexy self-portraits and had the bad taste to tease him about them or—worse—her choice of titles.

Forced Mate was the most embarrassing, but *Persephone, Abducted,* and *Igraine and the Incognito King* were pretty bad, too. Each was an attempt to capture her disturbingly erotic nightmares on canvas in order to make sense of them.

She'd always assumed that her dreams were an expression of her fears about her wedding night, but she never could be sure. She hadn't seen J-J since she was five, and, try as she might, she could never recall her dream seducer's face when she woke up.

It might help if she could paint J-J's face on her villains, but she could never remember it. If only she could, she might show J-J her artwork as a tactful way to warn him that she was afraid of sex. Except there was nothing tactful about the title of *Forced Mate*.

Not only was it an unflattering reference to their arranged marriage, but it was disloyal, and J-J would know it.

On the other hand . . . Djinni glanced at the big Knight who crouched in her garden, intent on her and unconcerned that his unbelted and unbuttoned black Burberry trailed in the dirt, or that his bold tie dangled outside his three-piece suit and hung low between his powerfully muscled, bent legs.

What if her bad-dream lover wasn't meant to be J-J? What if her nightmares were psychic warnings about someone else?

"Well?" The black-business-suited stranger spoke with the impatience of someone accustomed to instant obedience.

"Sorry. I was wondering what to do about the usual toasts. Would you mind using tea?" Djinni played for time, wondering where she could take him at seven in the morning. The college canteen was a possibility. Public, too. "I don't have—"

"I've wine in the car."

"What luck," Djinni quipped, unwilling to give him credit for planning ahead. She shouldered her holdall bag. At once, he cupped his right hand under her elbow, ostensibly to help her up.

Having straightened to her full six-foot height, Djinni noted that he was a good foot taller. And big, much too big for her to take on. His size didn't bother her, since she had no intention of getting into a physical confrontation with him.

"Not luck, little one. Destiny," he retorted, opening the wrought-iron garden gate and steering her through.

"How strange that you should say that." She hesitated. Most men scoffed at fortune-telling. "You see, last night I asked my runes a question—about ethics—but drew the Rune of Destiny. It didn't make sense, although runes may address a wish that's on a questioner's mind rather than the question she asks."

"And what is your secret wish?" His deep voice deepened.

"To prove myself worthy of my Saurian Knighthood, preferably by bringing Tarrant-Arragon to his knees. Perhaps it's my destiny to do just that."

"Perhaps," he agreed with an enigmatic smile and bent to open the near-side passenger door.

Djinni grinned back, struck by the best reason so far to ignore the warning prickles in her wrists, apart, of course, from her natural obedience to her father, the Dragon.

J-J assumed that he was the Royal Saurian Djinn of prophecy, who'd bring an end to Tarrant-Arragon's tyranny. But suppose she beat J-J to it?

If her father had given her this chance to earn credibility as a Knight in her own right, perhaps—if she succeeded—he'd let her renegotiate her old betrothal contract and marry J-J on her own terms.

She tossed her bag onto the thick, gray carpet, turned, and slid onto the back seat with the dignity of a supermodel, leaving her feet on the pavement.

"Skittish, my dear?" The Knight's drawl was distracting, like

the yawn of a bad big cat. Something belied the bored aristocratic roll of his Rs, but she couldn't put her finger on it. "If
the Dragon hadn't been so insistent, I wouldn't dream of taking a girl on a quest of this importance," he said, eyeing her
exposed ankles with apparent interest. "I don't mix girls and
business. Girls never take vows seriously."

"You're wrong about me!" Embarrassed by his scrutiny,
Djinni tucked her legs as far away from him as possible. "I may
not have the raw strength and ferocity of a male Knight, but I
am the equal of any warrior-diplomat in resourcefulness and
integrity."

"Oh, I hope not," he murmured. The car dipped under his
weight as he swung himself in after her with feline grace,
slammed his door, and sprawled beside her, thighs splayed, fabric stretched taut. His leg nudged hers.

There could be no innocent interpretation of his words.

Something wasn't right. Djinni scanned the car interior and
noticed the raised, black glass divider. Presumably, a visitor
from another world wasn't driving himself around on English
roads. He must have a chauffeur. Why wasn't the driver earn-
ing his hire, leaping out to open doors, and so on?

"Perhaps I should pack a bag. I'll just run back inside—"
She fumbled for the other door handle.

"We can't jump into Hyperspace for four more Earth rota-
tions. You'll have time to pack. After you've proved who you
are. After the toasts."

He lunged forward to the built-in, burled walnut cabinet
from which he took a decanter and two cut-glass tumblers,
splashed a generous measure into each, and pressed one into
her hand.

"Here's to the Saurian Dragon." He raised his glass and
watched her over its rim. He'd passed the third and final test.

"The Saurian Dragon!" Djinni responded, and took a sip.
The wine tasted sweet and mellow. It made her feel invincible.
Or perhaps it was the invocation of her formidable father, whose
protection extended across galaxies and even into this car.

Her father, the Dragon, deserved proper respect from her, so she took a second mouthful and saluted her drinking companion.

If eyes could smile, her brother Knight's did. Like the glint of sun bursting through purplish-gray storm clouds, his gorgeous, tarnished silver eyes dazzled her.

"Your turn to prove who you are," he prompted in his molasses voice, all erotic menace. "The countertoast should be . . . ?"

"Death to the evil Emperor, and impotence to his wicked son!" she rattled off in a daring rush.

"My dear, we should drain our glasses and perhaps smash them, don't you agree? Nothing else would do that most interesting toast justice, now, would it?" His eyes sparkled with amusement.

He was right again. It was an all-or-nothing toast, not for the dainty or weak-headed. So, although she wasn't used to wine, she tilted back her head.

As the last of the wine blazed down her throat, her head began to spin. In a burst of clarity she knew what had happened. She also knew that it was too late to do anything about it.

There had been a drug in the wine. Now that she thought about it, she hadn't seen him drink—at least, not to Tarrant-Arragon's erectile dysfunction. She'd been right to mistrust him. Oh, why had she flinched from reading his mind? Because he'd had vigorous sex on it!

Her head cartwheeled. Firecracker thoughts exploded and scattered. Why a sleeping drug? A truth drug would make more sense if he meant to use her to get at her father. Or J-J. But he couldn't know about J-J. Outside family, no one knew. . . .

Reality, like her glass, seemed to float out of her grasp, and a strong arm cradled her against an unyielding chest. Her recurrent nightmare world swirled like a dark snowstorm in her head and the rational part of her mind could not decide whether any of this was happening, or whether it was a dream within a dream . . . part of her last bad dream.

"No! No! You promised my safety," she protested as she did every night in sleep talk.

"You're safe with me," her abductor breathed into her hair. His voice was deeper than in her dreams, and he was gentle with her. He slid a band of something heavy, jointed, and as soft as gold-leaf around her throat and stroked it under her neckline with a touch that was firm, and sure, and sensually thrilling.

Perhaps she trembled, or tried to push him away. Perhaps he kissed her hand.

For some reason, her wrist lay on his chest. Under her help-less hand, she felt the slow, steady throb of his heart and sensed that she was indeed safe, though it was illogical to feel safe with him—even for a moment. . . .

Tarrant-Arragon cradled his precious prisoner as she slipped further into unconsciousness. He saw no reason why he shouldn't, so he pressed kisses onto the top of her head and whispered, "Checkmate, my dear! *Now* I truly have the advan-tage of you."

In response, she uttered a dreaming mew and nuzzled her nose between his shirt buttons. Her small fist clutched his tie.

He felt an irrational urge to exult, to indulge in small-scale triumph. He lowered the dark-glass privacy barrier.

"Look at this. Now I know why Englishmen choke them-selves with strips of silk when they want to hunt down a mate."

The two Tigrons twisted and looked. The human conspicu-ously concentrated on driving.

"Is the tie a mating display, my Lord?" the warrior-gynecologist asked. "Would you say the ends form blunt points in order to direct female attention downwards?"

At the wheel, the Earthling snorted.

"She never showed even the mildest interest in my person." Tarrant-Arragon raised one eyebrow. "Anyway, the tie is floppy. That's not what I'd call suggestive. No, I think it's crafty reverse psychology. The tie suggests a guidance leash."

He tossed his head gently, enough to make a point, but not to disturb the sleeping girl. "She thinks she's got me like a noosed stud beast. Behold the rampant bridegroom! Eager to be tamed."

A wildly improbable notion. The Tigrons laughed, and his naive young conquest stirred. Tarrant-Arragon held his breath, but she didn't awaken. In her dream-state, his delightful little mate-to-be twisted his tie around her hand as if she held the reins of a fiery bull Hunnox and she intended to control him.

The Emperor's wicked son was enchanted.

Chapter Two

From the moment Gregory Bodley Harmon, aka Grievous, saw the UFOs land on Salisbury Ridge he knew that he'd got himself into some seriously nasty business.

He'd thought himself too smart, too upper crust, to drive London taxis as other mercenaries did. He'd assumed that the college porter who'd placed the advertisement in both mercenaries' magazines was the sort of racist who calls all foreigners "aliens." Trouble was, the "aliens" really were aliens!

Now his life was very probably on the line.

He shifted gears to overtake a lorry on the A 505, and his leather-patched elbow brushed against the mean-looking warrior wedged in the front seat between himself and the doctor. The nasty customer kept his shark eyes fixed forward and said nothing. Grievous recognized the ominous signs.

What's more, their Prince Tarrant-Arragon frightened the living tar out of him. The devil only knew what His Alien High-and-Mightiness would do to the girl. Apart from the obvious.

"If she is an impostor, we'll abandon her at the Gog Magog golf links," the prince had said as they sped up to Cambridge.

Grievous had been cheered by Tarrant-Arragon's humanity until he heard the chilling rationale: "It'd be embarrassing to provoke interstellar war over an unremarkable Earthling."

War and embarrassment notwithstanding, Tarrant-Arragon's attitude had changed during the drive to the Gog Magog Hills.

According to the plans, the prince had brought along his Empire's best warrior-gynecologist—a contradiction in terms if ever Grievous had heard one—to examine the girl and determine her genetic and sexual status.

Inexplicably, by the time they drew to a gravel-spraying halt in the visitors' car park, the boss alien had turned dog-in-the-mangerish. He refused to let the doc touch her except to draw blood, and snarled that the penalty for touching an Imperial Djinn's mate was death.

To Grievous's surprise, the doctor had protested, "My Lord, she may not pass the Imperial bride's virginity test."

"She won't," Tarrant-Arragon retorted, "by the time I get her to Tigron."

"But, my Lord, the blood tests only—"

"They show that she has Djinn DNA, she's free of diseases and not pregnant. Anything else is my business. I'll examine her. At the safe house. On the Imperial wedding sheets."

Poor little miss! For her, it wasn't likely to be what Shakespeare would call a "consummation devoutly to be wished."

And therein lay another rub. Grievous hadn't reckoned on feeling a powerful sympathy for the girl. He wasn't a sentimental man. Far from it.

From the no-nonsense buzz cut of his worn-down, bristle-doormat hair to the steel tips of his bovver boots, he was one rugged son-of-a-bitch. He'd been up to his cleft chin in trouble all the four decades of his life, and there was probably no way on this Earth he was ever going to make good.

Expelled from Eton, dishonorably discharged from the Special Air Services, his officer's sword broken and his pips torn off, convicted of Grievous Bodily Harm, Gregory Bodley Harmon called himself Grievous because his initials matched his crime.

Even tough nuts need money. He couldn't afford to be squeamish about what he did, or for whom he did it. Which was why, at his second interview for the job of driver and tour guide, he'd shrugged and acted as if it were an everyday occurrence for alien war-lords to seek his assistance in abducting young misses.

But he didn't like it.

"Slack damn, it was a mild sedative! It should have worn off by now," the prince said, suddenly breaking the awkward silence that had reigned since the U-turn at Gog Magog.

Grievous smiled at the sounds of rummaging, the castanet clicking of what was probably the girl's makeup as the alien searched her bag. Then His Highness passed something forward to the doctor.

"What do you make of this, Ka'Nych?"

Carnage? Grievous thought. Now, there's a name to inspire confidence in your doctor. Carnage!

Ka'Nych sniffed, then tasted the leaf.

"My Lord, it's possible she uses leaves such as this when she is ill. Earth medicines may not suit her unique system."

"Are you going through her bag, Sir?" Grievous had long since decided to seize every opportunity to impress these aliens with the intelligence and friendliness of your above-average human being. "Mind you put it all back, then, Sir. Ladies get touchy about that sort of thing."

"Do they? Well, I should very much like her to get touchy with me. My poking around in her bag is hardly going to be her most pressing problem, is it?"

"Unbelievable!" someone said, sounding as close to her, and as far away, as an explosion in fog.

Reality was returning . . . and fading.

Djinni guessed that her Djinn immune system was fighting a seesaw battle with the drugged wine. Her head hurt. She needed a feverfew leaf from her bag. Where was it? Where was she?

Eyes closed, Djinni focused her other senses. She was lying

on her side on a hard surface; she could hear the brake-drum roll of wheels, the hum of tires. She was on the car floor.

So was he.

"What've you found, sir?" This was a clipped, military-educated English voice, with a faint Dorset burr. "The proverbial mouse? My great-grandmother used to threaten me with a snappish little rodent that might nip my boyish fingers if I stuck them in her handbag, sir."

"No, Grievous. I've merely discovered her taste in reading matter." Pages riffled. A very male chuckle. "She shall have stacks of the stuff if it makes her fertile and happy."

Fertile and happy? Stars! Next the oversexed oaf would suggest that infertility clinics should invest in Fabio-wallpaper. Djinni would have gritted her teeth, except that he might hear—or feel—her. All she could safely do was count imaginary stars until she felt calmer.

"What's this?" Apparently, the false Knight had lost interest in her romance novels.

"Tights, sir. Also known as panty hose. They're covering for the legs and nether regions. Ladies wear them for color, but they're surprisingly warm which isn't an advantage if one has them on one's head in order to commit a bank robbery."

"Xirxex, take note." Djinni noted the new name. That made at least two enemies in the chauffeur's compartment. "We'll need some black ones. Grievous, are these things durable?"

"It all depends how often you take them off, Sir. And how carefully. They tear very easily."

"Then we will get eighty." Her abductor chuckled. "I don't suppose I'll invariably destroy her underwear when I want to make love."

Djinni forced herself to breathe softly until he resumed his search of her bag.

So he wanted to make tights-ripping "love," did he? And presumably, he wanted her conscious and fighting. Therefore, the longer she seemed to sleep, the better for her.

Her karate sensei hadn't taught her what to do when trapped

in a confined space with a sprawling great oversexed boor. No doubt Sensei Scott would say that no fate is worse than death, so she should submit and survive.

Except, "submit" and "survive" might be mutually exclusive.

"My dear, you are subject to a one-sided chastity clause. Although I do not say that Prince Djetthro-Jason would resort to Tarrant-Arragonian unpleasantnesses, violent passions run in the bloodline," Grandmama had warned all too often. "Never forget what Tarrant-Arragon did when he learned that his first fiancée had cheated him of her virginity."

Djinni suppressed a shudder. Grandmama Helispeta might protest that J-J was not Tarrant-Arragon, but the more she said, the more she gave the impression that the late Emperor Djohn-Kronos's grandsons were very much alike.

"Males of the Imperial family have ungovernable tempers," she'd go on, as if unaware that she'd said enough to frighten a girl off sex for life. "At their best, they are overbearing, ferociously possessive and jealous. Their nature does not improve when they are determined to mate. I need not remind you how Djohn-Kronos served me. Nor of how savagely Djerrold Vulcan used Tarragonia-Marietta. Do not disappoint Prince Djetthro-Jason in any way. Especially in bed."

Grandmama was always hinting at dire consequences if Djinni didn't save her innocence for J-J. But what if she couldn't?

Her captor was distracted and thought she was asleep. It might be the ideal time to read his mind, if only he'd think something useful. . . . Unfortunately, he seemed to be enjoying some very depraved and inappropriate thoughts about her.

Djinni told herself that, owing to the drugs and—of course—the personal stress she was under, her telepathic impressions might be unreliable, but she couldn't talk herself out of the blush that crept warmly over her chest.

Perhaps mind-spying wasn't such a good idea.

Instead, she should concentrate on a Tibetan meditation technique that would slow all bodily functions and make it possible to play dead-to-the-world for hours on end . . . until she got a chance to escape.

"By Jove, he's horny!" Grievous thought aloud, without reflecting that he might give offense.

"What is the meaning of 'horny,' Earthling?" the one called Xirxex rasped. It was the first time he'd spoken.

"Outstandingly and aggressively sexual," Grievous ad-libbed.

"Aye? Horny. Good word, Earthling. Horny, horny, horny."

"Be glad he is pleased with her," the doctor known as Ka'Nych said. "It may explain his uncharacteristic friendliness, and also his desire to make the most of his short visit to your planet once he's taken her to the Cerne Giant."

Grievous nodded. He'd been briefed on the provisional itinerary, and had mugged up on the hundred-and-eighty-foot hill-figure dug into the white chalk of a Dorset hillside.

"Aye, Earthling. Tarrant-Arragon has hunted for his desired mate almost a third of his sexually active life. While he's here, it'd be slack-logic not to let the Giant's influence work on her."

Surprise, surprise! Xirxex could be quite chatty.

"Though he needs no help. Tarrant-Arragon is considered the ultimate authority on debauching nervous maidens. Heh, heh! I don't blame him for izzing horny."

"Being horny," Grievous corrected automatically. "Look here, may I call you Xirxex? If he's so popular with all the young ladies back home, why does he have to come to Earth and pinch one of ours?" Grievous thought he'd managed to combine appropriate macho indignation with an escalation of friendliness.

"That's the point, Earthling. She isn't one of yours. She's his! Of course, all virgins are his if he wants them." Xirxex sniggered.

Ka'Nych explained. "She is only half Earthling, as you heard on the spy tape. Djinni-vera is descended from the fugitive Empress Helispeta and the Prince Devoron-Vitan. Well, it must be the same with your royal families. The first duty of the heir apparent is to secure the succession."

"Aye. Ever since the broken-betrothal scandal, more than four conscription cycles ago, the High Command has urged Tarrant-Arragon to take a mate and sire lawful heirs." As he spoke, Xirxex reached forward and ran his fingers suggestively along the dash-mounted cassette slot.

"Hey, mind that," Grievous warned, speeding up a little for emphasis. "He's expecting her to wake up anytime now. Right? We don't want to wreck his good mood by accidentally playing that bloody tape for her to hear, do we?"

Xirxex shot him a dirty look, then continued. "Aye, the carnal comings and goings of our Emperor's horny son have fascinated the Star Forces, our allies, and our enemies, not to mention every virgin in the Empire. They all want to be his Empress in spite of his terrible reputation."

"But Tarrant-Arragon wouldn't settle for a willing subject. He decided he had to find a breeding mate of his own bloodline," Ka'Nych interjected, "It is her pedigree he's after. The fact that she has been hiding from him adds a certain, ummm—"

"Loin-buzz!"

Grievous noticed the doc's shocked expression and guessed that Xirxex had supplied a more graphic word than Ka'Nych sought.

"Thus, Earthling, the trouble-taking. Normally, our prince doesn't exert himself to get what he wants: not at the negotiating table, certainly not in the bedroom. The twitch of a Ring finger or the lifting of an eyebrow is threat enough. Heh. Heh."

"Occasionally," Ka'Nych said, "out of princely courtesy, he will ask for what he wants. There's never any doubt about the outcome. He never negotiates, except from a position of strength. He never requests, unless he has the power to take. Now he's in the characteristic courting mode of his kind. Tarrant-Arragon will win his mate by stealth if possible, by force if necessary."

"By stealth?" Grievous echoed. Having seen and heard a great deal more of the feminist little miss than was in the photos and on the spy tape, Grievous's private opinion was that His High-and-Mightiness was more likely to get his royal arse kicked than he was to "win" by "stealth." Force would be the order of the day.

"By stealth, eh? I'd like to see that!"

Tigron Imperial Space: The Trojan Horse

"Tarrant-Arragon suggests I wed and thoroughly—he underscores 'thoroughly'—bed her," Commander Jason confided when he and Horn't were alone on the secret stairs.

Jason couldn't contain his high spirits, not because he felt flattered by Tarrant-Arragon's friendly advice, but because of an irony he could not share, not even with Horn't, his trusted lieutenant and brother undercover Saurian Knight.

"Not necessarily in that order, since my long-standing betrothal contract and my newly approved wedding permit give me full legal rights to her before the marriage takes place." Jason paused to open the hidden door to his state-suite and ushered his friend through a wardrobe's worth of action-stud flight suits. "He advises me to perform all the 'dirty deeds' in my 'limited repertoire' before I flaunt her under his Imperial nose."

Jason flung himself onto his stomach on his sleeping couch and reached for the very personal letter that Tarrant-Arragon had enclosed with the signed wedding permit.

Flaunt her under Tarrant-Arragon's nose? He'd do no such thing. He'd kept Tarrant-Arragon off her scent, metaphorically speaking, for thirteen Earth-years. And literally? It thrilled him to imagine the sexually inflammatory effect his bride would have on Djinn nostrils. On Djinn male saturniid glands.

"The nasty bastard isn't referring to his 'god's Right,' is he?" Horn't hissed in sympathetic indignation. He made a beeline for Jason's well-stocked bar.

"By sinister innuendo, he probably is. Not that I've ever heard of Tarrant-Arragon exercising his Right with an unwilling subject. He'd better not start. Not with my girl."

Frowning, Jason skimmed through Tarrant-Arragon's letter. On second reading, it didn't seem at all funny.

Horn't passed Jason a goblet of fermented Tigron cactus brew. "Aren't you going to read his letter aloud?"

Jason heard the disappointment in Horn't's voice. He scanned the handwritten page, from the snarling tigerskull of the Imperial seal to the bold signature, looking for something he could share without being disloyal to his betrothed bride.

"On second thoughts, no. On the surface, Tarrant-Arragon's ideas on the proper management of virgins aren't so different from the stag night teasing all bridegrooms get. But she'd be distressed if she caught us thinking about this. I won't tolerate any disrespect. I wouldn't even if she weren't telepathic."

Jason tugged a locket on a chain from his neckline, prized it open, and stared at a portrait of Djinni, angelic at five years old, with her reddish baby-blond curls, and hero-worship in her passion-meter violet eyes.

"Jason? Is that her? May I see?"

Jason closed his fist possessively. He couldn't help it. "No! No one sees. No one touches. She's mine."

Horn't's chameleon eyes swiveled in alarm. He held his six palms and the soles of both feet out vertically in front of him in an exaggerated version of the universal "Fend Off" gesture. Since Horn't looked like a cross between a body-armored Buddha and a flightless insect, the effect was highly comical.

"Oh, Horn't! I didn't mean to dismay you," Jason said between laughter and remorse. He'd never grown used to inadvertently frightening his friends. His stronger emotions viscerally affected them, yet no one suspected that he was a Great Djinn.

Admittedly, he minimized his physical resemblance to Tarrant-Arragon by wearing contact lenses, growing his hair to shoulder-blade length, dying it blond, and shaving his chest.

Jason fingered the genuine scar that slashed from the high

bridge of his nose to the angle of his jaw. It dominated people's impressions of his face. Nevertheless, he counted himself lucky that Tarrant-Arragon had first seen him when the scar was fresh and at its most dramatic.

"Tarrant-Arragon kept asking to see a picture of my childhood sweetheart. I lied. Said I didn't have one," Jason went on, subtly rerouting the subject. "He'd choose the most damnable moments to ask about her, like at a crucial stage in a chess match."

"He meant to distract you, hmmm? The unprincipled cheat!"

"He succeeded. While I worried about my girl, he'd use one of my moves against me and set up a Forced Mate."

"Then he can't have known you were lying. He hates being lied to." Horn't fell silent, then mused. "It's a good thing Tarrant-Arragon and his dissolute family have had the ability to read minds accidentally bred out of them, isn't it?"

Jason watched narrowly as Horn't dipped his flylike, hollow tongue into his drink. Horn't was most likely thinking about the prophecy that a royal Djinn who was also a Saurian Knight would end the oppressive rule of the Tiger Djinn Princes of Tigron.

"It's a damn good thing," Jason agreed. "If Tarrant-Arragon could read minds, he'd know that he has a rival, wouldn't he?"

It was a dangerous thing to say. A test.

"Mmm. But that's all he'd know." Horn't passed the test. "None of us knows who this secret savior is, or where he is."

Jason knew, of course. He was one of a privileged few who knew that the present Emperor's father had impregnated his second Empress—Helispeta—before she ran away and was given conditional sanctuary on the Saurian-protected planet Earth.

Nor had anyone outside the lost branch of the Royal family heard of Helispeta's first son's son, Prince Djetthro-Jason. No one suspected that the safest place for a legitimate throne-contender to hide out and to gain a warrior-Emperor's education was right where he was, within Tarrant-Arragon's Star Forces.

Smiling sardonically, "Jason" turned his thoughts back to his promised bride. Yes, it was a very good thing Tarrant-Arragon couldn't read minds. The Tiger Prince would be intensely interested in Jason's thoughts, and in Jason's girl. He'd go after her, because Djinni was exactly what Tarrant-Arragon wanted.

In that case, however much he, Djetthro-Jason, grudgingly respected his cousin, Tarrant-Arragon, he'd have to kill him.

Chapter Three

Djinni felt the odds, at four to one, were heavily against her, but improving. Two things were in her favor. First, her kidnappers were so overconfident they were likely to be careless. Second, in their carnival mood it wouldn't occur to them that a female could be a force to be reckoned with.

Eyes closed, feigning sleep—which wasn't easy now her clumsy abductor was carrying her uphill over rough ground—she strained her senses for clues that might tell her where they were going.

Four sets of feet swished through coarse grass, stirring up scents: the warm whiff of cattle, the pungency of dog fox on the damp evening air, squelching mud. As they swaggered across the fields, the human named Grievous gave a very male account of local pagan practices.

"Sir, I daresay you've heard that this is the site of an Earth-force that makes animals and women fertile and healthy—"

Does he think of nothing else? Djinni thought.

"I expect you'd like to know the history of the place. Orgies and whatnot," Grievous continued. "I don't suppose you'd be interested in the rumor that couples who visit the Cerne Giant are blessed with marital happiness. Not you, sir."

So that's where they were! But why? Djinni had seen aerial photographs of the hill-figure at Cerne Abbas in Dorset. The Cerne Giant was prehistoric pornography: a hugely aroused male nude, ditch-drawn into the white clay beneath a grassy hillside.

"Mind!" Grievous's voice sharpened. "On your left. Barbed-wire fence, meant to discourage people from trampling on the Cerne Giant's person. We'll step over it. Watch out for a ditch."

Grateful for the warning, Djinni let her face roll into the hollow of her captor's shoulder.

"That ditch should be our Giant's left outer thigh. Is everyone over? More history anon, sir. It's time for accuracy. Anyone spot a second ditch? Uphill, to our left, curving towards us. We're looking for His Mightiness's grassy gonads, lads."

He lowered his voice. "Legend has it, a virgin who sleeps on our Cerne Giant will give her proud husband a fine brood of children. But, as I mentioned at the last rest stop, a girl's got to still be a virgin, and she can't just lie any-old-where.

"Here we go!" Apparently, Grievous had oriented himself. "Straight up, our Giant's privates cover thirty linear feet of hillside if you want to count his big grassy ones. Most do. Originally, he sported a twenty-two-foot erection, but the circle that used to be his belly button was accidentally added to his manhood during a ditch scouring."

She felt a change in her abductor's gait.

"No, no, Sir. Better leave measuring to me. Where was I? Scouring? Every seven years they clear the trenches of weeds. Otherwise, our Giant's outlines couldn't be seen. That's twenty feet. Should be about right. Put her on this, Sir."

Djinni felt herself being eased to the ground, onto a coarse wool blanket that smelled of spilled instant coffee and of the cheap-cigarette smoker who'd thoughtfully brought along the blanket, presumably from the boot of his car.

"Now, sir, you might be wondering if it's pure happenstance that the Earth-force is most potent where the head of our Giant's manhood used to be. As I understand it, many invisible lines of magnetic force come together and form a spiral—"

He was talking about "blind springs" and she was on one! She recognized the Earth-force, the *Chi,* beneath her. Feelings of health, vitality, and confidence flowed through her.

How to escape? Djinni's mind took on the clarity of crystal. She couldn't take out all four of the men with her bare hands, but she might fell one. Not the sex-mad one, but if he were fool enough to move away, she'd have a chance . . . and he was a very great fool to have placed her on a powerful "blind spring."

"There's a mystery about this hill-figure, sir," Grievous was saying. "Who's the Cerne Giant supposed to represent? Some say he's Helis, a god of health and fertility. Mind you, any of the old gods could qualify as that: Most of them were excessively fond of the ladies. Some did their seducing in a stealthy sort of way, in disguises; others were all but rapists."

"You interest me extraordinarily, Grievous."

Djinni's abductor spoke like a knife in silk. No threat could have communicated "Be-silent-or-else" as effectively as the soft menace of his compliment.

She'd had time to consider why his voice was so unsettling. He turned certain words into a growl or a sinister purr. It was partly his Royal Shakespeare Company enunciation of hard last consonants, as if lives depended on his words being understood. Perhaps they did.

Then, too, he deepened his tone on long-drawn-out last syllables, turning them into inappropriate caresses, like a tiger licking the gazelle beneath him in the long grass.

"Er, quite so, sir." Grievous sounded shaken. "As I was about to say, a lot of people like to think our Giant is Hercules, on account of his notched club. Farther up the hill, to your left, sir. Of course, you can't see it from the ground."

Whoever Grievous was, Djinni thought, he was good value as a tour guide. The other males in the party seemed to think so too, judging by the encouraging grunts whenever he paused.

"I prefer the theory that he's Saturn, whom we Brits also called Kronos. He's the god who castrated his father with a sickle and tidily put the evidence in a sack."

Appreciative male grunts.

"Why do I think our Giant is Saturn? Well, in A.D. 700 Saint Augustine came to Cerne and piled up a great deal of dirt over something that was supposed to be dangling from our Giant's other hand. What, you might wonder, could be more troubling to the holy saint than our Giant's monumental male erection? Perhaps you'd care to see the mystery mound, sir?"

Yes! Go! Djinni had never attempted mind control before.

"Watch her!" her captor growled.

She heard him stride off, but waited until she could gauge how far voices would carry on the evening air.

Her dark-voiced abductor murmured something that Djinni couldn't quite make out.

"Never do, sir. We've enough local legends and controversies without putting it about that His Mightiness is your ancestor—" Grievous's objections to gods from outer space grew faint. They were far enough away.

Djinni slitted her eyes and turned her head to locate her guard. He was standing downwind of her, heavily muscled legs apart, back toward her. She heard a splash and realized that he was vandalizing the Cerne Giant's trenching with uniquely male disrespect. The Schwarzenegger-sized alien was in no position to fight back. She was in no mood to be chivalrous.

Djinni rolled over and advanced in a power-building crouch. She focused her strength and braced herself. She dared not use the karate *Kiai* cry, which would have added psychic force to her attack. It was essential to incapacitate him quietly.

She struck, kicking the relaxed side of his right knee. The blow might cripple a nerve bundle or dislocate a joint. All she needed was to make him double over.

He crumpled. His head came down, and she drove her elbow into his neck. She felt the resistance of alien musculature, but he fell: Her attack was enough to temporarily paralyze him.

Djinni turned and ran.

★ ★ ★

Tarrant-Arragon felt remarkably godlike as he surmounted the mound. He closed his eyes, spread his arms, and prayed. Or, more accurately, as one feared as a god in his own worlds, he extended professional courtesy to the local deities.

He'd do almost anything to improve his chances of a happy marriage, and to ensure that his future Empress was the first in three generations who did not run away. He didn't mind having his time wasted—within reasonable limits. But he was not prepared to be made to look like a romantic fool.

As an afterthought, he thanked the God of gods, the Great Originator, for Djinni.

Tarrant-Arragon glanced down at Grievous, who was discreetly kicking the base of the saint's mound. The Earthling acted as though they were on a pleasure foray. Which was good. It was an embarrassing business. By coming to the Cerne Giant, he'd tacitly admitted that, apart from frequent, vigorous sex, he hadn't the first idea what a male was expected to do to make his mate happy.

He doubted that he knew any happy couples. Happy Tigron lords had the sense not to bring beloved mates to their Emperor's Court. However, he hoped the site held enough Earth-power to make her happy and counter any curse-power in the Saurian toasts.

Remembering how his shy mate-to-be had blushed as she unknowingly drank to his impotence, Tarrant-Arragon felt his smile crinkle the corners of his eyes. It was ironic that circumstances obliged him to conduct his sex life like a military campaign.

He was definitely going to enjoy doing his dynastic duty with Djinni! Pleased at the thought, he glanced down the hill and saw his gentle girl launch an efficient attack on Storm-Master Xirxex.

The warrior in him appreciated her tactics. The male in him didn't like it. A male should protect his mate. It was an insult to his machismo that she should flee his protection.

Stand and submit! For an instant he considered halting her

flight with Djinn-craft. However, the consequences could be
fatal if he revealed himself to her as the last of the Great Djinn,
Tarrant-Arragon, the Terror of the Tigron Dodecahedrons.

He calculated distances. Mathematically she couldn't make it
out of the field. Tarrant-Arragon let her run and ran himself, at
an angle, to intercept her.

Ah! the exhilaration of the chase. Intent on swift, silent re-
capture, Tarrant-Arragon hurled himself down the hill. He'd
never—literally—run after a female before. Perhaps he should
have. The excitement far outweighed the indignity of the
pursuit.

He raced, confident of catching her, reveling in the certainty
of mating. Physical pursuit. Marvelous exercise. Primal
courtship! If running felt this good in Earth's light-heady atmosphere, this night's mating would be sensational.

Djinni ran. For her honor. For her life.

Leap the ditches. Helter-skelter with flailing arms, down the
steep and slippery gradient between the Giant's spread legs. A
flying hurdle over the dimly seen barbed-wire fence.

He'd seen her . . . was swooping down the hill after her, his
unfastened coat spread like the wings of a well-groomed raven.

She shouldn't have looked back. She stumbled; felt her ankle
wrench—a high heel snagged in a tussock of coarse grass—ran
on without the shoe. With every thud of her stockinged foot,
cat-o'-nine-tails of pain lashed her right ankle.

Grit teeth. Run. Though knives of fire twisted in her ankle,
she had to keep going. Even ground, now. Trees overhead, the
cold squish of mud underfoot.

The cow-churned mud by the five-barred cattle gate was
too deep, her footing too uncertain for a fancy takeoff. Oh,
Stars, how ever was she going to get out of the field?

There was a kissing gate. Too complicated, too slow. He was
closing, she didn't have time. She'd have to vault the wood
fence. Cack-handed. No choice. Launch off the left, twist in
the air, land on the left. That's what she had . . . to . . . do.

He was on her. He launched himself at her at full stretch.

Midair, Djinni held her breath and closed her eyes. His arms closed around her. Half a heartbeat later, his chest slammed into her. Her breath burst out of her.

Time did something weird. She thought he took her on an impossible tumble through time and space, crashed her through the fence she'd been trying to clear. More pain, more breathlessness, and she landed hard on her back in prickly, wet, ungrazed grass.

She gasped, and felt his mouth on hers, and stars that never were in a March evening sky pulsed on Djinni's closed eyelids. Her heart began to pound. It hurt. Breathing hurt.

"I want to mate. To mate!" he rasped.

He'd tackled her brutally. Winded her. Was on top of her. She was so dazed she could hardly think straight, and he was trying to make out.

"Oh!" She fought for breath to make a suitable retort and was amazed at how angry she was. He wanted to do the worst thing in the world. She should be terrified, but she was fighting mad.

"What unsense to run," he chided, running gentle hands over her. Djinni couldn't make up her mind whether he was checking for broken bones or groping her. "What slack-logic to panic over mating! I'm experienced. I know what I'm doing. I won't hurt you more than absolutely necessary."

"Am I supposed to find your . . . remarks . . . reassuring?" she croaked with all the indignant force her winded lungs could muster. "Your lack of tact . . . reminds me of . . . my grandmother. Get off me, you clumsy great . . . oaf!"

"Oaf? Is this how you speak to your lord and master?"

"Squash me to death, then! I'd rather die than undergo what you have in mind."

"What I have in mind? Mating?"

Djinni forced herself to remember what her karate sensei taught about avoiding conflict. Although she might not be able to talk him out of mating, he might agree to a postponement.

"I know that what you want to do to me is an expression of male power, and you don't care about romance. But cows have been here!" Even if he didn't understand the euphemism, she hoped he'd move.

"You care about romance, little one?" He stroked away a strand of hair that had stuck to her cheek, and Djinni noticed the prickle and pressure of what must be the start of a bruise.

At last he shifted his weight off her. "I seem to want you very much. Beware. Your struggles inflame me beyond reason. Fighting excites me. Be still and I may manage to control my, ah, inclination."

Djinni wasn't sure what he'd promised, but she knew she was shaking. She didn't want him to think she was encouraging him.

"I'm c-c-cold," she said.

"Indeed, you are." Her unpredictable abductor shook his head in apparent concern, seemed to forget about mating, and helped her to her feet. "I see you've lost a shoe. Shall we look for it? Yes, this region is slack damn cold. The air is thin and damp. Come with me. I'll make you happy."

Djinni didn't believe him and didn't intend to let him try to make her happy. While he supported her against his side and they joined the others scanning the dark field for her missing shoe, a reasonable escape plan occurred to her.

"I need to powder my nose." She hoped he'd take her to a hotel with a choice of exits and lots of scene-making potential.

"Sir. She wants the little girls' plumbing. It's been a long day for her," Grievous's voice interceded. "We could go to the Royal Oak. It's a public house, but the facilities are in an out-house across the courtyard and car park. We can stand outside the Ladies'. If she makes a fuss, and anyone in the Gents' hears her, I can say—with your permission, sir—that she's drunk."

Djinni's stomach growled.

"And some of us may be hungry. I can get bottles of bitter lemon and hot sausage rolls to tide us over until dinner. Will you carry her again, sir? I don't think we're going to find that shoe."

Djinni's suitor swept her off her feet. "My good Grievous,"

he drawled as he strode toward the village, "I think you've missed your vocation."

For once, Djinni found herself agreeing. Grievous should have been a butler. Or a busy princess's equerry. What a pity he wasn't on her side!

The Royal Oak, Cerne Abbas, Dorset

Djinni's shameless captor marched right into the Ladies' with her and checked it to ensure that she was trapped.

"Remember, my dear, I'll be waiting outside," he said.

Once alone, Djinni examined her temporary haven. It was ill lit with a naked bulb hanging from a time-frayed cord. The tiny mirror had lost some of its silvering. The whitish porcelain hand basin was chipped and crazed with age. A single, corroded brass tap dripped cold water into a green-rimmed, brown tearstain that slid into the plugless plughole.

Djinni put her throbbing ankle under the tap, eased her pants leg up her shin, and blasted her stockinged foot with numbingly cold water while she splashed mud and blood from her face, before patting her grazes with crackling, folded sheets of toilet paper.

Then, leaving the water running, she sat down and scanned the bleak room for potential weapons. There was nothing. Someone had even taken the chain from the toilet's overhead tank.

The jonquil walls had had generations of graffiti scrubbed away, leaving faint vein-blue hieroglyphics where patronesses of the establishment had scrawled their lovers' names, and described their amatory achievements and equipment in diagram and slang.

Djinni felt tears spike her lower lashes. Who'd have thought she could be brought so low? She'd been brought up to have the manners of a Djinn Empress and to be a Saurian Knight.

Very well. Enthroned as she was, she'd fight with what she

had: a hairpin. She'd score a runic message in the plaster. What she wrote wasn't important. That she wrote was. Even the smallest gesture of defiance gave her some sense of control.

Besides, her message might be found.

Djinni blinked away her tears and concentrated on basic plotting. Runes. Read from right to left. First: her own runic signature. Two symbols. First symbol—

She sounded like a prime-time game show. Well, good! At least she hadn't lost her sense of humor.

First symbol, then: Ng, for the Inguz, sign of an intuitive nature, like two *X*s on top of each other. She scratched it in four quick strokes.

Her second rune-sign was the *F*-shaped sign of favors, signals, and warnings. Too bad that she hadn't pulled her Ansuz out of the bag last night; it would have warned her to beware of tricksters and people wiser than herself.

It was a poor description of her captor. Djinni grinned. He was very, very stupid. She no longer felt guilty about the few quick glimpses she'd had into his mind. After all, he was an enemy, so it wasn't dishonorable to use her powers against him.

What a mind he had! She'd never encountered such an archetypical one-track mind. Either it was completely blank or he was thinking about sex.

"SEX SEX SEX—blank blank blank—SEX SEX SEX." One could write an S.O.S. in Morse code out of his binary thought sequence!

A sense of her intellectual superiority made Djinni feel more optimistic, and she had an idea for her secret message. For a start, she'd reverse her Ansuz. It would be her personal S.O.S., meaning she was in a bad corner and cut off from communicating.

Three strokes completed her reversed Ansuz, which also meant "You may feel inhibited about accepting the gift that is being offered to you." Djinni doubted that any Saurian White Knight would read this meaning into her reversed Ansuz. Which was a good thing, considering her abductor kept offering to mate every five minutes. Some gift!

A deep voice rumbled outside, reminding her of the grimness of her plight. Djinni lifted her chin. When consulted, the Ansuz rune would suggest the Viking equivalent of "When life hands you a lemon, make lemonade!"

Fat lot of help that was! As a prospective lover, he was most certainly a lemon. But how was she going to squash him?

Tigron Imperial Space: The Trojan Horse

"I'll give our newest recruit the 'Welcome to the largest and least reliable war-star' speech. What do you think, Horn't?" Commander Jason said as he and Horn't sauntered into the secret area known as the "Trojan Horse."

"I think you take too many risks and give too much away, Jason," Horn't hissed. "One day, Tarrant-Arragon's agents will master the Saurian handshake and infiltrate us."

Jason couldn't read minds, but he could and did read body language. He was confident that any spy would betray himself, if not by a faint smirk, then by a glazing of the eyes as he—or she—struggled to memorize a scatter-bombardment of information.

"Gil!" Ignoring Horn't's pessimism, Jason approached the newly arrived Saurian, holding out both hands in greeting. "Welcome to the largest and least reliable war-star in Tarrant-Arragon's Thirteenth Star Force."

He might have been referring to the age and poor maintenance of the An'Koori war-star, or he might have meant something more sinister. He never elaborated, never introduced himself either, until newcomers got the secret Saurian handshake right.

The newcomer took Jason's hands in twelve tentacle-like fingers and his cool skin seemed to shrink at the contact.

Jason guessed that Gil hated to be touched, which was awkward for a mute who wanted to be a Saurian Knight. Gil's nervousness was not unusual. Many previous recruits had been intimidated by Jason, particularly since he was over seven feet tall, powerfully built, and his eyes were hypnotic and unreadable.

After a brief hesitation, Gil passed the test, performing the secret greeting correctly.

"We're glad to have you with us, Gil. We need a virtual reality engineer. I'm Commander Jason." Jason smiled. "As you can see, I'm not An'Koori. I'm a mercenary from a rim world, like yourself. Gil, I'd like you to meet Horn't."

Following Gil's startled eyes, he smiled, remembering his own first impression of Horn't, as Horn't stepped forward on two spindly legs and waved a six-armed salutation.

"Horn't runs this area. My superior officer is happy to polish his expensive and temporary badges of office, so I command this An'Koori war-star in all but name."

"Greetings," Horn't said in a humming voice. "Welcome to the part of the war-star that we Saurians call the 'Trojan Horse.'"

Gil made the Star Forces sign for *Why?*

"Do you want to know why we call it the 'Trojan Horse'?" Jason guessed. "We took the name from Earthling history. All things Earthling are highly fashionable these days. Horn't, you tell the history. You do it so well."

Horn't ticked story points off on his jointed fingers as he spoke. "Once upon an Earth-time, a prince ran off with a king's wife. The king was so zzz'ed off about it that he made war. The cuckolded king's men used a decoy hollow horse to trick the wife-stealing prince and to get the queen back. It's not so different from the way the Great Djinn carry on. Except the old Emperor Djohn-Kronos didn't get his second Empress—Helispeta—back, and though he's dead, the war that resulted izzn't over."

"As for why this part of the ship qualifies as a Trojan Horse," Jason resumed, "it's because no one knows it is here, ready for the day we overthrow Tarrant-Arragon. The tyrant has no idea we Saurians have set up this secret base, right in the bowels of one of his An'Koori war-stars."

He saw Gil make the *How?* sign.

"How? It wasn't difficult. I erased this area from the Ship Map. Star Forces auditors assume that a large and antiquated war-star like this still has to carry unreasonable quantities of fuel. Who wants to inspect fuel? Not a fastidious An'Koori. Moreover, no quivering An'Koori wants to serve his full conscription cycle. He'll gladly go home early if I find a mercenary like you whom he can pay to take his place. Thus, since I have served four gestates, I've been here longer than anyone. No An'Koori has ever questioned my Ship Map or any other records. Gil?"

Gil was staring at his eyes, which—thanks to his Las Vegas party-store contact lenses—were like black opals, with streaks of electric blue and green streaming across Stygian pools that held no sign of a pupil and revealed nothing.

"Would you like to join the others, Gil?" Jason dismissed Gil, who made the circle sign for Perfect, scuttled over to a beckoning Saurian engineer, and began signing excitedly.

A horny elbow dug Jason in the ribs.

"I hear you sent for your two favorite courtesans." Horn't rolled his eyes. "Don't tell me you need consummation practice?"

"What else?" Jason grinned.

The Royal Oak, Cerne Abbas, Dorset

"She's been in there a long time," Tarrant-Arragon remarked as soon as Grievous joined him outside the Ladies'.

"I'd say we've frightened her, Sir."

"I cannot imagine how, or why. I told her I wanted to mate."

"Yup. That might've done it." The Earthling tapped two cigarettes out of a battered paper packet. "Want one, Sir?"

Tarrant-Arragon accepted it, and watched Grievous to see whether it mattered which end of the cigarette went into his mouth.

The human cupped his hands, lit Tarrant-Arragon's cigarette, and took a long draw on his own before speaking again.

"This mating talk of yours, Sir. You might try varying your

vocab a bit. For one thing, the little miss may not share your notion of what 'mating' means. It's a strong word. We Earthlings tend to associate 'mating' with, er, animal activity. Ladies like a fellow to use the socially correct terminology, even though they know it all amounts to the same thing. Sir, if you mean marriage, say 'marriage.'"

Tarrant-Arragon raised an eyebrow.

"You say you told her, Sir? This masterful stuff is all very well, but most ladies feel they've a right to be asked properly, begged even. Ladies are funny about the little niceties."

Tarrant-Arragon was not accustomed to such impertinence. "Do you presume to advise me how to seduce my mate?"

"Ah, well, I daresay you've had more young ladies than I've had cups of tea, Sir. But does this one know your ways, Sir? Eh? Or does she think like one of us Earthlings?"

Tarrant-Arragon didn't reply. He blew a perfect smoke ring and watched its wavering ascent.

"Oh, splendid, Sir! Where did you learn to do that?" Apparently, Grievous thought flattery was expected.

Tarrant-Arragon grinned. "I've watched Earthling movies off your satellites, mostly for pointers on your courting customs. I find this smoking somewhat intoxicating. Will it adversely affect my breath for kissing?"

"It might, Sir. I shouldn't let that worry you. A girl will put up with all sorts of ill treatment if she knows she's going to marry a prince."

"No doubt," Tarrant-Arragon said, savaging the cigarette under his heel.

"Oh, that's right." Grievous slapped his forehead. "You don't intend to inform her of her great good fortune, do you, Sir? It's going to be romantic like *Beauty and the Beast*. Next thing we know, you'll be wanting her to love you for your sweet nature and kind heart."

"Will I? I see you've formed an astonishingly accurate opinion of my character and morals," Tarrant-Arragon replied with the same heavy sarcasm that Grievous had used.

The Earthling kicked gravel. Tarrant-Arragon smiled slightly and cocked his head in mock thoughtfulness.

"The sweet-natured approach hadn't occurred to me. In fact, the idea of her loving me hadn't entered my calculations at all. You suggest an interesting challenge. I must consider the possibilities."

Having nothing better to do, he pretended to consider until Grievous coughed into his fist.

"Er-'hem. If I might make a suggestion, Sir? The ladies generally like to know a fellow's name before they, er, put out."

"I'd assumed she would call me 'Sir' or 'my Lord' until some more affectionate term seemed appropriate to her."

"Sir, Sir. That'll never do. Only princes expect that," Grievous said disapprovingly. "You'd give the game away. Can't you use your real name, Sir? Would she recognize you by it?"

"I can't risk it." Tarrant-Arragon lowered his voice to a whisper: "You heard the spy-tape. She'd rather die violently than mate with me. Yet the fate of an Empire depends on my success with her."

"Well, where the security of the State is at stake, it's justifiable to use deceit and ruthlessness. According to Niccolo Machiavelli." Grievous spoke in what Tarrant-Arragon suspected was a Sandhurst-trained-officer voice. "Then we must come up with another name for you. Take John. There's a nice, dependable name, Sir. And a popular one. I suppose you'd like that image?"

"Start the car, Grievous." Tarrant-Arragon had had enough of waiting. He twisted the Ladies' dented brass doorknob.

Suddenly, he was struck by a preposterous image of himself.

"Nice, you said? Dependable? Popular? Me?" He laughed. "Oh, Earthling! Why not add 'lovable' to your list?"

Chapter Four

"You promised!" Tarrant-Arragon's exasperating little prisoner squeaked and squirmed in his arms as soon as she saw their bed.

"Did I? Generally, I'm quite scrupulous about limiting and qualifying promises." He feigned polite surprise.

The short drive to the rented Great House had been silent and malodorous. Even when he'd gallantly carried her up the grand staircase to the master suite, Djinni refused to look at him or speak to him. That was, until she caught sight of the bed.

"What, if anything, did I promise?" he said, punishing her a little for her coldness. "I do recall saying that I intend to mate with you."

"Oh! You promised to c-c-control yourself."

The discreetly lit but sadly undersized four-poster bed had not been Tarrant-Arragon's immediate destination. With supreme-princely tact, he'd decided to let Djinni wash off the stink she'd picked up in the field.

He'd expected her to notice their sleeping arrangements and get used to the idea of going to bed with him while they ate a civilized—and probably prolonged—evening meal downstairs in the Great Hall. He had not expected an argument.

Tight-lipped, he strode past the offending bed and into the bathroom with her before responding urbanely.

"Ah! That promise was conditional. And qualified. I didn't promise to control myself, only my 'inclination.' It might have been a gentlemanly offer to control the force of my thrusts."

Tarrant-Arragon thought his wordplay was rather amusing, but little Djinni looked so distraught that he felt it would be cruel to tell her what he could do with a powerful "inclination."

He'd show her. Later.

He set her down, on her feet, but close enough to the tub that she could sit on its off-white porcelain rim if her swollen ankle wasn't strong enough to support her weight.

"My dear, you're dirty. Would you care to bathe?" he asked, though there was no question. She was going to wash.

"On what terms?"

Now what was going on in her mind? Surely she hadn't decided to question his every word, had she?

"Does my being clean or dirty affect your 'inclination'?"

"By all the—" Tarrant-Arragon stopped himself mid-oath. He shouldn't swear at her. Not when he had initiated the wordplay.

He sat sideways on the tub's narrow rim and turned the taps to fill her bath for her, while he considered a more appropriate response. Her wit surprised him. He'd never expected her to consider the strategic implications of basic hygiene as she might a move in a chess match. This might be amusing. He'd play.

He smiled lazily up at her.

"I was about to remind you that you're in no position to refuse my demands. These are my terms. I will not molest you because you bathe, nor while you bathe. However, if you refuse, I will bathe you, and I will be thorough."

The water-chatter of the slowly filling bath had deepened to a state-banquet roar before she nodded, as if she'd decided that he could be trusted, and held out her hand.

He was about to take it, pull her between his bent legs, and kiss the fight out of her, when her lips parted and she spoke.

"Persons of honor shake hands over an agreement, as a sign of good faith," she instructed him. "I'm not surprised that you don't know this."

No one had ever dared to imply that he, the greatest legal authority in the Tigron Empire, was not a person of honor. Amused, he gave her his hand and waited.

"You surely don't expect me to undress in front of you?" she demanded. "Go away. Shut the door behind you."

His dominance was under attack. Again. He would set a bad precedent if he let her eject him, so he stayed.

In the flickering fire- and candlelight, he calculated the burn-rate of the logs in the bathroom's fireplace. He counted the elegant bottles of herbal oils and artistic little baskets of colored soaps. He tallied the toes on the clawed feet of the bath; estimated its fillrate and how long he could sit where he was before he'd have to back down or suffer the indignity of a wet bottom. He was looking for something else to count when her trembling fingers slid to the first fastening.

"I didn't know I was so generous," he said, rising. However, he paused with one hand on the painted porcelain doorknob and set the door open even wider, before retreating out of sight.

He knew his interesting little adversary wouldn't dare to shut it.

Having changed into a more comfortable upper-body garment and a fresh pair of English gentlemanly dark trousers, Tarrant-Arragon checked his messages on his forearm communicator until he heard a faint slap of water.

Good. She was immersed. It was time to saunter back into the bathroom. Inspecting his new property didn't count as molestation as far as he was concerned.

Her outraged squeal assaulted his Djinn-sharp ears. Djinni snatched up one of the fluffy bathtowels and flipped it into the water to cover herself. Her face was so expressive of betrayal that he felt vaguely uncomfortable about his playful treachery.

It wasn't as if he'd broken a promise. He crouched over her

discarded clothes to give himself time to think, and picked up her still-warm camisole. He took a deep breath.

"Don't you dare!" she stormed. A palmscoop of scented bathwater splashed his bent knee.

Excited by the mix of fragrances and hopeful that this was the start of a stirring water game, he leaned over the tub. "Are you throwing me perfumed lures, my wet siren? Shall I join with you?"

She sank lower in the water, crossing her arms over the wet towel. Not an invitation.

"No? You're right. It would be more efficient if I shared the water after you have left it. I understand there's a water shortage in the South of England. So please leave as much water as possible *in* the bath. Now I'm going to confiscate these horrible things."

"Then what am I going to wear?" She sounded frantic.

"It hadn't occurred to me that you'd need clothing. I'd assumed we'd go to bed wrapped only in each other's arms." He gave her a predator's smile. He couldn't help himself. Her unique mix of shy panic and reckless courage aroused the worst in him. "I still think it'd be appropriate."

He slowly unfastened his upper-body drape. Three tugs undid the ties that held the Tigron silk crossed over his chest. His eyes never left her face, and he enjoyed her wide-eyed alarm as she misunderstood why he was undressing.

"You look stunned." His voice dropped to a husky whisper. "Are you starting to find me interesting? Under that sodden towel, is your heart beating faster?"

He didn't expect her to admit it. If he'd wanted to know, he could have checked her heart rate on the readout from her tracer necklet, but he didn't. The less she knew he knew, the better.

She turned her face away. As he watched, a blush spread like a lover's fingers over her delicate collarbones and kissed what little he could see of her breasts above her white towel.

He wanted her. Badly. But, with the patience of a heavy-world superpredator, he placed his drape and a dry towel where she could reach them.

"If you insist on taking my clothes, you might as well take them away right now," she hissed. "Then I can get out of the water. Otherwise you're going to have a cold bath. . . . Although a cold bath might be just the thing for you."

Slack damn. She was attempting to usurp control again. He'd teach her a lesson. He took his time gathering up her clothes while he composed an intimidating reply. When he was at the door, he turned and let her have it.

"You don't have to worry about my sexual stamina, my dear. After a bracing cold bath, I shall be able to stay up all night. You'll see."

We'll see who sees what! Arrogant, overbearing, *stupid* oaf! He was determined to mate. He couldn't get it through his thick skull that she didn't want to have sex with him. He spoke and acted like a stranger, yet he behaved as though he thought he had every right to her. Well! If he thought he could seduce her with his alpha-male ways, he had another think coming.

Djinni stormed inwardly as she limped across the bathroom and knelt in front of a heavy piece of furniture to look for weapons, medical supplies, and something decent to wear.

She'd show him. . . . She gasped with outrage at what was in the left-hand drawer. Lingerie she wouldn't be seen dead in, still with the price tags on. Very expensive lingerie.

Djinni ran her hand down the front of her abductor's silky, black, kimono-like top. He might be stupid and single-minded, but he'd known exactly what he was doing when he gave it to her. The fabric clung. Everything showed.

There was no way she could conceal a weapon . . . even if she could find something. She opened the dark oak double doors. A Welsh dresser was incongruous in a bathroom, but it held almost everything a virgin bride could need—in alarming quantities.

Almost . . . Djinni's sense of humor kicked in as she dabbed witch hazel on her cheek. There were no knockout drops, emetics, or fast-acting laxatives to put an overeager male out of action.

But there was rubbing alcohol.

She eyed an unopened magnum of Dom Perignon on ice, tempted. It would be sauce for the gander . . . but she had no idea how much it would take to incapacitate him. He was so large. Stars, he must be over seven feet: about J-J's height.

Djinni frowned. If she were in a charitable mood, she might concede that he'd been thoughtful. And generous. Djinni looked around the room with new eyes. Under other circumstances—if J-J had brought her here for a sort of prenuptial honeymoon, for instance—she might find it romantic.

Although she wasn't so sure about the necklace. Djinni cocked her head at her reflection in a darkened window. It looked like something from a royal Byzantine mosaic. Or like a token of ownership, that a god-king might weld around a love-slave's neck.

A god-king? A honeymoon? She blinked at her thoughts.

No! He couldn't be J-J? Could he? She recalled the angry epithets she'd used a few moments before. "Arrogant, over-bearing, determined to mate." They were Helispeta's warnings about J-J.

She thought about it while she sorted out what she needed to tape her twisted ankle.

Stars, she couldn't even remember the color of J-J's eyes. How embarrassing! But one couldn't keep photos of people who weren't supposed to exist. It just wasn't reasonable to expect her to remember . . .

Then again, Great Djinn males weren't reasonable. And J-J had always loved suggestive puns and practical jokes. Was he playing some stupid, macho, practical joke on her?

The arrogance! It'd be just like J-J to think he could take up where he'd left off when she was a child and that it was acceptable for him to supervise her bath time. Apparently, he thought he could still select her clothes and what she read, too.

Djinni giggled over a flood of memories.

At five years old, she'd had none of it. She'd had no idea—then—of the consequences of thwarting a Great Djinn.

"You've no awfullity over me, J-J," she'd lisped defiantly

when her big half-cousin cornered her in his bathroom with some girly magazines of his that he didn't want her to see.

"No awf—?" He'd glowered. Then he'd grinned. "Oh yes, I have. I've all the authority in a thousand-thousand worlds over you, baby. I'm lord of your life, twice over. When you're all grown up, I'll come for you, and you'll see."

So here she was, all grown up. And here he was, perhaps, still using the same vaguely sexual threats.

It was terribly risky for her eldest half-cousin, the secret prince, to come—in person—to claim her after thirteen years on the other side of the universe, infiltrating Tarrant-Arragon's An'Koori Star Forces.

How very flattering! No doubt he now expected her to drop everything and adore him.

Tall, dark, and dangerous, he really was gorgeous, but that didn't mean she was in any hurry to have sex with him. But marrying him mightn't be so bad. Perhaps, if he'd take "it" slowly, everything would be all right.

Then again, perhaps it wouldn't. . . .

She pulled the tape into a tight figure eight to support her injured ankle, and cried out. Hell's teeth, it hurt.

If he was J-J, why hadn't he said so? Even if he had to pretend to be a stranger in front of the others, he didn't have to keep up the charade when they were alone.

He surely wouldn't frighten her like this as punishment for not recognizing him. Nor for questioning his virility when he hesitated over the Saurian handshake. No, his motives must be more sinister.

Furiously, she wound the rest of the elasticized bandage around her waist to keep the slinky kimono in place.

There was only one reason why J-J would come after her like this, unannounced and incognito. To test her. To find out if his promised bride flirted with sexy strangers. Or slept with them.

How dare he! Damn males and their double standards. Djinni gave another furious sob of rage.

He wanted chastity? She'd give him frigidity like the March

night air. Given the emphasis her family put on the chastity clause in her betrothal contract, J-J could hardly complain.

That is, if her abductor was J-J. And if he wasn't, she was as good as dead, anyhow, if she got taken to bed by the wrong man.

She wouldn't cry, damn it. She limped to the window, tears streaming down her face. She was going out of the window.

"Damn it all, Grievous!" Tarrant-Arragon swore into the corridor. "She's crying. What the Carnality does she have to cry about? I've been kind. I've been sensitive. I've made my intentions clear, haven't I?"

"I'm sure your love talk would make any young lady swoon with happy desire, Sir," the Earthling retorted. "I was just on my way to make myself some nice, soothing cocoa when I heard you crashing about. Shall I bring you a couple of mugs, Sir?"

"I haven't touched her. That's not why she's crying. Slack damn! I was folding my white wedding sheets at the entry points to make the bed look inviting, and I heard her sobbing in the bathroom," Tarrant-Arragon defended himself.

"Well, how ungrateful of her, Sir. I'd say that'd be enough to send any sensitive man into a furniture-smashing rage. Still at it, is she? I don't hear her."

"What you heard were the legs of that yellow sofa scraping—"

"I believe it's a valuable Regency piece, Sir."

"It's damned bad taste. Too many toothy creatures grinning at one! However, I suppose it's going to be my slack damn couch for the night, so I took the top cover off the bed and tossed it at the sofa. I forgot to compensate for Earth's lower gravity. Ah, Fewmet. Earth-gravity makes it hard to know one's own strength."

Tarrant-Arragon had no idea why he felt the need to explain himself. "I tell you, Grievous, Tigron girls aren't this troublesome. I can't understand how my Djinni's part-Djinn blood could be so frigid!"

"I daresay it's the Earthling in her. English too! Reserved lot we are, Sir."

"That must be it. She's inherited a cautious libido from her Earthling mother. What vile luck! I wonder how my Djinni's sire managed to seduce his Englishwoman."

Tarrant-Arragon scowled at his reflection in the massive mirror above the gold-inlaid marble mantelpiece. The low light from the fire threw shadows that emphasized the grim angularity of his features. "I seem to miscalculate at every turn. Do you think she's afraid of me?"

"She might just be tired, Sir. It's been a long day for all of us, Sir. If there's nothing else, I'll be—"

"Not for her. She's been asleep."

"Lucky for her too, Sir. I can't think she'll be getting much sleep tonight."

Tarrant-Arragon lifted a warning brow at the impertinence.

"Er, I mean to say, because her bed's an abomination, isn't it? Beats me why they say a four-poster is romantic. I wouldn't be surprised if the mattress was lumpy. They used to stuff 'em with horsehair and sawdust, you know. I shouldn't think she'll be comfy. Even alone. I'll be off, now. Good night, Sir."

Tarrant-Arragon nodded a curt dismissal.

Was he being too aggressive? Alone again, Tarrant-Arragon paced a complicated circuit around the grinning furniture. Grievous seemed to think so. No doubt the Earthling thought he should promise to wait until Djinni felt ready for sex.

Damn! He kicked a burning log. Sparks flew up from a fire-cradle resembling a monstrous, blackened rib cage, and he grimaced at his reflection in the big gilt-edged mirror over the mantel. He couldn't promise to wait. When it came to sex, he never made promises. It would be ridiculous to start. With Djinni, of all females, it'd be a promise he couldn't keep.

Never in his life had he forced himself on a girl who didn't want him. Of course, he'd never encountered one who wasn't eager to share his royal bed. He'd never had the rut-rage, either!

Poor little mate. From the powerful and contradictory emotions Djinni aroused in him already, she might be Djinn enough to inflame him with the distinctive mating frenzy when she came into her fertile time. That time might come all too soon for her. And it might make him behave very badly indeed.

History had shown that, crudely handled, the Djinn rut-rage was the fatal flaw of the Imperial bloodline. At least, these days, there were no rivals he'd have to fight to the death over her, but—still—seven days and nights of vigorous mating might be too much for a frightened little virgin to enjoy.

If, and when, Djinni gave him the rut-rage, he'd do his best not to be crude, but, whether or not she wanted him to make love to her, he'd have no choice. He would have to.

Chapter Five

Serve him right if she caught her death . . . out there in the March night with wet hair, bare feet, and no decent clothes on—

Djinni wrenched at the painted-shut double casement windows.

Serve him right if he caught his death from her—

Again, she tugged and shoved. With a chewing-gum crack, paint came unstuck. Another push, and the windows swung outward in a breathtaking rush of icy night air. Open.

As Djinni leaned forward onto the broad stone sill, she glimpsed a flash of movement in the leaded panes.

"No!" he roared, and time froze.

Djinni didn't dare to move. Before her eyes, reflected in the dark diamond windowpanes, she saw a white-faced demon with rage-flared nostrils and locomotive breath. She was bent over; he was on top of her, as intimidating as an angry movie-cop who'd forced a fugitive from justice to "assume the position."

Awareness shot sparks into her belly. Acute awareness—of a masculine knee, hard against the backs of her legs; of his hands splayed on her hips, pinning her down; of the sexually submissive position in which he'd caught her.

"I told you how cold water affects my person," he growled, and his voice was a rough caress in her hair. "What do you suppose cold air does to me? Do you want to find out?"

Too frightened to speak, Djinni shook her head.

"Shall I show you?" Djinni heard him take a deep breath and expel his temper in a controlled rush.

"Hmmm?" His tone softened to almost a purr. His spread fingers slid up her sides. Djinni held her breath, prayed that she'd taped her waist tightly enough, that her silky garment wouldn't ride up under his hands.

Warmth skimmed every trembling inch of her rib cage, flickered into her underarms, and stroked the outstretched length of her bare arms. In the terrified closing of an eye, strong hands closed over hers on the slender dolphin-shaped metal latches.

"Cold hands," he murmured, disengaging her reluctant fingers from the window fixtures.

"C-c-cold heart!" she retorted, and crossed her arms. Her options for defiant gestures were becoming more limited with every leap of her heart. There was an ominous finality to his movements as he snapped shut the casements and secured the hole-punched horizontal bars over their upright pegs.

She was locked in with him.

"Come to bed." It wasn't an invitation, it was a promise that she was mistaken about her sexual coldness and he'd show her. No predictable, puerile jokes about warming her up. He went directly for the erogenous jugular. Just like the ravisher in her nightmares.

Before she realized what he was going to do, his slightly rough lips rasped just behind her ear and set off a rushing sensation, as if she'd swigged brandy and it had dropped to her pelvic floor.

"You mustn't," she gasped, sure she ought to be revolted, appalled at herself for liking his caress. "It isn't safe—"

If ever she was going to scare him off, now was the time. She'd exaggerate about all the communicable human diseases that might be deadly to an alien. Either he'd be put off, or—if he was anything like the J-J she remembered—he'd make a joke about what catching the mumps could do to a boy.

"I must!" His wicked hands went after her cold ones. Oh, Stars, why had she crossed her arms? She'd given him the perfect excuse to "accidentally" touch her bosom.

"For thirteen of your years, I've looked for— Ahhh."

Looked for . . . what? Djinni's mind raced. Or looked forward to . . . what? Sex? What male waited thirteen years for sex? But 'thirteen years' was how long it had been since J-J went away. So, he was J-J. He must be! Relief, righteous indignation, and angry confusion impelled her to confront him. She turned in his arms and glared up at him.

"Well, you utter idiot bas—"

His lips came down on hers, stopping her from saying something she'd regret, and she was too surprised to fight him. Or too confused.

How big he was! How shockingly masculine!

Sensations besieged her. The rugged smoothness of his abs. The fact that her palms were caught against his muscular belly. He moved his mouth over hers like a deliberate lion starving its struggling prey of air. His cheek grazed her nose.

He smelled . . . of a man who played with fire? Of sinfully expensive macadamia nuts. Of old-fashioned English Christmas. Her head soared. A sensation of peace and warmth enveloped her. She wanted to surrender to the feeling of perfect love, total safety, absolute protection. . . .

If this was a test of her chastity, she was failing, and—shockingly—she didn't care.

His tongue thrust between her lips. He tasted of dark-demon-dream kisses . . . a gray-blue taint of cigarette. . . . How could J-J have forgotten that cigarette smoke made her heart race? A detached part of her mind fought free. Was he? Or wasn't he? There'd be hell to pay if he wasn't J-J.

Djinni struggled, and his arms ratcheted tighter. His kiss grew fiercer. He lifted her, and held her so her thighs were pressed against the inexorable, aching hardness of his body.

Aching? How could she possibly know . . . ? She didn't want to know whether or not he ached.

She was his. All his.

All wrong. Djinni shook her head but could not shake off the possessive, masculine thoughts that penetrated her mind. His mouth rode hers. His passion rose. A tornado roared in her ears, a bright white light flashed, and blizzards of multicolored stars shot across her eyelids.

He loved this! What fire! He couldn't wait to—

No! Djinni screamed in her mind. She shouldn't feel what it was like to kiss herself. If this was going to happen every time, well, she never wanted to be kissed again.

He'd dock in her, and dock, and dock—

Alien thoughts, explicit, terrible words she didn't know but understood all too well. It was too much. She couldn't cope. Not with all his thoughts and feelings on top of her own. There was to be no escape from it . . . unless . . . into oblivion.

Despising herself for her weakness, Djinni felt herself sink into the black quicksands of unconsciousness.

Tarrant-Arragon lowered his excitable little mate onto the bed and thrust a pillow under her hips. Though he hadn't intended it, his action pushed up her black hem.

Already breathing hard, he made the delightful discovery that her long, auburn hair wasn't the only place she used herbal shampoo.

He tested the softness of her skin with a gentle finger. Exquisite girl!

"Let me awaken you!" he urged, stroking her. "Ah, I was right about you. You may be very sexy, but you're inexperienced, aren't you?"

How sweetly passionate Djinni had seemed. He smiled and bent over her fascinating legs. This must be the happy swoon that Grievous had mentioned.

He kissed her thigh. Nothing happened.

"Such an innocent," he teased, in case she'd revived under

his lips and was too shy to respond. After all, she didn't seem to know any of the techniques he'd assumed all girls were taught.

"How long should a happy swoon last? Poor little one, nowhere near the moment of truth and already out of your depth. Surely you haven't exhausted all your fire over the first kiss? Hmmm?"

Silence. Except for the crackle of the fire, the muffled roar of their dueling hearts, and the fizz of skin on skin.

"I've had infinite experience." He tried a different line as he moved up her body to kiss the hollows of her throat beneath the tracer necklet. "I know what I'm doing. Ours will be a perfect bonding. Scientific. Lots of touching. However, you ought to be awake for it. . . . What's this?"

Her skin tasted of fear. Damn!

"Oh, Djinni! Have I frightened you? Did I go too hard and too fast for you?" Still astride her, he sat back and studied her. She was much too tense, her eyes shut, her mouth open in a mute plea, but apparently not for what he'd hoped to give her.

"My dear girl, you're not supposed to react like this. I want to dock. In you. With you," he whispered with something like remorse clogging his throat. "I'd no idea a girl could be so un-prepared. I'm going to have to teach you everything, aren't I? But perhaps not tonight?"

He tried to pat her chest as he would to comfort a winded pursuit-steed. Impossible! How could he pat her there without stroking her soft-and-firm figure? Glorious curves. He'd never laid eyes—or anything else—on such beautiful breasts! By All The Lechers, what must it be like to put his mouth on them?

He had to! He shouldn't. He couldn't. Not when he'd just offered her the sexual equivalent of a temporary restraining or-der. He groaned.

So distracting was she, he didn't at first notice her heartbeat under his fingers. Her heart rate was much too fast for a Djinn. At that rate, she might die of fright.

"Hush, my precious," he tried to croon, without betraying his inner panic. "Don't you want me tonight, little flutter-heart? Really and truly not? Did I misunderstand? You confuse me with your mixed-up signals. Hush. It's all right."

It might improve his credibility if he got off her bed.

"See, I'm gone. I'm harmless. I promise, no more tonight. Be easy, little one. I will not proceed with you in this state."

He gently tugged the Tigron upper-body drape back into place. How else could he demonstrate good faith? A symbolic barrier might help. He placed a lacy pillow lengthwise so she was covered from her belly to midthigh.

"Is there anything I can do for you?" He stood over her, feeling helpless and anxious. "No?" Reluctantly, he backed off, assuring her, "There will be no bedding, my fragile little mate. Sleep. I will not molest you, now."

Djinni felt exhausted. She wanted to dive into water, as if she could physically wash away the feeling that her mind had been violated. She still felt overwhelmed, and exhausted, and blown-away in a bad way. Though her throat was dry and her insides felt strangely tight, she didn't dare move. She wasn't going to let him see that she'd recovered her senses.

"Not *now*. Not *in this state*. Not *tonight*," she replayed his words in her mind and thought of an unwisely feisty retort: "You talk like a lawyer: Your promises are full of loopholes."

As her lurching heart steadied, she watched him through the lattice of her lashes. He was watching her, wolf-eyed by the fireside. From time to time he glanced at his forearm device, and his lips moved as if he were counting.

Suddenly, he rose. She held her breath. He advanced and loomed over the bed. His fire-shadow slid onto her body.

"Djinni?" He sighed and gave up. "Ah, my dear, I hope you'll like me better in the morning."

The click of a switch, a yellow explosion of electric light. He'd taken his "inclination" off to the bathroom. Djinni took mental stock.

One thing was sure: He wasn't J-J, otherwise he'd have known about her Earth-rate pulse. Her distress wouldn't have put J-J off having his wicked way as it had this lesser male. A panic attack or faint wouldn't stop the juggernaut advances of a Great Djinn like J-J. Nor would a Great Djinn apologize.

Djinni remembered her runes' advice about the power of humor over fear, and managed a wry grin. Her disappointed suitor hadn't apologized either. He'd expressed regret that she was ignorant, but there was one thing she did know.

I've known Great Djinn, she thought. *And, Sir, you're no Great Djinn!*

Imperial Space: The Pleasure Moon of Eurydyce

Seduction and danger were in the cards!

Seduction, Madam Tarra understood. In her line of work, it happened all around her, every day. But she couldn't think why she was sensing danger. She had it on the best of authority that none of her appalling son's Imperial Star Forces war-stars were anywhere near the neutral pleasure moon of Eurydyce.

If she really used psychic ability to make her predictions, this would be the perfect time to impress a client: no excitement, no personal involvement, and no strong emotions to confuse the few psychic perceptions she had.

"You're no help," she told the Tarot card in her hand, the seduction card! She threw down the eight of Swords. It landed in a position to threaten the Queen of Wands.

"Again?" She gave up and looked back on her life. In the seventy-six gestates since the Djinn princess Tarragonia-Marietta was born to privilege, wealth, and a girlhood in dazzling royal Djinn circles, she'd had many identities.

The Knights of the Saurian Orders knew her as the spymaster Salamander, named after a mythical lizard. The gallows humor behind her choice of Saurian name was known to only the Saurian Dragon's four most trusted Knights.

Since her escape from the Emperor Djerrold Vulcan V and his vile family, she'd ostensibly made her living as Madam Tarra, the most accurate fortune-teller on the pleasure moon of Eurydyce. She was well known to the lonely officers of the

Star Forces as the steely-eyed, veiled procuress of the most cultured and most expensive courtesans in the Communicating Worlds.

In her role as bad-tempered prophetess, she entertained her star-going patrons by prophesying their fortunes in love with palm-readings, runes, or crystal balls, but she preferred user-friendly cosmic Tarot cards. She liked the vivid pictures.

The sexual brutality and violence she'd suffered at the hands of Imperial Djinn males had neither ruined her aquiline beauty, apart from her legs, nor quite destroyed the romantic in her. Over time she'd come to associate certain Tarot cards with the few people who were special to her, and she thought of them even when she was pretending to read a paying client's totally unconnected fortune.

The King of Wands or Clubs always represented her rakishly handsome nephew, Djetthro-Jason. Her aunt Helispeta's troublesome granddaughter, Djinni-vera, whom she'd yet to meet, she naturally visualized as the Queen of Wands.

When the seduction card, the eight of Spades or Swords, first linked the Queen of Wands (Djinni-vera) with the King of Swords, it hadn't troubled Madam Tarra. She seldom admitted that she was a charlatan clairvoyant and often misread her cards.

Eleven gestates ago, the conjunction had become a regular pattern and Madam Tarra had to face the troubling truth. She couldn't explain why the Tarot cards never showed Djetthro-Jason lying with his betrothed, Djinni-vera.

It was no comfort to tell herself that she might be wrong about Djetthro-Jason, that he might have a dark and treacherous side. Perhaps he was more a King of Swords than of Wands, who knew? Given a little power. . . . After all, he was the Emperor Djohn-Kronos's other grandson.

Nevertheless, she sent a secret message to her aunt Helispeta, to warn her that someone other than Djetthro-Jason might deflower Djinni-vera.

She and Helispeta had decided to thwart destiny. Helispeta began to exacerbate Djinni-vera's fear of male passion, to keep the girl away from all males. When Djetthro-Jason sent for Djinni-vera, she would be brought to Eurydyce, where Madam Tarra was expected to undo the conditioning and to prepare the girl to be an enthusiastic but virginal bride.

The problematic time was imminent. Gossip about "Commander Jason's" wedding permit had reached Eurydyce, no doubt before the document reached Djetthro-Jason himself. She could guess why "Commander Jason" had sent for Petri-Shah. This time, the message pricked onto a condom would be his demand that Djinni-vera be brought to him.

Madam Tarra shook her head over the strange irony of fate. She was the least suitable female in all the universe to tell a nervous bride the Great Djinn made kind, considerate lovers and husbands.

The Great House, Cerne Abbas, Dorset, Earth

Djinni woke screaming. Her eyes flew open. For a confused moment, she thought she was having a layered nightmare, one in which you dream you're dreaming. Then she realized she was unable to brush off her treacherous suitor. Nevertheless, she struggled to get away from him.

He stroked her hair, and Djinni thought she knew exactly what was on his mind. He was going to try again. He'd already snaked one heavy leg across hers and his weight pinned her down.

"Hush, my dearest. Don't wriggle. You know what that does to me. Be calm. Feel, there's a pillow and all manner of bedding bundled between us. Are you awake now? You were dreaming."

"You promised not to assault me. I remember it distinctly."

"Is this assaulting? No," he purred, snuggling closer. "You cried out in your sleep. I'm comforting you."

"No, you are not. Having you on top of me is more of a threat than a comfort."

Djinni had the impression he was amused. Indeed, it was

ridiculous of her to be emboldened by two layers of silk and some feathers between his hardened wickedness and her soft innocence.

"How argumentative you are in bed," he marveled. "Are you sexually frustrated?"

"No, I'm not. Leave my hair alone," Djinni snapped, but she couldn't prevent him from helping himself to a handful of her tresses and rubbing his cheek on it, like a territorial feline scent-marking his personal catnip. So she kept quiet.

"I know what I did wrong," he said. "I forgot to give you my name. You can call me John, if you like."

Djinni was so dumbfounded by his alien reasoning that she felt compelled to turn her whole body to face him. By fire-ember light, she strained to read his expression.

"Then it'd be all right for you to put out. I give you my name: You put out. That's the proper prelude to mating on Earth."

"No, it isn't! You've a talent for misunderstanding English when it suits you." She switched to her probationary-teacher's voice. "There's a difference between giving your name by way of a polite introduction and giving your name in a civil contract. And, however you're offering it, I don't want it."

Her rejected suitor was looking altogether too pleased with himself. Suddenly, Djinni understood that he'd maneuvered her into having a face-to-face cuddle.

"Furthermore, you've been keeping some very low company. 'Put out' is a terribly coarse expression. I don't want to hear you repeat it. Don't even think about it."

"Yes, my dear," he sighed, sounding chastened. "If the deed is not even to be thought about, do you think we might sleep?"

He rolled onto his back, used his linked hands for a pillow, and shut his eyes.

Djinni wondered how he'd set up a trap like that. It was almost Chess-Masterly. Her impossible choice was to keep him awake and thinking about sex, or let him share her bed.

She considered it. She could tolerate him for the remainder of this one night. He probably thought he'd set a bed-sharing precedent for future nights. She smiled sleepily. That needn't cost her any sleep. There weren't going to be any future nights.

Tarrant-Arragon lay very still, staring at the ceiling and listening to her breathe. He was determined to prove to himself that he could keep his word.

It wasn't easy to let the little mate sleep. Her exhaled sighs fluttered the fabric of his upper-body drape and played like a warm sea breeze over his bare chest. The innocent eroticism made his loins sizzle.

With boa-constrictor care he eased an arm around her, drew her against him, and noticed—not for the first time—the paradox of her aura. When he held her close, her nearness calmed his savage lust for her until it was merely a pleasant tingling.

He was wondering how to exploit this discovery when she cried out in her sleep.

"My dear Djinni, I wish I knew what made you scream so?" he murmured, not expecting an answer.

"It. But I always wake up before he does it . . ." Her voice trailed away. Astonishingly, her reply was almost lucid.

"Who is 'he'?" he prompted gently.

"I don't know. I'm supposed to negotiate peace with him, I think. But he's an impossibly lecherous tiger-person. He chases me. He wants to—" Her dream-voice broke. "But I'm afraid."

"You mustn't be afraid with me. I'll keep you safe."

"That's what my tiger-lover says."

The Great Tiger Prince, Tarrant-Arragon, understood her dream as she could not. It was as if the Great Originator had painted the word "Yes!" across the cosmos, his burning finger joining the dots of distant stars, until the karma of Tarrant-Arragon and Djinni-vera was confirmed in a positive blaze of supernovae.

Chapter Six

"Did you hear his High—er—Horniness taking his prisoner?"

The coarse voice rose as clearly on the crisp morning air as the scrunch of gravel on the driveway below the open bathroom windows. Djinni glanced around the door to the bedroom. Thank the stars! His so-called Higher Horniness seemed to have gone back to sleep. She didn't want him to live up to that nickname.

Her abductor's henchmen were betting on why she'd screamed in the night! Djinni moved closer to the open window to hear which of the horrible men thought she'd screamed in the night with pleasure, and who swore that the screams had been karate-fighting cries as she fought for her virtue.

"His Horniness" hadn't ravished her.

Djinni hugged a bath towel around herself and mulled over what had happened since she'd woken in her large abductor's arms.

Perhaps he'd intended more than a wake-up kiss. He'd tilted her face into kissing range, but then he'd seen her puffy cheek.

His sharp intake of breath had sounded more like the sibilance of physical pain than high arousal.

"Your poor face," he'd grieved over her, and he'd seemed genuinely shocked and remorseful. "Damn! I should never have neglected your injuries last night. Does it hurt very much?"

Taking advantage of the sudden realization that her bumps and bruises from the previous night's escape attempt must have colored up dramatically overnight, she'd nodded and submitted to an examination. He'd winced in sympathy when she flinched, and tutted and berated himself with soft expletives while he probed. He was more talkative than a good—but foulmouthed—dentist.

After stroking the bruises on her bare legs, he'd wanted to carry out a more thorough inspection, but he'd accepted it when she refused to undress. She'd been able to extract his promise that she could soak her sore places in privacy.

Feeling victorious, she exaggerated her soreness and stiffness as she staggered to the ensuite bathroom. But perhaps he hadn't been taken in. He'd called out a dire warning, just as she opened the first bathroom window.

"I hope you're not planning to escape through that bathroom window. You really don't want to break your lovely long legs."

"You mean, you don't want me to. It'd wreck your plans," she'd shot back, feeling absurdly safe behind the half-open door.

"If you broke your legs, it wouldn't wreck my plans for you at all, my dear. In fact . . ."

"But you'd have to take me to the hospital." She had been startled into betraying the germ of her Plan B.

"Why do you think we have Ka'Nych?" he'd said in the most chillingly civilized of voices. Now, thinking about it, she had the impression that he had left a great deal unsaid.

"Callous, sadistic bastard!" Since he was asleep again, she voiced her opinion of him, but quietly. Enveloping her elbows in her towel to ward off the chill of the broad, stone windowsill, she assessed the facade below. It should be a straight-forward climb down. If only she could be sure her slightly sprained ankle wouldn't give way.

She leaned farther out of the window to study the gang, and recognized Grievous. He might turn a blind eye if she shinnied down the ivy. But there were at least three others, and they were behaving in an ostentatiously guardlike fashion. Some of them were dressed as if they had taken wardrobing tips from a Schwarzenegger action movie. The stately-home owner must think he'd rented out a "location" to Universal Pictures.

A film set. How perfect for aliens! They could have weapons, satellite dishes, even a fleet of UFOs parked on the lawn, and the people of Cerne Abbas would think nothing of it.

She might have been explained as a spaced-out starlet, high on drugs, prone to screaming tantrums. The locals would think it was a chase scene if she were seen running away. If she were recaptured, her abductor could do whatever he pleased with impunity, whether or not cameras seemed to be rolling.

Wait. There was a delivery taking place. A load of costumes, by the look of it. If they left the truck unattended, that might change everything.

Tarrant-Arragon glowered at the display grid of his forearm communicator, where a pulsing blue dot represented the troubling little mate. Her coordinates showed that, despite a warning, she was close to the bathroom window. Too close. Surely Djinni wouldn't do something unsensical.

He swore. She'd almost died of fright over her first deep kiss. Whatever had possessed him to speak as he had to such a girl?

Tarrant-Arragon couldn't stand it. Djinni was halfway out of the window. He couldn't keep his promise.

He insinuated himself sidelong in the bathroom doorway, steeling himself to put down a feminine rebellion. The next instant, it was a very virile uprising that he had to suppress.

His Djinni was leaning innocently over the broad win-dowsill. Her long bare legs were casually parted and braced in

such a way as to present a perfectly uptilted and aligned rear el-
evation. He was crazy to imagine she'd decided to entice him.
She didn't know what she was doing. She couldn't. So, what
was she doing?

"Where d'you want this lot, mate?" An uncultured voice
drifted up from the driveway. Presumably, a gesture informed
the deliveryman, but he went on in thick Dorset accents. "Got
a fetish for black, has he, your boss?"

Tarrant-Arragon stared as Djinni continued to lean on the
windowsill, unaware of his appreciative presence. His dear,
feminine heart's-delight, he could hardly wait to dress her up
in his all-black personal livery . . . and then undress her.

"He's got fifty dresses. Stone the crows! Did you see the labels on them, Xirxex? You wouldn't know who Valentino,
Mané, and De La Renta are, would you, old son? Those are de-
signer gowns—"

Tarrant-Arragon eased himself out of the doorway, hoping
his future Empress was as impressed as Grievous seemed to be.

Possibly, the Earthling was right after all; Djinni was unre-
ceptive toward him because she hadn't understood that he was
going to marry her. He'd set her straight forthwith. But what
had Grievous said about girls wanting to be asked properly?

Very well. He'd dress her. Then he'd feed her. And then,
when she was calm and attentive, he'd tell her—correction—
he'd ask her for her hand in marriage.

Tigron Imperial Space: The Trojan Horse

Commander Jason eased an extra-large condom—which re-
joiced, as much as condoms can rejoice, in the brand name
"Triumphant Magnificence"—from its radiation-proof foil
packet.

He grinned at the two exhausted courtesans who lay flut-
tering on his sleeping couch, where he'd left them some moments ago.

"Again, Jason?" panted Feya. "It's good for morale."

"Yours? Or mine?" Jason chuckled to soften his rejection of her offer. Then, bending over his desk, he copied a password until he had filled every square of a twenty-five by twenty-five grid with the password's characters. Substituting the characters from the grid, he encrypted his message to Madam Tarra.

"Send Djarrhett . . . ," he wrote. 'Rhett was the only Djinn he could trust to fetch Djinni from Earth.

It'd be a couple of months before she arrived. He'd have time to think of an explanation for Feya's and Petri-Shah's visits. As a married officer, he couldn't entertain courtesans as he'd done for the past thirteen years with no questions asked. Not with Djinni in his marital bed. The crews would draw disrespectful conclusions about his wife.

Which also ruled out saying that Djinni needed lessons. Besides, within a month, he'd have had the rut-rage and she'd be pregnant.

Jason massaged the bridge of his patrician nose. How would he explain to Djinni about Petri-Shah's and Feya's visits? Maybe he'd admit that he'd been keeping his hand in. Marking time until she grew up. A bride should be glad that her mate was a thousand-world-class lover whom courtesans begged for gratuitous sex.

However, he didn't want Djinni to think she was marrying an old roué. At thirty-five, he wasn't old. He wasn't a roué. He simply gave an excellent impression of being one.

After Djinni's liberated life in England, what would she make of her cramped life as a war-star wife? What would she think of him? What kind of first impression would he make on her?

He ran his fingers over the scar, and wondered whether there was a place in her dreams for a scarred hero who would come charging through her nightmares and save her from what she feared most.

He wondered whether she'd outgrown her nightmares.

She'd been eighteen months old the first time he'd been left to babysit. He'd had his head full of seventies rock music and hadn't heard her scream in the night. Djinni had been determined that he should comfort her. She'd escaped from her crib and toddled through to his room, dragging her stuffed toy dinosaur, presumably for moral support.

The first he'd known of her distress was when a drooled-on "Saur" was slammed between his legs. That got his attention.

Djinni followed "Saur," clambering resolutely up the Niagara of his tumbled bedding, her underlip trembling with indignation at her bad dream. She crawled trustingly into his bed and into his heart, and fell asleep on his chest.

"Hey, Petri-Shah, do you think this'll frighten my bride? She was always a sensitive little kid. I was wondering whether I ought to try to conceal it somehow."

"Definitely, darling. You're a very alarming sight. It's so fearsomely large! In our line of work, we're used to that sort of thing. . . ." Petri-Shah hesitated, and Jason recognized her trying-to-be-tactful look. "Your childhood sweetheart may not be."

"I'm talking about my scar," Jason said with great dignity.

Feya looked him up and down and pouted critically. "Well, that's noble, dashing, and devilishly sexy, too."

"We think so, Feya, because we know how he got it, and we're grateful," reasoned Petri-Shah.

While the girls argued about the right cosmetics to camouflage his scar until Djinni got used to it, Jason copied his coded message into a microprocessor, which automatically pricked the miniature symbols into the purple condom.

"Is it a love letter?" Feya asked.

"Not quite, sweetheart," he said, tolerantly uncommunicative.

"It's nothing to do with your wedding permit, I suppose?"

"Does everyone know my business?" he retorted, and reinserted the ruined condom into its packet, took a needle-fine soldering pen, and heat-sealed the foil.

"Not the business you entrust to us," Petri-Shah interjected.

Feya burst into sophomoric giggles. "It seems so funny to stamp information onto a condom and then seal it up again."

"It's perfect," Petri-Shah said. "Who'd be suspicious of a courtesan carrying condoms?"

"No one, I hope," Jason interrupted before Feya could make a predictable joke about condom failure. "Darlings, I have to ask you to leave. Stagger out of here looking shockingly plundered and totter back to your shuttle. I don't care what impression of me you give to the eager An'Koori, but you are now in no condition to see any other clients. Take this to Madam Tarra."

Jason gave a parting kiss to his two favorite courier-courtesans, whose shuttles shot through Hyperspace faster and more safely than an electronic message could be transmitted.

"Come again. You hear." He chuckled.

After the girls had left, Jason stretched out on his sleeping couch, a triumphant smile on his lips. Seventeen Earth-years ago he'd staked a legal claim to his "Baby Dragon." Now she was almost of lawful marrying age.

His waiting time had been used well. True, Tarrant-Arragon had anticipated and countered every Saurian plot. In so doing, he'd neglected his prime responsibility—to mate. With every passing year, Tarrant-Arragon's ability to beget gifted Djinn diminished. If he mated with a commoner now, the child would be weak, might be a girl. Moreover, a commoner might not survive the Great Djinn's repeated attentions. After a couple of gestates, Tarrant-Arragon would have to find a new Empress.

Meanwhile, Prince Djetthro-Jason had only to wait. He owned the last perfect bride.

The Great House, Cerne Abbas, Dorset

Djinni had never thought of trophies of arms as being phallic, until her abductor carried her down the grand staircase and remarked that the artistically arranged lances were all degrees of erect.

She hadn't wanted to be carried. She'd have preferred to walk in case they came across the nasty-minded members of his gang. However, he insisted. Since she'd decided to humor him as graciously as she could in minor matters, she shyly slipped her arms around his neck and tried to make polite conversation.

First, while really looking for a telephone, she'd admired a fine landscape painting on the upper landing. Unfortunately, he took up the topic of the arts and ran away with it. His idea of small talk verged on the pornographic.

Sober portraits of historical husbands and aristocratic wives lining the dark-paneled corridors and hallways excited her would-be lover's low opinion of their noble sex lives.

Djinni watched him prowl the magnificent breakfast room and wondered what further lewd inspiration he would find among the heraldic devices and paintings of classical subjects.

He'd already ruined her appetite with his observation that a writhing nymph was enjoying a crossbreeding experiment with a "stallion-man," followed by a tasteless discourse on what sorts of intergenetic breeding were scientifically possible.

As she helped herself from an array of silver chafing dishes, Djinni tried to imagine what Grandmama Helispeta would make of her suitor, who was contemplating a painting of satyrs and probably working himself up to another verbal atrocity.

Tarrant-Arragon grinned at the object of his not entirely dishonorable intentions as she took her heaped plate and limped to the far end of the formal dining table.

She hadn't appreciated his ideas on centaurs. He wondered how she'd react if he described a satyr as a "genetically enriched goat-man" and suggested that the satyr was debating essential family-planning methods with a laid-back goddess.

He wasn't sure why he was being so unsubtle, but he knew why Djinni had chosen a steaming pile of yellow food that smelled like his third equerry's breath: in the hope of discouraging kissing.

Moreover, she was playing with it instead of eating it, because she must think she was safe from sex for as long as she could make the meal last. Unsense. He'd make his play.

He stood at the head of the table, one leg relaxed, and leaned forward on his hands, rather in the manner of a movie mafioso making an offer she couldn't refuse.

"Would you like to marry me?" He sounded rather growlish, but it was an acceptable proposal.

"No, thank you." She refused him as casually as if he'd offered to pass the blackberry jelly.

"What? No? Raging Carnality!" Tarrant-Arragon didn't care to cap his explosion of fury. "By all the Lechers of Antiquity, I made you an offer of marriage! Marriage, do you understand?"

He rampaged across the room, slammed both the double doors, and gave vent to his choicest curses. "Damn and Do-Deca-Damn! Fewmet! You dare refuse me? Me!"

Recalling his pose as a common nasty bastard, he attempted to moderate his rage. He paced around the thirty-foot dining table and continued to fume in silence.

Slack damn! Even Lucinthe had squealed with excitement when he ordered her to marry him. She'd flung herself at his feet, kissed his thighs and Ring hand, and gave every indication of humble gratitude.

"Sizzling fireballs! You show more appreciation for that fishy concoction on your plate." His rage boiled over again. "You don't have the excuse that you love someone else."

Which was the excuse Lucinthe ought to have used. The lying traitoress hadn't said a word about her secret lover. And she was full-Tigron. She knew the purity rules.

Lucinthe ought to have confessed before anyone lost face. It was High Treason of her to continue her clandestine sex liaison, while telling him she was a virgin and pleading with him to be patient. Fool that he'd been, he'd believed her, until he heard the sound track on the tracer-necklace he'd given her for an engagement token.

"Or do you?" Tarrant-Arragon turned back menacingly. "Are you in love with some damn Earthling? I'll kill him."

Ah, damn his temper! Whether he meant it or not, that was hardly a remark likely to win her regard.

Djinni's frightened eyes were the silver of sea at ice-dawn. As white as royal wedding sheets, she shook her head.

"Interbreeding is forbidden to me," she whispered.

He dropped a fiercely possessive hand on her cold shoulder, and his temper evaporated. Djinni was definitely inexperi-

enced. Unlike Lucinthe, she would never sneak away to be un-
faithful, though she might do her damnedest to avoid him.

He watched her sip the infusion beverage that she seemed to
like so much. "Tea" she called it. He'd get her crates of it.

She might be unflatteringly reluctant, but he was delighted
with her. She was unlike the ambitious virgins of Tigron. Far
from being more responsive, Djinni would be horrified if she
knew that he was the most eligible bachelor in the Communicating Worlds.

He was effectively the ruler of an Empire; staggeringly rich;
extensively titled; formidably intelligent—qualifications that
made him every maiden's fantasy and every male's nightmare.
His future Empress, however, would not be impressed. No, if
she knew who he was, she'd probably try to disembowel herself with her paring knife out of misguided loyalty to her
Saurian Dragon.

Nevertheless, he would win her over. But, first, he had a situation to retrieve. Lacking experience with disappointment,
he'd handled rejection badly. He'd behaved like a sulking,
spoiled boy. What the Carnality was he supposed to do?

"You should try the kedgeree. It's a traditional breakfast of
turmeric-yellowed rice, fish, eggs, herbs, and spices. This is a
particularly good recipe, though it seems rather decadent to
serve it with caviar on the side," she suggested in a quiet
voice.

She was going to ignore his juvenile tantrum! She'd offered
him a face-saving excuse to retreat. Ah, Djinni had beautiful
manners. He silently congratulated himself on his good fortune while he helped himself from the warming trays.

"My dear, I mean to marry you," he ventured at his most
civilized, and he seated himself opposite her, his legs on either
side of hers—which were primly together, her vulnerable bare
toes tucked under her chair. "How do I change your mind
about me?"

He watched Djinni watching him over the rim of her
teacup. Apparently, a suitor who could not pull rank and influence had to put considerable effort into the chase.

"Tell me how an Earthling stalks his mate."

His little mate reacted as if he'd taken a decaying rodent by its bald tail and slapped it on the highly polished oak table.

"He does not stalk her!" she objected.

"No?" He flashed her a small skeptical smile and tried a heaped forkful of fishy rice. "Then tell me what must be done before a male succeeds sexually with his chosen mate?"

Djinni took another sip of tea and told herself that it was just talk. Grandmama Helispeta would be in her element in this situation. She'd pretend she was Helispeta.

"A strange male, such as yourself, would find a trusted acquaintance in common with his intended mate," she began Helispetorially.

She tilted back her head and half closed her eyes in a deliberate insult-signal. Her single-minded suitor settled lower in his chair, grinning as if he were enjoying himself immensely.

"Ahhhh. What for, my dear?" he said with the calculated innocence of Red Riding Hood's wolf.

"To have himself recommended to the lady's notice." Djinni mimicked Helispeta's sneer, implying that he was not only beneath any lady's notice, but also beneath contempt.

"Haven't I made myself sufficiently . . . noticeable?" He raised one eyebrow. "For the sake of argument, let's imagine that someone could be found to vouch for me."

"In that unlikely event, the lady might agree to meet the gentleman for a meal."

"A meal?" Her ungentlemanly suitor leaned back in his chair and flourished his wrong-choice, wrong-way-up, silver fork halfway to his mouth. Apparently satisfied that he'd made his point, he resumed his traditional English breakfast.

"Ah, did you think I might be an inconsiderate lover because I failed to feed you properly on our first night together?"

It was her turn to lift an eyebrow. "I'm not prepared to offer an opinion of you as a lover," she said haughtily.

"Very wise." He grinned. "I'd prove you wrong. Seriously, though, I did want to feed you, I meant to wine and dine you—"

She could imagine what he'd meant to put in the dessert wine.

"But you slept the whole damn day. Then we had to make an unplanned detour to the Cerne Giant. If not for a chance remark by Grievous during a motorway rest stop, I might not have known in time that a bride-to-be has to sit on the Giant's potent male member before she is eased onto her future husband's. It's like a symbolic form of the ancient Right of the Lord."

"I don't wish to know that," Djinni snapped, and gave him a glare that had always withered college campus wolves.

Unfortunately, he was another breed of wolf, and seemed to enjoy baiting her. He chuckled impenitently.

"You don't like talking about sex, do you? And you blush so delightfully, I cannot resist it. My dear, if I'd given you food after your bath, instead of kissing you, would you have let me talk you into bed with me?"

"No!" She shook her head emphatically.

"No?" Tarrant-Arragon found himself fascinated by the way her eyes changed color. They were like a private scoreboard that told him how successfully he'd stressed her. He just couldn't decide whether he felt victorious or ashamed when he said something truly disconcerting, and registered a silver glare.

"So, little dagger-eyes, is eating together an important preliminary?" This time, he was careful not to draw attention to the fact that they were eating together.

"Yes. In a public place. After which, we'd part."

"Is eating and parting all that you'd consent to?"

"Considering your manners and adult interests, yes." Then, as he watched, his quarry's eyes shaded darker to a color that reminded him of the lighting on the Bridge of a war-star at Battle Stations. She went on the attack. "Don't you know anything at all about proper behavior?"

"I thought I did. Apparently, I was wrong." He tried to feign meekness, but couldn't sustain it for grinning. "How many times must we go through this rather pointless routine of meeting, eating, and parting before we copulate?"

"Courtship . . . is . . . formal," she said distantly. A pulse began to throb two finger-breadths above the tracer necklet and directly below her ear. He memorized its position for future attention and allowed himself to imagine all her kissable places.

Either she knew what he was doing and it made her even more nervous, or she was trying to lie to him. She stammered as she listed rules that bore little resemblance to the behavior he'd studied on Earthling satellite television. Her rules sounded more like Tigron customs, except she omitted to mention the law that a male who deflowered a virgin had to marry her. He understood why. Nor did she mention that the "Tiger" Djinn Princes of Tigron were exempt from the law, but then, she wouldn't think it relevant.

He waited for her to make a mistake.

"A gentleman," she decreed, "may not kiss a young lady until he has proposed marriage."

Check!

"I've already proposed marriage. Therefore I may kiss you, by your own rules, dictated voluntarily by your own lips." He got to his feet, swept aside the silver clutter of his place setting, and leaned teasingly across the thickly waxed table. "I told you, right from the first, that I wanted to mate. What did you think I meant? Shall I explain mating to you?"

"You . . . are . . . no . . . gentleman!" she gasped, as if she thought this minor detail might disqualify his claim on her.

"Very true. I'm your determined mate. As such, it will be my pleasure and my duty to instruct you in the practical aspects of sex." So saying, he vaulted the table. An easy matter for a Djinn in Earth's light gravity. "Besides, I'm tired of being misunderstood. I'm going to have to anticipate my vows."

"No!" she gasped. She rose as if to defy him, but her legs collapsed under her and she stumbled into his embrace. He saw that he'd gone too far.

He could see, and hear, that her heart was beating too fast. Her luminous eyes were about to overflow with silvery tears, and he felt strangely uneasy with the image of himself reflected in those swirling pools.

"I only meant verbally, for now. Unless you feel uncharacteristically adventurous?" With a well-judged kick he turned her chair so he could sit, and use the table for an armrest. Having placed her on his lap, he asked, "Can't you try to like me? Just a little?"

"*Like* you? Like *you*?" she spluttered, effectively varying her emphasis. She seemed able to handle "liking" as a topic. "Do you like people who lie to you and trick you?"

She had a point. He half-killed people he caught lying to him. To his knowledge, no one had ever dared to trick him.

"Or bullies who threaten you with dreadful unpleasantnesses?"

"Now, just you wait a heartbeat." Now she was being personal. "Are you referring to my sexual prowess as 'dreadful unpleasantnesses'? That's an outrageous mischaracterization—"

He mind-shielded his thoughts about how he might dispel her prejudices. He was beginning to see a pattern in Djinni's flashes of terror.

"My dear, I mean to marry you." Her head-shaking had freed a long curl from her bun. He caught it and coiled the silky skein around his forefinger. "Must I follow your tedious courtship rules without any obligation on your part?"

She nodded, and her hair tugged softly on his finger.

"You're going to make me suffer, aren't you?" he sighed, purposely giving her a false sense of control.

"We only met twenty-four hours ago," she reasoned. "It's all very sudden. May I think about it?"

"About making me suffer, or about marrying me?"

"Both!" She smiled tremulously.

Tarrant-Arragon wanted very much to kiss her, but he knew it would be counterproductive. She needed time. And courtship.

"Think about me all you like," he flirted gently. "Get used to the idea of being with me."

Djinni felt like King Canute, enthroned on the seashore to teach obsequious courtiers an object lesson in the limits of royal power. Her uncouth suitor courted like an incoming spring tide. The waves of his desires tugged at her hemline. Every seventh advance was a great, roaring breaker that crashed over her head and almost swept her legs out from under her.

She tried to concentrate. It wasn't easy. His fingers were like the sun in her hair. He was asking her out on a "date."

"We could go sightseeing together," he said. "Grievous tells me there are some charming botanical gardens at Stourhead, a vehicular museum at Beaulieu, a castle ruin at Corfe, and some prehistoric ring fortifications at Badbury."

While he listed Dorset's and Wiltshire's tourist attractions, Djinni mentally assessed the escape potential of each, and made plans of her own.

Chapter Seven

"Sir, she's up to something."

Tarrant-Arragon felt inclined to ignore his driver's warning. He liked the idea of going shopping for his little mate. He liked the astonishing greenness of the hedgerows alongside the narrow Dorchester Road, and the whistles of ridiculous birds that sang—sang!—to protect their territory and attract mates. It was all so delightfully inefficient.

"Sir, if you go into Boots-the-Chemists and ask for the items you've just read off her shopping list, you're liable to get us arrested."

"Exactly what is the problem with . . ." Tarrant-Arragon consulted the paper in his right hand, ". . . glycerine?"

"Well, that's harmless in itself, Sir, but if you buy both types of acid she's listed, you've got yourself bomb-making goodies. We wouldn't want the local constabulary getting the idea we're terrorists, would we? See, I was a demolitions expert back in my SAS days—"

"I see. And the 'Marijuana'?"

"Illegal substance, Sir. Drugs. So's the 'Morning Glory.' She probably hoped you'd think they were cosmetics because of the flowery names. Dropping names like those in sleepy Dorset would get our safe house raided for sure, if they didn't arrest us on the spot."

"Turn back."

"Yes, Sir. As soon as we come to a roundabout, or to a nice lay-by," Grievous said in an infuriatingly patronizing tone.

"Slack damn!" Tarrant-Arragon drummed his fingers on the sun-warmed, black paintwork.

"There's no use in committing a moving traffic violation in our haste. I daresay your little miss doesn't care how we get ourselves pinched, just as long as we fall foul of the law one way or another."

"No girl is that devious. Carnality!" Tarrant-Arragon swore in self-disgust at almost having been outwitted. "Well, she won't escape me!"

He rolled up his English man-of-affairs-style shirtsleeve, and contacted Xirxex on his forearm communicator. Xirxex's report was as expected.

"Storm-Master Xirxex informs me that all is quiet and under control." Tarrant-Arragon kept his triumph out of his voice.

The alarmist Grievous did not seem to be convinced. "Still, we are going back, Sir? Because, strictly speaking, it isn't possible for Xirxex to have the situation under control."

"No?" Tarrant-Arragon glanced quizzically at his driver. "Do you have second sight too, Grievous? Don't tell me all Earthlings are clairvoyant."

"No, Sir. Er, Xirxex tells me he's not allowed to touch the little miss. I'd say he'd be severely handicapped if she did try to escape while we're out of the way, wouldn't you, Sir?"

"Xirxex's mere presence and size should be a deterrent," he said, not wishing to admit that Grievous had a point. Tarrant-Arragon checked the mate-tracer function on his communicator.

"A deterrent? To her? Nah! It wasn't in the Cerne Giant's field, now, was it, Sir? And at that stage, she didn't know what you had in store for her."

Tarrant-Arragon overlooked the insolence. Grievous's caustic sense of humor amused him.

"I hadn't considered the difficulty Xirxex would face if my little mate were to lay violent hands on him again." Tarrant-Arragon smiled. "She seems to have no concept of her own physical limitations. I'm surprised she hasn't attacked me."

"Now that, Sir, is an absurd—"

"Be warned, Grievous." He held up a hand to silence the Earthling, who presumed a little too much. "I can't allow other males to touch my mate. Our royal females are exceptionally precious and rare. We manage to breed—and keep—so few.

"The no-contact rule is officially a precaution against the contact poisons an assassin from my worlds might use. However, I'm sure you've heard of our deadly jealousy. One cannot predict when a Great Djinn will become impassioned. There is a reason for our tendency to kill off perceived rivals—"

"Yes, Sir. Consider me well warned. Ah-ha! Public house up ahead. I'll turn the limo around in its car park."

The driver turned. Tarrant-Arragon noted that the little mate had been very still in one part of the bathroom for a very long time. He might have suspected that she'd found a way to remove the tracer necklet if not for the fact that only a special sort of laser could cut through the rare golden metal.

"As I was about to say about your little miss, she is resourceful. Daring too. If she were my daughter, I'd be damned proud of her for putting up such a jolly good show of virtue and resistance, Sir."

"I don't know what you're talking about, Grievous," Tarrant-Arragon snapped. But he had a very good idea. He had been fully alert when Djinni opened the bathroom windows that morning. He'd heard the "High—er—Horniness" conversation.

"Well, Sir, have you made it clear to her that you propose to marry her?" As he asked, the driver made a great show of looking to the right and left and right again before crossing into nonexistent traffic.

"I told her." Tarrant-Arragon smiled wryly and crumpled

the shopping list in his hand. "And she sends me out on an impossible quest for bombs and drugs."

"And speeding tickets!" Grievous snorted with mirth. "She may not want to get married. Or perhaps she doesn't believe you. We all know you've told her one or two major whoppers. And you say she's psychic? I'll bet she smells a rat, Sir."

Djinni wasn't surprised that her abductor had posted guards. She'd expected elementary precautions. She'd already torn and knotted the white bedsheets into a rope, and while she secured it to one of the freestanding bathtub's clawed feet, she congratulated herself on how well her multilayered plot seemed to be working.

She'd made inspired improvements to her shopping list. Her suitor had received it from her hand like a five-star bellhop accepts a tip—without examining it. He'd gone away humming. Then Grievous stopped for an indiscreet chat with Xirxex outside her door, which alerted her to the presence of the sentry.

The gritty-voiced Xirxex complained about being left "alone" to guard "Herself." Although Djinni didn't believe that an overgrown male could really be afraid of her, his unhappiness had given her morale a much-needed boost.

When she heard the start-up scrunch of the limousine's tires, she'd leaned out of the window, ostensibly to wave in a wifely fashion, while she checked whether or not there was a guard below. There was. Thus informed, she carried out Escape Plan A.

She opened a faucet and let the water trickle. When the sound of running water sent the guard off to investigate the plumbing, she dropped the sheet and took up her position behind the bedroom door until her "escape" was discovered.

She didn't have long to wait.

An outraged yell signaled the discovery of the dangling sheets, and was closely followed by shouts. The uneven thunder of hobbling heavy-worlder feet, a peremptory thud on her bedroom door, and Xirxex burst in to investigate.

While she flattened herself behind the open door and willed

her ruse to work, she heard Xirxex storm the bathroom and comment in alien immoderation on his findings.

Djinni listened to his floor-creaking progress and could only guess at the effect that the apparent proof of her escape had on him. Xirxex was too dismayed to think of further searching the room. He followed the bolted-horse-and-barn-door principle and charged off, at a fast limp, leaving the bedroom door unguarded.

Djinni slipped quietly along the corridor to where she assumed the back stairs would be.

"Grievous"—Tarrant-Arragon kept his voice enigmatic— "never in my life have I been called a rat—never mind a malodorous rat."

He was using his smooth interrogator's tactic; its open-ended menace invariably elicited far more incautious honesty than any direct question. Tarrant-Arragon expected that, if he was any judge of character, he'd receive a piece of Grievous's mind.

"Hell's Bells and Buckets of Blood, Sir. You've been at her like some damned rutting animal ever since you caught her! I did warn you, Sir. Nice young ladies don't like chaps coming on to them like blasted satyrs. If you don't mind my saying so, I'd recommend something anti-aphrodisiacal in your tea. Sir!"

It was a startling idea. Most original. One he'd never have thought of for himself. Nobody else would dare such an impertinence. However, Grievous had no way of knowing that Djinn males did not inhibit their sex drives in any way, neither for contraception nor for social convenience.

Tarrant-Arragon eyed Grievous thoughtfully. The Earthling spoke his mind and he didn't pull his punchy opinions. Tarrant-Arragon liked that quality.

"Grievous, you're refreshingly unlike my 'yes-saying' Warstar Leaders and equerries," he began. "I have time and space for warriors who aren't afraid to give an unfavorable status report, even if it is hardly flattering. To tell the truth, I could use a devil's advocate at my side. Would you consider coming to work for me permanently?"

Grievous nearly swerved into the ditch.

"What was that, Sir?" he said, flabbergasted.

"Join my staff as my Earthways Advisor. I can profit from your distressing insights into how my half-Earthling mate may be perceiving me and my actions," said the prince.

Suddenly, lights flashed on the prince's forearm.

Grievous realized it wasn't a good time to inquire further about the job offer. So, while Tarrant-Arragon dealt with an emergency back at the house, Grievous considered his future.

The title sounded impressive. The job description was right up his alley. He'd take it. For one thing, it probably wasn't healthy to refuse Tarrant-Arragon. For another, he liked both the compelling sex-fiend and the bewitching little miss. He'd like to be along to see romance flower between them.

He didn't understand what Tarrant-Arragon was saying to Xirxex, but his tone was unpleasant and decisive. So Grievous put the pedal to the metal and listened in discreet surprise when Tarrant-Arragon became very particular about how Xirxex should enunciate phrases like Search The Orchard and Try the Rhododendron Shrubberies.

Then Grievous looked up and met a mischievous glint in the alien's coal-ember eyes.

"Ah, Grievous. It seems my unsettled mate wants to play cat-and-mouse." The prince's eyes gleamed with amusement. "Guess who gets to be cat? I am very good at it."

Djinni listened to the hue and cry going on outside and in the rooms below the one from which she'd fled. From the shouts in English, she knew that the garages and the kitchen gardens had been searched and the maze, the orchard, and the rhododendron shrubberies were next.

The delivery truck had long gone. Still, she might find a car in the garages, or a working telephone. It was worth a try.

All clear!

Djinni eased the scullery door outward and couldn't help grimacing when the hinges creaked. She turned and used both hands to close the door so it wouldn't bang in the March wind.

Stars! He was right there! Arms folded, leaning against the wisteria vine behind the door. Almost on top of her. Watching her like a big, smug cat.

"When we agreed that I might try courting you, I thought there was an implicit understanding that you'd be physically present." His tone suggested that he would make certain nothing was ever again left to implication and inference.

Djinni shivered. Literally, she'd only promised not to climb out of a window, but she had broken the spirit of the promise. Before he revoked all of the concessions to her personal privacy that she'd already won, she'd have to outwit him.

"Sir, if ever you were a gentleman, or if you wish me to think of you as one, we should settle our differences honorably," she began, hoping he didn't have a chess-playing sort of mind.

"I'd love to." Tarrant-Arragon uncrossed his arms, pushed off from the wall, and captured her cold hands in his.

"My precious, you've no idea how much I want to—" With the exquisite and well-practiced tact of the conqueror accepting an honorable surrender, he kept the rest of his thoughts to himself.

He was delighted that she was being sensible at last. Presumably, she had satisfied her sense of how far a captured Saurian Knight's duty to escape went.

Perhaps he'd overreacted, back on the Dorchester Road, when he called ahead to order the foray-shuttle pilots to stand by, ready to take them back to the Ark Imperial.

"You're shivering. Let me take you inside, to the fireside, where we can be warm. And we'll talk."

"I don't have any friends to act for me," she said as he guided her toward the Great Hall's hearth, with a firm hand in the delicate curve of her back, "so I must act for myself."

The businesslike little mate! She wanted to discuss their marriage contract. Her quaint formality was enchanting.

"If I win, you must let me go. Also, you tell your men to let me go if I accidentally kill you."

"Slack damn!" He was startled into swearing.

What now? Single mortal combat? That decided it. Even if she was only half serious, this wild talk proved she was ready to try any dangerous folly for as long as they remained on her world. She wouldn't settle until he had her safe on the Ark Imperial.

He looked for Xirxex, located him by the front door, nodded a prearranged signal, and returned his attention to Djinni.

"Fierce child, you can't even walk without limping. How did you come to the absurd conclusion that I agreed to fight you? You've been warned—amply, I should have thought—that fighting stiffens my, ah, inclination."

Her eyes turned the color of Tigron's lilac sheet-lightning.

"Quite so. Must I remind you that I am a great deal bigger, heavier, and stronger than you are? When I have won, as I inevitably shall, are you prepared to yield willingly to me, as a Knight and as a maiden too? Or will you try to beg off, on the grounds that it was an unequal contest?"

Her agitated breathing was putting a fascinating stress-pucker between the third and fourth buttons of her new dress. She must think he truly meant to take her on. She couldn't be reading his mind, or she wouldn't breathe like that.

"Oh! How dare you imply that I'd renege on an affair of honor!" she stormed, standing her ground in spite of her obvious terror. "You, 'sir,' have accepted my challenge."

He caught her wrists below her clenched fists and pressed her onto a fireside Chesterfield, then took his time settling on the rug at her feet. He glanced at his forearm communicator. The Ark Imperial was, as requested, transmitting a local weather forecast. Low cloud cover was moving inland from the Dorset coast. The launch window would open in an Earth-hour or so. He had plenty of time to amuse himself with her impractical aggression.

"My dear, I did no such—"

"Oh yes, you did! You said you'd love to," she hissed. "And, since you hold me prisoner, you have constructively chosen the place and time. That gives me the right to select the weapons, by all the conventions governing dueling."

Her logic was a delight. As Tigron's Lord Prosecutor, he'd never come across a female with the mind of a defense attorney. Of course, her argument was faulty, but she didn't know that, weather permitting, she'd soon be in his bed, on the Ark Imperial, and in his Tigron jurisdiction where he had Rights she would not believe. And where she had none.

"Bully! Your boasted weight and strength are of no advantage if we duel with pistols," she argued, and her passionate eyes shaded to the purple of distant mountaintops.

"How dangerous! You can't expect me to arm you? Where would be the advantage for myself? What I want to fire into you won't harm you. However, if I gave you the means, I've no doubt you'd try to make me incapable of enjoying you."

"No," she gasped. "I would not. Ever since I was little, I've made it a hard-and-firm rule: I never hurt someone in a place I wouldn't want to kiss better."

Did she know what she'd said? It seemed uncharacteristically bold. From her virginal panic when he'd kissed her, he could have sworn she'd never heard of oral sex. So she didn't want to kiss him? He'd soon see about that. His thoughts coursed off in five directions all at once.

"Anyway, it wouldn't be sporting. My weapon of choice is a pistol," she continued, unaware of how provocative she was being. "What do you say to that?"

"Ah, mine should be the 'choice weapon'; yours should be the choice of place and time." It was the only pun that sprang to mind that wasn't unacceptably risqué.

"So you refuse my offer of a fair fight?" she said, ignoring his wicked wit. She used the same tone of voice that he might use when asking one of his nephews whether he was quite sure he wanted to make a certain (bad) chess move.

She extended a hand. "Then I've no choice but to accept your counteroffer. Shall we shake hands on our new contract?"

He had her consent! Triumphantly, he took her hand in both

his. Her moods shifted like the wind-whipped weather vane on the stables' roof, but one couldn't expect to understand a female.

"We're agreed, then," she said, and battle colors flared in her eyes. "You'll keep your choice weapon to yourself until I choose the place and time."

Tarrant-Arragon's Personal Shuttle

Tarrant-Arragon ruled out forcing himself on her. It would be poor strategy to show her his worst side before he had to.

Naturally, he thought about what he wasn't going to do to her as, weightless, he lay back in his throne-and-a-half-sized shuttle seat, his precious little mate deeply cowled and dressed in a protective "courtesy suit," and securely buckled to the front of his seven-point seat harness.

He'd stroke her clothes away from her breasts and trail his lips down the soft curve-lines of her cleavage, intoxicating his explorer senses in this deep virgin valley, then sucking on her to the beat of her sheltered heart, until . . .

She was trembling.

Was she perhaps reading his mind? He fervently hoped not! How else would she pass the time in his arms, hooded as she was?

"You're very quiet, little one. You do understand about the courtesy suit and hood? They are to protect you from radiation. Also to shield your poor bruised face from prying eyes when we reach our destination. Here, let's push it back a little."

The hood will also stop you seeing the warlike parts of the war-star and the Imperial scale of my suite when we get there. Mind-shield that thought!

"Shall I tell you what I'm thinking? I'm making passionate and very thorough love to you. I'm taking all the time in the Empire. I'm patient and very, very generous. I'm thrusting you into wild, wonderful female ecstasies, over and over again."

"If you break your promise," her whisper was harsh, and raw, and final, "I'll make it a point of honor to hate you for it."

The idea of being hated by her was depressing.

On the other hand, after that little conversation, she probably wouldn't be interested in his private musings.

"Ah, what a volatile and delicate situation. Can we talk about it?" he murmured, his chin on the crown of her head. "What are we going to do about your very peculiar phobia? And what if I can't keep that damned impossible promise?"

His train of thought was interrupted as a puff of solar wind buffeted the foray shuttle. She gasped and tensed. Tarrant-Arragon protectively hugged her tighter with one arm and nudged a Mars bar toward her lips.

"Are you feeling ill, my dear? Try some chocolate fudge. Did you hear Grievous say that the British Royal Lifeboatmen swear by Mars bars for seasickness? He thought they might help you. And I've heard that chocolate helps females to relax."

He felt her shake her head against his chest. She wouldn't eat from his hand, and now she wouldn't talk to him. Sulking, he supposed. Childish behavior, but then—under Djinn law—she was still three cycles shy of her coming of age.

Possibly he'd made a tactical error with Djinni. He'd tried too hard to arouse her unawakened sexuality, and she felt threatened.

"How am I supposed to overcome your fear of sex without having sex? That is the question. Ah, little one, what a ridiculous quandary!" he sighed. "Do you think we should make friends first?"

He'd never tried to befriend a female before, apart from one lovable little tigress. He'd won his pet cat's confidence and trust, which he'd failed to do with Djinni. Certainly, if he'd been training an Imperial tiger, he'd know how to deal with her.

Tarrant-Arragon knew all about cats because, just as most great Houses keep exotic, intimidating, or impressive beasts, his family kept black, saber-toothed tigers as household pets.

The big cats were a reminder of the Imperial Djinn motto "the rapacity of tigers" and of their traits of ferocity and strength. Who but a god could control a tiger with a word? Therefore, petting black tigers was living proof of dominance.

Could he make his experience with tigers count?

"Would you like to be friends?"

Silence. Exactly like an offended cat.

Looking back over the past thirty or so hours, there were similarities between Djinni and his little pet tigress, Euterpe. There were the word games: Djinni's bold, verbal darts into dangerous territory, and hurried retreats to safe subjects; her way of batting at sparkling wit, and then frightening herself when the topic ricocheted.

Take Djinni's penchant for running away. That was comparable. His small tigress had explored where she should not and scampered away to hide when he wanted her. At other times, when he was busy, she came uninvited, redeployed his model star-fleet with her big, clumsy baby paws, and speared black holes in his star-maps with her saber teeth.

In matters of personal grooming, Euterpe would have snarled him away just as Djinni had done.

Was this a valid line of thought? It was hardly respectful to compare house-training a big cat with seducing his future Empress. And yet the first rule—"Never force a cat to do something that frightens her"—seemed applicable to Djinni and her phobia. As did the second: "Encourage her to do things that she likes to do and is good at."

"First, we're going to have to get you used to being in bed with me," he whispered half to himself, since Djinni wouldn't respond. They'd begin by doing nonsex things in bed that she enjoyed, or at least tolerated reasonably well. "Won't you tell me what you like to do? No? Too shy?"

Ah, well. With a cat, all one had to do was wait and see. It might work. For lack of a better strategy, he'd resort to what he knew, and try tiger-taming principles on his mate.

Part Two
The Ark Imperial

Chapter Eight

"So this is Prince Tarrant-Arragon's personal spaceship." From the Clearance mezzanine Grievous squinted in the dim fuchsia light at acres of shuttle bays and starfighter ports. "Stone the crows! He is heavy duty, isn't he?"

"Aye, the Ark Imperial is the most sophisticated, most impregnable war-star in the Communicating Worlds," Xirxex gloated.

Grievous leaned on a convenient railing. Stopping-to-admire was a great excuse to take a breather in the Tigrons' leg-dragging gravity. Xirxex seemed happy to limp from sight to sight, though the tour was limited to the route from their arrival port via Decontamination and Medical to top-curveside and the highest officers' quarters.

"Well, Xirxex, I'm so impressed, I'm gobsmacked," Grievous said, clapping his open hand over his mouth to demonstrate the literal meaning of the term.

"You've seen nothing." Xirxex sounded gratified. "It'll take me half a gestate to show you everything."

"What's a 'gestate,' then? It sounds, er, reproductive."

"It's the equivalent of forty Earth weeks. Don't quote me,

because moon's a dirty word, but Tigron isn't a planet, it's a moon in a tidal lock orbit of a gas giant like your Jupiter, which is in an elliptical orbit of a class of star you'd call a Red Dwarf. Our year lasts about four Earth days."

"I'm sorry, old son. Science never was my thing. You've lost me." Sorry to disappoint, Grievous scratched his head.

"Never mind, Earthling. The point is, we don't have seasons that are regular and predictable. Our females do. That's the third thing Tigron girls are good for: timekeeping," Xirxex said, deadpan and smugly patronizing.

"You're pulling my leg. An advanced civilization like yours? Nah!"

"Heh-heh. We weren't always civilized, but once Tigron began to dominate multiple star systems, marking time by the female cycle became impractical. Still, the old names stuck. Also, the associated Imperial wedding customs, such as the Imperial brides' chastity test, public consummation—"

"That sounds bloody barbaric!"

"It ought to be both, Earthling, but who knows?"

"How d'you mean?" Grievous didn't want to know, but had to ask out of common politeness and a morbid sense of guilt that he'd helped get the little miss into this mess.

"We know he's already done his worst to her, don't we? How's he going to pass her off as a virgin at the wedding?"

"Beats me," Grievous grunted.

"His Horniness wouldn't be the first—" Xirxex hid his mouth with his hand and whispered, "to flout the Imperial wedding laws. Now, move along, Grievous. We've twenty decks between our wing-sails. The Ark Imperial bristles with advanced weapons. You'll be Deca-gobsmacked when I show you."

"Will I, by Jove! What've you got?" Grievous asked enthusiastically.

"Coil guns, unmanned smart-craft, particle-beam projectors. Everything state of the art. Our arsenal only had to be used once. Now, when rebel worlds see us, they surrender. See, the Ark Imperial looks like one of your devil-ray fish: It was designed to inspire gut-twisting terror on sight. We hardly ever use the Virtual Invisibility systems. I can't remember the last time Tarrant-Arragon chose not to advertise his presence."

"Not to . . . ?" Grievous echoed before it dawned on him that this visit to Earth was a departure from Tarrant-Arragon's standard operating procedure. Covert ops, in fact.

"Aye. *Not* to. That's why we're lying dark at Battle Stations until the Plunder unit returns. Our presence in your solar system is illegal. Tarrant-Arragon doesn't want the Saurian Dragon to know about this raid. See that?"

Xirxex pointed to three sinister black fighters.

"Tarrant-Arragon's personal Thorcraft. He's deadly, when he is pleased to fight. Heh! And when he's pleased to dock—"

"Poor little miss!"

"Don't fret, Earthling. He'll take good care of her. If he doesn't, you'll be fourth to know. You and Ka'Nych are to share War-star Leader's quarters. Tarrant-Arragon made Slayt give up his rooms—"

"Slayt being a War-star Leader?"

"Aye. Your biggest on-planet war-units are led by admirals, our interstellar ones by War-star Leaders. Feel honored. His Horniness wants you and Ka'Nych close by the Imperial suite in case she makes difficulties on the sheet. Heh! You look doubting, Grievous. Want to bet—"

Grievous shook his head.

"Unsense to bet anyway. We'll be at Battle Stations for at least the next six watches. What else is he going to do in the dark but dock?"

"I hope you don't think this purple gloom is romantic."

Tarrant-Arragon's lips twitched. His Djinni was just like a frightened cat. As soon as he'd loosened her hood, the swatty little mate came out hissing and staggering.

"Sit!" he commanded, taking her upper arms and power-guiding her down onto the wide, polished pumice ledge of the murk-bath.

"This feeble lighting is dangerous and inconvenient," she

snarled, having made a furtive assessment of their surroundings. Presumably, she felt brave enough to cast aspersions because she didn't think he'd ravish her in his bathroom.

She lacked imagination.

"Our light quality is nowhere near as dangerous and inconvenient as your escape attempts," he fired back. "We could have had two days exploring your interesting home world. Instead, we must lie in the dark until the others return."

"Others?" She looked up, her face kissing-close to his as he bent over her, her perfect lips parted in surprise. "Oh! Of course, there are other abductors and other unfortunate abductees."

"What makes you say that, my dear?" he asked, intrigued.

"Well, you can't be important enough to have an intergalactic spaceship at your service. You only had one car and three henchmen. A cosmic 'Somebody' would delegate a kidnapping."

A provocative argument. However, he could hardly tell her that "the others" were a Plunder unit, under orders to bring every last chess pawn and bead from her home to the Ark Imperial.

Instead, feeling wicked, Tarrant-Arragon embellished the lie.

"How perceptive you are, my dear," he drawled. "What do you suppose this spaceship is? A galaxy-going condominium complex, financed by a consortium of lonely bachelors?"

"Like interstellar Vikings? And you all plan to kidnap 'mates'? That's wicked!" she spluttered. "Will I meet them?"

"No, you won't, my dear. I shouldn't be popular with 'the others' if you organized a sex strike."

Her eyes flashed in the semidark. She smiled. By all the Lechers of Antiquity, she must have taken his evasion as a compliment. He was lucky she hadn't read his thoughts recently, because her organizational skills were not uppermost in his mind.

How strange, he reflected as he went to the tray left for him on the dressing bar and poured wine into two goblets. When he'd first encountered her, he'd deliberately thought about sex to shield his more dangerous thoughts. Now he couldn't banish sex from his mind: Sexy thoughts came unbidden, every few minutes.

"Oh! Disgusting!" she launched another attack. Apparently, she'd made a discovery. "Dirty, filthy bathwater, left standing."

He sauntered back to the murk-bath with the wine, and sat beside her. "Ah, sometime I'll explain about ram scoop technology and lumps of water-ice adrift in deep space. This isn't a bath as you know it. It's a murk-bath, which I put in for you because you may have trouble adapting to our slightly heavier gravity." He paused to gauge the success of his technical remarks and saw her glance at the goblet he'd placed by her hand.

"That's An'Koori wine. It's much too fine to pollute with drugs," he reassured her. He hoped.

"To return to the bath, the murk-water is dense, a little like your Earthling Dead Seas, only not with salt but with soft, rounded Agamottite particles which are continuously purified by ionization. Your body will feel almost weightless."

Djinni sipped her wine but said nothing. Instead, she trailed an experimental finger in the murk-bath water. The antigravity "murk" was more like burst-teabag water than her idea of a German spa mud bath. The tub was extravagant in size. A small corps of water ballerinas could form a floating daisy in it.

She couldn't begin to calculate what such a thing would cost, but the implications were daunting. Her single-minded suitor had invested a great deal of thought and alien cash. He must be serious about keeping her.

Frowning in the purplish semidark, she discerned that the bathroom was large, luxurious, and starkly designy. The vertical surfaces were high-gloss black, complemented by matte charcoal planes and purplish-black detailing in the beveled edges.

There was a shower, and two of everything else, and, as she'd noticed when her abductor put away her hood and antiradiation bag, there were clothes closets behind the paneling. She'd very much like to know where the water closets were.

"Come here." He stood, and strolled over to two glossy

black pedestals that looked rather like chess pieces. Bishops. "I'll show you how to use the plumbing."

How unromantic. And how necessary. Djinni set down her wine, rose, and spread her arms for balance. At once, he was by her side, an arm supportively around her waist.

They tripped what she assumed was a sensor, and both of the Bishops' mitre-lines opened, revealing stepped arrangements of airline efficiency that included a mirror, a small wash-basin, loo and integral bidet, each with tiny waterfalls.

"The smaller one is for you. Hold my wine." He passed his glass and sat on the padded seat.

"Weight: three hundred pounds." Her loo told his weight! In American English.

He explained. "I had your toilet programmed to use English for your, ah, convenience. It's pressure-operated, and responsive to weight, temperature, and so forth. Pour my wine into the bowl and observe." He parted his thighs invitingly.

Djinni obeyed and the liquid was sucked away.

"We harness variable gravitational tow for tidiness and for the separation of resources," he said. "We recycle everything. For example, we extract yeast from urine crystals, for baking—"

Djinni experienced unwarriorly squeamishness about recycled cuisine. Then her loo spoke again.

"Increase water consumption." There followed a detailed urinalysis of wine, and, "Levels of fermented sugars: high. Performance impairment probable—"

"It's dangerous if star-crew are unfit for duty. Drunkenness on watch is a court-martialable offense." He gave a twisted grin. "An interfering Imperial High-Up, ah, Tarrant-Arragon himself, decreed that diagnostic plumbing should be standard equipment for all star-craft. To, ah, void the usual plea of ignorance as a legal defense."

"Do not pilot a starfighter for forty-eight hours," the loo interrupted him.

Djinni had an inspiration. His loo ought to make the same recommendations, but in his alien language.

"I didn't ask Maintenance to feminize the suggestion bank. What should an inebriated female avoid?" he teased.

"Men!" The quip slipped out.

"Ah! And would-be gentleman, too? I'll respect your privacy. In return, you'll give me your word that you will harm neither yourself nor my very expensive bathroom. Agreed?"

"Agreed." She nodded. She couldn't wait to be left alone. As he sauntered into an adjacent room, Djinni barely noticed his remark about getting into something more comfortable. She was planning to memorize a word-for-word translation of "Do not pilot a starfighter for forty-eight hours," and then sort out the alien grammar so she could demand a pilot for a starfighter.

Before she could use this lavatorial vocabulary, she'd have to get away from her unwanted suitor. No easy task, that. If the saying "To have a tiger by the tail" applied to anyone in serious trouble, it applied to her.

However, he'd have to sleep eventually. And she wouldn't.

Tarrant-Arragon mentally debriefed himself while he changed into loose, black satiny robes, then settled on the bed to wait for Djinni to come out of the bathroom.

He was still bothered that she'd managed to trick him into making the one promise he'd been determined not to make. However, his immediate challenge was to implement his tiger-taming plan and to win her trust and acceptance before he bedded her.

It went against his predatory nature to wait, and wait, and wait for Djinni to come to him. Tarrant-Arragon resisted the temptation to monitor his mystifying little mate's bathroom activities closely. He simply checked on her periodically, electronically, to be sure she was all right.

The tracer necklet provided an upgraded readout on his bedside computer screens. She'd been into his closets. She'd also inspected his pedestal. Used it. Like a cat claiming territory. Tarrant-Arragon grinned. He hoped this was a sign that she was settling. With a cat it would be.

At last! She peeped around the bathroom doorway, exploring her new environment with wide eyes. He worried that despite the Battle Stations gloom, her half-Djinn eyes would make out the slight variations in shade where the black walls had been stripped of Imperial trappings.

He regretted that his robes might have been better fastened, but it was too late to adjust them now. She might have felt safer if he'd kept on his human trousers, and sat in a chair instead of sprawling on what must be the biggest and strangest-looking bed she'd ever seen.

Though acutely aware of her, he acted as sexually nonthreatening as possible. He called up his Pending Archives to his bedside computer screen and read royal documents of state.

A sudden flurry of black and a frantic gasp alerted him to her difficulties with his gravity. He vaulted off the bed and was across the room in nanoseconds, but was too late to catch her before she landed heavily on the carpet.

She made no effort to get up. She simply sat, her heart thudding, looking as dazed and dejected as a night bird that had flown into the palace force field.

"Oh, Stars. I can't believe I drank enough to—"

"You didn't. Don't be embarrassed, my light-worlder love." He crouched over her. "The heavier the gravity, the harder and faster all objects drop to the ground. You're going to be tired, accident-prone, and clumsy until you're used to my gravity."

"Oh, dear. Can we just sit for a bit? You too," she whispered, accepting his closeness but shyly averting her gaze.

He felt a surge of tender protectiveness. If his little mate felt tired, he'd carry her. He'd been carrying her around most of the time, for one reason or another. He'd enjoyed doing so. It was compatible with the Imperial Machismo. . . . But it might be tactless to carry her straight to his bed at this juncture.

"What's this?" He stroked her cool little hand which was clutching a hairbrush. Djinni reminded him of a teasel-clawed tiger cub raising a defensive paw. "My poor kitten, that's a very blunt instrument for stabbing me."

"I wanted you to brush my hair for me. Would you, please?

I usually give it a hundred strokes, but my arm feels like it's dragging through deep water."

Her request blindsided him. He'd never dreamed that she might want him to groom her. Flattered by her sudden trust, Tarrant-Arragon set about the unfamiliar task.

Such intimacy was new, and exquisitely sensual. His chest felt like it was expanding, as though his body refused to breathe normally for fear a heavy breath on her shoulder might break this enchantment. His heart pounded. His belly tightened.

Radiating paradoxical tranquillity, the temporarily docile mate sat cross-legged between his bent knees. Her glorious reddish-brown hair cascaded down the full curve of her hips, and slipped silkily between his fingers and over his bared thighs.

"Ah, my Djinni, what spectacular hair you have. A Scythian chief would prize such an unusual scalp as yours for his virility-rite groin mantle!"

"My *scalp?*"

It hadn't been the most appropriate of compliments.

"Be easy, little one. I'm not Scythian. I don't scalp prisoner women after I've docked them to death." Slack damn, he'd made it worse! In view of her phobia, he might have refrained from casually callous remarks about Scythian practices. Now he'd probably put a new fear into her mind.

"It hadn't occurred to me that you might," she gasped while snatching a fair quantity of temptation away from him and plaiting it with trembling fingers.

"No? But you are afraid of me." It was an effort not to caress the exposed nape of her neck, but he controlled himself and resumed brushing the fistful of hair that remained in his possession.

"I'm not afraid of you," she retorted. Then, it seemed, her innate honesty caused her to modify her outrageous allegation. "It's just, I am afraid of 'it.'"

"Ah, 'it,'" he repeated. "Not me, just 'it.' Though I imagine the unspeakable 'it' is something you think I'm capable of doing to you?"

"Do you know what frogs do?" She flew off at a conversational tangent. "The male is smaller than the female, but he has specially developed thumbs which he locks around a female. Well, usually he does, but he's stupid and single-minded, too."

Tarrant-Arragon raised an amused eyebrow at "too," and waited for her to reveal her motive for comparing him to a frog.

"Sometimes a male frog gets hold of a fish. Of course, they're incompatible species, but he clings to her for days, hoping she'll lay frog-spawn for him to fertilize. She doesn't, so he squeezes and squeezes to encourage her—until he's killed the poor fish."

It was an interesting concept, desperate males trying to mate with another species. He might borrow from it to explain his "consortium's" quest for Earthling mates. Djinni might swallow such a lie.

"Ah, what would you say if I told you our own females are large, aggressive, and demanding? Naturally, we desperate males find sex more satisfactory with small, submissive females, and seek relief on a planet where there are little mates for the taking. Rather like your fish-hugging frogs, in a way."

"I'd say you miscalculated when you took me," she answered with a flash of her earlier defiant spirit. "I may look small to you, but I'm not submissive."

Tarrant-Arragon gave a shout of laughter. "No, you aren't, are you?"

"And I might remind you," Djinni said, "the stupid, oversexed frog hugged the life out of the unfortunate fish."

"I was afraid you were identifying with the fish," Tarrant-Arragon sighed. "What a tragedy of miscommunication," he mourned. "Your fish didn't know what the male wanted, and the male didn't understand why the female didn't respond to his lovemaking. I'm so pleased we're having this talk."

"Frogs are lousy mates," she continued crushingly. "They kill their own females too. When the male gets hold of the slow, heavy female frog, she has no choice but to bear him on her back all the way to a pond. If she gets there without being eaten by a predator, there may be more males than females. In which case, other males get on her too, and their weight may drown her, but they won't let go until they've got their froggy rocks off."

Tarrant-Arragon stroked Djinni's hair and struggled with the information. "If there's a comparison to be made here, I assure you, I'm not going to allow other males near you." He visualized the impossible scene. "I think I have more strength, and more wit, than a frog."

He thought he heard a snigger and a whispered admission, "Just a fraction, perhaps."

He tugged her hair. "Are you damning me with faint praise? Perhaps I should warn you that I'm savagely jealous. I want you all for myself, and I'm going to have you. You needn't worry that I might share you. I won't."

"Good. I don't like the look of your friends." She tilted back her head and gave him a cheeky upside-down smile. His heart leapt. Did she like the look of him?

"You may sympathize with frogs, but moles are the worst things in the world," she added as if unaware that she'd sent his ever-hopeful hormones into overdrive. "They live underground, in small tunnels, and they can't turn around. Anyway, the female doesn't want 'it,' and the male does. She runs away down a tunnel, and he comes up behind her and he bores into her velvety skin with his you-know-what, which is very hard indeed: There's a bone in it. Wouldn't that be dreadful?"

He wasn't going to touch the subject of penile bones. There and then, Tarrant-Arragon decided that his courtship of her would suffer a serious setback if she saw his own princely endowments.

"I'm beginning to understand why you think males are unpleasant bedfellows. So, my gentle girl, do you conclude that sex is a perilous activity?" He hoped he sounded sympathetic.

"Yes, and not just for females. Female spiders kill the male for doing it. And look at the male bee. He gets his little member ripped off. The queen bee flies away with it inside her, and he falls to the ground to die," she concluded.

"My little romantic, do you feel better for having advised me of these horrible hazards?" Tarrant-Arragon inquired, smothering a laugh in her hair and wondering just how much she knew about Djinn sex. "Was this most instructive conversation intended as a warning?"

Fascinating little Djinni twisted around to glare at him. "I am trying to explain . . ."

"What? That you'd like an exclusive relationship with me, unlike frogs, but you'll rip my head off if I attempt to mate? If you wish to discuss sex with me by using animal examples, we should consider the love-ways of the Tigron Hunnox."

"No," she protested faintly. "I do not wish to!"

"I insist. Hunnoxen are dimorphic: the males are much bigger than the females. Like us. When the big bull Hunnox sets his heart on a little cow, he lumbers after her until she's exhausted from his relentless pursuit. Then he stands quietly and lets her rest. She's grateful, but he doesn't mount her, not even slowly and carefully, although he wants to very much. He loves her with his big tongue all along her soft belly, to show her she's the most marvelous female in all creation; and he uses his persistent tongue all over her precious—"

"You play chess?" Djinni squeaked a challenge. He'd been expecting it. He'd seen her scanning the bedroom, desperate for a diversion. She'd focused upon the ancient chess set that he displayed on the massive communications unit at the foot of his bed. "Did you know that chess may have been invented by a Cretan queen, back in 4000 B.C.? She needed something to distract an overly amorous husband."

It was a Djinn Empress, four hundred thousand of your years ago, Tarrant-Arragon thought as he fetched the chess set. And, my cherished wife-to-be, you think you're going to distract me, don't you?

Chapter Nine

"Sooner or later I'll get you to mate. . . ."

Djinni looked up reproachfully. They were lying on her abductor's carpeted floor, on their fronts, their heads the width of the chessboard apart. He lay low and predatory, like a polar bear on pack ice, a large paw masking the lower half of his face. Above his hand, his eyes smiled.

"Ah, check and mate. I can't see how you can get out of it," he amended as if the double entendre had been accidental. Djinni wasn't deceived. She knew his hand hid a wicked grin. "Beware. A well-placed piece of mine is simultaneously threatening two of yours. Even you would call it a 'fork.'"

Her response would have appalled her diplomat brother 'Rhett, who did not advocate attack as the best form of defense . . . at least for females.

"You'd be a good player if you didn't put so much thought into cheating—" Her voice cracked, and she felt her lower lip puff into a sad pout.

As she moved her Queen out of danger, her hand shook. And no wonder! She was angry and tired, heavy-eyed, and her suitor showed no sign of going to sleep. Perhaps he had two brains, like a shark, and never slept. He wasn't normal! He hadn't even been to the bathroom. He was used to the dim light and the eyelid-dragging gravity, and he was going to wait her out.

"You accuse me of cheating?" He reared up, his weight on one elbow, disbelief and soft menace in his voice. He could be very, very intimidating when he chose.

She didn't back down. "You are a cheat," she said, nodding severely. "You've done everything you can think of to distract me."

She'd wound herself up, was almost ready to fight to the death rather than give in . . . and her nose was beginning to run. She sniffed. What else could she do?

"I've never known anyone who took such delight in turning a harmless game of chess into a minefield of erotic pitfalls. . . ."

Hot, shameful tears of frustration blurred her vision. She dashed at her cheek with the back of her hand. For good measure, she then dashed the pieces from the chessboard.

"You set up chess positions for the sake of all the lewd comments you can make." As she made the accusation, it flashed into her mind that considerable intelligence would be necessary for such behavior. However, she was too far into her tirade to stop and think about startling new insights.

"It's sad," she raged. "I might have liked you very much. Under other circumstances. If you weren't what you are, and I wasn't who I am, and bound by vows. As it is—"

"What fury!" he marveled, looking as startled as a huge bull discovering a small cat swinging by her teeth from the end of his tail. "All because of a play on words. I've upset you, haven't I? My dear, you are adorable when you're angry."

"But . . ." She was thoroughly bewildered. "You said your kind couldn't enjoy sex with aggressive females."

"Ahh! I thought that's what you were up to." His big hand cupped her cheek, and his thumb smoothed away her tears. "Djinni, I think you're the exception to every rule. I've been enchanted by you ever since you first put your hand in mine. You make me feel protective, and potent, and very male—"

"You distracted me on purpose, so I declare a Grand Master Draw. I demand a new game," Djinni cut him off. She reset the board with much clicking of pawns, and avoided his searing stare as he tapped his upper lip with two long fingers.

Suddenly, his hand darted across to her side of the board and captured hers. In the dim purple light, she thought she saw blue flashes of static electricity spark between them.

"If you're going to demand a rematch every time I upset you," he growled, and she knew she was in trouble, "you must agree to transfer from the floor to the bed."

Djinni eyed the bed. High and huge, it looked like an ultra-masculine version of a boy's inflatable truck bed. The thick sides were built up, and padded on the inside, suggesting the marriage of a rolltop desk with a Chesterfield. The head of the bed was armed with more swing-into-position equipment than a Harley Street dentist's couch. Including twin Anglepoise-mounted computer stations. It'd be like getting into bed with NASA.

"I don't think I'd feel safe up there," she objected.

"And I think I'll grow stiff if we stay on the floor. Will you feel safe then?"

"I'm going to take another bathroom break," she said with all the dignity she could muster. She waited until she reached the safety of the doorway, then turned for a TV detective–style parting shot. "By the way, that was blackmail."

"All's fair in love and war." His eyes had a wicked glint.

"No, it isn't," she returned fire. "That's just the sort of thing the despicable tyrant Prince Tarrant-Arragon would say."

His face was the picture of baffled frustration.

What did she mean by that? Tarrant-Arragon bounded to his feet, ready to compel an explanation, but she'd slipped into the bathroom. No doubt she thought the Great Tiger Prince resorted to dirty tricks on every occasion. What made her think Tarrant-Arragon would waste his time quoting Earthling aphorisms about a fool's emotion—love—foreign to his experience and expectations?

"My dear, the saying has been in common usage since—"

She probably wasn't listening. Nevertheless, he'd have the last word. He crossed to his bedside computer and keyworded "Fair."

"Ah, since Earth's seventeenth century, according to a document called 'A Lover's Progress.' Note the propitious title."

Tarrant-Arragon smiled. He was immoral, despicable, a tyrant, and she liked him very much!

Surrounded by yes-sayers all his life, and flattered and courted due to his royal rank, he'd never imagined he could be honestly liked by anyone, let alone a female. He'd never troubled himself to be likable. But Djinni couldn't help herself. She liked him. This, he had to share with Grievous.

"Open!" he commanded in High Court. Computers responded; a section of wall between the master suite and main room slid aside. He entered the main room, activated the master computer, and fired off a series of commands. To the duty engineers in Fabrication. To the duty officers' kitchens. To Grievous.

While his subjects prepared to await his pleasure, he crossed the reception area and made use of his guest bathroom off the dining area. Since Djinni had confessed to virginal terrors, he'd tacitly ceded her the master bathroom. It seemed expedient, not only because she'd taken a lot of breaks, some of which, he suspected, had been excuses to get away from him. However, she was unaccustomed to the drag of his gravity. He wouldn't invade her bathroom privacy until she settled.

Back at the main computer, he checked on the mate monitor. She was sitting quietly, no doubt sipping the wine she'd taken with her and thinking of ways to stay out of his bed.

Grievous was awake. "Female trouble, Sir?"

"My little mate plays chess too well to be stupid." Tarrant-Arragon came straight to the point. "I'm re-evaluating my opinion of female intelligence."

"High time you did, Sir."

"Do you understand how Earth-girls think, Grievous?"

"Er, not really, Sir. Never claimed I did. But I never underestimate the feminine way of thinking, just because I can't follow it. Ladies' minds jump—"

"Precisely. My Djinni's behavior isn't as random and nonsensical as one might think. No wonder she confused me at first with her sexy, out-of-character come-ons. She makes a bold advance followed by two side-steps. Or two deceptive forward moves and a last-minute diversion. She plots conversation like a chess Knight's moves."

"Eh?" Grievous's sleep-reddened eyes blinked. "Are you telling me you're playing chess, Sir? In Battle Stations light? In the middle of the night? Doesn't she know it's bedtime?"

"She knows. She's determined not to go to bed with me. I don't usually respond mildly to defiance, so it's a good thing she found an elegant way to avoid a confrontation. According to her arcane Earthling rules, if I say anything suggestive, I'm guilty of cheating." Tarrant-Arragon remembered the games he might have won if he hadn't cheated, and smiled. "I've never been called a cheat to my face before."

"I'm not surprised, Sir. Have you ever played chess with someone who thinks herself your equal?"

"Probably not. Although, now you mention it, there is one arrogant rim-worlder, Commander Jason—"

"I was asking rhetorically, Sir. What I meant to say is that she doesn't have the, er, advantage of knowing who you are and that it's more than a man's life's worth to anger you, Sir," Grievous blundered on. "You may have any number of horrible little habits which no one's ever dared mention. She may even take it into her head to tell you that you don't quite float her boat in bed, Sir."

"Then I'll learn to enjoy criticism." Tarrant-Arragon swiveled in his chair. "My dear little mate can't carry off an insult. She calls me terrible names to my face, but she is too cross to realize what she's saying. I'm sure she didn't intend to tell me that she likes me."

Grievous goggled. Tarrant-Arragon might have savored the effect of his casual boast, but just then a discreet beep alerted him. Djinni was on the move.

"Thank you, Grievous. Go back to sleep. Conference ends."

Surveillance of the corridor outside the main portal

showed an unnecessary number of engineers showing tray-bearing chefs and the duty sentries what they'd rigged up on short notice.

Tarrant-Arragon opened the outer doors by computer override, then intercepted Djinni. He scooped her against his side so his voluminous robes and the angle of his body sheltered her from curious Tigron eyes, and walked her back into the bedroom.

"On the bed," he ordered the chefs in commoners' Tigron. "Are you hungry, my love?" Watching her, he saw her head turn as she caught the aroma of Imperial delicacies. Yes, she was hungry.

Tarrant-Arragon grinned. He was about to execute another tiger-taming strategy.

Tigron Imperial Palace

"If my big brother can abduct a mate for himself, why can't he bring home an Earth man like that for me?" sighed Princess Martia-Djulia, thinking herself alone.

She moved closer to the window wall in Tarrant-Arragon's suite. Between the layers of glass were liquid-crystal and gas, so the window doubled as a viewing screen. Enhanced from a grainy newsprint photograph to full size on the screen, a god-gorgeous male seemed to scan a ballroom for the next object of his healthy lust, even as he danced with a willowy girl who looked like a Djinn.

"Oh my! I'd lose weight just looking at that . . ." Martia-Djulia frowned with the effort of reading an overenlarged *Indianapolis Star* headline. "That . . . Fabio."

"You get your lecherous tendencies honestly, my dear."

Martia-Djulia snatched her hands behind her back, appalled that her raid on Tarrant-Arragon's office had been discovered.

"I doubt an Earthling would be tall enough for you. Few males are," her father, the Emperor Djerrold Vulcan V, added with careless cruelty. "It's a pity the idea of sister-marriage disgusts Tarrant-Arragon. If only you'd been able to give him the rut-rage. Unfortunately, you take after your mother. She never gave anyone the rut-rage, either."

"I could attract a new mate," Martia-Djulia said in defense of herself.

"Then do so." The Emperor raised an eyebrow.

Martia-Djulia lowered her gaze and stared at the stylized tiger motif in cold-ember black woven into the border of her brother's pumice-gray carpet while Djerrold Vulcan V assessed her figure with pursed lips and a connoisseur's eye.

"Gravity can be unkind. Control your obvious charms and lure an unsuspecting male into bed. Take surveillance footage, and ask Tarrant-Arragon to frighten your lover into marrying you. My terrifying son has more power than I since I gave him control of the Star Forces."

While Martia-Djulia gaped, her father swept across the office. With a glance, he raked over the disorder she'd created on Tarrant-Arragon's smoked mirror desk, saw what he wanted, and took it.

"I presume you want to see Djinni-vera?" As he spoke, the Emperor flashed on the light marker he'd appropriated and drew a slashed circle of light around the Djinn-featured girl in the enlarged photo.

"This slender, young, dark-haired beauty," the Emperor said, cruelly stressing all the Earth-girl's physical advantages, "is not your new sister, Djinni-vera."

The thin light beam arced away to dance around an isolated figure in the background. "Enhance!" the Emperor said, and the computers brought the face into focus.

"That's Djinni-vera? What an insignificant little thing!"

"Her looks are irrelevant."

"Oh?" Martia-Djulia did not bother to hide her skepticism. "Why was this photograph taken?"

"Our lazy-minded equerries cataloged every tall, dark-haired female in the Communicating Worlds and beyond, on the assumption that a girl who looks like a Djinn might have Djinn genes."

"So he saw Djinni-vera by chance?" Martia-Djulia suddenly understood how unlikely it was that even Tarrant-Arragon's roving, wolfish eyes would see a small face in a crowded ballroom.

"He was tormenting an equerry. He might have claimed to want any female in the crowd: any one the harried assistants couldn't hope to procure. Then he saw this. Enhance!"

The light marker played on the girl's bosom. The computers brought a name tag into focus. "Earthlings cannot recall names, so they wear little labels at functions. 'Djinni' appears to have competed in a chess tournament, after which she attended this motor-racers' ball in Indianapolis."

"The little fool!" Martia-Djulia hissed.

"Somewhat indiscreet, I agree. Presumably, 'Djinni' had no idea that my son has spies on Earth. Nor that he'd want her."

"I'll bet this Djinni is an impostor." Martia-Djulia didn't feel she was making mischief by saying so, until she saw ominous amusement glittering in the Emperor's heavy-lidded and faintly bloodshot eyes. The left lid had a slight droop, giving the impression that His Imperial Majesty was winking lecherously, even when he was not.

"Tarrant-Arragon thought of that. It is one of many reasons why we can't promise our subjects the spectacle of a royal mating. Although I've no doubt my son knows everything there is to know about her by now, we won't know if 'Djinni' is what he wants until he returns—with or without her.

"Unfortunately for you, what he doesn't know now, he will find out at that time," the Emperor added nastily.

Martia-Djulia followed her father's eyes to the surveillance lenses mounted in all three corners of the highly organized room.

Oh, fewmet! Tarrant-Aragon would see footage of her making free with his things. Worse—he might misinterpret her remarks about his mate being a fool and an impostor.

"What shall I do?" she whispered, her throat rasping at the thought of her brother's fierce displeasure.

"I'd recommend you leave the planet," the Emperor said.

"But I need you to oversee the wedding, coordinate arrangements for the honeymoon resorts, seating at the banquets, and so on."

"But—"

"We'd suffer massive loss of Imperial face if guests come to Tigron a second time expecting to see Tarrant-Arragon marry, and once again the bride is, ah, unpresentable. So we must keep the nature of the festivities as secret as possible. With your involvement, the inevitable gossips may suppose that, if there's to be an Imperial wedding, it might be yours. Or Henquist's. Or Thor-quentin's."

"No one would believe that either of my sons is old enough to want to settle down," Martia-Djulia protested.

"No one is ever old enough to want to settle down. When the time comes, We do Our royal duty. We select the prettiest and most docile breeding-bay. We formally take her to mate, and continue to dock in her until she is well and truly impregnated. And then We resume Our natural pleasures . . . unless, of course, one's mate is a true-Djinn."

His insinuation that a Princess was somehow less than a true-Djinn if she hadn't given anyone the rut-rage was all the more hurtful because she knew he did it deliberately. She could not argue about her hormones, but she could refuse to do favors for the pretentious Djinni-vera, who dared to taunt her betters by calling herself True-Djinn.

"You're asking me to do equerries' work. I won't—"

The Emperor raised his right index finger.

Martia-Djulia was too angry to heed his warning to be silent.

"Why should I? If she is not an impostor, she's a bastard's daughter! And what does she do to merit precedence over me at Court? She spreads her—"

"My dear, your jealousy is entertaining, but unwise. Tarrant-Arragon, ah, commands us to be kind to Djinni-vera. He has a theory that the disposition and intelligence of children is affected by the happiness of the breeding mother. Presumably, he made a negative extrapolation from our history, since the last two Empresses who were royally bedded ran away."

The Emperor Djerrold Vulcan V rubbed his jaw. "Since I don't imagine he'll wait for his wedding day, I've no idea how he plans to avoid the witnessed consummation. For once, he may have a problem which he has not thought through. . . .

"I digress. Your remarks have not been kind, and you know how exceedingly nasty your brother can be. He won't be pleased to see that you broke into his office." His Imperial Majesty stooped smoothly to blackmail. "And he will see. Un-less— Help me with the wedding and I might show you how to erase this surveillance footage."

"Can we? Even with Tarrant-Arragon's sophisticated systems?"

The Emperor shrugged. "Let us hope so for your sake, my dear. Tarrant-Arragon can be very dangerous when he is annoyed, as Djinni-vera will discover, if she hasn't already."

Ark Imperial

Djinni recognized manipulative behavior when she saw it.

"When I commissioned this bed, the convenience of a small female wasn't uppermost in my mind," her unsubtle suitor said, as he installed steps on either side of the unit at the foot of his bed, which made it look like a graduation platform.

She didn't think her convenience was his prime consideration now. By making entry and egress easier for her, he pre-empted all her reasonable objections to the bed.

Resentfully, she glanced at the door-wall that had closed off the adjoining room, which seemed to be part of his suite. So far, he had only given her the run of the bedroom and bathroom.

Meanwhile, he mounted his new steps, threw himself on the bed, and began to crunch nutlike fruits that smelled of raw peas.

Djinni had no doubt that he knew what he was doing: Food was the oldest and most effective lure known to man or beast.

Something smelled delicious. If she wanted to eat, she had to join him on the bed. She did. Then, remembering Grandmama Helispeta's advice about the power of exquisite good manners, she searched for something to praise.

"I like your wine. Where did you say it came from?" She hadn't forgotten, but it seemed a good way to get him to talk about J-J's adopted base-world, which might one day be her home.

"From An'Koor," he responded, seeming pleased. "An'Koor is a young, fast-spinning planet. Its days are shorter than Earth's and its surface temperature varies less. Yes, try those. They're balls of spiced ground meat in a smoke pit sauce. Where was I? Ah, yes. Until my ancestors colonized it, An'Koor was covered in water and too newly cooled for anything to have evolved except single-celled aquatic life. We reclaimed it with gigatons of what you'd call hydroponic fill—"

Was he from An'Koor?

"What do you generally do during the day?" she abruptly interrupted his explanation of how the arrivals and departures of asteroid-sized space-freighters affected An'Koor's water table.

"Generally? I work at my computers, or exercise in the gyms. Have another meat ball." When she took one out of politeness, he grinned. "But there won't be much of that from now on. I want to spend all my time with you. Mating with you. Feeling your heart beat with my rhythm, your long legs wrapped around my waist. Or my neck.

"I think we should do it in the murk-bath. It would be easier on you until you're used to my gravity and my weight."

"Please. No!" Djinni took a shuddering breath.

At once, the wicked gleam in his eyes clouded over. She had a strong impression that he was remembering how she'd passed out when he kissed her.

"This sort of . . . talk is too . . . stressful." She panted for effect and wondered whether she'd be able to fake a heart attack. "Being with you is like . . . playing Tag or Off-Ground Tig with no Home. No subject is safe. Nothing is off-limits with you. I can't . . ."

"Explain this Off-Ground Tig. Is it a game? I had a lonely childhood. No one taught me games."

"Oh, how sad." Djinni remembered a teacher's psychological profile of the classroom troublemaker: a sullen boy, filled with anger because he didn't know how to be lovable. Who got attention the only way he knew. If her abductor had been a child, she might have put her arms around him. But he was a very large, dangerous male, and after his remark about her legs, there was no way she was going to try to comfort him.

"No wonder you're so bad! Yes, Off-Ground Tig is a chasing and catching game. One person—the He—chases all the others."

"He's the Tigger?" he interjected, as if eager to prove he was paying attention.

"Yes. Everyone else gets chased. There's always a sanctuary or 'Home' where the 'Tigger' isn't allowed to tig the chased people while they rest." Djinni used his made-up word and hoped that if being ignored made him worse, a little judicious mothering might encourage him to behave.

"Why don't the chased people stay in the safe place all the time and balk this Tigger?"

Typical! He couldn't understand why everyone didn't cheat.

"Because there's a code of honor. And a time limit. Then they have to make a dash for a different sanctuary."

"I see. You're casting me in the role of the wicked Tigger, aren't you?" He looked askance at her. "It doesn't seem fair. Have you told me all the rules? Why should I be condemned always to be the Tigger? We could take turns. You can chase me."

"But I have no desire to maul you," she pointed out.

"Ahhh, I wish you did." He reached across the buffet tray to stroke her forearm with his forefinger as he spoke. To her horror, his gentle touch and his wistful expression set off a feeling of free fall in her insides.

"We'd still need the safe places," she reasoned in her best kindergarten-teacher manner.

"What exactly must I not do when you are in a safe place?"

She was conscious of his appreciative scrutiny while she considered her response. No doubt he thought it was a fine game to make her list objectionable behavior. She decided not to risk exciting him by being specific.

"No groping, and no kissing. Where will we designate as 'Home'?"

"In the bathroom, you may have your pedestal." He grinned.

"That's no concession at all." Djinni gave him her most quelling stare. "You'll have to do better than that."

"Will I?" He tapped his upper lip thoughtfully. "Very well. In the main room, you may share my chair in peace."

"Another dubious proposition." Djinni raised a skeptical eyebrow. He mirrored the gesture. A standoff. She crossed her arms. He stared at her breasts.

"Lastly," he purred, "I'll allow you one designated cushion, which will constitute a portable safe place, as long as it's on the floor. Do you agree?"

She nodded. Considering her bargaining position, she'd done well.

"Of course, I demand a concession in return," he said.

"Of course," she agreed with a nonchalance she did not feel. She felt like a casino novice learning midgame that her opponent can raise the stakes. Her heart began to thump.

Chapter Ten

And the concession is . . . ? Djinni wanted to ask, but didn't, for fear that her inexhaustible suitor would demand sex.

He did nothing to dispel the tension. Nor did he set up the chessboard on the bed, despite his earlier suggestion that he'd like to play with her all night. At chess, of course.

Judging it wiser not to ask him questions, Djinni borrowed from Scheherazade's tactics of telling night-long tales to preserve her virtue and her life and began a recitation of *1001 Arabian Nights.*

"I wouldn't tolerate one-thousand-and-one sexless nights of stories," he interrupted. "If it were my story, the Sultan would let Scheherazade live because she's exceedingly good in bed."

"I'm not talking about you—"

"No? Given that we are not talking about me—and assuming that the Sultan's enemies didn't greatly exaggerate his earlier wives' fate—would you prefer me to say that the Sultan was unable to, ah, perform and had to kill his brides so they couldn't gossip about his humiliating difficulty?" He paused. "Scheherazade gave him an excuse to rest, without having to explain himself, until his problem corrected itself."

"You shouldn't make fun of sexual problems," she chided, but couldn't help remembering some of J-J's jokes about the An'Koori.

Did his Sultan theory explain his own inaction? Was her would-be lover . . . unable? Djinni peeked through her lashes at her captor. He reclined on the vast bed, like an ancient Roman at a badly lit midnight feast. Or like a big cat. He always sprawled, and she hadn't decided whether it was due to despicable laziness or super-predatory energy conservation, but it might explain how he'd grown so tall in his heavy gravity.

He looked relaxed, but there was a grimness about his jaw, and his lean cheeks looked flushed, even allowing for the purplish Battle Stations light.

"I don't consider impotence a joking matter." He flicked his right index finger with his thumb as if to spark a flame—a gesture she'd noticed before when he was annoyed. "Have it your way, then. Did Scheherazade come to love her Sultan?"

"Tyrants who kill unsatisfactory wives don't deserve anyone's love or respect," she retorted, thinking of what Tarrant-Arragon did to his first prospective bride, and what J-J might do to her if she lost this bedtime battle of wills.

"I will tell you this. Human girls prefer to be in love with a man before they have sex."

"Hurry up and fall in love with me, then," he teased.

Instead, she told him another story, and another after that until exhaustion slurred her speech. Her eyelids closed. She felt warm, welcoming arms draw her down and turn her, so she lay on her side against him. His cool, silken, quilted robes billowed around her as she snuggled closer. Where was the harm? For all his macho posturing, her self-styled Tigger was all talk and bounce. A sexual paper tiger.

"Well, my Tigger, what did I agree to?" she whispered, made reckless by relief.

"You'll sleep in my arms." His husky whisper kissed her hair.

She must have slept, because the next thing she knew, it was light, and her whole body felt as if she'd been in bed with a bad case of the flu. Still lying on her side, she closed her eyes, concentrated, and began a long, slow, self-healing stretch.

Tarrant-Arragon caught his breath. She'd woken as relaxed as a sunbathing cat, he thought, stilling his fingers at the computer and lying perfectly still behind her back.

As he stared, transfixed and very turned on, she arched her body from the heels of her hands to the spread-wide tips of her toes. Every curve and swell was visible through the clinging fabric of her dress.

He had to touch. Very gently he splayed his left hand and settled it on the soft, taut sweep of her rib cage into her waist. To his delight, she gave a breathy murmur of pleasure.

"Hello, little dreamer. We've slept long and hard!" He chuckled. In truth, he'd slept lightly, much disturbed by her. "A short time ago, we made the jump into Hyperspace. The effect makes novices ill. How do you feel?"

"I feel like I've been bedridden for a week," she groaned.

"Do you know how that feels?" Not for the first time, he was too aroused to calculate the consequences of his words.

Her eyes, her uptilted mouth so close below his, opened in innocent bewilderment. The Great Originator be thanked, she didn't understand what he'd said! Perversely, this excited him even more. He felt his lower-body sash give way, and his heavy arousal thudded against the small of her back.

Panic in her eyes, nervous as a prey animal, she shied away, scrambled to the edge of the bed, and almost fell down the improvised steps. "Must go," she gasped, fighting the heavy gravity all the way to the bathroom.

Tarrant-Arragon silently cursed himself for losing control of his person. By pure coincidence she'd dramatized her soreness by a reference to a week in bed. Djinni couldn't know that in the aristocratic form of the Tigron languages the literal translation of *bedridden* was explicitly and exclusively conjugal.

What to do? Neither lies nor hard truths would reduce her horror of aroused males. She believed that big animals had big sex organs. And she was right.

He needed to distract her, perhaps lure her into learning his language. Rolling back onto his stomach, he searched the archives for some reassuringly dull and very old news to use with English subtitle software he'd prepared to help her learn High Court.

Treating her like a cat among strangers, he didn't look at her when she left the bathroom, and he was eventually rewarded by the feel of her shy weight settling beside him on the bed.

Djinni frowned at the huge screens behind Tigger's bed head, upon which six-armed men in hooded robes were waving their limbs at each other. "This looks interesting," she said, assuming from the English subtitles that she was expected to be interested.

"It is. The Coppellusian Senate is debating whether to secede from the Tigron Empire. Do you know what that means?"

Djinni couldn't tell him that her brother had been involved in the secession negotiations, any more than she could reveal that she had a full-Djinn fiancé and a living father.

"Secede means withdraw from a political group," she replied. "It's immoral to pay tribute of any kind. Do you know that some worlds have to send virgins to the lecherous Emperor and his vicious son? How can any civilized world not want to secede?"

"It's my understanding that the virgins are volunteers. And not everyone is ready for the uncertainty and chaos of self-rule," he gritted. "The Senators voted for the status quo."

"Rot!" Djinni tried not to sound as dismayed as she felt. "They must have been bribed. Or threatened. Well? Were they?"

"Both, I imagine. They probably justified their vote by engineering an alarm just as the Senate rose to vote."

"A false alarm? You mean, a rumor that a Tigron war-star was approaching?" she suggested, eager to show she was capable of discussing diplomatic chicanery at the highest levels.

"Nothing so unsubtle. If I were in their place, I'd report a convoy of nasty, nomadic, scalp-taking Scythians was entering the Coppellusian galaxy."

"But if the Coppellusians were protected by the Saurian—"

"No, my love. The Scythians don't respect honorable, law-keeping Saurian Knights. Fortunately, they're convinced that the much-maligned and misunderstood Tarrant-Arragon is worse than they are. They hesitate to annoy him." He stroked her cheek with the knuckle of his left hand. "A Scythian threat would allow the bribed Senators to reluctantly vote in favor of the prosperous calm under a strong and fair Tiger Prince."

"You can't think that Tarrant-Arragon is strong and fair!"

"Given a chance, he might be."

Djinni was starting to understand Tigger. Judging by his reaction to the bedtime stories she'd told him, he took a perverse delight in arguing the cause of the villain—any villain. But his willingness to defend the awful Tarrant-Arragon worried her.

Tigger knew something of her ancestry, she wasn't sure how much. The question was Did he know she was related to Tarrant-Arragon? He surely wouldn't dare to rape her if she fibbed and told him she was Tarrant-Arragon's much-loved cousin.

The thought of being much-loved by Tarrant-Arragon made her queasy. According to human myths, bad djinn were ugly. She had no idea what Tarrant-Arragon looked like, but he was a very bad Djinn, so he must be very ugly. Not to mention old and cruel.

Her ambition might be to cut short Tarrant-Arragon's career, but it'd be a disaster if she fell into his hands. Which might happen if she were to threaten Tigger with her most powerful male relative's wrath and Tigger called her bluff and restored her to her appalling Imperial family.

"Judging by her stuff, there's more to your little miss than meets the eye, Sir," Grievous greeted Tarrant-Arragon, who was making his way toward him across the Ark Imperial's brightly lit storage bay. "Eclectic taste. Makes taking inventory a pleasure. And I'm glad of a sitting-down job."

"Are you having difficulty adjusting to our Tigron military

living conditions, Grievous?" the prince asked, squatting beside him amid the little miss's yet-to-be-sorted possessions.

"Actually, Sir, I must confess, I'm amazed at the human body's adaptability. I've been aboard—what?—a good sixty hours by my body clock. Getting about in your gravity is really no worse than marching uphill through knee-high dune grass, into a headwind, in a downpour while carrying a full fighting-man's kit."

"Is it that bad?" Tarrant-Arragon laughed. "I won't ask you to join me on a weight-training circuit today. However, you'll have to exercise for the sake of your bone density and muscular integrity, and so will my Djinni when her bruises have healed."

"Poor little miss! Er, what do you make of this sword, Sir?" Grievous rushed to less tricky matters. "Lovely bit of kit! Ceremonial, I'd say."

"That is a Saurian White Knight's sword. May I?" Tarrant-Arragon took the weapon and tested its weight and balance. "Ceremonial? Not exactly. It is worn as a symbol of civilized behavior, rather in the same way that your kings carry a scepter but seldom attack anyone with it."

"Gotcha, Sir. Yours is a bit like a James Bond type of world, isn't it. Cold war. Secret elites. Cool code names. Shadow governments and shadowier kingmakers. Enemies pretending to be civilized. Cultural attachés you can't touch . . ."

Tarrant-Arragon's smile twisted.

"As long as they wear their virtuous white uniforms, which is the reason I've never captured a Saurian sword before."

Space travel was making Grievous's eyes go funny. He could have sworn he saw green sparkle swarm out of nowhere and shimmer down the blade and up Tarrant-Arragon's extended arm. As though the sword was some sort of benign lightning conductor.

Grievous shook his head, assessed the prince's all-night eyes, and went back to sorting the little miss's household contents, which the returning Plunder Unit had handed over to him.

Whatever the Tigron warriors thought of their god-prince's Earthways Advisor, they'd accepted Grievous as the logical choice to identify Earthling substances that were dangerous, unsanitary, or perishable. In return, Grievous felt it behooved him to put a positive spin on his new shipmates' efforts.

"Er, your chaps were very thorough. Followed orders to the letter, Sir. They even packed up her rubbish out of—"

"Ah, damn it!" Tarrant-Arragon swore softly. "Since she has the sword, there's no doubt she is a White Knight. Damn. She's kept me so focused on her frailties and fears, I'd almost forgotten that she may have taken a chastity vow."

"How's that?" Grievous kept his voice neutral and began to empty the top drawer of a slender games table, which was labeled as having been beside the future Princess Consort's bed.

"There's a rumor that Saurian White Knights take a vow of chastity," Tarrant-Arragon said as he sauntered over to the table. "If Djinni has taken such a vow, it would explain a lot."

"I'll say," Grievous agreed, shaking alien scrabble-like game pieces out of a purple, quart-of-whisky-sized pouch.

Still holding the sword, Tarrant-Arragon used a forefinger to sort the twenty-five game pieces into a five-by-five block. "Do you know what these little stone tablets are?"

"Not the foggiest, Sir. Unless they're some kind of game pieces?" Grievous picked one up and studied it. "Interesting patterns, Sir. I've seen that shape somewhere."

"She's given me a pet name. Is that a promising sign?"

"It might be," Grievous agreed just as casually. "It depends what she calls you."

"Tigger!" the Great Tiger Prince said.

"Tigger?" An A. A. Milne character leapt to mind. Grievous was appalled. He racked his brain for something to say that wouldn't get the cheeky little miss into trouble. "Er, that's pretty close to your title. How do you stop her from reading your mind, Sir?"

"Mind-shielding. I learned to do it because my great-uncle Django has mind-probing talents. Mind-shielding is akin to auto-alignment of one's own electromagnetic brain-field. To

put it simply, one relaxes and thinks of something pleasant."
Tarrant-Arragon smiled inscrutably. "I think of sex."

There was no answer to that. Grievous looked for a reason
to change the subject and found something.

"I knew I'd seen that pattern. Look!" Grievous held one of
the game pieces against the decorated blade under Tarrant-
Arragon's hand. "Same designs. See? There are inscriptions
like these on the scabbard, too. You want to pass it, Sir? To your
right, in the umbrella stand. Maybe they're good-luck charms,
Sir."

Tarrant-Arragon pounced on the turned-oak umbrella
stand, the contents of which included a five-iron golf club labeled "Rapist Masher," fencing foils, and several poster rolls.
Items of fascination for any male, they were, though surprising
property for a virginal miss.

"I could use a charm." His Highness opened one of the
poster rolls marked "J-J" and fell silent.

"That's what I need." Tarrant-Arragon smoothed out a
rolled calendar, *Body Armor Through the Ages*, at a cross-sectional
study of Tudor armor.

"King Henry VIII's cod armor, Sir? Why ever would you
want something like that? Still kicking, is she?"

"No, Grievous." A twitch of the prince's eyebrow suggested
His Highness was enjoying a private joke, possibly at the little
miss's expense. Grievous found it heartening that the prince refrained from sharing it. "I've a little reverse psychology in
mind. Inspired by your flaccid Earthling neckties."

"Reverse, my eye. A thing that size . . . ?"

"I'll have Fabrication pad the interior. Extensively, to suggest that the usual wearer is much less well-developed than in-
cidental contact through daily clothing might lead my
innocent girl to, ah, fear." Tarrant-Arragon's smile became a
distinctly Machiavellian grin. "If I leave such a monstrous decoy lying around for Djinni to examine, perhaps her false conclusions about me will make her bolder in bed."

"Is this deception worth the talk it's bound to cause, Sir?"

"You will bear it, Grievous. My people think Earthlings, like

An'Koori, are inferior beings and self-conscious about their penile shortcomings. They'll assume the cod armor is for your private enhancement."

"Right ho, Sir," Grievous enthused. "Er, wouldn't it be simpler to get her drunk?" He felt like a cad for suggesting it. "Get the business over, Sir. Then tell her that she loved it."

"I'm sure she wouldn't believe me, Grievous. Besides, you have told me how my gravity feels. Multiple drunken ecstasies might be too much for her fragile heart right now."

"Well, Sir, there's no sense in rushing her," Grievous approved heartily. "There's no hurry, is there?"

"There may be." Tarrant-Arragon's mien darkened. "If she gives me the rut-rage, I'll have to do something about it."

Tigron Imperial Palace

" 'Commander Jason and (nameless) bride'?" Martia-Djulia hissed, stabbing Tarrant-Arragon's guest list with a stiff finger. She was helping her father with the wedding arrangements, albeit with bad grace, since he hadn't kept his side of their bargain and taught her to erase the damning footage. "I'd like to know why a paltry Commander is on the wedding list."

"Commander Jason is a trusted friend of your brother's. His war-star will be the near-orbit guardian of the honeymoon resort. Ah, you reserved the ice-pole for the happy couple? Charming, Martia-Djulia, considering Tarrant-Arragon dislikes the cold."

The Emperor smiled tauntingly from his observatory, where he was observing the violent electrical storm that—as usual—accompanied the Royal Side's daily eclipse.

Djerrold Vulcan V was in a good mood, because, Martia-Djulia suspected, he had several young virgins staked out in his bedding chamber, anxiously awaiting his pleasure.

"As for the 'paltry' rank, Commander Jason is a rim-worlder. Only Empire-born patriots may hold the rank of War-star Leader."

"Is 'nameless bride' a euphemism for 'mistress'?" Martia-Djulia sought a softer target. "Or do we really not know her name? And must I warn this 'bride' not to wear Tarrant-Arragon's black or the wedding-day silver of the Princess Consort?"

"Her name may be unpronounceable. Alien names sometimes are. And Jason knows how females who wear black are punished because of a long-ago dispute over a female."

Martia-Djulia couldn't contain her curiosity. "How can Jason and Tarrant-Arragon be friends if they were involved in a sex triangle?"

"I know you adore gossip—" Her father paused tantalizingly. "And it is an enlivening tale. Ah, yes. The sanctions used to be more stimulating when a female was caught wearing my personal purple livery. After we invested Tarrant-Arragon as First War-star Leader of the Star Forces, he decreed that offenders who wore his black were merely to be publicly stripped of it."

Martia-Djulia nodded.

"A mercenary Enforcer in command of an An'Koori patrol-craft captured a Saurian vessel. There was a female aboard. A whore. When Enforcer Sris arrested her, she tried to cover herself with a black sheet. Sris shredded her sheet with his whip, gave each of his crew a strip of it, and challenged them to use whatever ramming apparatus they deemed appropriate to—"

Her expression seemed to silence him. He raised his right eyebrow just as a jag of lilac lightning highlighted the three faint scars that raked into it. A long-forgotten virgin with very good nails and terribly poor judgment had missed his eye.

"The joke is, the crew were quivering An'Koori, sexual tiddlers, most improbable rapists. One appreciates Sris's sadism so much more if one knows this detail."

"Did she survive?" Martia-Djulia did not find it funny. All the Worlds knew that the An'Koori were quite capable of rape in a gang, or if they were sure their victim was helpless.

"There was another mercenary aboard. The young barbarian was a stickler for 'due process.' He objected violently and attacked his superior officer. Sris attempted to flog him. A mistake. The barbarian wrested Sris's whip from him, intimidated the An'Koori crew, and released the female and the Saurians. Sris demanded a court-martial. Naturally, Tarrant-Arragon presided.

"Considering how raw he was from Lucinthe's treason and the broken betrothal, I was amazed he sided with the barbarian."

"Perhaps Tarrant-Arragon thought Sris showed the greater disrespect to his black livery." Martia-Djulia feigned a yawn.

"Possibly. Sris was transferred to Terror and Interrogation, but he fell foul of Tarrant-Arragon for damaging the prisoners. Sris has since been sent to create a diversion while Tarrant-Arragon pursues Djinni-vera. Now, you really must excuse me. Speaking of Sris's excesses has made me eager to see to my own love life.

"Ahhh, it's high time I allowed Henquist and Thor-quentin to do more than watch. . . ." Martia-Djulia did not waste her breath on a protest. Her sons' sexuality was beyond her control. She rose, but had to ask, "What became of him?"

"The barbarian? He was promoted and assigned to an An'Koori war-star." The Emperor ushered her to the door. "He's Jason. I suppose you'd like to meet him? Too bad. He's the right height for you, too. Alas, he's taken by a nameless bride."

The Pleasure Moon of Eurydyce

"Djetthro-Jason! Words fail me," Madam Tarra hissed. "Why are you dressed like"—she made a fly-shooing gesture with a hand that remained beautiful despite years of pushing her antiquated wheelchair over the soundproofed brothel's thick carpets—"this?"

Jason felt his blush all the way to his six-pack abs. It didn't show under his makeup: He checked. His Djinn machismo called for a display of male assertiveness before he explained, and he didn't have to look far for an excuse to be offensive.

"Are mine lying around in there?" He jerked his head toward her bowl of condoms.

"I am neither stupid nor careless. The best hiding place for dangerous letters is in plain sight," Tarra said with all the reproachful hauteur of the former Empress Tarragonia-Marietta. "And I've passed on your demands for Djinni-vera."

Stalemated, Jason turned back to one of the full-length mirrors his hostess kept hidden behind smoky gauze curtains and used for séances. He studied his reflection from the crown of his tight, black leather hood and mask to the come-dock-with-me heels of his flame-and-spit-polished thigh boots.

The Rocky Horror Picture Show meets the Caped Crusader; he summed up his disguise with no great regard for accuracy and struck a pose, his left hand on his hip, much in the manner of his paternal uncle Ala'Aster-Djalet, the Saurian Dragon.

"Stegosaurus has been arrested." He dropped this bombshell almost casually and observed Tarra's reflected reaction.

Since she already looked shocked and offended, her expression didn't change enough to indicate either guilt or horror. Perhaps her thin lips tightened. Her knuckles might have whitened as she wheeled herself to her usual place at her fortune-telling table.

"Ah, I suppose you haven't had a visit from Tarrant-Arragon?" He parodied his infamous cousin's smooth menace phraseology.

"I infer that Stegosaurus might have betrayed me under torture?" she said. "If he had, I doubt if my appalling son would come here to arrest me personally." She began to shuffle her Tarot. Her hands shook.

"He might. This moon is neutral. It'd hardly be a diplomatic outrage for a male to call on his long-lost mother." Jason spelled out her peril. "Of course, while he's here, he'd give you Loquacity, and you'd tell him about me, and Djinni—"

"And about Ala'Aster-Djalet being the Saurian Dragon," she agreed. "So? What will you do?"

Until he saw the way she looked at a skeletal reaper card, he'd never considered killing her to silence her and safeguard the others. Nor had he thought she'd think of it.

"Rescue Steg before he talks, of course," he said more kindly. "Sris is making for the Eften Detention Moon, so—"

"Sris? Carnality!" Tarra spat out a most unfeminine Imperial oath. "I thought that pervert was on freighter detail for the rest of his unnatural life."

"So did I. It's a spot of luck. We know what Sris is like, and what he likes." Jason swept his hand over his belt, causing whips, chains, large dildos, and other tools of a dominatrix's unwholesome craft to swing obscenely. "This is the perfect way to get Sris to invite me aboard. And allow me to be masked and carrying, ah, weapons!"

"Why can't you impersonate Tarrant-Arragon, as you did when you wanted untraceable starfighter parts from a wreckers' moon?"

"For one thing, he pilots an Imperial Thorcraft. I can't get one. For another, I don't want to provoke a grudge-ruthless investigation. Rescuing Stegosaurus must involve maximum dishonor and humiliation for Sris, and no loss of life."

She still looked doubtful.

"This way,"—he gestured at himself—"I'll be taking advantage of Sris's known sadistic tendencies. He won't see me until we're alone in his suite. His crew won't interfere. The nature of our appointment guarantees that shrieks and cries for mercy will be expected, and will be ignored by his quivering An'Koori crew."

At last, Tarra understood. "Did Sris request black leather? Ah, I see. Does Petri-Shah know? It's double vengeance! Sris expects to give another inexperienced courtesan a surprise. But Sris will be the one to get a nasty surprise. You!"

Ark Imperial

"Tarrant-Arragon's Inquisitorial pleasure? Oh, typical! But of course the depraved beast takes pleasure in it," muttered little Djinni over her computer-aided lessons.

NAME: _____

ADDRESS: _____

_____

_____

TELEPHONE: _____

E-MAIL: _____

_____ I want to pay by credit card.

__ Visa   __ MasterCard   __ Discover

Account Number: _____

Expiration date: _____

SIGNATURE: _____

*Send this form, along with $2.00 shipping
and handling for your FREE books, to:*

Love Spell Romance Book Club
20 Academy Street
Norwalk, CT 06850-4032

*Or fax (must include credit card
information!) to:* **610.995.9274.**
*You can also sign up on the Web
at* www.dorchesterpub.com.

Offer open to residents of the U.S. and
Canada only. Canadian residents, please
call 1.800.481.9191 for pricing information.

If under 18, a parent or guardian must sign. Terms, prices and conditions
subject to change. Subscription subject to acceptance. Dorchester
Publishing reserves the right to reject any order or cancel any subscription.

"What's that?" His name spoken with such loathing shook Tarrant-Arragon out of his contented reverie.

He'd made a breakthrough. After four blissful days, Djinni had giggled in her sleep. He could guess why. Even so, every time he thought of his mate giggling in her sleep, his ruthless war-engine of a heart rolled over like a playful tiger.

Absurd. He hadn't had the rut-rage yet, hadn't even had sex with her. How could he be in love?

Pondering this mystery, Tarrant-Arragon paid little attention to the badly padded An'Koori accounts on his screen. Nor did he keep a close eye on the quick little pupil on the bed beside him.

"I'm sorry, Tigger. I didn't mean to disturb you," she said sweetly. "Tarrant-Arragon likes torturing people—"

This horrible slander eclipsed all other thoughts.

"What the star-blazes are you looking at?" He rolled over to her side of the bed and threw one arm around her shoulders, his hand draped against her neck so he could feel the pulse that he'd originally used to check how her runaway heart was responding to his gravity, but which he'd discovered was a reliable lie-detector.

"I'm not sure. This news program doesn't have subtitles. I think the naked male has been arrested. The whip-swinging male in body armor must be describing what they're going to do to him."

Tarrant-Arragon saw at once why his censorship and subtitle-translation software hadn't functioned. Somehow, she'd pulled up an Imperial broadcast from An'Koor.

Replaying the footage, she repeated An'Koori words that she shouldn't understand. It reminded him of the way alien new subjects uncomprehendingly echoed the pledges of loyalty that were dictated at a swearing-in ceremony.

But she must be guessing at the meaning. Since he hadn't taught her An'Koori, she could not possibly understand what was going on.

"He's saying, 'White Knight . . . of the Saurian Orders, you are a spy.' " After a hesitant start, she translated confidently. "He goes on, 'You have forfeited the right . . . to a hearing or to any appeal . . . to your ambassadors.' "

Against his fingers her pulse pounded rhythmically. She was upset and outraged, but she was not guessing.

" 'You'll be taken to . . . ' " She shook her head. "I think he names a prison. ' . . . to await Tarrant-Arragon's Inquisitorial pleasure.' "

Obviously, she understood the nastiest parts all too well. Therefore, much as he'd like to know how she knew An'Koori, his top priority was damage control. Her prejudices must be refuted.

"Torturing people is the only way he gets sexually aroused," she speculated. "I expect his terrible diet has clogged his arteries. Or it might be his age; he's nearly forty."

Tarrant-Arragon had difficulty keeping his tone amused.

"The usual meaning of 'awaiting someone's pleasure' has more to do with convenience than with alleged sadism, doesn't it?"

"Tarrant-Arragon isn't a normal person. You have no idea. As a Saurian Knight, it's my business to know. These wickednesses are the reason I'm ready to die fighting the Tiger Princes of Tigron." She patted his cheek. "The bloodthirsty beast eats girls alive. You look shocked. You should be."

"Where the Carnality did you get that revolting slander? Tarrant-Arragon does not—"

"Yes, he does. It's common knowledge, though they suppress the beastly details within the Tigron Empire," Djinni said airily.

"No, my little ghoul. He does not." Tarrant-Arragon realized what she was talking about. "You have misunderstood your sources." He dipped his head and took her earlobe between his teeth. "You're referring to some deliciously sophisticated love-ways. Think of what I told you about the Hunnox, and I will show you what Tarrant . . ."

"How would you know what Tarrant-Arragon does in private?" she squealed, and tried to wriggle away from him.

"Whereas you have firsthand experience?" he growled, and rolled on top of her. Pinning her down with his weight, he traced the outline of her ear with his tongue. She shuddered. Exquisite response! Instantly, he wanted to do more to her. Much more. He flicked his tongue into the delicate recess and blew lightly.

She jerked free and turned on him. "Don't be ridiculous," she snarled, glaring as fiercely as a tigress who isn't ready to mate. Then, apparently, she decided he'd attempted irony.

"Oh dear, I deserved that." She giggled. "It's bad manners to argue about politics. But you must agree, Tarrant-Arragon is losing his touch."

"Must I? Why?"

"Look at this public arrest. It's terrible diplomacy and bad psychology. He has nothing to gain by such tyrannical behavior."

Tarrant-Arragon didn't contradict her. He thanked the Great Originator that he'd taught her only the spoken word, and made sure all negatives and Imperial Wedding and Consummation vocabulary were censored out of anything she might see or hear.

He'd underestimated Djinni for the last time.

Now he was going to make sure of her. Since she had a good ear and could duplicate An'Koori pronunciation almost exactly, she could certainly echo unfamiliar phrases in the Royal language. She was going to swear her irrevocable love, obedience, and loyalty to him. This very night. Before she knew enough High Court to understand what she was saying.

Chapter Eleven

Tarrant-Arragon memorized the ancient and irrevocable vows while Djinni took her evening murk-bath. Next, he activated his surveillance systems in the main room, where the acoustics were better, and set up the chessboard.

Phase One of his game plan was to confuse and infuriate Djinni. To that end, he began a chess game without her, moving the White King's pawn to King 4, and the Black pawn to Queen's Bishop 4. Trap set, he waited for Djinni to join him.

"Are you good enough to take over Black against me?" he said, and advanced his White Knight to threaten the Black pawn.

As he'd hoped and anticipated, she moved her King's pawn forward one place to protect her endangered Bishop's pawn.

"The so-called Sicilian Defense?" Tarrant-Arragon raised an eyebrow to suggest she'd made a bad move. "Do you think that is advisable, little lover?"

"I'm not your lover," she objected.

"You will be." He deliberately leered at her. Disregarding her defenses, he moved his Queen's pawn.

"How do you know Earthling names for the standard openings?"

A dangerous change of subject. One he'd purposely invited. "My best friend, a Commander in the An'Koori Star Forces, has an encyclopedic knowledge of all known forms of chess. He's the only person I know who has . . ." He paused to emphasize a vulgar term likely to upset her. ". . . the balls to play a Queen's side game."

"Don't be coarse," she said, and took his aggressive pawn.

Apparently, his blatantly male figures of speech no longer distressed her. He'd have to try harder, Tarrant-Arragon told himself as he took her pawn with his Knight.

"Shall I tell you why it takes testicular fortitude to play the Sicilian Defense?" he teased. "You see, most of the boot-kissing courtiers and career warriors are afraid that favoring a Queen's side game would be seen as disloyal to the Tiger Emperor."

"How stupid!" she said, and Tarrant-Arragon was delighted to have offended her feminist sensibilities. "Why would anyone associate a chess move with disloyalty? Is the Emperor paranoid?"

"He might have good reason to be. Neither he nor his father was able to control his Empress. To save face, the Emperors claimed that their Consorts, or Queens, were physically and intellectually weak, untrustworthy, and slack-witted. In fact, genetically defective . . . because of their female hormones."

Success! The darling little mate was so outraged that her hand shook, tapping her King's Knight on the board. Tarrant-Arragon hid a grin behind his hand before he personalized the attack.

"Logically, this defect—having female hormones—renders all females unfit for social, financial, or political responsibility, and for decision-making of any sort, including choice of mate."

"No one in their right mind could believe that!" she stormed. "Do you mean to tell me I am deprived of my rights just because two Empresses refused to remain married to repulsive lechers?"

"Strictly speaking, my love, an Empress cannot 'refuse to remain married.' Once a Tiger Prince's intended mate says the Imperial Wedding Vows in his presence, she's his till death."

He reached across the board to still her trembling hand.

"Pedantry aside, Djinni, you must agree that the Emperors are right. You prove their case by your unwillingness to make love with me. It's unsensical of you to reject me. I'm eminently desirable, both financially and sexually. Admit it, I'm supremely attractive. I'm strong, virile, passionate, healthy—"

"And you are insufferably vain, boastful, and arrogant!" she shot back, and he noticed she was careful not to challenge his masculinity. "Which reminds me, Tigger, I've been meaning to ask you how I say 'No' in your language."

"You don't, my love. It's grossly improper for females to use cudgel words. A blunt refusal can get you into big trouble— Ah, you've bounced that Knight halfway across the board. Can I take it you've moved?" he interrupted himself to taunt her on another front. "I'm teaching you the feminine-submissive speech forms." He advanced his Queen's Knight and smiled patronizingly.

Djinni could hardly see straight for fury. So Tigger thought he could teach her to talk like a submissive, did he?

Well, that explained one mystery. No wonder the An'Koori she'd learned with J-J seemed different. A Djinn god-prince like J-J had no use for anything except male-superior speech.

Stars! She'd like to tell Tigger what he could do with his "cudgel" words. But . . . all this male-supremacy talk sounded ominous. Tigger had been acting strangely ever since their conversation about Tarrant-Arragon's unnatural sex life.

She eyed him warily. He seemed to be trying to browbeat her; perhaps he was working himself up to some macho misbehavior. Given what she suspected about him, it would be sheer folly to give him the fight he seemed to be asking for.

Tigger had probably been exaggerating when he boasted that fighting aroused him. Then again, J-J once told her that the mild-natured An'Koori find female resistance sexually stimulating. So Tigger might find an unequal struggle exciting.

Given his size and strength, if Tigger assaulted her, she wouldn't have much hope of fighting him off. But she'd try.

"You're still afraid to dock with me, aren't you?" Despite the appalling obscenity, Tigger spoke with tenderness. "Little love, don't look so anxious." He gently tilted her face, forcing her to look at him. "I try—really I do—to respect your beliefs and values, but respect doesn't seem to get me anywhere with you." He sighed. "If you're not willing to make love, would you do me the honor of reciting a duet poem with me in my language?"

A poem? All this aggravation, and he'd settle for poetry instead of sex! Intoxicated with relief and suddenly unnecessary fight-or-flight hormones, Djinni shook her head in disbelief.

"I'll teach you your part phonetically," he said, taking her consent for granted. "The poem is a favorite of mine. It is, ah, a love poem."

From the husky timbre of his voice and his formal manner of asking, he must be embarrassed, Djinni guessed.

Still distracted with relief and confusion, her thoughts fluttered like summer butterflies, while Tigger directed her to stand, facing him, her palms flattened together like Durer's *Praying Hands* between his.

She'd had no idea he was so fond of ritual, or that he'd make such a production of a mere love poem, and insist she flawlessly imitate his pronunciation of each beautiful, momentous-sounding syllable, as if it really mattered.

Poetry, parrot fashion! Djinni grimaced inwardly. At any other time, she would have rebeled against his "Repeat After Me" method of teaching her the female part, and would have demanded to learn meanings to match the elegant phrases.

But her choice was sex or poetry. So she humored Tigger without protest, and as she listened to him speak the majestic male parts, her resentment shifted into more complicated feelings.

It was endearing that this stern-faced, alpha-acting male secretly loved poetry and children's stories. And intelligence in his female. A girl could easily fall in love with such a male.

One thought led to another, and Djinni couldn't help wondering whether "The Great Unpleasantness" might not be so terrible with him, if only she were free and not promised to J-J.

"Thank you, my love," Tarrant-Arragon murmured in English, and a feeling of tender euphoria swept over him. "If you can bear it, the poem ends with a kiss." He traced a fingertip along the curve of her lower lip. "Just one chaste kiss."

Of course, there was no such thing. However, for the first time in his extensive experience of seducing awe-inspired and nervous females, he gave careful consideration to how he was going to close the distance between her lips and his.

Not that he cared how he'd look on surveillance footage, but because he didn't want to frighten her this time.

Slowly, inexorably slowly, he bent over her. Smiling, he ignored the uncertainty in her eyes and lowered his head, lips slightly parted—just enough to close his mouth completely over hers.

She gave a gasp of surprise and—he hoped—pleasure, and took his breath. Heat slammed into his groin like the heavy thunk of a leap out of an atmosphere. Passion flared his nostrils. Senses fired, he breathed in the brackishness of murk-bath tangling sexily with the soft fragrance of herb in her hair. And lying under her hair and clothes was her natural feminine scent.

Don't breathe heavily. Don't press. Give her time. Let her get used to it, he warned himself.

Much as he wanted to thrust and invade and possess, he exercised heroic restraint. He used his lips and tongue-tip the way he'd like to teach her to use her mouth on him, but infinitely more gently. Just to taste, and stroke her lips with his, to make them part for him. And then, if she didn't open her mouth within a reasonable time frame, he would make a strategic withdrawal.

He waited. It was the most languorous, lingering kiss he'd ever achieved, and he thought he detected the faintest responsive tremor in her lips under his. But she didn't invite him in.

Remember her inexperience, her fragility. Tarrant-Arragon

groaned. *Remember you promised. Just one kiss.* A heartbeat before she struggled, he lifted his head.

"There are many ways a male can kiss his mate," he whispered, smiling down into her dazed eyes and cupping her flushed cheek with his palm. She'd been so sweet, so good, he had to see how far she'd let him go. Scanning her expression, he noted that her mouth was pink and puffed from what he'd done to her, and he couldn't help fantasizing about more delicate places he would kiss and taste. One day. Soon. "May I show you, my reluctant love?"

He was not surprised that she fled.

"You say you got her to marry you, Sir? How absolutely marvelous!" Grievous exclaimed while he sized up Tarrant-Arragon's air of shamefaced triumph. He nodded his guest to a chair in War-star Leader Slayt's former quarters. "Congratulations, Sir."

"She doesn't know it. She thinks the Imperial Wedding Vows are a love poem." The prince began to pace.

"So congratulations are on the premature side." Grievous stuck to pleasantries. "You're going to catch it when she finds out you've cheated her of a big wedding, Sir."

"The royal wedding is scheduled to take place at the Imperial Palace in just under twelve Earth weeks' time. If I have my way, she'll never know about this, ah, preemptive marriage."

Beneath Tarrant-Arragon's affable velvety purr, Grievous had a sense of steely implacability. The prince was determined to have his way. And Grievous was beginning to get the idea that he was supposed to simply lend a sympathetic ear while Tarrant-Arragon examined his own motivations aloud.

"I leave nothing to chance." His voice hardened. "Djinni may refuse to cooperate for the Imperial ceremony. Unfortunately, she thinks I'm a monster, Grievous. My enemies have told her horrific untruths about me. I know it's standard campaign procedure to demonize the enemy, but these are gross distortions. I'd probably confirm her ill opinion of me if I waged war over her."

"War, Sir? Isn't that rather far-fetched?" Grievous passed his hand over his eyes as he spoke. Tarrant-Arragon's caged tiger circling was making him queasy.

"That depends on the Saurian Dragon. If he could, he'd persuade my enemies that my treatment of her is cause for war. Technically, I've given him sufficient provocation. Not only is it illegal to abduct Earthlings, but my little mate is one of his Knights, and it's an act of war to 'draw first blood.' Her deflowering would be a rather interesting interpretation—"

Grievous thrust out his lower lip to indicate that he understood the problem. He hoped a bloody rape wasn't what was troubling His Imperial Highness's conscience.

"But the lawful consummation of our marriage can't be defined as an act of war." Tarrant-Arragon threw himself into a chair, and protocol allowed Grievous to sit too. "It ought to be an act of love, oughtn't it?" The prince smiled enigmatically. "I hope it will be. However, an Emperor's heir is not obliged to obtain his bride's consent." Tarrant-Arragon raised an eyebrow, as if he knew how he sounded and did not wish to be advised.

"If the Saurian Dragon makes trouble before we cross into Imperial space, I'll prove that Djinni is already my lawful mate. I have footage of us reciting the Imperial Marriage Vows."

"Well, Sir, you have the most puzzling scruples." Grievous scratched his head. He was sure Tarrant-Arragon had omitted to mention some vital and nasty bit of information. "Let's see if I've got this straight. You've put up with agonies of lust for a good two or three weeks"—Grievous hoped he was still using the correct tense—"because you respect her Saurian vow of chastity—"

"My bride takes all vows seriously and expects me to do so, too," Tarrant-Arragon interrupted, and rose. No further explanations would be forthcoming.

As he saw Tarrant-Arragon to the door, Grievous came as near as he dared to asking whether His Highness had had his way. "Sir, you can't expect her to obey vows she didn't know she was taking."

"I can't?" Tarrant-Arragon answered him with a knowing grin. "You're right. I'll seduce her if I can, but I'm not going to tell her I've married her until I'm sure she loves me too much to care who I am."

"Asgaard"—Stronghold of the Saurian Dragon

"Tarrant-Arragon grows aggressive." The Saurian Dragon dispensed with the usual formalities of a meeting of the Inner Circle of the Saurian Assembly. "He must be distracted. We all know what he wants more than anything in the known worlds."

A delegate interjected a succinct gynecological term.

"Just so, O-Garr." The Saurian Dragon inclined his masked head. "My Lords, I suggest we let Tarrant-Arragon believe it has fallen into his sexually excitable lap. Unfortunately, the female will be unlikely to survive his—ah—attentions."

The highest-ranking Saurians were silent. Their expressions were hidden behind stylized dinosaur masks and courtesy suits, which were worn in memory of the Saurian Orders' founders and which not only gave anonymity to the members of the intergalactic organization, but also provided for the communications and life-support needs of those who were not air-breathing.

"What would happen if Tarrant-Arragon were suddenly smitten with the notorious rut-rage? Publicly?" the Saurian Dragon asked.

Masked heads shook. Venerable delegates might dimly remember the scandalous events before the last rut-rage-exciting female vanished from the Empire. The idea of a public rut-rage defied the virile imaginations of most of the younger White Knights.

"Highly discreditable behavior?" an ambassadorial Knight suggested through his simultaneous-translation device.

"At the very least," the Saurian Dragon concurred.

"A murderous rampage?" a more imaginative delegate spoke up.

"Indeed. Especially if the public occasion were an important Imperial ceremony."

The Saurian Dragon lifted his arms in a sorcerer's gesture and a star map of the Tigron Empire lit up across the planetarium ceiling of the vast chamber. No one gazing up would imagine they were deep within a space ark that was disguised and sheltered beneath a mile of crushed asteroid and ice.

"With all the Tiger Princes present? Would they all fight?" Members of the Saurian Assembly suggested enthusiastically.

"To the death," agreed the Saurian Dragon. "The victor would be Tarrant-Arragon. He would then attempt to mate with the source of his rut-rage."

"She could flee, and lead him to one of our less salubrious colonies." Garrot of Altaeres left the rest of his dishonorable suggestion to his brother Knights' imaginations.

As if plotting the rut-rageous female's flight, the Saurian Dragon conjured a brilliant blue beam of light from a staff hidden among the ribbed folds of his trailing sleeve and flash-marked a dotted line from Tigron to the Altaeran wreckers' moons.

"Presuming a Djinn-line girl exists, we surely wouldn't place her in such peril?" a hoarse-voiced Knight said.

"I'll send him an impostor." The Saurian Dragon paused for effect. "Our impostor will wear an undergarment once worn by a Djinn female during her rut-rageous time, and which I subsequently . . . ah . . . confiscated."

"Does a pure female exist?" Excitement caught the others as they began to fully understand the plot. "Where? Who is she? Why isn't she safe on Asgaard?"

"We swore to defend the vulnerable and virtuous; to protect disadvantaged and emerging worlds; and to oppose oppression and injustice," the hoarse Knight objected above the computer-modulated uproar. "Doesn't the sacrifice of a female violate our fundamental principles?"

"My impostor volunteered," the Saurian Dragon said. "Her actions will be legal. Neglecting to wear fresh underwear may be antisocial, but it's not a crime. The Tiger Princes will scent her and mistakenly assume she's a Djinn. Do I have a seconder?" The Saurian Dragon nodded at the Altaeran. "Thank you, Garrot. My Lords, I propose that we disrupt the next Imperial ceremony on Tigron in the manner discussed. Cast your votes."

Voting knives were driven into the assent or dissent slots. Unemotionally, the Saurian Dragon intoned, "It is not unanimous, but the majority is in favor. An expendable female Knight will take the rut-rage to Tarrant-Arragon."

Ark Imperial

"We'd have had the rut-rage by now," Tarrant-Arragon remarked with studied nonchalance. "If she were pure enough to cause it."

He glanced toward the fighting mats on the far side of the gym where Djinni was doing firming exercises and showing more interest in the wall-display of weapons than in him.

"She hasn't bled, either," he added quietly. "I suppose it's not possible that she's pregnant?"

Emotions played across his advisors' faces. Tarrant-Arragon watched with informed predatory interest. Since Djinni had shown him that social intercourse was like chess, he took grim pleasure in predicting what others would say.

Doctor Ka'Nych, no doubt, was professionally offended and would like to remind all concerned that he hadn't been permitted to conduct a pelvic examination. But he wouldn't dare say so.

Grievous might want to say that the little miss probably had been rut-rageous in a very ladylike way, back on March 30, which explained Sir's horribly horny conduct that first day.

"From what I've heard of your rut-rage, it's just as well for her," grunted Grievous over the free weights. "As for the other matter, a lady from Earth doesn't function with Swiss watch precision. You can't time your Star Forces maneuvers by her."

"Possibly not," Tarrant-Arragon agreed, "but I'd hoped to do some forward family planning." In a show of machismo, he swept up a bigger weight than Grievous could manage and began an impressive set of biceps curl repetitions.

"In Queen Victoria's reign, men thought overwork or too much intellectual activity would wreak merry havoc on the delicate female system." Grievous warmed to his theme. "I'd think stress and fear would upset her timing, too. You, Sir, specialize in frightening the living daylights out of grown fighting men. You've probably scared her frigid."

Frigid? Tarrant-Arragon glanced at her. She looked flushed. He hoped she wasn't eavesdropping. Frigid, he could deal with. But what the Carnality was he going to do if she was infertile? Every day he spent with his funny, clever, delightful little mate, the notion grew more horrifying.

"It's too early to reproach yourself, my Lord—"

"I've no intention of reproaching myself, Ka'Nych."

"Too early! That's it!" Grievous announced, and slapped his freckled forehead. "I read somewhere that anywhere between twenty-four and forty-two days is considered a normal cycle."

"A change in gravity could affect all her bodily functions, my Lord, including her hormones." Ka'Nych blamed the environment. "I'd recommend a blood test. Also, a nutrient may be lacking in her diet. And, my Lord, I'd advise regular sex—"

"As opposed to 'irregular' sex?" Tarrant-Arragon growled at his sarcastic nastiest. For reasons he couldn't fathom, he was suddenly so angry that, if Djinni weren't present, he'd have spat fire. A cheap illusion. "I'm tired of hearing my subjects repeating my enemy's propaganda about my sexual excesses."

What's yours like? Sizewise?

Djinni blushed to think of asking the other abductees about their abductors' anatomy, but she would, given half a chance.

Tigger was watching, and he tended to respond to her blushes like a shark to blood in the water. Djinni clasped her hands behind her head, added a twist from the waist, and hoped that he'd think her high color was due to the effort of doing sit-ups.

As she touched each elbow to its opposing knee, she puzzled over the magnificently equipped gym and its equally magnificently equipped occupants. Certain discrepancies bothered her.

Tigger exuded sexuality. Yet he let her sleep in his arms unmolested. Dauntingly male, he wore a scowl, a bulge-hugging, black bodysuit, and a broad cummerbund, presumably to hold up his cod-armor. He exercised with the lazy grace and controlled economy of a feline superpredator. Djinni refused to let him see that she was impressed. But she was, even though she knew all about his endowment padding.

Why didn't the other abductors treat their mates to blatant displays of their masculine attributes? Where were they? In the communal showers? The sunken combat pits? No. And no.

In fact, she couldn't imagine why there were combat pits on a civilian spacecraft, or why one wall was covered with trophies of arms, from elaborate multiblade weapons to simply deadly sticks. A lot about the gym didn't fit the mental image J-J had given her of the lazy, cowardly, draft-dodging, sex-scavenging An'Koori.

All the more reason to compare notes with other abductees! *Did he hurt you?* she'd want to know. And *If an An'Koori raped you while you were unconscious, would you know he'd done it? Or wouldn't you suspect anything until you missed your period?*

She didn't think Tigger had taken advantage of her the first day. But she wouldn't be half-human if she didn't wonder, and try to count back. She thought she'd been past the fertile stage of her cycle when he abducted her, which would be about three weeks ago, if she could judge time by the fading of her bruises.

Which meant she was late. It didn't mean she was pregnant. She couldn't be. Not with an An'Koori. Pregnancy might be a concern for the human abductees, but not for a half-Djinn.

When in doubt, Djinni tried to imagine what the exiled Empress Helispeta of Tigron would say if consulted.

"Sexual congress with an inferior being is forbidden to me, as it is to you." Helispeta always prefaced any discussion of sex with a reference to her own enforced chastity.

Then, while Djinni was speechless at her hypocrisy, Helispeta might justify the ban on human boyfriends.

"A vigorous and persistent human might manage to impregnate you, since you are half-human. But I think it improbable. Your pheromones, at least, are Djinn. You proved that conclusively when you 'set off' your twin half-cousins and broke up my family."

Djinni sat up, hugged her knees, and shuddered at the memory of her first ovulation. J-J had been long absent. Her father happened to be out of range. And, of course, 'Rhett had no sense of smell that way. So it could have been much, much worse.

The twins noticed her rut-rageousness simultaneously. If the "boys" hadn't happened to have been skinny-dipping, she'd have had no warning. As it was, she was able to climb a tree.

If her terrifyingly rut-enraged cousins had cooperated to get her out of the tree instead of wrestling each other half to death for the honor of having her first, 'Rhett wouldn't have been able to step in and break their noses, and save her.

More distressing was the rejection that had followed.

Her rut-rageousness made her a pheromonal time bomb, her father had told her. Her dreams of being initiated as a Saurian Knight and eventually joining her cousins on the Asgaard were at an end. At the age of eleven, she'd understood only that her adored father didn't want her within fifty Earth-miles of his fully functional, Djinn nostrils until she was safely married and pregnant.

Be careful what you wish, Father! Djinni seethed.

Her head on her knees, she looked sideways across the gym at Tigger and tried to visualize what he might be like under his endowment padding.

How terrible could it be? Djinni's cheeks burned. She ought to be ashamed of herself for wondering whether J-J would notice if Tigger preceded him in a very small way.

How could she not wonder what An'Koori lovemaking

might be like when Tigger's kisses were so terrifyingly wonderful?

She must be mad. Tigger's kisses were to die for in every sense.

J-J might laugh at quivering An'Koori for their cowardice and remarkably small penises, but he wouldn't be at all amused by Tigger's sexual advances. J-J was a Great Djinn. One day, he'd be god-Emperor. Djinn Emperors didn't permit themselves to be preceded by or compared—possibly unfavorably—with lesser lovers. J-J would kill her. He'd certainly kill Tigger if he found out. He wouldn't be able to help himself. Rival-killing ran in J-J's blood.

And what of her? Did infidelity run in hers?

Chapter Twelve

The Pleasure Moon of Eurydyce

"A visit to an expensive brothel is never a waste of time!" Commander Jason threw his voice like a drunken punch in the dark, so anyone listening would assume that the two An'Koori officers were well primed for a night of timid lechery and were arguing about the high price of Madam Tarra's girls.

"I thought you were taking me to Salamander," Steg complained.

"Speak a little louder, why don't you? I don't think those Scythian pirates heard you," Jason drawled in a good imitation of Tarrant-Arragon at his sarcastic nastiest. "While you're about it, perhaps you'd like to tell every Star Forces officer taking his pleasure on this moon that you're an escaped Saurian."

"But this moon's neutral," Steg hissed. "Aren't we safe?"

"No one walks in safety on Eurydyce's moon." Except Great Djinn, but Jason saw no reason to tell Steg so. The moon of Eurydyce had always been a space Vegas. Ironically—since the Earth word "vegas" meant fertile plains—it had once been green, until one too many thoughtless orbits by visiting G-class war-stars interfered with its rotation. Now the moon had a hot, arid, bright side which was good only for jet-racing, and a dark side lit by the reflection of the local star on Eurydyce.

As it turned out, the darkness was good for the sin business, and led to the burgeoning of booths, bars, and gamblers' halls in the debauched adult playground, where literally anything could be bought or bartered, and any excesses could be gratified.

As he passed a deeply shadowed niche between noisy booths that smelled of attics, Jason flicked a mind-numbing glance at the Scythians. Under the influence of Djinn-craft, they crouched, gray as gargoyles frozen mid-retch on an English country church.

All they would remember was that the big An'Koori was a depressingly uninviting target, his luxuriant blond hair not worth the trouble of scalping him.

"Need I remind you, Steg, we aren't dressed as Saurians?" Jason continued. "Our An'Koori uniforms are a flag of surrender to any darkside prowling pirate in search of easy prey."

Jason lengthened his stride, forcing Stegosaurus to trot in his wake, where Steg was sheltered from the low-level vibration Jason projected to warn off attack. Jason didn't want Steg's mind numbed before Madam Tarra had her chance to interrogate him.

"It was you who rescued me, wasn't it?" Stegosaurus blurted out.

Steg didn't know, and there was no way that Jason was going to enlighten him. The fewer people who knew, the better. It would hardly dignify a future god-Emperor's biography if his part in the escapade became known.

"When you stalked into my cell, I thought you were Tarrant-Arragon, come to torture me."

"Tarrant-Arragon?" Jason snorted. "I've heard he's sexually creative, but I can't see him wearing high-heeled thigh boots and feminine underwear. His enemies would have a field day."

He mentally revisited Stegosaurus's antibacterial-fresh cell. Steg had been naked, chained, somewhat emaciated, but uninjured. Which was remarkable, considering he'd been in Sris's custody for quite some time. At the time, Jason had been relieved that Steg was physically whole and healthy enough to impersonate a hooded Sris.

They had escaped with ludicrous ease.

"Come, Dog Sris. Heel," Jason had warbled, and, hooded and leashed as if Sris and his dominatrix were playing a sado-bestial game, Steg had crawled unchallenged past the bemused An'Koori guards and into Jason's shuttle.

Perhaps it had been a little too easy. Belatedly, Jason had started to wonder about the absence of whip welts and had become seriously concerned that Stegosaurus might be a traitor to the Saurian cause.

"For all his faults, Tarrant-Arragon is not crude," Jason said to see how Steg would respond. "He doesn't resort to physical torture. He's more into mind games. Sris, on the other hand, is notorious for using the whip."

"You can't understand why he didn't use it on me, can you? It looks suspicious, I admit. But I wasn't asked anything." The past master-spy protested a little too much for Jason's liking. "If I'd talked, Salamander would've been uncovered long ago. Are you sure that Salamander's not a double agent?"

"Yes, I'm sure about Salamander."

Since Steg had never yet indicated that he knew Salamander's gender, Jason was careful not to give the game away, but avoiding feminine pronouns was tiresome. He was glad when they arrived at the tented frontage of Madam Tarra's den of aphrodisiacal quackery.

To outward appearances, Tarra's secret-pleasure palace was as full of sensual subtleties as a god's harem, but, there was no sign that it was as well guarded. In fact, behind the potpourri-scented smoke and two-way mirrors, it was better fortified than the old American presidential nuclear-war bunker under Greenbriar.

"She'll want to read your palm," he warned. "I don't know if Madam Tarra really thinks she can tell from a horny guy's hands whether or not he has dangerous carnal proclivities, but nobody gets to spend his docking credits on her girls unless he's had his fortune told," Jason said in the manner of one who knows, explaining the etiquette of getting laid on Eurydyce's moon.

Jason lifted a curtain, and seductively mixed aromas of lust-inducing herbs and love-potion-laced wines caressed his senses. Dark, passionate colors and glitter drew him in, even though he knew about the fish-eye mirrors hidden among the galactic zodiac signs and the metal detectors in the upright members of the lewdly fascinating fertility gods who guarded the entrance.

"Two loveless An'Koori officers, Mother." He hoped the formal greeting would warn Madam Tarra not to trust Steg. He did not want her to call him Commander Jason or Tyrannosaurus Rex or Djetthro-Jason. "We're on Eurydyce's moon for the jet-racing, and ready to be relieved of our silver." He couldn't resist the pun.

Her crystal bowl of condoms was still in plain sight, as colorful as it was appallingly indiscreet. It was a breach of security waiting to happen, in more than one sense.

Madam Tarra, aka Salamander, not widely known to be Tarrant-Arragon's long-lost mother, turned a short row of cards.

"You must be the King of Wands," she said as if she'd never seen him before. "I've been expecting you. Give me your hand."

Amused, Jason stood over her, avoiding the lumpy client's chair, which was overstuffed with magnetized feathers the quills of which could deliver a nasty prick and dose of Loquacity. With a mock bow, he placed his open palm across hers.

"I see a long voyage. Very soon."

An obvious prediction for a uniformed Star Forces officer. Jason doubted she knew that he'd been ordered to Tigron. Or was she hinting to him that he could leave Steg with her for the debriefing Steg didn't know was taking place?

"You may go to your pleasure, my son." She waved her hand in the general direction of the passage that led to the girls, and also to a secret exit, and to a well-guarded hotel. His choice. Her steely gaze was already on the unsuspecting Stegosaurus, who was gaping at an icon of a fierce Scythian god.

"Will I find the love of my life at the end of this voyage, Mother?" A coded way of asking whether 'Rhett would be back with Djinni by the time he'd done whatever he had to do at the great event—whatever it was—about to take place on Tigron.

"I won't ask you to cross my palm with your silver." Her thin lips lifted as she threw his smutty Earthling pun back at him. She traced a long fingernail over his heart line. "You'll find the Queen of your Heart—" Her voice faltered. For a flicker of an eye she looked puzzled. "Sooner than you think."

Ark Imperial

"There's something you should know, Sir," Grievous blurted out before he could change his mind. "Though to my way of thinking, it's water under the bridge, so why rat on the little miss?"

"Why indeed?" Tarrant-Arragon agreed, as worryingly cordial as the devil himself. For an instant, Grievous thought the little miss was present. Then he noticed the stewards laying the table for dinner.

He got the message, clammed up, and amused himself by looking over the public room of the Imperial suite. Gobsmacking, it was. Medieval baron's great hall meets Bond-movie villain's luxury yacht.

Meanwhile, Tarrant-Arragon prowled over to the massive refectory-style table, selected a viand, and fed it to one of the lads. A sinister touch. Shades of ye royal food taster, Grievous thought.

There followed an exchange of smiles, a lazy, imperious wave, and the stewards left Grievous alone with the tyrant.

"Well, Grievous?" Tarrant-Arragon gestured to him to sit in a sunken conversation pit. Before joining Grievous, the prince touched a recording-studio-style bank of controls. Doors clicked locked. "My little mate won't disturb us. She's taking her evening bath. So, what mischief of hers has come to light?"

"We-e-ell, Sir, apparently there was a bit of a hoo-hah in Britain over so-called alien writings. Your chaps picked it up while we were at Battle Stations. Now, you said you wouldn't be watching the Earthling satellite TV, so you might have missed—"

"Six Earth-weeks ago?" Tarrant-Arragon queried sharply. His Highness didn't miss a trick.

"You'll be wondering why I didn't bring it to your notice before now, I daresay?" Grievous knew damned well he'd be wondering. And worse. "See, Sir, I only just heard about it, myself. You know how your chaps love our talk shows? Especially, it seems, when some alienologist shares his theories."

Tarrant-Arragon smiled. "I confess, I'm amused by your human fellows' slack-logical idea that we aliens won't have any more to do with Earthlings until they elect a single-world government. I also enjoy James Bond movies. Ah, but we digress, don't we?"

"I was asked to explain why heterosexual humans write sexy messages on lavatory walls where their lovers can't go to read them. I couldn't. That's how I came to see the talk show about so-called alien writings. Found at Cerne Abbas. In the ladies' room of the Royal Oak, Sir."

"I see," drawled Tarrant-Arragon. "Are you saying that my Djinni left a message for someone? Perhaps I should see it."

He rose, strode to the big CEO's desk in front of a glassed-over wall of computer screens, flung himself into the throne-and-a-half sized chair, and winced.

Grievous could guess why. He'd been privileged to see Tarrant-Arragon in warriorly action that afternoon: being attacked by Tigrons armed with wicked-looking sticks during a "Zurkehd Threshold Training" session.

"The Zurkehd are a dwarf-warrior race who inure themselves to pain by repeated exposure to it," Tarrant-Arragon had explained as they strolled away from the combat pits. "However, I don't think I'll ever get used to the discomfort of, ah, denying myself sex. By making myself sore all over, I'm less preoccupied with a very singular ache. Do you realize I've been in a state of sexual anticipation for almost six Earth-weeks?"

Grievous hadn't known what to advise. Instead, he'd expressed surprise that a prince of Tarrant-Arragon's power needed to practice hand-to-hand combat at all.

"I am not, ah, popular, Grievous. Assassination is a real danger in my worlds. The Rings of Power I usually wear are effective weapons, but there are environments—such as a high-oxygen or methane atmosphere, or on worlds where it rains pure petroleum—where it wouldn't be suitable to throw laser-ring fire at my enemies. And situations—"

The tyrant had grinned.

"It might be undiplomatic to incinerate Saurian assassins in front of my loyal Princess. Loyal to my enemies, that is."

"It might help if her loyalties could be shared honorably, instead of divided," Grievous had suggested, nonplussed.

The prince had not taken to the idea.

Now, as Grievous watched his boss stab in access codes with one finger, he thought he ought to attempt damage limitation.

"There's something you should understand about our talk shows, Sir. They do go in for high drama. Exaggeration, Sir—"

"What makes you think these rune-writings have anything to do with my Djinni?" Tarrant-Arragon had found the broadcast, and was glaring at the talk-show guest's translation of the Viking runes found in the Royal Oak's lavatory.

"J-J, I am sorry, A," the expert had scrawled on a studio-set wall, and then added an upside-down Ng.

"Only that the symbols match those markings on her sword," Grievous said, all too willing to back down. "On the other hand, Sir, the lady archaeologist thought J-J must be a lad's name. Well, that can't be right. Not when the little miss is Djinni the Djinn."

"It's unoriginal bathroom graffiti," the soundtrack reported. *"An apology. What any heartbroken girl might write after falling out with her boyfriend."*

For a moment, the prince sat still while the implications sank in. The atmosphere seemed to crackle with elemental fury. Then the storm broke.

"Raging Carnality!" Tarrant-Arragon snarled the fiercest of his expletives. "So she rejects me because she's pining for some damn Earthling. Some lover! She might even be pregnant."

"Let's give her the benefit of the doubt, Sir," Grievous said without much hope that Tarrant-Arragon would take any notice. He had no doubt where the ferociously angry alien was going, or what he meant to do.

"If she has made a fool of me, I'll— Ah, damn! I have to know. And there's only one way to find out for sure."

"How does someone who is so self-conscious that he wears endowment padding to bed get nicknamed His Higher Horniness?" Djinni mused as she floated in the black-lace waters of her murk-bath.

"How? Oh Stars, he must have a friend with J-J's warped, English sense of humor; the sort that calls a tall man Shorty and a timid man Godzilla."

J-J. Djinni closed her eyes and sighed. Dark syrupy murk-water ebbed, then flowed heavily back over her chest.

When she was five, she'd thought J-J was the essence of romance and infinite wisdom distilled into one godlike being. A crack shot with his collection of pistols, he could shoot the pips out of playing cards—which she held up for him, having trained her Djinn-sharp eyes by watching throwing knives, then darts and arrows until she could see J-J's bullets coming.

Apart from pistols, puns and pornography, J-J enjoyed rock music, politics, and chess. Chess was a potential problem. From what Tigger had let slip, his chess rival—the Commander in the An'Koori Star Forces—might be none other than J-J.

After about six weeks under Tigger's regrettable influence, she'd become less idealistic about truth and honor. She'd decided that J-J need never know what might or might not have happened between herself and Tigger. She wouldn't tell him.

Unfortunately, she could wrap a male, even a sexual paper

tiger, only so far around her finger. There was nothing she could do to curb Tigger's An'Koori tendency to stretch the truth and to boast. If Tigger met J-J across a chessboard, he'd boast about her. To J-J's face. Then, friend or no friend, there'd be bloodshed. And they might meet very soon, now that Tigger's love cruiser had entered An'Koori-patrolled space.

Of course, he probably wouldn't boast about a girl who'd left him. She had an escape plan. She was ready. At the first starport, she'd simply leave. Make a clean break. . . .

Djinni sensed a shadow move over her. How long had he been there? Had she spoken J-J's name aloud? Opening her eyes, she looked up into the thunder-and-lightning gaze of Big Trouble.

Tarrant-Arragon felt his emotions roil as he looked down at her. Poor little mate, had he taken her away from someone she loved? Was it fair to be angry with her for that?

Her golden tracer-necklet glinted through the murk-water in the hollows of her collarbones like a flat eel trapped between shallow tidal pools. He leaned over her, paddled two fingers at her throat, and began his fishing expedition.

"I had not anticipated indefinite abstinence, little mate. I've waited over forty of your Earth-days. I want to know why," he began gently.

Her violet eyes paled and searched his face. There was a swirl of flustered movement in the thick, dark water as Djinni tried to cover her breasts with her hands. She said nothing.

"I asked you once if you were in love with an Earthling. You denied it. Did you lie?" He was being too aggressive, he knew. He ought to make her want to confide in him. He was too jealous. Too angry. Too much in love with the faithless little wretch!

"Of course I didn't," she gasped.

"Do you have sexual intercourse with people you don't love?"

"How dare you!" She splashed him emphatically.

"I dare much more, my dear. White Knights who don't respect their own truthfulness-pledges can't expect others to respect other pledges." He paused, expecting a panicked reaction. Djinni didn't seem to understand his reference to her vow of chastity. Provoked, he asked harshly, "Are you telling me you're a virgin?"

"I'm not telling you any such thing. It's none of your business," she retorted and folded her arms over her distractingly buoyant breasts.

"Oh yes, it is. I've made it my business. You're my mate, and where I come from, we value virginity."

"So much so that you've run out of it on your home world and have to raid others to find the rare commodity?" she answered with spirit. "If it mattered to you, Tigger, you ought to have asked me before you abducted me. Besides, I very much doubt *you're* a virgin." Djinni dared to shake her finger at him. "Therefore, you've no right to expect me to be one."

"What a very novel concept," he sneered, and leaned threateningly over her. Impossible girl! Here he was, being kind, and she was trying to attack his morals. Slack damn! The effort of attempting to give her the benefit of the doubt made his blood simmer. He'd swear it was hissing in his head.

"Are you pregnant?"

"If I were, who do you think would be responsible?"

Her logic baffled him. Damn, damn! He could've sworn—Then he noticed that the hissing sound was coming from the pedestals. It wasn't his blood pressure. She'd done something to the plumbing. He rounded on her for a confession.

She'd made an island of herself in the center of the murkbath. Doubtless she thought she'd be safe there, until his temper had spent itself. Well, she was mistaken.

"That hissing is my loo, Tigger. I tried to mute it. I didn't think you'd be able to hear it. It seems to be some kind of alarm-function," Djinni said. Her nonchalance was a little strained.

Tarrant-Arragon narrowed his eyes. A blush spilled over her face and chest, betraying her agitation. She was hiding something. He went straight for the pedestal's diagnostic readout. What he learned horrified him. He'd been badgering her about her chastity, and beneath the black waters she might be letting herself bleed to death.

Had she somehow worked out who he was? Was she keeping her Saurian vow to kill herself before he could make her his mate?

"Precious little mate, don't you understand, I need you?" He flung himself into her murk-bath. She squawked and plunged. "You will not die. You hear me? I will not allow it." As frantic as she, he made a second grab, caught her from behind, locked an arm around her waist, and drew her back against his body.

"What have you done to yourself?" he demanded.

Instead of answering, she kicked up black turbulence. His pale, slippery nymph wriggled and squeaked. She bucked against his belly. She flailed and fought, and tried to scratch him when he captured her arms in his free hand and inspected her wrists.

"Ahh, little love!" She did not need tourniquets. Relief washed over him.

Tarrant-Arragon forced himself to be calm. If her injuries were internal, he'd need her cooperation. Gently, he wrestled her into a sitting position on his lap in the dense water.

"Be still, fierce little one," he insisted while she struggled against him. She seemed intent on dislodging his forearm, which was wrapped tightly around her waist.

"Am I hurting you? Is this heavy gravity crushing your insides? Are you in pain?" he asked, trying to slacken his hold without letting her twist around for a frontal attack. "Ka'Nych is a gentle gynecologist. The best in all the Communicating Worlds. I won't let him hurt you. You must see him, Djinni. You must."

"No, Tigger," she panted, still trying to push herself off his lap. Suddenly, he realized why. He was clasping her like one of the damned horny frogs from her stories. And, of course, he had an erection; he always did. She probably feared that mating was imminent.

"May I put my arm around your shoulders?" he asked as if her consent weren't entirely redundant by that stage. He shifted her to his side so they could share his robe. Lying back, he held her in the hollow of his arm. He relaxed. Waited.

She accepted an available corner of his robe and pulled it around herself. Quiet at last, she continued to tremble, making little ripples in the dense water.

"Do you think it's 'soft tissue fissures'? Or 'bleeding ulcers'?" He repeated her pedestal's varied diagnoses in what he hoped was a concerned but conversational tone.

"I'm in perfect health," she said, sounding shy. "You forgot to feminize the computer banks, that's all."

For a moment, his overloaded brain did not make the obvious connection. Then he understood. His sweet, shy mate was in perfect feminine health. His fear that she might be pregnant could be forgotten.

"Is this normal for you? Or did I frighten you so much last cycle that I unsettled your feminine system?" She threw him an indignant look, and he did not persist in his inquiries.

As for her "past," she'd been prevaricating. Now he thought about it, he understood why she didn't want to tell him about her relationship with the Earthling J-J. Look how he'd behaved. His jealous tantrums couldn't change her past. However, they might interfere with her delicate fertility.

Tarrant-Arragon cocked his head, hoping a kiss would be possible. She turned hers—away. No wonder! He'd been a self-spiting fool. He could adjust. If he made love to her in the next few days while she still bled, perhaps he'd never know whether or not he'd been the first to dock in her bay.

He could live with not knowing for sure.

"I don't see why we shouldn't make love now. This would be a good time," he murmured against her earlobe.

A nonvirgin would surely have appreciated his generosity and his exquisite tact, but the love of his life said nothing until she noticed that he'd slipped a loving hand under her breast.

"Don't, Tigger." She grabbed his thumb and tried to push him away. "Suppose I like it with you?" she added beneath her breath, as if this were a terrible possibility.

"I'm going to make certain you like it." He knew her last, baffling objection hadn't been intended for his ears, but he was pleased to infer that she hadn't liked it with the wretched J-J. "It's all right to like it with me. Think of our lovemaking as the consummation of our marriage—as I do. It'll be like your first time, only more so. We'll pretend it is your first time."

"It would be my first time," she snapped.

"It would?" He cupped her throat between his hands. Her pulse thumped against his palm, and he waited for the telltale racing of her heart to signal that she was lying. As far as he could tell, she'd told the truth.

His heart began to sing a new—and a very ancient—song.

"Of course it would," she reiterated. "But it's not going to be. I'm not ready to break my vows."

Her damned Saurian vows! What was he to do? He could hardly retain credibility as the future lord of her life if he encouraged her to break solemn Saurian chastity vows, yet expected her to take her wedding vows seriously.

Djinni might have been tempted to read Tigger's mind, if it weren't for the fact that she was naked and he wasn't. He smiled, and his eyes flashed speculatively at her.

"Quite right, little Knight, you must keep your vows—every one of them," Tigger said, removing his hand from her bosom. It was an extraordinary remark for someone as amoral as Tigger, particularly since it went against his self-interest.

"My dear, in another week, we'll reprovision at Eurydyce. A Saurian Knight-spymaster who lives on the pleasure moon owes me a favor, and has the rank to give us an Unbinder for your vows." Tigger smiled, as if he'd solved everything. "Then you'll be free to love me with a clear conscience."

Djinni felt dishonorable for not telling him that her vows were vows of betrothal, but she couldn't without betraying a greater trust. As far as she knew, only her father or J-J could "unbind" those vows. Suddenly, Djinni's mind began to race.

Could Tigger's White Knight-spymaster be J-J? It was unrealistic to hope that he would release her from their betrothal even under the best circumstances. But in a week's time she'd be rut-rageous.

A week from now would be a particularly bad time to expect a Great Djinn to be reasonable. The timing couldn't be worse. If J-J was on the pleasure moon of Eurydyce, she'd be jumping out of Tigger's frying pan and into a Great Djinn's fire.

Chapter Thirteen

"I'll never let you go. You're mine. Mine!"

Dream lovers could be very confusing. In Djinni's nightmare the shadow-faced J-J held her, facedown, and raged at her for asking him to release her from their betrothal.

"You're mine," echoed a fiercer, sexier J-J, and she felt the coarse caress of his hair-darkened thighs astride hers as he mounted her from behind.

Two dream lovers at once. Arguing over her; sharing her; one holding her down, the other easing something that might—or might not—be a wickedly skilled finger between her legs.

What he did with it felt so sinfully good that honor swooned, overwhelmed by the sensual onslaught. Her senses swirled with the part of him that stroked hypnotically inside her, and with the unrelenting eroticism of an open mouth moving against her neck.

Her nape! He bit, gave a long, hot, seductive suck. The sharp nip of his love-bite awoke her good sense. She tensed.

"Ahhh. Tight! I don't know how I'm going to . . ." J-J's voice slurred into a growl of very virile frustration. Which was all wrong. The lover of her recurrent nightmares always knew what he wanted to do and how to do it, though she inevitably awoke before he could.

"No. Please. J-J!" Reality shifted. Part of her mind knew she wasn't with J-J, even as she cried out to him.

"J-J?" The outraged roar was Tigger's, and he was jealous. "Who is this J-J? Forget him. I'll make you forget him! He'll never give you babies. I will."

His finger—if that's what it was—emphasized his point.

"Can you feel . . . this?" He thrust slowly into her again as he spoke. She gasped at a sudden discomfort.

"Don't. That hurts," Djinni protested, fully awake now and uncomfortably aware that her nightdress had been pushed up around her waist, and that Tigger's hand was inside her knickers.

"In future, dream only of me," he growled. The invading whatever-it-was was even more slowly withdrawn.

"Thank you," she breathed, very relieved. Then she felt a tug, and heard her knickers rip. "What are you doing?"

No answer. None was necessary.

His abs brushed her back as he reached across her. She heard the opening of a drawer, the shush of heavy fabric unfolding and sliding over silk. Curious, she raised her head and watched him cast an embroidered white sheet like a sudden snowdrift over a tumbled heap of cushions and bedding.

Tigger wanted to have sex on a fresh sheet. Part of her mind tried to poke gentle fun at his perfunctory concession to romance. Another part remembered his obsession with her virginity. The sheet was white. His actions took on a barbaric significance.

"No, Tigger. We c-c-can't . . ."

But, of course, he could and he knew it. Which was probably why he smiled down at her as he flipped her onto her back, bounced her hips high into the mound of pillows, and bent over her.

"And now, my love." His voice was rough. "I'm going to dock with you."

End of conversation. He was determined, he knew his physical power, and he flaunted it in the menacing way he threw open his robes, let them slide off his shoulders and down over their hips. He braced one hand by her head, held her by the throat while he repositioned himself astride her thighs and the mound of pillows.

Now his weight pinned her spread legs. He took his hand from her chest and reached between them, between her legs and his. . . .

Djinni tried to meet his eyes before he stroked himself into a frenzy of pleasurable savagery, but he gazed down at her with such fierce intensity that she feared for her life.

This was it. Nothing else would stop him. She'd have to threaten him with her wicked second cousin.

"Tarrant-Arragon—"

Hr reared up over her. Their gazes locked. In the dark-on-dark of the bedroom, his eyes seemed to spark. "I didn't want it to be like this. . . ." He sighed, and lowered his handsome face to touch her forehead with his. "Ah, so be it."

He wasn't going to stop. For some reason, he was too aroused to fear even Tarrant-Arragon. Only one thing left. . . .

She drove her fist up. Hard. As hard as she could.

The impact sounded sickening. It felt awful. She felt awful. His eyes had been shut when she lashed out. *Oh, Stars!* She watched him recoil. Would he retaliate? She'd never seen him like this, didn't know what he'd do.

His eyes widened. He brought a hand to his nose, held the fingers up to his eyes, and stared disbelievingly at his own blood.

"Get off me, you big Hunnox!" She took charge while he was still too surprised to think for himself. The instant his weight shifted, she scrambled off the bed, grabbed a cushion, and hugged it for symbolic protection.

"By the Stars, Tigger," she scolded him from a safe distance, "anyone would think you had a fit of the rut—" She closed her eyes, as if she could shut off the thought as abruptly as she bit her lips together. He wouldn't know what she'd been about to say, but if he had, he might ask awkward questions.

"Dju bwoke by dnose!" he mumbled, and Djinni heard his

bare feet hit the floor. Fearing what he might do, she opened her eyes and saw him clutch the nearest sheet to his face and stalk out.

It was time to go.

Djinni changed into the most businesslike of her dresses: a black coat-dress. Her first sewing project had been to move and reinforce bodice buttons. When Tigger lost interest in her modifications, she'd opened side seams in case she ever needed a little number that she could run or kick-fight in.

Now she might need to do both. She really couldn't wait to see if Tigger would keep the promise he'd made over a week ago and take her to his friend, the White Knight on Eurydyce's moon.

Who might be J-J. But she'd worry about that later.

Her honor, as a Saurian Knight and as J-J's pledged bride, demanded that she leave. They were a mere shuttle trip from a pleasure moon on the borders of An'Koor. There was no better starting point for finding J-J. No better time.

No time to try to cut off Tigger's necklet, even though J-J would take a very dim view of another male giving her jewelry. No time . . . but she took time to throw the quilt over two pillows. A tired truant's trick, but probably not one Tigger knew.

She snatched up Tigger's robe. Her first thought was simply to distance it from the bed; her second, to take it with her.

And so, to open the door. She'd studied it for weeks, or rather, she'd studied how Tigger opened it. She wasn't sure that his fingerprints were the key, but she'd lifted them from his computer and silently thanked her stars for the cellotape in her overstuffed carryall bag.

The next hurdle was reaching the touchpad over the lintel without leaving a telltale pile on the threshold. The obvious answer was to pack her bag tightly—vertically—reinforce it with paperbacks in the ends, and stand on that.

Precarious it was, but it worked. The doors opened! And she almost tumbled into the stiff back of a guard! There'd never been sentries when they'd gone to the gym, but perhaps guards were posted when the spaceship was in an unfriendly starport.

But wasn't Eurydyce's moon supposed to be neutral?

The guard stamped to attention. Djinni circled him warily and tried to read his mind. It was impenetrable. All at once, she realized that people think in their own language. So she spoke in Tigger's language to ask, "Which way?" Without moving his head, the guard flicked a diagonal downward glance at the black robe, which she'd bundled over her bag like so much dirty laundry.

Djinni held her breath.

The guard nodded almost imperceptibly, his face rigidly expressionless. He'd probably noticed that Tigger had stormed out of the suite wearing no more than a thunderous expression, and trailing a sheet. He rolled his eyes to the right, indicating the way Tigger had gone.

No matter how dangerous it might be to follow Tigger, it was even more dangerous not to. There was no point in deliberately arousing suspicion. Whatever she did, the chances were good that she'd be caught and returned to Tigger.

A "good" chance? Djinni acknowledged her secret ambiguity about running away, but she had no honorable alternative: If she could, she had to find J-J. While she was still intact. Even though she might be rut-rageous.

"Dju're duh dnearest!" Tarrant-Arragon announced as he unceremoniously flooded Slayt's former quarters with light.

"Trouble, Sir?" Grievous sprang up from a deep day-couch in the living room that doubled as Dr. Ka'Nych's examining office.

"Bery 'barrassig drubble," Tarrant-Arragon confirmed through his nasal congestion and the sheet he was holding to his nose.

"You bloody cad!" Grievous snarled in unprovoked and unwarranted hostility. "Come to gloat, have you, Sir?"

"Gload?" The Earthling's remark made no sense. Annoyed, Tarrant-Arragon lowered his fists, preparing to glare.

Grievous's gaze dropped. Tarrant-Arragon glanced down.

"Thad's blood!" And, indeed, the bunched white sheet in his hands was dramatically stained with fresh blood. His own.

"You've got a bloody nose!" Grievous stated the obvious as if he'd only just noticed. "Er, sorry about my initial comments, Sir. I, er, jumped to the wrong conclusion."

"Slag dab, Griebbous. Thad was my last weddi'g sheed!"

"In that case, if I were you, Sir, I'd hang on to it," the Earthways Advisor suggested robustly. "Only the Doc and I need to know it's your nosebleed. The bloody-minded guests at your Consummation Banquet can think what they jolly well like."

Tarrant-Arragon raised an eyebrow. He was impressed.

Ka'Nych emerged from the bedroom and bustled forward. "If you will be pleased to sit, my Lord?" He indicated a chair, reached for his handheld gynecological flashlight, and began his examination. "The imperial septum is greatly bruised, my Lord."

"As is my bride."

"You mean to say 'pride,' Sir?" Grievous translated. "You wouldn't leave her in a sorry state and monopolize her doctor."

"Griebbus, your good opidion douches me. Gaaahhh! Slag-Dabbit!" Tarrant-Arragon protested at Ka'Nych's exaggeratedly careful treatment of him. "She bested be."

"She bested you, Sir? Good for her! Particularly obnoxious, were you, Sir?" Grievous said with cheerful insolence.

"My Lord, I can give you a vitamin-rich cactus extract to reduce the swelling," the doctor offered nervously.

"Doh! Bust thingk!" He flung up a hand to ward off Ka'Nych.

"By Jove, I think he's thinking, Doc!" Grievous remarked.

What had she said? *"The rut-"* . . . ? Tarrant-Arragon suddenly became aware of the sensation of little white flowers unfurling in his mind. She was right! Of course!

"Rud-rage. Inconbenient!" he groaned. And his heart sang.

"The rut-rage! Congratulations, Sir. It's just what you were hoping for, isn't it, Sir? What a pity the little miss has taken to it so poorly!"

Tarrant-Arragon did not appreciate Grievous's sarcasm. He glared at his Earthways Advisor. "I thingk, Griebbus, you should cultibate a more symbathedic bedside banner!"

"You do, Sir?" Grievous retorted. "Ah, but, I ask myself, do you deserve it, given your own rather questionable bedside manners? Perhaps you should tell us what happened."

"What habbened is— Ouch-damn!" Tarrant-Arragon swore at Ka'Nych, who was dodging and ducking as if the rumors about a Great Djinn's basilisk stare were true. "She hit upon—"

"Ha, ha. Very witty, Sir," Grievous interrupted dryly. "I'm glad to see that your inimitable sense of humor is returning, along with your consonant and vowel control, Sir."

"About the only tactic that had a chance of stobbing me."

"How fortuitous, my Lord!" Doctor Ka'Nych joined in.

"Fortuitous? That she blocked my saturniid gland?" Tarrant-Arragon considered. "What would one expect my Tigress to strike, if she thought it was in her best interests to fight me off?"

"We-e-ell, Sir, she's got a karate black belt, so she knows better than to go for the usual soft targets. And let's not forget she's telepathic. Perhaps in your excitement you weren't mind-shielding, and that's how she knew that her scent set you off. In which case it'd make jolly good sense to bung up your breathing apparatus, wouldn't it?" Grievous reasoned.

"Ah, but at the time, I had no idea that the rut-rage was upon us." Tarrant-Arragon smiled. "She recognized it. Why? And, perhaps more significantly, how?"

"My concern, my Lord," Ka'Nych said, "is that you'll impregnate her a full female cycle before the Imperial Wedding. You could give her the usual drink, but in view of her reaction to our drugs and her unreliable general health—"

"Drugs are out of the question. Ka'Nych, go to my suite and get me something to wear," Tarrant-Arragon dismissed him, then helped himself to Ka'Nych's medical supplies. "I can't avoid her indefinitely, Grievous, so for the next few days I must keep my saturniid gland blocked to minimize my, ah, tell-tale enthusiasm. We'll say I have a sinus infection."

"Won't wash with the men, Sir," Grievous said.

"True, but we need an official story," Tarrant-Arragon agreed, ruefully examining the damage to his face. "The, ah, scuttlebutt version should be that I attempted an advanced level of lovemaking and, in her inexperience and excitement, she let her foot slip . . . off my shoulder, I think." He grinned.

"Grievous, have a pilot stand by. I'm supposedly unwell, so I shouldn't pilot my own Thorcraft." He raised an eyebrow. "As I'm somewhat crossed in love, I'll go down to the pleasure moon and consult the local fortune-teller."

Djinni was lost. If only she could find some of the other abducted mates . . .

As if conjured up by her wish, she rounded a corner and found an exotic female. Far from looking like a submissive abductee, the painted alien fitted Djinni's mental image of how a Neoclassicist would have painted Cleopatra. This Cleopatra was checking her dramatic dark eyeliner in a device that looked like an all-in-one credit-card swipe, cell phone, and makeup case.

"May I join you?" Djinni said in her best feminine An'Koori.

The Cleopatra stared at Djinni's dress. Her reaction was unnerving. She seemed aghast. Something was obviously very wrong with what Djinni was wearing. She tried to read the Cleopatra's mind but could only identify vibrations of warning and fear.

"A pilot? The pleasure moon of Eurydyce?" Even if Cleopatra didn't understand feminine-submissive An'Koori, she'd surely recognize the name of the reprovisioning planet.

Cleopatra stepped closer, frowned, and reached for Djinni's throat. Did she want the necklet? It was the only thing she had of value: She'd no currency to pay . . .

Djinni blushed, realizing she had love-bites on her neck.

Since Cleopatra didn't seem to understand feminine-submissive An'Koori, Djinni sighed and said, "Forty-eight hours," the only unit of time she knew in Tigger's unfeminized bathroom-fixture language.

"Forty-eight hours!" Cleopatra echoed in scandalized tones. She sounded like a women's issues activist. How ironic it would be if all females—except the last of the Djinn-line—already had rights in Tigger's world, after all.

"Pilot a starfighter?" Djinni persevered, encouraged.

Then Cleopatra gripped her by the upper arm and it was too late to reflect that someone who talked "male talk" might keep unsavory company, and perhaps she oughtn't to trust her just because she was female and knew her way around.

They set off for the unknown at a heel-clacking pace.

The Pleasure Moon of Eurydyce

"I'm playing a dangerous game," Madam Tarra muttered half to herself, half to the Tarot cards on her dark, velvet-draped table. "Oh, not with you, although that's bad enough. I wonder why I didn't warn Djetthro-Jason. . . . Though I couldn't have known then that Djinni-vera had vanished."

The urgent message from Helispeta, now seven Earth-weeks cold, had been delivered that day. Apparently, Djinni-vera hadn't answered her telephone one midnight, and the college porter never returned after being sent to Djinni-vera's home to check on her.

Now Helispeta wanted Djarrhett to come to Earth to find Djinni-vera as much as Djetthro-Jason wanted Djarrhett to go to Earth to fetch his promised bride.

She'd speak with the Saurian Dragon. Ala'Aster-Djalet might recall Djarrhett from his secret mission, since Helispeta insisted. However, she couldn't use the holo-link for a few days. It was always unsafe to conduct Saurian business during jet-racing events. Now the Ark Imperial was in the Star Roads. Just when Stegosaurus was being smuggled out, too.

"What brings Tarrant-Arragon to Eurydyce so inopportunely?" she demanded of the Tarot. "He's hunting Stegosaurus, I suppose. Drat the boy, he's dangerous. Anyone would think he had an evil djinn-nose for knowing when and where he's least wanted."

She turned over The Lovers, and then two more cards. Madam Tarra stared unseeingly at her Empress card, and dreamed about what might have been if she had made different decisions when she was the romantic girl named Tarragonia-Marietta.

She had no idea how long the heavily robed and cloaked figure had been by the door before she noticed him.

A psychic should know at once what preoccupied her visitors. Madam Tarra knew how much time she needed to fake it. She routinely gave her clients time to hide wedding bangles, necklets and rings, to twist their debt-notes, or to react to icons of the gods they feared the most.

While he examined her display of dried aphrodisiacal herbs, she studied him indirectly, using the fish-eye mirrors hidden among the galactic zodiac signs. This visitor had an aggressive, dangerous presence. His body language told her that he might want help but probably was too proud to accept it.

"You are troubled, my son?" Her standard open-ended welcome to a male. She gestured to the client's chair.

"Troubled, Mother? You could say that." He flung himself into the chair and sprawled his long legs in the uncomfortable attitude of a male who has been bested by an unscrupulous kick-fighter, or who has been denied by a female.

"You're angry?" It was a reasonable guess. "And sore?" She looked into bandit eyes masked by fresh bruising. There was something familiar about him.

"My own mother doesn't recognize me," he snarled.

"Tarrant-Arragon!" She'd been distracted by his battered state. Swelling puffed his upper lip into an involuntary sneer more alarming than any she'd ever seen darken his father's face. "What have you done to your face? And what do you want?"

"I want advice." He rubbed his damaged nose as he spoke. "I am, ah, troubled by a female. I've been courting her for almost two cycles. However, I can't be very good at it."

"I find such an admission hard to believe," Madam Tarra said carefully. She'd heard of her son's reputation.

"Ah, but she's a fighting Saurian Knight." He put a slight emphasis on "fighting" and smiled self-deprecatingly. "Getting her into bed is more work than turning a Gravity-class war-star."

"Are you telling me that she fought you? You?"

"My Imperial Machismo forbids me to confirm or deny something so damaging to my reputation," Tarrant-Arragon replied with a mocking twist of his lips. "I will admit, she doesn't know what she's up against. I'm conducting an experiment to see whether I can get a virtuous girl to love me—not the next Emperor, but me—for my sweet nature and sense of humor."

His half-sheathed-weapon smile became a sudden chuckle.

"My fierce little Saurian would probably try to castrate me if she knew who I am. She cheerfully toasts my impotence."

Madam Tarra knew the toast to which he referred. "How very provocative of you to choose one of the Saurian Dragon's Knights for your carnal experiments," she replied.

"I didn't take her because she's a Knight." He threw back his head, half closed his eyes, and tapped his upper lip with two fingers. No doubt the wicked boy was deciding how much of the truth to tell her. "Ah . . . I think I've fallen in love."

More likely he was feeling a potent mix of pique and lust.

"I'd heard that Saurian Knights took vows of chastity, but I never thought a girl would take her word of honor so seriously—"

He stood abruptly and began to prowl the room. Watching him, Madam Tarra fought an urge to glance toward the secret alcove where murky drapes hid her Salamander mask. She sat still.

"She means to keep her ridiculous vows until she is given an honorable release. Mother, I want an Unbinder."

Madam Tarra suspected a trap. In their previous dealings,

Tarrant-Arragon had given no sign that he knew she was a spy-master for the Saurian Dragon. Did her devious son think she'd admit she was Salamander? She wasn't that much of a fool!

"What do you want of this girl?" The sharpness of her voice belied the nervous clench-unclench of her hands, hidden by the deep, mysterious folds of her table coverings.

"Something she doesn't want to give me."

"Don't all males? Be specific. Novelty? The sadistic pleasure of breaking her heart?"

"Her love. Well? You owe me this. Can you annul her vows?"

"I'm sorry, I can't," she said, thinking rapidly. His story was so out of character, it almost rang true. There weren't many female Knights, but a new female had been initiated recently. Tarrant-Arragon's Knight must be too junior to be important. "Even if I could unbind Saurian vows, there are none pertaining to chastity. In my line of business, I speak with authority. Some of my best clients are Saurian White Knights."

"Really? How in-ter-est-ing." Tarrant-Arragon flashed a cold-steel grin.

She'd said too much. In future, her premises would be watched. Thank the Great Originator, Stegosaurus was with the twins. By now, the Lounge Lizards' number-two pilot should have staged the spectacular jet-race accident they'd planned. With no hope of qualifying for the jet-races, the teammates wouldn't arouse suspicion when they left early, taking with them the bandage-swathed and unconscious Stegosaurus, whom they'd claim was a crew member burned by invisible fuel in the "accident."

"Do these work?" Tarrant-Arragon picked up a jar of Hun-nox gonads and raised an eyebrow.

"Like a charm." Madam Tarra shrugged.

"How do I give them to her? No, don't answer that. Instead, satisfy my curiosity about the rut-rage. When a male wants a girl with all his heart and she is . . . hesitant, his long-pent passion must be very similar to the rut-rage, mustn't it?"

"No, not in intensity, frequency, or duration," she snapped. "The rut-rage is a reversion to the basest of male animal behaviors, a perversion of natural law, a vicious, vicious circle that grows more tragic with every inbred generation of our deadly kind."

"In other words, my saturniids may be a curse?" he said, closely scrutinizing the Hunnox testicles from below.

"Suppose you pick up the scent of a female Djinn." Provoked by his inattention, she spoke bluntly. "Being most ruthless, you force yourself upon her. In your heat, you neither know nor care whether you could love the fragrant girl who inflames your glands. You want only to mate, and mate again."

"You make our aristocratic rut-rage sound like a dangerously potent aphrodisiac." He put down the jar.

"It is. After raping a Djinn Princess, how can you hope to persuade her that you love her when you yourself won't know the truth?"

"Ahh, but there are scientific studies of this sort of thing." Tarrant-Arragon draped an arm patronizingly over one of his mother's very large love god's projecting parts. "On Earth it is called the Stockholm Syndrome. In the Eurydycean dodecahedron it translates as Abduction Syndrome—"

"Bah! Irrelevant unless you plan to abduct and ravish an Earthling or an An'Koori. Did your studies factor in the Djinn rut-rage? Have you *no* idea how very unlovable the rut-rage makes a Djinn?

"Take my advice. If you want to be loved for yourself, as I did, let go of your yearnings for a true-Djinn mate."

To indicate that she'd say no more on the painful subject, she pushed herself back from the heavily draped table, revealing her primitive mobile chair.

"Why are you sitting in that thing?" Frowning, Tarrant-Arragon came to crouch beside her. "I paid for you to have state-of-the-art legs. Did you break them? Do you need replacements?"

"I know you paid." She spoke ungraciously, but Tarrant-Arragon's concern seemed like a threat. "You've been generous, especially in not telling Djerrold Vulcan where I am. But I don't trust you. You might have had transmitters put in my new legs."

"I might." He grinned, tacitly confirming that he knew about his mother's subversive activities. Something—or someone?—had changed Tarrant-Arragon. She would never have expected to hear him admit to wrongdoing or to make a joke at his own expense.

Tarrant-Arragon in love. Was he capable of it? Madam Tarra watched him rise and resume his roving inspection of her love-aids. She was indulging in romantic speculation when an audible transmission came in.

"I've rescued the most pathetically incompetent whore from the Ark Imperial . . ." Petri-Shah, normally her most reticent courtesan, had chosen the worst time in her life to throw caution to the winds.

Madam Tarra was on the wrong side of the room, unable to warn Petri-Shah that she was in bad company, and that he'd have no compunction about listening to every word.

She'd make matters worse if she sounded alarmed. Luckily, Tarrant-Arragon had become engrossed in his glossy forearm device.

Tarrant-Arragon scowled at the unexpected difficulty he foresaw from the blue blip on his forearm communicator. Djinni's tracer-necklet confirmed the identity of the "incompetent whore" whom Petri-Shah had presumed to "rescue" from the Ark Imperial.

How surprised Djinni would be to find him waiting for her! But how ever was he going to avoid introductions?

"Tarrant-Arragon?" His mother's shrewd eyes raked him.

"Yes, Mother. It seems you are about to meet the love of my life. Are you sure you can't give me an Unbinder? No? Then would you pretend to do so for her benefit?"

"Why don't you assert your 'god's Right' and be done with it?" she sneered. "Your father would. Everyone thinks you do."

"I prefer a girl to think she has a choice, even if she hasn't.

Moreover, asserting my 'god's Right' would rather ruin my experiment." He feigned interest in a penile restraint.

"Don't tell her who you are. Be-djinn her."

"No! Apart from my desire to be loved, I'd be a fool to mess with my little love's mind. She blurts out anarchic, mind-booting things that make me see our Tigron ways through new eyes."

He noticed his mother's expression soften, and realized that some truth was an effective strategy. So he added, "She holds up a distorting mirror to the natural order of things and challenges me to justify the way things are. When I can't, I have to reexamine my values. And my beliefs about females."

He grinned, imagining how his mother's credibility would plummet if she passed on this bit of intelligence to his enemies.

"She means to reform me of my wicked ways. And, Mother, I want her to succeed. If you won't give me an Unbinder, at least help me to convince my skittish girl it's her destiny to love me."

Madam Tarra ignored his request, which Tarrant-Arragon took as a fairly positive indication. He guessed she'd save face by pretending to consult her Tarot before she agreed to help him.

He gave her time. The colorful contents of a bowl caught his eye. "That solves one problem," he murmured, estimating the fit of the purple, massive-size condoms. "May I—?" He glanced toward his mother, saw she was engrossed in a fortune-teller's reference book, and took what he wanted, as was his custom.

Having pocketed several handfuls of condoms, he sat beside her and amused himself with the half-told Tarot on her table.

The Lovers card gave him an idea.

"James Bond—a fictional Earthling action-stud—may be an unreliable role model, but he played a trick on a superstitious virgin who was afraid to dock. Much like my little Knight. His stratagem might work. He produced a pack of identical Tarot cards, all with the picture of The Lovers, and persuaded the virgin to draw one card and abide by its meaning."

"That's not how you tell the Tarot," his mother said. "And

your lecherous hero would have been in deep fewm if the girl had pulled out The Lovers—Reversed."

"Have you a better suggestion, Mother?"

"Yes. The unprincipled bastard should have used Viking Runes," she said, tossing a cloth bag of stones to him. "Observe. Nine of the twenty-five runes are not reversible."

Obediently, he began isolating the nine symmetrical symbols.

"The Daguz, rune of Breakthrough and Initiation, might be fitting." His mother leaned forward and tapped a sign made up of equilateral triangles in a Bond-style bow-tie configuration. "Or, if you'd like her to trust you, you might make her choose a blank Rune of Odin."

"Blanks would be efficient," he agreed. "I don't have much time. Do you have twenty-five of them?"

"Make your own."

Sizzling fireballs! Tarrant-Arragon felt his temper rise. It was a logistical impossibility to call Fabrication, and she knew it. Even if the duty Engineers knew how to make runes, they didn't have time to make them and get them here before Djinni arrived. Damn! What a waste of a great idea.

"I'll tell you how," his mother compromised, having turned over the first of three cards. She turned the others and fell silent, staring from her cards to the book in her lap.

"Tarrant-Arragon!" she gasped. "You're never going to marry her."

Chapter Fourteen

"Was that a prediction, Mother? Or a question?"

Tarrant-Arragon had weighed the advantages and disadvantages of telling his enemies—by way of his mother—that he'd already married the love of his life.

"Astonishment." Madam Tarra gestured, palms up, fingertips down, at the Tarot cards on her table. "Three Eights indicates new family ties." She shrugged. "Besides, you've been humming the Imperial wedding anthem. So. Are you going to marry her?"

"If she'll have me." Tarrant-Arragon looked up from kneading his rune-stone dough and smiled. "I may have to cheat, but I'll have her. One way or another."

Receiving only a steely stare, he asked a technical question. "I've crushed out the air bubbles. Now what do I do?"

"Use the heel of your hand to flatten it to about a finger's thickness. Tarrant-Arragon, make a rectangle of the dough, not a square. You want to make a six-by-four grid."

"We want twenty-five units, not twenty-four. Logically, that means a five-by-five grid," he argued.

"This, son, is mystics, not mathematics. A Rune of Odin is

made from a tiny portion of all the other twenty-four runes."

"What does it matter? They're all blanks."

"Why not make one real Rune of Odin? If there is good in you, and magic in you, the runes may work for you. I hope they do."

Tarrant-Arragon liked the idea of good magic. He took great care as he pinched out and set aside a fraction from each, before shaping twenty-four roughly rectangular runes between his fingers.

In the companionable silence, he steeled himself to press her about the rut-rage. "Mother, why did you run away? Was the rut-rage so very bad?"

"It was," she choked out. "The one time I was its victim."

"One time?"

"I suppressed my pheromones. Your father never— Like you, I wanted to be loved for myself—There are herbs—" She broke off her disjointed account and shielded her face with one hand.

"Somehow, Django knew. Beware of your great-uncle Django-Ra. He knows too many dangerous, ugly secrets."

"I know. He hasn't lost as many of the ancient powers as the rest of us—that's why we all mind-shield."

"Bah! Mind-shielding!" she sneered, angered and distracted by his complacency.

"What secrets?"

Tarrant-Arragon kept his head down, held his breath, and hoped she might tell him something he didn't know.

"The Royal Genealogy isn't accurate. Some direct lines ought to be dotted. And some dotted lines . . ."

"Illegitimacy?" Tarrant-Arragon looked up sharply, then lowered his gaze just as quickly. "Close to the throne? Who?"

"Martia-Djulia is not your father's daughter."

"She's not? Does he know?"

"Of course not! Not unless Django taunted him about it."

"She's Django's?" He could not keep the disgust out of his voice. "Mother, how could y—?"

But, of course, she hadn't wanted to. Fragmented childhood memories slotted into place. Her screams, her broken legs, the

Imperial Restraints all made sudden disturbing sense.

"I see." Tarrant-Arragon shook his head. "Why didn't you tell me gestates ago, when I found you?"

"You weren't safely in love with someone else." She glared boldly at him, daring him to take offense at the implication.

"The secret of Martia-Djulia's parentage is safe, Mother. And thank you for the warning. I shall keep my little White Knight well away from Django."

Tarrant-Arragon glanced up from molding the twenty-four scraps together into the Rune of Odin. His mother was looking misty-eyed. However, he doubted that she'd be so sympathetic if she knew he was having the rut-rage.

As a finishing touch, it seemed appropriate to make his thumbprint on the Rune of Odin. Then, feeling mischievous, he used his little finger to insert Ka'Nych's irritants into his nostrils.

"Charming! Most regal!"

"Sinus medicine," he lied sweetly. "Mother, I know the rut-rage is too painful to talk about—" He gave her his most winning smile. "But what am I going to do about my girl? She's afraid of sex, and I feel like I've a supernova in my groin. I'll explode if I don't make love to her. Ah, damn! I'll explode when I do, too. I don't want to frighten her with my passion; I want to thrill her with my prowess. What can I do?"

"Exhaust yourself with a courtesan, son."

"No. I only want her. And I intend to be faithful. Do you have any other suggestions?"

Madam Tarra knew the secrets of the galaxies' greatest lovers. Tarrant-Arragon never expected her to give them away to him. To his amazement, she did.

Asgaard, Stronghold of the Saurian Dragon

"Dirtier tricks are required, my dear. Your charms alone might not seduce Tarrant-Arragon to his death." Eyes darting cold blue fire behind his mask, the Saurian Dragon leaned forward in his throne.

Bronty stood tall before him in her new Knight's tabard. Her Brontosaurus mask was politely under her arm, but her face did not betray how violently she resented his opinion of her plan to assassinate Tarrant-Arragon.

"Brontosaurus, I doubt you have the internal capacity to conceal a bomb where you suggest."

"Outward appearances can be deceptive," she answered. She could have said more, but she didn't feel that it would be wise to tell the Saurian Dragon that she'd accommodated both Prince Django-Ra and Sris at the same time. It was humiliating enough that the Dragon had formed an opinion of her "internal capacity."

Bronty shivered.

She'd heard rumors about the Saurian Dragon. Sexually, he was almost as bad as a Djinn. He'd had three wives, not strictly sequentially, all of whom had expired of exhaustion, and he frequented an exclusive brothel on the pleasure moon of Eurydyce.

Naturally, he'd seen her boyish figure during her initiation, but it was unpleasant to think that he'd looked at her as a sex object.

Bronty's thoughts flew back. Naked, she'd entered the Planetarium Chamber, which was in darkness to symbolize the ignorance that made fools like Tigrons let themselves be ruled by an alien family of self-styled gods.

With the first of the six oaths to defend the virtuous and vulnerable, a single star had ignited into a pinpoint of light, and the first pure white garment was blessed and donned.

By the time she'd sworn, the Chamber was lit by simulated starlight and members of the Assembly loomed into imposing life in their dinosaur-shaped head masks and flowing courtesy suits.

"Indeed appearances can be deceptive," he conceded with a smile in his deep voice. "However, the point is not worth ar-

guing. You'd never get past the Palace's portal security with a
bomb in you. I regret to say, Tarrant-Aragon is efficient.
You'd be interrogated. He'd find out from you that I'd allowed
you to take part in an assassination attempt, and my other
White Knights would forfeit their ambassadorial status."

Bronty bowed her head in silent fury.

"Diplomacy is an intricate dance, Bronty. In uniform, one is
identified as a neutral Observer, or a well-intentioned enemy
diplomat. Out of uniform . . . one is a spy. These polite conventions only work as long as the presumption of neutrality
and goodwill is cultivated.

"However, my dear, you have the distinction of being a suitable volunteer for a more subtle trap. There is to be a ceremony
following the next Virgins' Ball. I wish to disrupt it. You can
help if you are still willing to be ravished by Tarrant-Aragon."

"I'll kill him first!" Bronty curled her fingers into claws.

"That would be an improvement on *during,* wouldn't it?"
The Saurian Dragon mocked her. "Though still suicidal. Of
course, suicide would be preferable to being forced into
Tarrant-Aragon's marital bed. Which you might be. He has the
technology to make an unwilling bride's consent irrelevant."

"He might marry me? If that's what you want, Sire, I'll take
my chances," Bronty said, feeling suddenly light-headed in the
sunshine of his approving smile. Or perhaps it was the glittering future that was unfolding in her imagination.

"You are sure? Good." He gestured and a tall, glacier-eyed
White Knight stepped out of the shadows. "Brontosaurus, I
want you to meet the ambassadorial Knight who will escort
you. His Saurian name is Leviathan, but he is known as
'Rhett."

'Rhett was not masked. He smiled at her.

"Masked and in an Altaeran courtesy suit, 'Rhett will pose as
a member of the Altaeran delegation to which you are attached
as an official Saurian observer."

The Saurian Dragon turned to 'Rhett. "Keep quiet about
her sex. Let our enemy suspect she's a female masquerading as
a male. Let him think we exposed her to him by mistake."

Bronty felt insulted that the Saurian Dragon thought she made a plausible boy, and that he had not consulted her about this convolution in his plot. While the males talked over her head, she seethed and resolved to have the last laugh.

"Take no risks." The Saurian Dragon lowered his gaze from the equally tall 'Rhett. "Brontosaurus, stay within sight of 'Rhett. That shouldn't be too difficult."

'Rhett gave the Dragon a secret-knowing smile.

"Leave promptly after the ceremony, whatever it is. Never be alone with any of the Djinn."

"Then, Sire, how am I—?"

"Show her the pouch, 'Rhett. Triple sealed within—No! Don't open it!" the Saurian Dragon roared as she took the pouch and turned it in her hands. "Do not dissipate the power of its contents by exposing them to air until you're in the Palace."

"It looks like a camisole," Bronty observed.

"You'd be astonished at the effect this slip of slightly torn fabric can have on a Great Djinn." The Saurian Dragon chuckled. "You'll smell nothing, but the Tiger Princes' saturniid glands will detect female Djinn copulins. They'll be frantic to discover the source of their arousal, and when they do, they'll know they can't legally touch you. You're protected by diplomatic immunity as long as you remain with your delegation and are dressed as a White Knight.

"They would violate treaties if they were to take a uniformed White Knight by force," the Saurian Dragon continued. "They'd lose many allies—which would suit us very well—but after smelling you, they might not be able to control themselves."

Bronty had noticed the Saurian Dragon's use of the plural. Princes. Yes, it would be pleasant to have her revenge on Django-Ra. But for the moment, she was interested only in snaring Tarrant-Arragon.

As for the other Djinn, she'd use her initiative. What a scandal it would be if old Django-Ra and the Emperor were maddened by the rut-rage! What a scandal if the old buggers attacked the Princesses or the wives of visiting heads of state! She'd take some lace from the camisole and attach it to an ordinary handkerchief or two, which she'd plant on some highborn breeding-bays who deserved to die anyway.

The Pleasure Moon of Eurydyce

Djinni circled warily, stalking her stalkers. Her posture was a classic defensive *kamei*. Anyone who knew karate would see she was ready to fight and would back off.

The conventions of human martial arts didn't seem to apply here. All rules were different on this free-for-all moon. No chivalry. No law and order. She'd have to fight for her life.

Her attackers had formed a loose ring around her. Their shuffling, three-clawed feet kicked up puffs of black dust. It smelled of gunpowder. They smelled of drains. Their long, hairy arms were spread, and they held curved knives in their hands.

For some reason, even with four of them, their overt menace wasn't as terrifying as Tigger in one of his rare, really foul moods. Perhaps it was because they were short. . . .

Still they circled.

"Precision, poise, posture," Djinni recited, keeping her feet slightly apart, one ahead of the other. Her parrying left hand smoothed the air at breast level; her fighting right she fisted, close to her body at midriff level.

Breathe deeply. Draw in oxygen, use the mind to strengthen the body. Good. Her *Chi* was strong here.

Djinni tried to identify the leader. If she fought the most powerful one—and won—the other three might leave her alone. But which . . . ? They all wore skirts—of horse tails—she thought, and squinted to see better in the dark of the garish gaming-hell night. No! The hair was attached to scalps.

Scalp-taking Scythians!

Images flashed in her mind. They thought in simple picture

language. Djinni nodded. Scythians probably wouldn't attack in a pack. Only one could wear her scalp—

One lunged, snatching at her hair.

Djinni's heart lurched. Everything slid into slow motion.

Flex knees. Aim. Kick the side of his right knee. Hah! He staggered forward and she hit him in the face and stomach, twin blows, each delivering two hundred pounds of fisted force. He screamed and fell, retching green.

Respite. Everyone watched him crawl away on his hands and one buttock, dragging his kneecapped leg sideways.

No use to look for help among the strangers sidling like scum around the action. People here looked at her as if she had some kind of black plague. She didn't understand—

Movement. She braced herself as another rushed her. Steady. Go for his kneecap, too.

He blocked, shattering the heel of her shoe as it slammed into his palm. He was still howling and shaking stiletto slivers of heel from his hand when the second part of her scissor kick drove her other heel deep into his matted abdomen, and left it there.

Kick free. Balance. Djinni resumed her *kamei* in stockinged feet. Number Two hunched over and staggered out of range.

Next one. Dodge. Grasp his outstretched right wrist. Good! Now twist his arm over the back of his shoulder. And—yank.

Number Three wailed and dropped. So far, so good. Stomp on his ankle and he won't get up. Three down. More had arrived.

A knife! Someone's throwing a knife. Concentrate. . . .

Got it! In thirteen years, she hadn't lost the knack. J-J would've been proud of her. She'd plucked the knife out of the air as easily as a ballplayer catches a slow-ball.

What to do with it? She'd never killed anyone. Doubted she could, even in self-defense. The world was screaming. And what's that stench? Couldn't look, but someone was burning some foul kind of hairy meat.

Number Three groveling beneath her foot was leaking fear

in nauseating waves. Disgusted, she released him and looked around. A fourth pirate's nose gushed green bottom-of-pond scum. Stank like stirred pond-scum, too. Why? She hadn't touched him yet.

Surely she hadn't done that to him by Djinn-craft? She'd refused to learn . . . thought it was unethical. But Djinn-craft might explain the strange vibration—

Tarrant-Arragon removed his still-warm Rings and thrust them deep into a pocket.

He exhaled hard through his flared nostrils and concentrated on subsiding before Djinni noticed him. He didn't want her to see him revealed as a furious Great Djinn with his many-caped cloak and robes billowing and snapping about him.

He hadn't needed Petri-Shah to tell him that the little mate was in trouble. He was already storming to the square to rescue her, only to find her holding her own. She never ceased to amaze him. However, enough was enough, and when fresh Scythians lined up to join the fray, he'd incinerated one of them and frightened the slack damn, quivering sphincter out of everyone else.

His presence was a knife in the nostrils, a white-hot claw in the bowels. Everyone felt it and wanted to die. Except Djinni.

Djinni gave the fourth Scythian a four-fingered fighter's "Come On." Instead of charging, he squinted past her left ear. His scalping knife was suddenly red hot, clutched in a black charred fist. He gave a strangled cry and stumbled away, hugging himself as if he felt he'd been slashed open and needed to hold his entrails inside his belly.

Around her, the air prickled and sparked. Maybe the volatile black dust really was gunpowder; maybe spontaneous combustion was a reality on this moon. Or maybe one of her ruthless cousins with Djinn-craft had blown his cover for her.

J-J? One of the twins?

What a time to be rut-rageous! Ready to run, Djinni looked

around. People tumbled and scattered like autumn leaves on a night gale. Tigger stood alone, legs aggressively apart, looking like a witch's cat puffed up with fright.

Tenderness and relief flooded her. She was so glad to see him that she didn't feel at all awkward about the shocking shape his face was in, or that she'd left him. She sauntered over.

"Hey, Tigger. Were you worried?"

"Have you any idea of the danger you were in?" he snarled, grabbing her by the shoulders as if he wanted to shake her.

"Well . . ." She shrugged under his long, strong fingers. "Some idea. Of course, gravity is on my side here, but there were a couple of bad moments when I wished I'd had my Saurian sword with me. Then I realized that they had to take turns to attack me."

"You read their minds, did you?" Tigger smiled grimly.

Djinni nodded.

"They would have raped you to death, then taken your scalp."

"I know." She made a short pass with the scalping knife before shoving it into her pocket. "With this nasty toy."

"You are coming with me." As if nothing had changed, he swept a hand under her knees, lifted her, and strode off.

Electric sensations jolted through her, as if her system had thrown a switch and turned her emotions back on in a surge of power. Her pulse began to pound slowly and heavily, everywhere, even between her legs.

It must be the erotic combination of winning and of being in her man's arms. Not that he was a man. He was An'Koori. Whatever he did with whatever he had under his excessive endowment padding, he couldn't possibly get her pregnant.

"Where are we going?" She nuzzled her face against his bruised, unshaven cheek and felt his jaw muscles tighten.

"To settle your conscience," he growled. He meant to get the Unbinder, she supposed. "Then, my love, I'm taking you home."

Home. An'Koor. Her heart bumped. Go home with Tigger: such a seductively simple proposition. After all, it'd be much easier to start looking for J-J when they got to An'Koor, where she knew the language and people would understand her.

But if she went to An'Koor with Tigger, she might have to go all the way in bed.

For once in his dissolute life, her appalling son might have told the truth. Madam Tarra stared at the love-bitten girl with bruised knuckles, torn black hose, a Scythian lord's scalping blade poking a hole in her pocket, who, calm as a housecat, was sitting on The Terror of the Dodecahedron's lap. This girl was good for Tarrant-Arragon, a much better influence than even he realized. If anyone could tame The Tiger Prince, it might be this street-fighting young beauty.

At Tarrant-Arragon's gentle prompting, his girl had greeted her in High Court, which she spoke in carillon accents with the Imperial inflection and a distinctive growl on the end of certain consonants. Madam Tarra was amused. Clearly, Tarrant-Arragon had taught his girl Imperial elocution. Which implied that he meant to keep her at Court in one capacity or another. Why else would he teach her the aristocratic speech of The Tiger Princes?

Depraved boy! He could hardly keep his hands off her, but at least he was being subtle—a finger tracing circles on the nervous virgin's wrist, his Ringless ring hand splayed possessively across the no-man's-zone between her magnificent low-gravity bosom and the apex of her slender thighs.

At first glance, he seemed to have his passions under control. Closer scrutiny told a different story. Ever since he'd returned, carrying his shoeless young Knight, he'd held her firmly on his lap as if he'd never let her go. And he wouldn't, until he'd had what he wanted, which might be the best years of her life.

"I thought we were going to get a . . ." The girl hesitated, as if her vocabulary failed her.

"An Unbinder?" Tarrant-Arragon supplied. In English, Madam Tarra noticed. With typical arrogance, her son made no apology for switching to a language he'd no reason to think his mother understood. "I tried, little one. I'm told we don't need it."

The girl nodded. Her eyes sparkled with unshed tears. Of disappointment or feminine reaction to the danger she'd been in? Danger, victory, fear, surprise, an exotic world: All the right circumstances for love had fallen into Tarrant-Arragon's lap.

"I came here to have my fortune told." Tarrant-Arragon reverted to High Court. Surreptitiously, he dabbed his nose on his wrist, then nodded at The Lovers card, where he'd left it on the velvet-draped table. "Now we'll have yours told to be sure. With runes. You trust them. The fortune-teller specializes in runes."

"A girl needs a protector, dear," Madam Tarra said, following Tarrant-Arragon's lead and speaking High Court. "You should stay with this big male who loves you."

"I do love you," Tarrant-Arragon growled, making an announcement not heard from a Djinn in generations. "Ah, slack damn my nose."

Was there ever a less romantic declaration of love? Madam Tarra frowned at her son. He'd just sabotaged the most important words any girl could hope to hear. Why?

"Tigger, please use a handkerchief." The girl tilted her head against his chest, frowned up at Tarrant-Arragon, who was using his forearm, and passed him a square of white cloth.

Tellingly, her hand shook.

"Take a rune, dear." Madam Tarra smiled and pushed Tarrant-Arragon's rune-pouch across the table.

What was the matter with Tarrant-Arragon? Presumably the byplay with his nose was meant to distract attention from his declaration, in case the little Knight did not respond in kind. He had no idea that his girl was trembling on the brink of falling in love with him.

What was so different about this girl that he should bother with his "It's destiny" charade, when he could dazzle any girl into bed with his wealth, Imperial rank, and power?

His idea of stealth, no doubt.

Just like a Djinn! "By stealth if possible, by force if absolutely necessary." Archetypical Imperial courtship behavior.

Djinni kept her outward calm, but her thoughts whirled. Tigger loved her! It changed everything and it changed nothing.

"What am I to do?" she asked herself as she ran her fingers over the warm rune-stones in the pouch. "I can't trust my psychic perceptions when I'm under stress. Tigger isn't going to take me to any Saurian Knights. I must decide."

Trying to escape again here would be a mistake. She'd no money. If she stayed here, she'd be raped and killed before she could find J-J. So much for the honorable course of action.

The alternative? Tigger. His lovemaking might be erotic and unforgettable, but, if An'Koori males were as underendowed as J-J said, it wouldn't really count as sex. J-J need never find out.

An unworthy notion, Djinni mused. Suppose Tigger gave her some non-insertive experience? Was it fair to him to let him make An'Koori love to her, when she knew she'd have to leave him? No.

Yes! Sex was all he thought about. He was thinking about it now, which wasn't surprising, considering all the phallic symbols and sexual stimulants about the place. Not to mention the pornographic diagrams. . . .

Anyway, it would serve him right for bringing her to a house of ill repute and pretending the madam was a fortune-teller.

It wasn't as if she'd break his overheated heart. He talked of love and his injured nose in the same breath! His protestation of love was the sort of thing every would-be seducer said.

Djinni nodded to herself as her thoughts came into focus and she began to frame her unspoken question to the runes.

Maybe he loves me, maybe he doesn't—but he can't do much damage. I think I can trust Tigger in bed. Is it time I did?

Her thumb came to rest in a depression that might have been formed for her. She drew the rune. As she did, she knew both sides would be blank. With a sense of déjà vu, she remembered the last time she'd consulted runes. She'd drawn the Odin's Rune. The following dawn brought Tigger.

The same rune! It couldn't be a coincidence. She must be

meant to go with him. The Odin's Rune confirmed what Tigger, Madam Fortune-Teller, and her own heart wanted her to believe. "Trust him. Trust your destiny."

Trembling, she slid the Rune of Destiny across the table.

"She's drawn the real Rune of Odin. My son, it is destiny!" Madam Fortune-Teller said, staring at the crude tablet.

"The real one? Are there false ones?" Djinni tumbled the rest of the runes onto the table. She was about to comment when she heard the fortune-teller gasp, and Tigger's fists clenched where they rested on Djinni's thighs. Her handkerchief tore.

Looking up, Djinni saw the furious snarl on his thinned lips. For a missed heartbeat, she didn't understand what had enraged him, or why the older woman had turned as white as antique lace; then Djinni felt very wise and very mystical.

Tigger must want her very much, if he'd gone to the trouble of getting fake runes. And "my son!" the older woman had said. She might really be the lovable bastard's mother. There was something familiar about her lips and eyes. . . .

Had Tigger really brought her to see his mother? Oh dear, perhaps he was serious, or thought he was. In that case, she'd have to hope that sex would be a fiasco. If it was, their hearts might not break when the time came to part.

"I might've guessed he'd cheat. He always does," Djinni said calmly. "Poor devious Tigger. He is . . . moral." Which wasn't at all what she wanted to say, so she added in English, "Not!"

Tigger and Madam Fortune-Teller were waiting.

She had to decide. Suspicion or Superstition? Head or Heart? An appropriately ambiguous saying from Shakespeare came to mind. Djinni quoted, " 'There's a Divinity shapes our ends rough hew them how we might.' "

"So, even if I'd had the time to make all the proper signs on all my runes, you'd still have picked the blank one made of the bits?" Tigger paraphrased in confident English. "You can't escape destiny, and you can't escape me. You have to let me have my way with you. That rune says so."

Speaking so much English in front of the fortune-teller

seemed discourteous. Djinni was embarrassed, but what she had to say was private. She gave the older woman an apologetic smile and took a deep breath. Teaching Tigger a lesson was risky.

"Tigger, you take too much for granted. You can't tell me what the rune says to me, because you don't know what I asked."

Defying him is not a good idea, someone was thinking. Someone else was contemplating violence if he didn't get to mate with her soon. Djinni swallowed hard.

"I don't want you to think that cheating gets you your way, Tigger. Next time you trick me, I may not forgive you."

"You will this time?" He pounced on the implication that there would be a next time. Tilting her face, he made her look him in the eye. "Constructive forgiveness? In bed and anywhere else I want it?"

Djinni gave him the best answer her conscience would allow. "Yes, Tigger, I forgive you. This time."

Chapter Fifteen

"Next time you trick me, I may not forgive you," his little mate had warned him. Her words haunted Tarrant-Arragon.

Carrying her through the Ark Imperial's Battle Stations–dark corridors, Tarrant-Arragon wondered how heavy a price he'd pay for what he was about to do.

He knew it was unforgivable of him to make love to Djinni without telling her she was consummating her irrevocable marriage. To "her depraved enemy Tarrant-Arragon," no less. But he was going to do it. What else could he do? He'd lose her love and trust all the sooner if he told the truth.

Discovery was imminent. She'd see that he was by no means hung like an earthworm as soon as he opened his robes. If he was lucky, she'd resent his trickery but would spread her legs because she'd promised him sex and she was incorrigibly honorable.

The alternative was unthinkable: She'd take one look and recognize the ravisher of her nightmares.

Knowing Djinni's horror of large male genitals, he'd be slack-witted to let her see him in advance. Time enough for tears and recriminations after the truth was thrust upon her.

Or even if it was nudged, and stroked, and eased in— Tarrant-Arragon groaned at his thoughts.

Once he was in, she'd know who he was.

"Your friends seem to know what we're going to do," his shy bride whispered, and her blush flamed against his chest.

"I must be an unusual sight." It was a gross understatement. He was a sight to stimulate a million domination fantasies: the invincible warrior prince, with his eyes blackened during questionable sex, returning his runaway princess to his bed, where she belonged.

His carnal amusements had always been unavoidably public, so he was used to discreet stares and hadn't noticed the interest he and Djinni had excited all the way from the arrival port to Top-Curveside.

Lust-enhanced senses in erotic overdrive, Tarrant-Arragon was more aware of the weighted swing of the condoms hidden in the sleeve pockets of his robes; the soft bump of her bulky bag on his buttocks as he walked made him think of frantic feminine hands urging him to thrust faster, harder, deeper.

"You will be careful? You won't be rough and clumsy, will you?" she whispered as if she knew his thoughts.

"Oh, my love!" he gritted, and swept into his suite.

Stars help her, "Oh, my love!" was hardly a solemn pledge, Djinni thought as the guillotine-shaped outer doors closed behind them like the silent blink of a three-lidded crocodile eye. Never had his suite seemed so alien. Never had she felt so trapped.

Psychic warnings flashed like paparazzi behind the protective cordon of her consciousness. She refused to "listen." She'd given Tigger her word. For better or worse, she just wanted to keep her promise and come through . . . it . . . intact.

Djinni took a deep breath, and her senses were inundated by scent-traces of Tigger's recent, violent emotions. Since the first time he'd kissed her, she'd become a lot better at tuning out his strongest thoughts, but it didn't always work.

Sometimes his thoughts were normal. Sometimes they weren't.

To calm her nerves, she tried to focus on the familiar, but something was different about the subtly lit bedroom. She was trying to analyze what it was when she saw that Tigger was taking her to the bathroom.

She supposed it was a good idea to go, before . . . But she'd have preferred a less direct approach to sexual hygiene.

"Tigger, it might be romantic to . . ." She closed her eyes in shyness. "Perhaps, we could bathe each oth—"

Fully clothed, not even breaking stride to kick off his high boots, he plunged into the murk-bath with her.

"My God!" she spluttered as soon as they surfaced and she could draw breath. "Do males of your species routinely half-drown your females during sex?"

It was a feeble attempt to make light of how much he'd frightened her. Shocked silly, she found her eyes adjusting faster than her mind. Below them, his robes drifted out in the slow, sinister diamond of a manta ray, casting shadows upward and effervescing tiny air bubbles like black sequins.

"I never knew the bath had underwater floodlights!" she added distractedly. "Look here, Tigger, I'm not at all sure about this. . . ."

"I know," Tigger said, breathing hard and stroking her throat with trembling fingers. "You're afraid of what I'm going to do."

"No. Yes. Well, you might have warned me. I agreed to let you have sex any way you want, but I need preparation—"

"I know you do." He unsheathed a carnal grin. Under murk-water, the fingertips of his left hand traced lines of fire over her belly, and her insides shivered. Then he dipped his fingers into the opening of her coat-dress and tugged. "Lots and lots."

"That's not what I meant." She didn't know how to ask what an An'Koori did when his moment came. "Tigger, don't you think this is dangerous? You may be in your element, but I—"

"I'm going to give you a very thorough seeing-to. But first . . . Ahhh, I come first." His thumb circled a button at her waist, and she felt the caress as though he'd stroked her between her legs. "Well? Your dress is ruined anyway. Shall I ruin it some more? A lot more?"

"I don't—"

"Don't talk. Kiss me."

He angled her face up to his, and Djinni had the oddest impression that she'd been ordered to do the sexual equivalent of rubbing noses with a tiger. However, she'd promised to do what he wanted, so she took his darkly stubbled jaw between her hands. Shyly, she bent forward and touched her lips to his.

Absorbed in the tequila taste and intriguing textures of his lips, she hardly noticed what he was doing until wicked fingers circled her areolae through her wet clothes. Sparkling sensations zigzagged through her.

She was so surprised, she looked down. He did too. Their foreheads brushed, and it seemed doubly indecent for them both to watch his long-fingered, masculine hands fondling her breasts.

"Oh, little mate. Oh, yes!" He sighed as the top half of her chest turned slowly pink with embarrassment.

His hands kneaded and stroked her, and she was too shocked to look away. Never had she felt anything like it. Never had she imagined . . . this. As though under conjurer's hands, her reinforced bodice buttons gave way. The front of her dress opened like a black peony, spilling forth inner petals of lacy petticoat and a white profusion of bra and bosom.

"Ahhh." He pushed his spread fingers inside her clothes and took her breasts in his hands. "Firm but so soft. Beautifully heavy. You fill my hands. You're wonderful. Gorgeous!"

It didn't seem right. It wasn't, of course. She was in over her head. She hadn't wanted or expected to feel the way she did. It was a complication. A disaster in the making.

"Tigger, this isn't right," she pleaded, conscience-stricken. "Something strange is happening to me. Can we stop for a moment?"

"No, we can't!" He sank lower in the water and put his open mouth on her. His tongue flicked over her like liquid fire, hot through the wet cotton and lace, and above it, and under it. One of his hands curved under her bottom from behind, with his spread fingertips pressed up into the soft gusset of her panties.

"Ahhh," Tigger groaned again, crushing her against him. All of a sudden, he surged up in the murk-water.

If this was "it," he'd got their positioning wrong, unless he expected her ovaries to be under her kneecaps, Djinni thought. She was wondering what she was supposed to do when a jolt ran through him. The length of him juddered against her. There was a vibration and a shiver in the water that seemed to last and last.

Had he just done what she thought he'd done?

He had!

J-J's scornful epithet "Quivering An'Koori" took on new meaning when Tigger trembled and jerked in the water. There was no further doubt in her mind that Tigger was An'Koori. It almost made sense that people from a water-world mated in water.

He subsided and lay on his back in the water, which now glittered and fizzed like champagne in black beer. Black and silvery waves radiated out, shimmering in the dark and suddenly peaceful room. Their thick slow slosh was a heavy caress.

Djinni adjusted her bodice and floated beside him. Her ear against his chest was filled with the muffled traffic roar of his heart, but gradually she recognized another rumble.

Tigger was purring. Which told Djinni that not only had he spent himself against her, but he'd done it on purpose.

"Tigger?" she whispered. But how does a nice girl ask her satisfied lover if sex was over for both of them?

"Yes, my love?" At her shoulder, his hand stirred. Long fingers slid over her much-ruffled bra, found a loose thread, and tugged. With a silken caress, her underwear unraveled.

"I was just thinking . . ." She thought quickly. "Oh, my Stars, Tigger, when I told you about frogs trying to mate with fish, I never dreamed . . ."

"That you'd lose your virginity in an amphibian mating?" he completed her thought. "You came close."

Strictly speaking, she hadn't lost her virginity, but if a quivering An'Koori didn't know the difference and was happy with frottage, was she morally obliged to tell him what he was missing? She didn't want to invite that sort of trouble.

Or did she? What they'd just done wasn't the mutual anticlimax she'd wanted, since Tigger seemed to be delighted with his performance.

"You're very quiet, little one. I haven't disgusted you, have I?"

"Oh, no!" she protested, although she was shocked. "How could your behavior be disgusting if you're doing what's natural and normal for you? But something is bothering me. I can't put my finger on what it is, and I'm frustrated about that."

"Are you?" he drawled.

"Tigger, about last night," she began, thinking that if the An'Koori mated in water, which they obviously did, something about his sexuality didn't make sense.

"Ye-e-es?" There was a world of alien sensuality in the way he watched her through narrowed predatory eyes. When he looked at her like that, her mouth went dry and a frisson of guilty excitement ricocheted through her insides.

The honorable-daredevil part of her wanted to ask whether she'd misunderstood his previous night's attempt to force himself on her. When she'd sucker-punched him, she'd been sure he'd been about to have sex in the normal way.

Had his sexual aggression merely been a bungled powerplay? The cautious martial artist in her didn't want to inquire. Either way, she'd be asking for trouble.

"Nothing." She shook her head. "I'm just confused. I need to sort out my feelings."

For a breathtaking moment, she thought he wasn't going to let her off the hook. His nostrils flared. Then he exhaled hard.

"I'll sort your feelings out for you," he said at last, with deep-voiced, casual arrogance. "You love me. Admit it."

"I'll do no such thing." This topic was almost as dangerous as analyzing his sexual preferences. "How do you expect me to love you when I can't trust you? Tigger, you can't even tell the truth about bathwater! You told me this murk-bath was to help me adjust to your gravity. When I look back at your misbehavior whenever I was around water, I could kick myself for not guessing that this bath was for mating."

Tigger choked and began to quiver. At it again, Djinni thought. What a pig!

"You once accused me of sending mixed signals. What about you?" She glared, saw that he was shaking with silent mirth, and splashed him. "How dare you laugh at a time like this? What about those things you said about wanting to spread my legs and bury your 'choice weapon' deep inside me? All you want to do is make love like a spawning fish."

Spawning fish? Tarrant-Arragon stopped laughing. What the sunblazes had his little mate convinced herself he was? Not a Great Djinn, that was for sure.

Yet on some repressed level she knew exactly who he was. She must have known last night. She'd cried out his name! Had she forgotten? Or did she not trust her insights?

A thousand worlds' tribute for your thoughts, Tarrant-Arragon mused, silently courting disaster.

Was it possible she knew who he was and loved him, despite all the vicious propaganda she believed about him? An entrancing supposition. That she'd just denied it, didn't worry him. She lied to him all the time.

He turned his head and smiled at her.

"I love you. You know that, don't you?"

He watched her changing expressions and recognized all the signs that she was desperate to change the subject.

"Human lovemaking must seem intriguingly unnatural to you," she blurted out, and Tarrant-Arragon couldn't decide whether she sounded wistful or patronizing.

"Very," he agreed. It was a stretch, but he thought he understood her. She was so afraid of the amorous unknown that she wanted to think that making love with him would be something less than having sex.

Why disabuse her of the notion? He was much too experienced to forfeit a strategic advantage in bed. And yet his heart had leapt when she'd started to ask, "About last night—?" If she hadn't backed down, he might have told her the whole truth. If only he could convince her that she loved him.

Heavy murk-water tugged at his boots. He kicked free, and congratulated himself. The murk-bath had been an inspiration for taking the violent edge off his passion. Off-camera. Moreover, the dense waters had dampened Djinni's fertile fragrance.

However, even if it was possible to stay in the murk-bath for the next five days and nights, he'd no intention of consummating his marriage anywhere but in bed.

"Very," he repeated huskily, and slid his hand under her dress. So far, so good. She parted her legs. It was the first time she'd welcomed his hand there. It might be the last.

This first-and-last he'd remember for the rest of his life— her first lover, his last virgin. He'd take his time and savor every nanosecond. Standing between her legs, dazzled by desire, he inserted a finger inside her panties and held his breath.

She didn't object.

He stroked her.

"Oh, Tigger!"

He yearned for her to sigh "Oh, Tarrant-Arragon!" and for there to be no secrets between them, no disguises. Next rutrage, he'd make love to her without inhibition and pretense; he'd inhale freely and glory in her fertile mystery.

"I've never felt this—" He couldn't continue. It was too hard to put his feelings into words. He wanted to tell his bride of his amazement and love, but he had to fight to control his sudden surge of passion and only partly succeeded.

He had to see her. He slipped his Fire-Stone Ring from his deepest sleeve pocket, laser-separated a seam of her dress, and smoothed her skirts into the depths of the murk-water, revealing sensible white panties, made semitransparent by the water and stretched over the knuckles of his left hand, until he took out another seam.

"So pretty. So sweet," he whispered. His comments seemed unimaginative and inadequate, even to his warrior's ears, but he knew the importance of reassurance and encouragement. "My love, you're like an elastic creature of the sea."

It felt like putting his finger into a sea-chrysanthemum: feathery fronds at the opening, and the slow clench of a satiny sheath, softly pulsing and resisting deep penetration.

Catching his breath in awe, he caressed her thighs farther apart and eased himself between her floating knees. She was almost ready. He added a second finger, gently stretching her, and felt her delicate flesh shimmer.

"Have you been reading my novels?" she gasped.

"Why?" he growled, exercising heroic restraint. Slack damn it, this was no time for small talk.

"I mean, Tigger, do you want to try it like a human?"

He gaped uncomprehendingly at her.

Misguided compassion lit her distant-mountain eyes. "Oh, dear. You need me to tell you what to do, don't you?"

Great swirling nebulae, what impudence. What an outstanding idea! What an erotic novelty! He'd erupt just at the thought of a girl telling him what to do in bed.

"I've never . . . you know." She hesitated, cheeks flushed. "So I'm not exactly sure what I'd like, either. Should we act out what they do in one of the novels' love scenes?"

Perfect solution! If Djinni didn't enjoy their first time, he'd blame some Earthling author. Tarrant-Aragon tried to look eager and innocent at the same time.

He nodded enthusiastically.

"But you've got to think of an in-bed scene." Despite her bold words, her voice cracked. His sweet, shy little mate was as nervous as the day he'd met her.

"To bed, then. Wet robes and all," he agreed, since bed had been his plan all along. He scooped her up, with her legs tight around his waist and her cool arms clinging to his neck. Behind her back he initiated a sequence on his forearm communicator, and with water streaming from the square corners of his sleeves, he carried her into the bedroom.

A glance satisfied him that his orders had been followed. On the bedhead wall, the twenty computer screens played one huge incoming tide borrowed from a Bond-film seduction scene. Movie moonlight was slivered and tossed off endless computer-generated waves that sucked and sighed over and over again.

A subliminally sexy sound-track. Tarrant-Arragon hoped it might inspire Djinni.

Having mounted the steps, he sank to his knees on the bed, braced himself on one hand and lowered her onto the carefully arranged mound of pillows, and followed her down.

"Ahhh, my love." He could have told her that she had the loveliest little docking bay he'd ever come upon, but he thought she'd rather not know how well he could see her in the semidark.

He looked as much as he wanted, with most of his upper-body weight on his forearms, and his arousal out of her line of sight and buried in the silken cushions under her hips.

Before he could decide where to kiss her first, she reached up and caught his face in her hands.

"Tigger . . . you mustn't expect excessive raptures—like in a book—for either of us."

"Why not?" He loved his excessively nervous mate. If she needed to chatter, he was male enough to love her and listen at the same time. "Hmmm," he prompted, easing down and humming into her.

"Oh, my! Because in novels . . . Tigger! . . . the hero is very experienced. He knows exactly what he is doing—"

"You think I don't?" He raised his head and smiled knowingly at her flushed face.

"Mmmm. Last night you said you didn't know how. . . . A little while ago you said you'd never felt . . . oh dear . . . down there. You're trying it human style for the first time—"

Great fiery balls, passionate half-sentences led to some extraordinary misinterpretations! Tarrant-Arragon stared at her in astonishment. No girl had ever flaunted such low expectations of his prowess and staying power, yet presented such a challenge.

He dipped his head again. He'd show her just how wrong she was.

Djinni didn't understand herself. Something perverse was

happening to her. Why did she want their lovemaking to be unforgettably good for Tigger? It made no sense. Disappointment was what she wanted. Needed. If sex wasn't a disappointment, she'd break his heart. He'd break hers. . . .

She wanted to talk it through. Tigger didn't. It was hard to talk to him when he was doing . . . what he was doing.

"Tigg-errr!" She grabbed his hair to make him look at her, but didn't have the heart to hurt him, so he continued to do as he pleased and she clung for dear life. "You've wanted this . . . so badly . . . for so long. I don't want you to be disappointed."

"I won't be, if I ever get to it," he mumbled, not stopping.

Stars, she was a fool to enjoy any of this. How could she live with her infidelity if she enjoyed it?

But this might be the best sex she'd ever have. No Great Djinn would ever—ever—lower himself to do . . . this. A god with his head lower than a female's bottom? No way!

But if this was what Tigger liked to do, hadn't she promised him . . . ? Didn't a girl deserve . . . to be made love to . . . once in her life?

Not that this was lovemaking. It was sex. Sex. Impure and complicated sex. Great sex. . . .

Djinni tossed her head back in sinfully soft pillows and let herself float on a guiltless sea of sensuality.

"Ohhh. How lovely!" She meant the An'Koori seascape playing on the wall, but Tigger must have thought she liked what he was doing with his fingers and his tongue. He did it even more thoroughly.

"I'm really and truly making love," he groaned against her.

It's not lovemaking! Djinni wailed inwardly.

Sure as water, Tigger ran a hand up her aching thigh. He was like an eager boy putting a well-licked finger in the icing of his birthday cake and claiming the whole confection for himself.

Sweet ruin to feel claimed by Tigger. Oh, Stars. . . .

"I've never made love before," his awed whisper undid her.

Stars, Stars, Stars! He'd found a chink in her armor. How could she not love him for making her his first love?

His mouth was as warm and gentle as sunlight. His tongue

made hot, wet animal love to her. It was getting to be too much.

"Tigger, I can't . . ." She tried to arch away, but he loved her relentlessly until—unexpectedly—flowers of flame burst into bloom deep inside her. Her senses scattered and wheeled like a startled flock of bright birds of paradise.

"You won't believe what you can take," Tigger breathed.

His finger reentered her and the sensation made her feel all white and tingly, and softly explosive—like a sunburst of 'Wishes' ready to float away on the summer breeze.

"Oh my! Oh my!" Swept up in the glory of his lovemaking, she wanted more. "Now, Tigger. Fill me!"

Chapter Sixteen

"I want to, my love. I will . . . fill you."

Tarrant-Arragon trembled with raging urgency to consummate their marriage, to thrust into her and feel her shatter, to feel the warm rush of her virgin's blood and to plunge and soar in her slick sweetness.

Ah, Carnality. He wanted to fill her, and fill her, and fill her, to pump his scalding seed deep into her in a torrent of savage, thrashing, liquid life. However, she was rut-rageous, and they weren't officially mated.

"Oh, Stars. Put two fingers in me or something. Tigg-errr!" his sweet, tight, little mate cried out. She had no idea—

"I've got to put on a condom," he gritted.

"It's . . . not . . . necessary."

"It is. Very." An Empire would—in theory—mark time by her pregnancies. He could not start the clock until after the Royal Wedding. He had to protect her, whatever the cost to his own pleasure.

"Uh, I'm too excited. I might frighten you." He panted the flimsy explanation as he forced a Triumphant Magnificence on as best he could without her seeing him.

"You can't think condoms are passion limiters? Oh—"

He was on her. In her. He crushed his mouth on hers in a fierce kiss before her sexy little moans, pleas, and protests drove him wild beyond control. As he did, he straightened his legs and pushed slowly into her.

"Stars, Tigger!" she cried out under his mouth.

He held his position. Every muscle shuddered with the effort, but he waited for her quivering body to adjust a little more.

"Stars," she gasped again. "This must be the point when I'm supposed to grip the bed, close my eyes, and think of something else . . . like bringing down an Empire."

"Hold tight, then," he warned. "We're committed now—"

She pushed against his chest, but he'd had the experience to cradle her with his arms so she couldn't flinch away from the full length of his careful consummating thrust.

"My life mate," he whispered as he felt the resistance shatter. Her scream might have kept his words of love and possession from her ears, but the ritual binding words were on record. Hers was the last maidenhead he'd ever take.

The thought sent him over the edge. Rivers of joy pulsed through him. White flowers exploded in fragrant brilliance. In blinding, white-hot delight. Silver streams teeming with life silently burst the dam of his restraint.

"It is done," he said, riding wave upon wave of exquisite pleasure and sweet torment. With a violence, he wanted to buck and thrust in her, and come again as soon as possible.

He didn't. He couldn't. To move would hurt her more. If he moved, he wouldn't be able to stop. Bad enough that he'd left her behind this time.

"I'm dead," his new-made Princess wailed. Her words ran the gamut of meanings—from erotic to desperate.

"Not in my lifetime," Tarrant-Arragon vowed in deadly Djinn earnest. He gently touched her forehead with his and smelled the thick, salty tears trembling on her eyelashes.

"I love you," he whispered. "What would you like me to do?"

She opened her eyes, which glared silvery pale in the Battle Stations darkness. "Don't move," she gritted.

"Thinking about an Empire didn't help, I take it?" Tarrant-Arragon teased very tenderly, hoping to distract her from his size. "Did you think you would, ah, bring down the Tiger Djinn?"

"You know I did. That's why I came with you in the first place." Her retort was a half-snarl. She reminded him of a panting, injured young tigress. Down, but dangerous.

"Somehow, Tigger, I don't think I shall after this." A wry note crept into her voice. She still sounded strained. Her sweet mouth suddenly contorted and hard-fought tears streamed into her hair. "Oh, Stars. He'll kill me."

Tarrant-Arragon wasn't sure what to say. Knowing of her fears, he assumed that he was the "he" who'd kill her, presumably with the size and force of his passion.

"*This* is normal," he lied to reassure her. It wasn't. A Djinn-on-Djinn mating was too rare to be "normal." *This* was quite extraordinary. "Virgins nearly always suffer—"

Her forehead wrinkled under his. As clearly as if her thoughts were drawn on crumpled paper, he knew she was puzzled. She thought he'd never deflowered a virgin before. So how might he know what was normal?

The challenge of being economical with the truth took his mind—somewhat—off the explosive lust that was starting to rake his sex, still deep and hard within her.

"Ahhh. In one of your novels, the long-suffering heroine screams when she sees the hero's male splendor. Like you, she imagines he's going to split her apart."

"Male splend—?" she began in a breathless but almost normal voice. One of her delicate brows arched in gentle mockery.

Sweet vice! Her sheath tightened around him. He could feel every sensitive little quiver as her inner muscles bore down on the source of her discomfort. Ah, damn, she was curious.

"Ohhh. You are rather splendid, aren't you? Tigger, are you larger than average?"

This was it. Tarrant-Arragon braced himself. She'd draw the

inevitable conclusion about his rut-enraged Djinn anatomy. Once she knew who he was, she'd withdraw her consent. He . . . would not . . . could not . . . withdraw from her, perhaps not for days. He'd rut and rage like the worst of his ancestors. And he'd love her forever. And she'd hate him.

"I can't really judge——" His beloved rippled on him, and he wondered how much longer he could bear this delicious torment. "But I don't think I could manage anyone any larger."

"You won't have to," he soothed, attributing her slightly unhinged reaction to traumatic shock. "Ah, my love"—it had to be said—"this is no time for you to be considering larger lovers."

"Serve you right if I were," his Tigress defied him.

Adjusting his weight on his forearms, he kissed the damp corners of her eyes and marveled at his own tolerance. Future Empresses simply did not taunt their mates with thoughts of infidelity.

This was not at all how he'd imagined the rut-rage would be. Maybe her soothing aura had something to do with it. Maybe it was because she was being so good.

He privately acknowledged the savagery of his determination to have her and to keep her. He supposed he might rage and rut if he was denied. So far, she hadn't denied him.

"Tigger, I suppose there's no way I can pretend this didn't happen, is there?"

"No way at all, little mate," he agreed, bemused but not greatly offended. He knitted his fingers through hers. "What we have done is absolutely irrevocable."

She nodded to herself, the way she did whenever she was about to be scrupulously honorable. "Then I suppose it's only fair to tell you that in novels, the hero usually does a bit of thrusting at this juncture, if the heroine can take it."

At this juncture? By all the Lechers of Antiquity, she had no idea what "this juncture" was or she wouldn't be in such a hurry. If he was lucky, they might mate three times an hour for the next twenty-one—correction, seventeen Watches, since her escape had cost him the best part of a day.

"Can you take it?" he rasped, thrumming with excitement despite his resolve to pace himself.

"I think so. If you take it slowly."

He obliged. "Is this good . . . ?" He breathed raggedly. "Am I thrusting . . . slowly . . . like a hero?"

"Ohhhh, yessss!"

Grandmama had lied. Tigger's lovemaking was nowhere near as horrendous as Djinn sex. Of course, there was no reason why sex with an An'Koori should be anything like the Great Djinn rut-rage.

Even J-J's porn magazines' letters from boastful readers and professional "confessions" didn't hold a candle to the erotic fireworks of Tigger's sexual experiments.

Though still trembling and throbbing from sex like nothing on Earth, Djinni was more wide awake than a girl had any right to be after as many aftershocks as Tigger had given her.

Wet were their wide-spread clothes, wet was her hair, wet bed, wet between her legs. . . . It was a wonderful, abandoned sort of wetness. It suited her devil-may-care mood.

She liked the feel of his big, muscular body on hers. His abs were sunbaked smooth cobblestones on her soft belly. The backs of her legs ached from the hard pressure of his powerful thighs. Even her toes ached from curling so often.

"Dear Tigger," she whispered, and patted his bare shoulder.

"My mate!" he murmured thickly, and a stray thought of his burst into her mind like a November the Fifth firework.

"Oh, Stars!" He thought *mating* was short for *consummating* and that they'd consummated a marriage, first in the murk-bath according to his An'Koori customs, then in bed according to hers.

What had she done? How could she possibly bring herself to tell him that she couldn't marry him?

She'd have to tell him. But it seemed cowardly to do it in the darkness. She'd wait.

★   ★   ★

"I just hope that double-dealing fortune-teller didn't put you up to trying Tantric Sex," the sore little mate muttered as she rested on his chest in the dark murk-bath.

"What's Tantric Sex?" Tarrant-Arragon asked, happy to try whatever non-insertive sex she might suggest next, especially since he'd almost run through his supply of stolen condoms.

"If you don't know, I'd be a fool to tell you."

"Tell me." He nibbled her neck. "Or I'll put you through every sexual act I can think of. Is this Tantric?" He darted the tip of his tongue into her ear.

"No," she squeaked, wriggling delightfully on top of him. "I only mentioned it to warn you off, if you were working up to A Thousand Loving Thrusts."

"What's that?" he demanded, immensely intrigued. "Tell me!"

"There's a school of ancient erotic thought which claims that a man can't experience true sexual ecstasy unless he can control his, er, ejaculations."

Tarrant-Arragon was strongly tempted to comment.

"Practitioners of Tantric Sex don't believe in wasting their life force, so they try not to erupt every time. A man performs A Thousand Loving Thrusts by alternating sets of shallow and deep thrusts. He is allowed to enjoy mini-orgasms, but he isn't supposed to withdraw or spill his life force. It is not written how the ancient erotic scholars' partners felt about all this frugal thrusting, but I think the idea was that the man had to go through the motions with a few score concubines each night."

"I'm confused, my love." *And very aroused.* "Are you telling me this because you do *not* want to try it?"

"I told you about frogs, moles, and spiders and we didn't copy their nasty ways."

"No?" He grasped her around the waist and moved against her. "What about the persistent-tongued Hunnox? Have we done that?"

He exploded out of the water and, ignoring her squeals, gave her a thorough licking from belly to breasts, especially breasts, until they both fell back, helpless with laughter.

Sex was a serious matter, a grim pleasure, or so he'd always thought. It had never been an occasion for laughter or irreverent conversation—until Djinni accused him of fishy mating habits, and since then he hadn't taken sex seriously at all.

Lovemaking had never been such fun. Much as he'd longed for her to know and accept the truth about him, he didn't want this blissful intimacy to end.

The truth could wait. She had given him an idea. A very wicked idea. A perfect excuse for the remaining rut-raged days and nights of debauchery and deception to come.

"I want to do it all," he breathed. "I want to make love to you according to the ways of every sexually reproducing species in all the Communicating Worlds. *Every* one. From frogs to Great Djinn. After that, we'll work up to thrusting Tantric Sex."

"Oh, Stars," she gasped.

"And I take that as informed consent."

One Thousand Loving Thrusts Later

"Tigger, this can't wait any longer. I can't marry you. In fact, I may have to marry someone else."

"Who?" Instantly jealous, Tarrant-Arragon grabbed her. Then he saw a way to turn matters around. "So you weren't joking when you made that comment about larger lovers? I suppose the only male who is virile enough for you is Tarrant-Arragon himself."

In chess terminology, his little mate was well and truly forked! If she argued, she'd undermine her arguments against marrying "Tigger." Agreement would end all lies and pretense. Tarrant-Arragon was tired of lies.

"Don't be spiteful. Having sex with Tarrant-Arragon is a vile idea." She turned her back on him.

Ah, but it was a beautiful, supple back. It still presented lots of possibilities. He touched. She shivered. "Tigger, promise you'll never let him anywhere near me."

"I can't promise that, my love." It was no time to laugh, but that hadn't stopped them anytime during the past eighteen Watches, and he couldn't stop his voice from shaking.

"No, I know you can't promise." Her voice softened and she reached behind her and patted his thigh. "Don't be afraid, Tigger. I don't expect you to protect me. I couldn't ask a quivering An'Koori—"

"You can't possibly believe that I'm 'a quivering An'-Koori,'" he expostulated. Where in Carnality had she got such a grossly mistaken notion? He decided to make her laugh. He might even tell her the truth . . . in jest . . . to see how she reacted.

"Slack damn! An An'Koori? Is that what you think of me? I might have been amused that you thought me amphibian in my masturbatory preferences, but to be mistaken for an An'Koori is an outrage. After my magnificent imitation of the Djinn—"

"It was a very watered-down imitation, Tigger."

"We spent a lot of time in a bath!" he said with great offended dignity. "Also in the showers, and on the wash-stand—"

"What are you, then? You speak An'Koori, do An'Koori bookkeeping, watch An'Koori news, and mate in water. You like poetry and puns. You're boastful. You pretend to be a sex maniac. . . ."

He gently bit the back her neck and moved against her.

She gasped. "I take that back. You don't pretend."

"Thank you." He didn't understand where she'd got the idea that the An'Koori mated in water, but he forgave her for the An'Koori slur. In all justice, he'd invited something of the sort with the cod-armor deception. However, they were drifting from the real issue. It was time. He stood up in the murk-bath and threw open his robes.

"Lights!" he commanded. The Ark Imperial lit up.

"Good gracious, Tigger!" The little mate goggled. "I had no idea. Did I—? No wonder I'm sore. You villain!"

"As you see, I'm not An'Koori." He gestured and grinned. Her anger was better than tears. "Will you marry me?"

"You complete and utter . . . bastard!"

Djinni burst out laughing. She didn't understand her own reaction. J-J couldn't possibly be any bigger.

Tigger looked puzzled and expectant. Djinni prevaricated.

"We'd still be genetically incompatible. I'm half Earthling. Aliens can't breed with Earthlings."

"Aren't you living proof that they can?" He advanced.

"My father was a Djinn. It doesn't work the other way around. Oh, do put it away, Tigger. You deserve a serious explanation." She threw up her hands to fend him off.

She hadn't meant for her palms to touch his penis. It had a mesmerizingly tactile quality, and such heat!

"Male Great Djinn have alarming reproductive power because they've more than the fourteen types of defender sperm and warrior sperm put out by ordinary beings." She eyed him suspiciously. "Who was your father? Do you know?"

"Leave my father out of this," he growled. "Stop trying to change the subject when I'm proposing. Your problem is, you're afraid of commitment. Being married to me will be all right, I promise. It'll be like kissing. Do you remember how terrified you were the first time I kissed you? You almost died of fright."

"Rot! I didn't . . . Have you any idea what being kissed is like for a mind reader?" Perhaps he hadn't, but thinking about it seemed to stir him behind the buffers of her palms, so she added hastily, "Besides, I can't marry anyone without the Saurian Dragon's permission, and he may not grant it to us."

Tigger indulged in verbal chest-thumping. "Leave him to me. I'll tell him how I forced myself upon you. Every time it occurred to me, several times . . . every hour of every day."

Djinni felt like weeping and laughing all at once. But of course, Tigger didn't know that the Saurian Dragon was her father, and she couldn't tell him.

"You can't swagger up to the Saurian Dragon, say you raped me repeatedly, and expect him to reply, 'That's all right, then.'"

"Oh, can't I?"

"Not unless you enjoy living dangerously."

"Perhaps I do." He put his big hands over hers and curled them around himself.

Silk on steel, she thought. It was very stiff, but she couldn't tell whether there was a bone in it . . . whether there was a little bit of rogue Djinn in him.

Perhaps he did enjoy living dangerously. Djinni remembered what she'd seen of Tigger's devil-fish stylish spaceship during her escape. One didn't have to know much about space to recognize cannon ports. Unmistakably military, Tigger's "love-cruiser" was a war-star, no less.

As for Tigger, he wasn't what he pretended to be. He ignored other males with the arrogance of a monarch in his own traveling kingdom. For all his protestations of love and adoration, he treated her with maddening condescension. Whatever she said, he remained complacently convinced that she was his by some undefined right that he'd chosen not to exert.

His suite was a VIP penthouse, and the An'Koori numbers that he pored over might well be his personal investments.

"I don't think the Saurian Dragon would be amused to hear how, or how often, we made love," she began cautiously. "But I'm sure he'd welcome you as an ally against the evil Emperor and Tarrant-Arragon."

As she thought, she stroked him. Up for the pros, down for the cons. He closed his eyes and parted his lips.

His power and wealth weren't honorable arguments for marrying him, but the Saurian Dragon never let noble sentiment cost him a strategic advantage. He might consider Tigger an eligible suitor. Especially if she could recruit him as a brother Knight.

In fact, from what she remembered of her father, he and Tigger were two of a kind. They'd probably get along famously together. She tilted her head at Tigger speculatively.

"How would you feel about becoming a Saurian Knight?"

Tigger's eyes flew open. He gave her an enigmatic look. "Ahhh, it'll give me great pleasure to think about it," he said with an unholy glint in his tarnished silver eyes. "Now, talking of pleasure . . . kiss me."

The Pleasure Moon of Eurydyce

"Some of your . . . collection is missing." Ala'Aster-Djalet, the Saurian Dragon, swirled the remaining condom packets in Madam Tarra's infamous crystal bowl—to save her the trouble of pretending she didn't understand him. "Are you not concerned?"

"The messages on them were of no interest." Interestingly, Tarragonia-Marietta's first thought did not appear to be of espionage.

He raised an eyebrow, the way all Great Djinn did, to suggest the many comments he'd refrained from making.

"Most of them were Djetthro-Jason's love letters," she was goaded into explaining. "Djetthro-Jason pricks his messages into purple Triumphant Magnificences."

Which was perhaps more detail than Ala'Aster-Djalet required. Naturally, he didn't believe that his little girl was ready for the enormous size—and purpleness—of a fully aroused Great Djinn. Not that Djetthro-Jason would wear a condom. No Great Djinn ever had, or ever would.

"*All* of them?" He replaced the bowl on its side table.

"Most. There were his demands that Djarrhett should be sent back to Earth to fetch Djinni-vera." Tarra dealt playing cards as she spoke, as if each card represented a missing message. "He also wanted Feya to give his An'Koori War-star Leader a smart-virus-contaminated view-disc of pornography."

"I know. The resulting black-over gave him the excuse to rewire the war-star." Ala'Aster-Djalet spread his ribbed Pterodactyl-tough leather cape over the chair opposite her and sat. "Now he can put virtual-reality images of anything he likes on the Bridge screens. And if I know Djetthro-Jason, he'll use Feya and the porn disc to . . . ah . . . bugger up other Imperial war-stars."

Tarra looked up from her card-dealing. "And Komodo?"

"I'm told our brother Knight Komodo had a weapon which might have been able to penetrate the Ark Imperial's defenses. The theory is that Komodo attacked the Ark Imperial and damaged it. We assume that the Ark Imperial returned fire, destroying all witnesses, then limped into quiet space near the Earth Exclusion Zone to make discreet repairs."

Ala'Aster-Djalet wasn't happy with this account of Komodo's disappearance. It didn't explain why Tarrant-Arragon had been on the wrong side of the Communicating Worlds.

"This was at least six cycles ago, wasn't it?" she said.

Watching her, he saw the conflicted look on Tarra's face and made a mental note not to take her into his confidence in matters concerning her son. In any case, he'd never intended to tell her about Brontosaurus and the camisole plot. Hormonal warfare wasn't something females should know about.

Ala'Aster-Djalet had an unpleasant thought. There could be a connection between the theft and a sighting of the Ark Imperial three Imperatrix-cycles ago, inside the Earth Exclusion Zone.

Tarrant-Arragon sniffing the wind on Earth?

For twenty-one days out of twenty-eight, Djinni-vera would be as hard to find as a hay-colored needle in the human haystack. For the other seven, a Djinn male would have to be within fifty Earth miles of her, and downwind. Statistically, she ought to be safe, depending on how much time the searcher had at his disposal.

"When were your condoms stolen?" he snapped.

"Less than two cycles ago. Around the time of Stegosaurus's rescue," Tarra said blandly, and resumed the irritating hocus-pocus with her cards.

He gave a sigh of relief.

Djinni-vera! He hadn't been able to stop Virginia from naming their daughter as she had. He'd been fighting in the Vygan annexation wars, unaware that his Earthling was breeding. By the time he returned, Djinni-vera's portentous names had been registered. Nevertheless, he should have had them changed, would have, if not for a deathbed promise to Virginia.

Tarra was looking at him askance. "Well, Ala'Aster-Djalet? When *will* you send Djarrhett to get Djinni-vera?"

Djarrhett and Brontosaurus were less than a quarter-cycle from Tigron, committed to the camisole plot. "Perhaps I'll be able to spare him soon." Then again, perhaps not.

"Hmmm. Djetthro-Jason is on a mission," Tarra mused, peering at three court cards. "With luck, Djinni-vera can be here when he returns. I ought to think about her trousseau. Is she dark-haired like all Djinn?"

"Her hair is reddish brown. She has her mother's coloring and fine figure, but Helispeta's eyes. Djarrhett tells me she's stunning. Do your cards tell you where Tarrant-Arragon is?" he asked, changing the subject abruptly.

"Not geographically," Tarra said. "But he must be nearing Tigron. I hear he's about to settle down . . ." She looked archly at him. "With a White Knight?"

Slack damn, so much for secrecy and the camisole plot. He'd thought 'Rhett was tighter-lipped. However, Tarra couldn't know the entire plot, or she wouldn't be behaving so peculiarly.

"Hah! I doubt he'll 'settle,'" Ala'Aster-Djalet grunted, rising. "Let him try to mount one of my female White Knights. He'll find it a very unsettling experience!"

As he thrust open the curtains, on his way to visit Tarra's healthiest girls, Ala'Aster-Djalet looked back. He didn't like her know-it-all smile one little bit.

Ark Imperial—the Tigron Star-Roads

Djinni faced facts. Making love with Tigger had changed her ambitions, her moral perspective, her nightmares. . . . Since making love, the nightmare lover of her bad dreams had Tigger's face and unleashed his magnificent body shamelessly on hers.

Strenuous lovemaking was said to use up a lot of calories. Maybe it did, but Tigger's heavy gravity was taking its toll on her tummy, which was rather surprising considering the amount of time she spent on her back.

Drifting off to sleep in the circle of Tigger's arms, Djinni prepared to confront all comers in her dreams as a rehearsal for the confrontations she faced in real life with all the powerful males who loved her.

Not least of whom was Tigger. In her What-If dreams she dreamed that he was an unofficial offshoot of the Imperial family tree. It would explain a great deal, not just his anatomy but his unhealthy obsession with Tarrant-Arragon.

Since making love, she'd begun to wonder what else—apart from sex—Grandmama Helispeta had lied about. She might be wrong about J-J. J-J wasn't going to kill off the last fertile female simply because someone else had debauched her.

She also knew that she couldn't marry J-J in good faith. She'd be forever comparing him with Tigger.

That didn't mean she could blow J-J off. J-J was still a future Great Djinn Emperor. Possibly, he was more powerful than her father and might even be the head of her family.

That troubled her. It would mean she'd need J-J's permission to marry Tigger if she wanted to do so with a clear conscience.

Home.

Tarrant-Arragon braced both hands against the opened viewing wall in the docking dark, while Djinni slept.

The Ark Imperial was idling in the Tigron star-roads, its inertia carrying them to join the war-stars and moon-docks that necklaced the common side of Tigron, glowing old gold and red-gold and silver depending on their positioning relative to the small red-and-white sun and the turgid "Body Imperial" primary planet.

The rut-rage was overdue. He'd hoped to get his bride safely pregnant within a week of the wedding, and before he had to bring her within range of his father, his uncle Django, and his nephews.

Instead, he hadn't even convinced her to marry "Tigger," let alone told her who he was. Thank the Great Originator he'd wedded her informally, as insurance against this contingency. However, pulling off the Royal Wedding without her consent would be his most monstrous trick on Djinni yet. She might never forgive him.

"Hypothetically, Tigger . . ." Djinni murmured in sleep talk so lucid that for an instant he thought she was awake. "Because legal trivia interests you . . ."

What irony. Djinni had chosen to pick the dirtiest and most devious legal mind in the Communicating Worlds. Inexplicably, she still had no idea that he was Tarrant-Aragon, Imperial Crown Prince, First War-star Leader of the Thirteen Star Forces and Lord Prosecutor of the Tigron Empire.

"Suppose that Helispeta was pregnant. . . ."

"When?" he prompted.

"When she ran away from old Emperor Djohn-Kronos."

"What if she were?" Though he spoke as casually as possible, Tarrant-Aragon was very interested.

"If that were so . . . and she had a son . . . would he be the head of my family?"

A legitimate branch of the Royal family? It hadn't occurred to him that Djinni-vera might be a Princess in her own right. Tarrant-Aragon didn't consider this legal trivia.

"Are we talking about your father?" he asked carefully. Awake, she had never once mentioned her father. "His status is irrelevant. Your father is dead, isn't he?"

She didn't answer.

Tarrant-Aragon did not like to think that Djinni's father might not be accounted for. The implications were far-reaching, but he didn't pursue that point. Instead, he gave her his legal opinion.

"If your father was Djohn-Kronos's younger son, the head of your family would be the present Emperor. You'd need Djerrold Vulcan V's permission to marry me, or J-J, if that's where you're going with this."

He was fishing in the dark. Everything he thought he knew about J-J was conjecture, some of which had been proven wrong. Tarrant-Aragon couldn't bring himself to ask whether she would rather marry J-J or himself, so he dangled the bastard's name and waited to see whether she would confirm that

J-J was a serious suitor, or whether she would volunteer any more dangerous hypotheses.

"Well, we can't ask the Emperor. He mustn't know about me," his evasive love murmured drowsily.

Tarrant-Arragon couldn't sleep after that. He paced the Imperial suite after Djinni had fallen silent, analyzing what little she'd revealed.

The most troubling factor in Djinni's hypothesis was that Djohn-Kronos had sired a legitimate son by his second Empress.

If the descendants of such a legitimate son were also legitimate, then he, Tarrant-Arragon, had a hitherto unknown rival with a serious claim to the Imperial Throne.

Why else would there be a question in Djinni's mind who was the head of her family?

Legitimate or not, one thing was sure: No son of Helispeta would ever give Djinni to Tarrant-Arragon. Helispeta's sons would support any rival, any action to prevent such a mating.

Logically, then, J-J might merely be a powerful enemy of the Tigron Empire—a Saurian, most probably. Or he could be a rogue Djinn.

Tarrant-Arragon made a mental note to make some judicious arrests. Take some hostages before the mating ceremony. Hope to net this bastard, J-J. Whoever J-J might be, however he fitted in, he had to be found and taken out of contention.

Part Three
Empire of the Tiger

Chapter Seventeen

"You want me to recite our poem for the Emperor? We'd be taking an insane risk!"

Djinni stood beside Tigger at the viewing wall, looking down at Tigron—the cratered, terrestrial moon of a superjovian gas giant. The lichen- and mold-colored terrain visible through Tigron's low cloud haze and volcanic smoke looked like trodden cardboard egg cartons.

"Not as great a risk as we'd run if we didn't appear." He smiled down at her with half-closed eyes. "The Emperor wanted to have you in lieu of my toll-tax payment, though I told him I'd thoroughly debauched you—which I have. Fortunately, he's giving a soirée. When I told him you were a passable poetess, he agreed that a poetry performance would satisfy him. The danger of your appearing at one of the Emperor's parties is not so great. Even his enemies come."

"Where's Tarrant-Arragon?" Djinni asked abruptly.

"Ah. I've heard—from a reliable source—that he is on the

Ark Imperial, bringing home a bride. Everyone will be thinking about that."

"And you say the Emperor's enemies will be there? Might I meet some important Saurian White Knights at this soirée?"

"You might," he agreed, showing more interest in the progress of his forefinger down her bare arm.

"We-e-ell, in that case . . ." Djinni saw the chance she'd waited for. "The only sane reason for me to go within fifty Earth miles of the Imperial Palace is to have a private talk with one of them."

Tigger didn't reply. Obviously, he was thinking of sex again.

"Tigger, promise me that you'll never attack a Saurian. No matter what happens, you must swear to keep your word about that."

"You're asking a lot, aren't you?" he drawled.

"It's for your own good, as well as for my peace of mind," Djinni insisted. "Please, Tigger. For my sake."

"Very well." Tigger looked thoughtful. "I promise, I'll never attack any Saurian unless I'm attacked first. I'll keep this pledge for as long as you live and love with me."

"That's three loopholes," Djinni objected. She'd learned to keep count.

"I'm negotiating from a position of strength," he said with all his old arrogance. "And 'love with me' is non-negotiable."

Djinni knew Tigger too well, especially when a certain calculating look was in his eye and his mind was on sex. "And you should understand that there will be no more tricks, Tigger. I'm going to put our agreement in writing."

The nearest paper was her yellow legal pad. She dropped to her knees on the floor with it. *As long as I live and love with you . . .* she wrote, then glanced up. "Moreover, there's to be no delegating. 'No attacking' applies to Xirxex and Grievous and everyone else you control." She held the pad up to him. "There, Tigger. Does that seem fair?"

Tarrant-Arragon, Lord Prosecutor of the Tigron Empire, cast an expert eye over her script. Then he read it again.

"Great swirling nebulae, you expect me to sign that?"

"Yes, I do."

He'd been playing with her. Humoring her. What she'd written down was tantamount to an intergalactic peace initiative, or would be if he signed it and it got into the wrong hands. On the other hand, peace wasn't such a bad idea.

"What do you want to do with this?" he inquired.

"I'm going to give it to one of the White Knights at the soirée," she said. "He'll take it to the Saurian Dragon."

"I'm signing this because I love you very much." *And because the document might have its uses.*

He pushed off the wall and strode over to his desk. If they were going to sign it, they might as well have proof. He activated his surveillance systems. "You first, my love."

She joined him, bent over the impromptu contract, and signed with two symbols that he'd seen before.

"Is that a legal signature?" he couldn't resist asking.

"This is my secret signature. The Dragon will recognize it. This is the Ansuz rune, and that's the Inguz rune. They double as the A and the Ng of runescript." The fallible little mate fell happily into his trap. "I chose those particular signs because I like their meanings."

Tarrant-Arragon smiled as she explained. His darling little mate couldn't help answering questions honestly—and in unwise detail. It was an adorable fault that made him want to cherish and protect her. She was a most unsuitable Knight. But she was going to be a wonderful mother to their children.

"Sign your full name, too, if you want Grievous and Slayt to witness it later. Why don't you use a rune for Djinni-vera?"

"I can't, because that would be the Jaera sign." She drew another sign that he recognized on a fresh sheet of her pad. "Jaera is for a 'J' pronunciation, however it's spelled. . . ."

She'd given Tarrant-Arragon another piece to the puzzle. So! It had been an inspired move to order Grievous to arrest a White Knight to be used as a hostage, if they could not identify J-J. Moreover, she had opened the door to the possibility that J-J might be Dj-Dj. A legitimate rival Djinn.

"The Jaera is reserved for the highest-ranking Saurian White

Knights," she continued, unaware that she'd virtually confirmed that J-J was the important Knight whom she hoped to see at the soirée.

Tarrant-Arragon watched her through narrowed eyes. If Djinni was not the only royal Djinn among the top-ranking Saurians, then he'd very much like to meet the Saurian Dragon.

Who the Carnality was this Saurian Dragon? What kind of being had the arrogance to think he could control Great Djinn?

"You know what, Tigger?" the little mate interrupted his train of thought. "That planet down there must have some very interesting tides." She sighed. "Oh-oh, I can't talk about it now. I have to go again."

After Djinni had gone into the bathroom, he reread their contract carefully and sat for a long time, tapping it on his upper lip. She had no idea what she'd just drawn up, because she still didn't know who he was.

It was quixotic folly to make peace. Yet this paper could also be interpreted as a marriage settlement. One that Djinni had drafted and signed. She'd feel obliged to honor it.

"Checkmate!" he whispered. Grinning, he signed his full name and all his titles, and removing his third Ring from his secret cache, he affixed his great Imperial Tiger-skull seal.

Imperial Palace—Wedding-Eve Virgins' Ball

Princess Martia-Djulia smiled at someone she didn't know, ignored the Virgins' Ball babble, and tried to overhear what was being said about her deliciously dangerous big brother.

"Does Prince Tarrant-Arragon shower with his warriors, too?" squealed a girl in the available-white of a virgin prepared to sacrifice her innocence. "Commander Jason, is he really large?"

So the warrior who stood head and chest taller than most of

the wedding-eve ball guests was the notorious Commander Jason! Intrigued, Martia-Djulia moved closer.

A ragged scar ran from Jason's high cheekbone to the angle in his strong jaw. He reminded her of a sexually aggressive tom-tiger whose battle scars showed he fought for and won his females and his territory. Except for some reason Jason wasn't with his no-name fiancée. And, from everything Martia-Djulia had been able to find out, he was far from faithful to her.

"Great starbursts! Is that all you young girls think about? But, my dear," the Commander continued in a low, sexy drawl that set Martia-Djulia's erogenous zones atingle, "would you want to meet him if he were?"

What girl wouldn't? Martia-Djulia thought. The supremely powerful Tarrant-Arragon was said to be as accomplished a lover as he was a liar, and impressionable virgins gladly gambled their honor and their lives for an hour in his royal arms.

Martia-Djulia looked down to hide a smile and felt her eyes widen at a thick contour that ought not to show in a loose-fitting Commander's uniform, whatever his degree of arousal.

The object of Jason's attentions was looking the wrong way: toward the empty throne-space. All girls glanced Tarrant-Arragon's way, even when he wasn't there. They were all waiting for the biggest matrimonial prize to appear, unaware that Tarrant-Arragon was to be married at dawn.

Jason was the male Martia-Djulia was determined to meet. So how was she to endear herself to him? If she were in Jason's large boots, she'd love to make the little rank-hunter regret showing a cold shoulder to someone important. Martia-Djulia knew just how to do it.

She surged toward Jason and deliberately crushed her bosom into his chest as she pulled his face down for a familiar kiss.

"Dearest cousin," she gushed, "are you pulling virgins without pulling rank? We missed you at the family party, and you promised this dance to me. Come. Dance."

Jason was horrified. He'd never met his half-cousin before. How had Martia-Djulia recognized him through his disguise?

Was she clairvoyant? Telepathic? Was it only the male Djinn who'd lost the power to read minds? Yet she seemed very friendly.

His thoughts swirled as she backed him onto the dance floor. Did the substantial Princess like what he couldn't help thinking when her generous breasts pressed up against him and spread a startling expanse of cleavage that smelled of Queen-of-the-Night?

What a soft, feminine armful! How perfectly his tall cousin fitted against him. His arms tightened around her as they moved together. Misty, snow-shadow eyes gleamed close to his own.

"Did you see her face?" Martia-Djulia whispered after a few stunned seconds. "I've made her think she spurned a Djinn Prince. So naughty of me. I don't know what got into me!"

Jason knew. He felt the princess's inner thighs quiver when his knee brushed between her legs, heard her heart pounding like an old star-drive. He knew what that meant. Jason felt the stern wariness leave his face.

The spoilt, sexy baggage needed a real male to spank her behind. He was Djinn enough to do it. If she was in the mood to play with fire, then so was he.

Grievous had a nose for trouble. Having been entrusted with the diplomatically ticklish task of arresting a Saurian Knight who might be J-J, he was shadowing a possible suspect through bright subterranean hallways lined with more aggressively posed gods than the pharaohs had erected at Luxor.

Not that his quarry was a satisfactory suspect, Grievous thought regretfully. Tarrant-Arragon had asked him to arrest a Knight who was humanoid, male, tall, and attractive. One whose behavior was unusual enough to justify suspicion.

So far, the lad met two—maybe three—of the criteria, Grievous reasoned. He was humanoid. He was in a Saurian Knight's white toggery. He appeared to be male, but he was not masculine.

In Grievous's manly opinion, the lad had been far too attached to a Djinn-tall member of the Altaeran delegation, until they'd been parted at Portal Security, where guests trickled in like controlled runoff at the base of a really big dam.

Given his druthers, Grievous would have followed the masked Altaeran. Though not a Knight, he'd be a prime candidate for detention if only he'd step out of line.

It was one thing to question Tarrant-Arragon's orders, but quite another to disobey them. Grievous had pushed the envelope far enough when he'd protested the attractiveness requirement.

"It's a mystery to me why you'd want a good-looking hostage around, if you don't mind my saying so, Sir," he'd grumbled.

"I don't want him around," Tarrant-Arragon had replied. "I'd like to think that my rival is a repulsive, sniveling youth not much older than my little mate. However, I assume the wretched J-J is more serious competition."

Grinning, Grievous cozied up against a god-sized statue of some Great Djinn of old whose stone erection inside his kilt would not have disgraced an elephant, and as he watched his suspect, Grievous pondered Tarrant-Arragon's unique bridegroom worries.

"I'd rather not have to confront J-J at my wedding," Tarrant-Arragon had said. "So I want you to keep him out of my way."

"Gotcha, Sir," Grievous had interjected. "Not very festive to be accused of stealing another chap's bride—"

"Festivity be damned! It's six weeks since the last rut-rage. By my calculations, Djinni might soon become rut-rageous, in which case, I may not be my usual, reasonable self. I don't want to kill the bastard. I doubt that I've unwittingly invited J-J to my wedding, but he may have come anonymously. If you can't identify J-J, arrest a suitable Saurian White Knight."

For the umpteenth time, Grievous pretended to adjust the swords in his belts. Not that the pantomime was necessary. The young Knight seemed to have no idea he was under surveillance.

★ ★ ★

"Excuse me, Your Imperial Highness. I think this is yours."

Martia-Djulia ignored the scrawny Saurian White Knight and the badly made lacy object he was trying to thrust at her.

She was leaning on one of the balconies of the Imperial Portrait Gallery and wondered whether Jason would rejoin her. He might not. He'd seemed reluctant to dance with her.

When he offered to fetch drinks, she'd suspected he planned to escape. "Shall I introduce you to a more virginal partner?" she'd countered, trying to keep her voice light, the way she always did at the first sign that a male didn't have the penile bone to be interested in her.

"Not yet, Princess." He'd lowered his voice like a cheerful conspirator. "I'm not here to look for a wife. Shall we move to a vantage point and criticize the crowd? I've seen some appalling garments, and I hoped you'd tell me what possesses these people to make such disastrous fashion choices."

Jason seemed to be a male after her own heart. A fashion hawk and a gossip hound. Martia-Djulia smiled to herself as she scanned the crowd below to locate badly dressed guests.

"Excuse me, Your Imperial Highness."

Martia-Djulia sighed. Since the importunate Knight had the bad manners to think she'd dropped something, he would no doubt persist in his alien rudeness if she didn't accept it.

She took the scrap of fabric, turned away, and was about to drop it into the crowd below when she saw that Jason had rejoined her. Her heart beat faster. She didn't want him to think she dropped litter on her guests, so she slid the handkerchief into her cleavage.

His gaze followed her fingers. He looked bemused.

"What am I doing?" he groaned. "Ah, what the Carnality! Princess, I've got to have you!" So saying, he swaggered against her, crushing her ball gown as he thrust a muscular thigh between hers. He seized a fistful of hair at her nape, and as she gasped at his insolence, he plunged his tongue between her lips.

No one had ever kissed her like that. In public, too. His masterful barbarity seared her senses. Martia-Djulia felt her shell of aristocratic confidence collapse in a cloud of stardust, leaving an aching emptiness.

He brushed the sides of breasts that her father said were too heavy, and his breathing grew hard. He kneaded her softness shamelessly. It had been so long. She'd forgotten. No, she'd never known anything like this. Resistance abandoned, she clenched her fists to make her flesh seem young and firm. She held her breath, felt his lust in her mouth, and kissed him back.

She knew where to take her sudden suitor, and was about to suggest that they adjourn to bed when Jason's hand was wrenched from her bosom.

Martia-Djulia glared over Jason's broad shoulder at the intervener. He had the elegant build of a light-worlder, but in his full Altaeran courtesy suit he was as tall as Jason. Icy green eyes glinted behind the eye-slits of his mask.

"We'd no idea you'd be here," the officious guest rasped. "It's a bad idea, Jason! Put her down."

"I think it's a fine idea. Stay out of it!" Jason snarled. Without warning, he turned and slammed his fist into the interfering Altaeran's helmet, sending him flying.

All hell had broken loose, and for no reason that Grievous could suss out.

He didn't think it was his business if the Altaeran got his comeuppance for trying to impose his alien morality on an overtly heterosexual couple. He was interested in the fallen Altaeran only because of the White Knight, who knelt beside him.

"Get away, Bronty," the Altaeran croaked, perhaps having trouble breathing owing to the damage that the Star Forces officer had done to his headpiece. "You're making that overgrown An'Koori worse."

"He had no right to do that," the one named Bronty protested, ignoring the order to leave. "We're White Knights!"

"We're"? Grievous switched his attention from Bronty to the Altaeran. This wasn't the royal "We" that Tarrant-Arragon used when he got on his high horse. It was plural. As in Knights.

The big Star Forces officer stalked across the Gallery and struck a stiff-legged attitude over his victim. They exchanged words, although the Altaeran's helmet had been knocked off. The Altaeran didn't seem to need it for communicating or for life support, which meant he must be using it as a disguise. It was a no-brainer that a White Knight out of uniform and in disguise was a legitimate arrest. Then a surprising thing registered in his mind. They were talking in English. And he distinctly heard one of them say "J-J."

Martia-Djulia had never been fought over before. It was gloriously disgraceful behavior, better than any sex she'd ever had, but she couldn't understand why Jason was wasting time talking. His wonderfully primitive aggression had made his intentions clear. Why allow the beaten Altaeran to dispute his right to kiss her?

They insulted one another in low, angry voices. Amid the obscenities, she heard toe-curlingly wicked allusions to sister-docking and group sex.

Burning with curiosity, she moved closer.

"You should know better than to interfere with me—" Jason stopped mid-jeer. He'd noticed her. Immediately, he swept her high in his strong arms.

No one had ever picked her up before, either. It was dizzyingly erotic. And, although she didn't understand what Jason meant, she felt faint over the rampant maleness of his parting taunt to the Altaeran: "I know she's not your sister, but at this moment, I don't give a flying dock!"

"Excuse me, sir." Grievous patted one of the swords in his belts meaningfully and stood in the way of the young man who had emerged like a White Knight butterfly from his smashed Altaeran chrysalis. "Could I have a word?"

The seven-foot-tall Knight frowned when he saw the engravings under Grievous's hand.

"I see you recognize this sword, Sir, as belonging to a White Knight. I was wondering whether you could read the inscription. I can't get beyond the Ansuz, Inguz. . . . Of course, I could ask the poor little miss."

"The poor little miss?"

Gotcha! The White Knight whom the Star Forces officer had attacked spoke perfect English with much the same accent as the little miss. Grievous managed not to crack his stony face, but he knew he was onto a winner.

"I know it must seem odd for a chap like me to call a young lady who's about my own height 'little,' but I've never got out of the way of feeling sorry for her . . ." He paused artfully. "Ever since Tarrant-Arragon towered over her and told her he was a Saurian Knight, and had come for her. See?"

"Go on," the White Knight croaked.

"There's not a lot of time if you want to save her. She's being held up at Moondock. See, I'm just a bloke out to save my own hide any way I can, and these Tigron Forces types weren't surprised when I threw my lot in with them—or seemed to."

He backed away. The tall fellow followed.

"But she's a Saurian White Knight, so no one would believe her if she pretended to turn her coat, unless, of course, they thought she was in love with one of them. She's a nice girl, is Djinni, so she couldn't bring herself to do that, could she?"

"Take me to her."

"Yes, sir!" Grievous turned with British military crispness. He'd hooked the big one. All he had to do was usher J-J out of the way before anyone got wise to what was about to happen.

If the Saurian Dragon had plotted a convential assassination, it would have been complicated by the fact that standing room was assigned. The Saurian White Knights were isolated from each other and from their delegations.

The assassin, Bronty, scanned the crowded throne room.

There was no sign of 'Rhett. Nor had her target made an appearance. Tarrant-Arragon hadn't been at the Virgins' Ball. In all of a night that was twice as long as she was used to, the only grimly handsome, seven-foot-tall male she'd seen had

been the sex-crazed Commander who'd carried off Princess
Martia-Djulia.

"Do you know what we're here for?" Bronty said to the
armed and body-armored War-star Leader standing beside her.

"Something your Saurian Dragon will not like, White
Knight. A royal marriage, I think." The War-star Leader
nudged her white-uniformed arm. "Hear the music? That's
the prelude to the sex act in song. By law, it's sung only for a
Dominator's nuptials, only by massed male warriors."

"I don't believe it!" Bronty shook her head. Inwardly, she
raged. Tarrant-Arragon, marrying someone else? If she got
close enough, the unknown bride wouldn't survive the Consummation.

A loud fanfare made further conversation impossible. The
pentagonal room reverberated with the thunder of massed
war-drums. Thunderhead clouds of roiling smoke erupted in
one of the throne-spaces—it had the cloying, head-spinning
smell of a hallucinogen. The first throne-stage rose like a
coldly glittering, ice-sculpted volcano thrust up out of a boil-
ing nitrogen sea. Fire. Ice. An impressive, expensive display, but
it was not magic.

The Emperor Djerrold Vulcan V appeared to stroll on the
smoke, high above eye level and master of the elements. The
lights flickered as if their own power dimmed in his presence.

Bronty watched and sneered. She'd dearly love to expose
whatever sophisticated conjuror's technology made Imperial
levitation seem possible on this heavy world.

Hugely bored Imperial black tigers spilled gracefully out of
the ominous smoke and poured themselves into niches and onto
pounce-off points around the newly emerged throne-scape.

Bronty noticed that even the most decorated of War-star
Leaders glanced assessingly from the Emperor to the unleashed
unsatisfactory-bride-eaters and back again, as if unsure which
presented the greater and more imminent danger.

"Dear friends," the Emperor began with affable menace,
"you are here to witness the exchange of vows between my
son and his bride. This, with proofs of her virginity, will con-

stitute the Short Form of the Imperial Wedding Ceremony."

His eyes pierced the assembly. His robes in vile colors of deadly night-shades swirled threateningly. He pointed his Fire-Stone-ringed forefinger around the room, and even those with theoretical diplomatic immunity shrank where they stood.

"Most of my guests have never attended the marriage of an Emperor's heir. Be warned. Tarrant-Arragon will ask anyone who objects to speak out. Anyone who does so will be incinerated."

Star-blue lightning sizzled and flashed from the Emperor's finger, as if His Imperial Majesty was itching for an excuse to burn an enemy. Bronty couldn't help being impressed. When Tarrant-Arragon married her, she'd have a trick ring like that.

"Out of consideration for your fellow guests' nostrils," Djerrold Vulcan V continued with supreme callousness, "I advise against any interference. Let the doors be shut."

High above, another fanfare blared from long deep-noted instruments. The voices of a thousand warriors throbbed from a low melodic growl and surged to a roaring, triumphant climax.

The second Tiger throne-stage began its eerily silent descent from the Imperial quarters above.

Chapter Eighteen

If testosterone could sing as it flowed through male arteries to swell a potent erection, this would be its song, Djinni thought. She didn't understand the words and couldn't identify the instrumental accompaniment, but it made her knees tremble.

At first she thought it was the sound of mature males in an ecstasy that was spiritual. Then she knew it was highly sexual. The music throbbed, thrust, withdrew, and surged to an explosive climax of sound, of conquest, of male satisfaction and sated lust.

"Stars, Tigger," she whispered, "that's the sexiest and most sexist music I've ever heard in my life!"

"Is it?" Tigger's voice deepened with amusement. "Are you excited? Stand closer." His hands angled her hips. "Face me."

Djinni felt her stiff, silvery dress scallop around his legs.

"My soirée costume is too ostentatious. Are you sure . . . ?"

"You look just right for the part, beloved. Trust me. Your Earthling standards of good breeding don't apply here. Now, be quiet. We're on."

It was too late to worry about the dubious protocol of looking like an empress in an Imperial palace. Their platform was moving.

Bright fingers of light clawed upward, making the silvery metallic threads in her dress shimmer and flash like lightning in a leaden sky, catching in an albino peacock's tail of a ruff and dazzling her peripheral vision. And, as if the costume wasn't heavy enough, there were magnets in the hem of the dress and its medieval-style trailing sleeves.

"What am I—?"

"Hush, my love, don't talk now," Tigger said. "The stage lights will be blinding. Close your eyes."

She did, and he kissed her eyelids. She heard the susurration of his clothes. Perhaps he adjusted his sleeves, the way nervous males do, and then he clasped her hands between his, just as he always did when they said their love poem together.

Djinni felt the strength in his hands over hers, and the metallic coldness of three rings on his right hand. Rings must have some significance for the male character in their poem. As must the spectacular black clothes he wore.

She'd never seen him look so magnificent. Blue-black was the quilted lining of his open Samurai-style fighting robe, which he wore over an ankle-length frock coat and tight thigh boots. Black on black, an iridescent slash of sash on matte planes. Softer than satin, sexier than velvet, she could have stroked Tigger's chest all day in tactile fascination. The layered effect was dramatic, mysterious, and subtly erotic.

Dear Tigger! He'd gone to a lot of trouble over their performance, but it must be hard for any male to recite poetry in public. How could she doubt that Tigger loved her? She couldn't! Whatever happened with J-J, she'd always love Tigger. If only she could tell him. Perhaps after today, after she'd spoken with J-J, she might be free to do so.

For now, she was glad to close her eyes, say her words, and trust Tigger to take care of her in this intimidatingly huge palace environment. Concrete-zoo architect of the Carl Hagenback school meets Siegfried and Roy to design a mountain lion habitat–cum–grand opera staircase: That was how she'd describe the full soundstage elevator they were on.

She sensed the curiosity of a vast body of people rising like a fog to meet them as they made their descent. Although her eyes were closed, the rotation of the stage was making her queasy. She took a deep breath, and Tigger's new, spicy-musky fragrance went to her head. She felt dizzy, light-headed. Her wrists tingled.

Tigger began. Majestic syllables rang out, sounding more spellbinding than ever, and she wondered why he'd never told her what the words meant in all the times they'd recited this love poem together.

A cold cobwebby sensation crept up her legs. Something wasn't right, but before she could figure out exactly what was wrong, it was her turn to speak mysterious words with theatrical enthusiasm.

Djinni hoped her English private school accent didn't seem distractingly alien. She winced inwardly every time her voice cracked with stage fright, but she got through her part.

"Good girl," Tigger whispered in English when she came to the end of her performance. Unexpectedly, he placed her palms on his chest. She felt the stallion canter of his heart, as powerful as his sex drive, as relentless as his pursuit of her.

She heard the rasp of stubble against the high, stiff collar of his frock coat. Tigger must have turned to the audience. He spoke in an alien language. She didn't understand what he was saying, but she recognized a triumphant throb in his voice and assumed that he was thanking them in advance for their applause.

In her mind's eye, she saw Tigger looking down his nose at the Emperor's guests, catching high-rank warriors and ambassadors in his glare, like the slow turn of a lighthouse in the night. Perhaps he flashed them a daggers-drawn smile.

Djinni wanted to see if J-J was among them. Why not? Her senses had stabilized somewhat. She opened her eyes but saw only a sea of shadowy heads bobbing like antique glass lobster-pot buoys in an unquiet bay.

Tigger took a sharp breath. "My love, my love." He groaned. "Your exquisite timing is a shade shy of perfect."

What had she mistimed? Before she could ask, he crushed her hard against his chest. His left hand splayed at the back of her head, his fingers thrust into her swept-up hair, ejecting pins and causing the auburn tangle of her hair to tumble over his arms.

Heart to heart he held her. He closed his eyes as his dry lips sealed hers on an indrawn breath. The poem ended with a kiss, but never with a kiss like this, even after they'd become lovers. She hadn't agreed to this. J-J might be watching. . . .

She struggled in protest. Tigger ignored her. Still he kissed her. Not like a lover. It was erotic suffocation, a ruthless big cat smothering prey with his hard mouth.

Her pulse was like the throb of helicopters. Through the thrumming in her ears, she heard shouting:

"Tarrant-Arragon Djustin Djohn Alexander Thor."

Was *he* here? Tigger had said Tarrant-Arragon wouldn't be there. Since he'd come—late—to the party, she wanted to glimpse her enemy. She twisted to see. Tigger would not permit it. His arms tightened around her. His fierce kiss proclaimed her his.

"Djinni-vera Persephone Berengaria Caissa Scheherazade Igraine." Her names! Why? Why would someone shout her names at all, let alone in the same breath as Tarrant-Arragon's?

The stage ascended. She was fast spinning into breathless oblivion, but she had to have the proof of her own eyes that Tarrant-Arragon was old, ugly, and on the other side of the room. Black spots swarmed dizzily before her eyes. An unthinkable thought whirled in the gathering darkness.

Tigger was Tarrant-Arragon.

"Do they still whisper about Tarrant-Arragon's broken betrothal?" Martia-Djulia asked, raking her nails through a light sheen of perspiration on Commander Jason's muscular bare chest.

"Warriors hide their sisters, and will do so for as long as his mate-hunt continues," he drawled. "No one doubts he'd maul another girl to death if he caught her in bed with another male."

"People assumed he did that to Lucinthe," Martia-Djulia said. "Or they say he threw her to the family pets. They're wrong. She had a lover. I heard whispers and told Tarrant-Arragon. For the longest time I thought he was going to ignore me. But it turned out he was just waiting for proof."

"Proof?" The Commander's dark-star eyes were almost closed. He was sated, languorous, and not really listening as he drew a damp scrap of lace from her bodice and sniffed it.

"My overprotective brother had given Lucinthe a transmitter necklace. She couldn't have taken it off if she'd wanted to. I imagine he hoped to hear her mutter his name in her virgin dreams. Ha! She wore it to bed . . . with her lover."

"I can imagine how he felt." Commander Jason sounded grim.

He'd be a jealous and possessive mate. Martia-Djulia could hardly believe her luck.

"Furious, of course. He sent for her. It's not romantic to speak of, but when my brother is angry, most people wait out his temper in bathrooms. Lucinthe took one look at him and ran. The slack-wit!"

"Did he run after her?" The Commander opened one eye.

"He never runs. How was he to know that she'd go into the Tiger Habitat, squeaking like prey and reeking of fear?"

"So her death was an accident?" Commander Jason asked, showing more interest in pushing the scrap of alien fabric between her legs. He'd played erotic hide-and-seek several times.

"Her mauling was an accident. Tarrant-Arragon saved her life. Then he sent her away, with her lover, to some backward rim—Commander!" she squealed in delight as he had his gloriously twisted way. "What are you doing?"

"I haven't the faintest idea," he muttered, and Martia-Djulia thought she heard a strange ambiguity in his muffled voice. "This is crazy. I must be out of my mind."

★ ★ ★

There was no doubt. No hope.

Djinni gazed numbly at the hangings of the huge black bed on which he'd deposited her. A sinister stranger's bed in the Imperial Palace. Motif beasts—three silver-eyed, black tigers—looped their long feline backs in the folds of a deep-space-dark canopy. It looked ominously like a Tiger Prince's Imperial coat of arms.

Water was running in an en suite bathroom. He was washing. Otherwise, the ambient white noise was like the soft, oppressive collision of thick snowflakes on a deep winter quilt of snow.

Through tears, Djinni scanned the room and focused on a wall display of alien instruments of torture. In his bedroom? Oh, Stars! It was true. It was worse than true.

The trembling began. She fought it. She couldn't afford the paralysis of despair. With a great effort of will, she slid off the high bed and approached the ghastly display. Plenty there to hurt with. Nothing she could kill him with. Or herself.

She snatched the first blunt instrument within reach, scrambled back to the heavily draped side of the bed, and collapsed on the thick, storm-gray carpet, finding a use for the integral magnets inside her skirts. Just in time.

"Problem with the bed?" he asked, covering several possible questions about why she wasn't where he'd left her. His loose, shimmering, new robe hung open as he twisted a short kilt around his hips. Damp, dark hairs curled and clung to his freshly washed thighs. He circled toward her, picking up a goblet on the way.

"With its owner, I think. Please tell me you're not . . ." Her voice cracked and failed.

"Tarrant-Arragon. Djustin. Djohn. Alexander. Thor." Each dreaded name brought him a long-limbed pace closer. "Lord of your life. We can't pretend otherwise any longer."

"I never pretended! I never knew."

"No?" With a predatory grin, he sat down beside her and handed her his drink. "I always hoped you did."

"I can't love Tarrant-Arragon," Djinni gasped, horrified by

the deeper implications. She'd sworn . . . what? To end the tyranny of his bloodline. To thwart him or die trying. But how? Castrate him? Kill him?

She had a shuddering image of putting martial arts theory into bloody practice. Of jabbing trembling fingers into his smiling, tarnished-silver eyes. Monstrous, monstrous disconnect! It was all very well in theory, unimaginable in real life. She could never bring herself to try any such thing.

"You can't, you shouldn't, yet you do love me?" He twisted her words. Only a heartless villain would try to flirt at a time like this. "I'm your first, last, and only love. However, I do hope you will be fond of our children."

"Oh, don't make fun of me!" Djinni wailed. "You are my f-f-fa—" A surge of nausea threatened to overwhelm her with the sick realization that, on top of everything else, she'd almost told Tarrant-Arragon that her father was alive and dangerous.

Enunciating carefully, Djinni corrected herself. "You are—by far—my greatest enemy. B-b-beware." She gulped the wine.

"Are you terrified of me?" Teasingly, he nudged her arm with his, then bent his head close to hers and sniffed. "Hmm. I think you are. Your maddeningly arousing scent has vanished again."

A wave of quesiness shuddered through her. Djinni dropped the goblet, and brought both hands across her mouth.

"I . . . am . . . going . . . to . . . be . . . sick."

He'd respected her distress long enough. The marriage had to be consummated, and—somehow—he still had to tell her that he'd married her.

Tarrant-Arragon grinned at a cynical suspicion as he strode from his stark office back to the bedroom suite.

Her violent reaction to his identity had been disconcerting. Deliberately so? In the past, Djinni had tried less extreme forms of tactical unromanticism when she wanted to avoid lovemaking. She'd risen to the occasion this time, or rather, her gorge had. What would she do when she realized that they were in his rooms for the express purpose of consummating their marriage?

He wondered whether she'd been impressed by his practical demonstration of love. He'd got her to his pedestal in time and had stayed with her, twisting her hair away from her face and murmuring jocose encouragement, until she begged him to go away and find her the Tigron equivalent of peppermint tea.

Tea! Flimsy pretext. He'd taken a calculated risk when he left her alone—not too great, since she still wore his tracer necklet. However, he'd seen the warning that someone had been in his office and had tried to interfere with his surveillance systems. He'd had to see about that. There would be no secret footage of him making love to his mate.

His precious little mate! Tarrant-Arragon leaned against the bathroom door frame and watched her wash her pale face in his waterfall washbasin.

Glancing back, to check that everything they needed was in reach of the bed, he noticed that a crude item from his antiques collection was missing. His heart beat faster until he'd run a rapid mental inventory and identified what she'd taken.

Did she intend to bludgeon him with Scythian toe-claw pullers? Ah! This was more like the mate he loved. He'd welcome a fight. If she attacked him, he'd wrestle her onto the bed, and romp and tumble her until she'd constructively forgiven him.

"You've made the floor very wet, my love," he commented evenly. Approaching, he examined the glossy black bathroom floor. No blood. She hadn't hurt herself. Wet by the pedestal, but she might have been ill again while he was taking care of business.

"That beautiful dress. It's soaked. Let me help you out of it." He took the opportunity to frisk her while efficiently unfastening her at the back, and pretending to grieve over the wet ruin of priceless fabrics. "Splashing everything with my State Occasion aftershave was counterproductive, my love. I'm afraid the Imperial wedding dress is beyond saving."

It was the kindest way he could tell her.

"What you are t-t-talking about?" Trembling in her dampened white underthings, arms crossed over her breasts, she looked chilled, frightened, and lost.

"You need to sit down." Giving her no choice in the matter, he lifted her by the waist and swept her into the bedroom and onto the bed, where she sat, slumped like a beautiful broken doll. "We exchanged wedding vows in front of all the Empire a short while ago. We're mated. Married."

"No! How c-c-could we be?" Her voice fluttered like a half-stunned bird's, struggling plaything of an idle tiger. "You said it was a poem. I didn't consent. I didn't know what I was saying."

"Only you and I know that. All the Worlds will believe the evidence of their own eyes. Look at what Propaganda did with the wedding footage—and with certain recordings I made aboard the Ark Imperial."

He threw himself onto his stomach beside her and activated his wall of computers at the head-end. As he did so, he ran his hand under the pillows. No blunt instrument. The toe-claw pullers weren't on her, and they weren't in the bed, so what the Carnality had she done with them?

"This is the Propaganda control room. See? I spy on spies. It compensates for my lack of telepathy."

She didn't seem to notice his self-deprecating humor.

"Once I patch something into my systems, no one can alter it, not my father—who tried—not even V'Kh, our Head of Security. He's that hairy male. He'd be mortified if he knew that his name sounds like an English sexual obscenity."

No response. Poor little mate.

"V'Kh depends on six assistant editors to feed him 'good' footage, from which he chooses what to show to the commentators."

"What can they choose from?" At last—interest!

"Heads of State; War-star Leaders; White Knights—there's a poor, thin specimen. Do you know him? Then there are four viewfinders on my father; two on Electra-Djerroldina, my elder sister; three on my younger sister, Martia-Djulia, who seems to have absented herself from the ceremony."

"Why me?"

"It was you or my sister, and I'm not—"

"That's not f-f-funny. It was a serious question. There must be lots of bastards . . . half-Djinn like me."

"There is no one else like you. Luckily for my sanity. Wouldn't it be a disaster if there were other unknown, untrained Djinn running amok?"

An incongruous flash of purple triumph streaked her eyes. Had she just tried to find out how many half-suitable girls he had rejected? Or how much he knew?

"Ahhh, my love, your intelligence is one of the many things I adore about you, so I should have thought you'd know—"

A teasing glance at her trembling, contemptuous pout told him that if he respected her, he'd give her the serious answer.

"Your Grandmama took such pains to vilify me, I'm amazed she didn't tell you our nastiest secret. Great Djinn can impregnate most Class Two mammalian females, but non-Djinn females don't tend to, ah, thrive after more than one pregnancy. So we don't."

"You assume that I'll survive?" The cold hatred in her voice chilled him. There was an elusive something else, too.

"I know you will." He slipped a reassuring arm around her. "I had your blood tested within an hour of meeting you."

"How callous!" She shuddered.

The broadcast showed the part of the ceremony when he had addressed the guests. He welcomed the obvious change of subject.

"At this point, I asked whether anyone wanted to object."

"I should have objected." A stricken look crossed her face. "Is this what the Dragon will see?"

"It depends where he is. However, what he sees now makes no difference." It sounded cruel, but it was true. "Look at the banquet, which is taking place as we speak."

He wished she'd ask why they weren't at the Consummation Banquet. Then he could tell her that they were supposed to be making love. Since her scent had gone, and with it his urgency to mate, he was strangely reluctant to mention the final formality, let alone force it on her.

What if he took pity on her and neglected to consummate? Would she think she had grounds to demand an annulment? *Mind-shield that thought.*

She didn't give him an opening, so he slid a finger up her neck onto her lie-detecting pulse-point. "Do you recognize anyone at all?" he asked, thinking of J-J.

"No, I don't." Djinni was glad she could answer truthfully. In all honor, she couldn't attempt an escape if it meant that a brother-Knight might be taken hostage and tortured until she surrendered. "I don't know any of your guests. You didn't consult me about the guest list."

"Ah, touché! Whom would you have invited?" It might have been a harmlessly condescending inquiry from anyone except His treacherous Imperial Highness.

"No one," she said with bitter honesty.

He frowned searchingly at her.

"No one." She pinched the bridge of her nose. "If you'll excuse me, I need a moment to compose myself. Don't . . ." She held up her free hand in a universal "Leave Me Be" gesture. "Please don't."

Hot tears prickled her eyes. She needed time to mourn the love she'd always known was impossible but had hoped . . . the love she'd never have because Tigger had never existed, and his love was a lie.

What could she do? It was futile to fight. This wasn't how she'd dreamed of thwarting Tarrant-Arragon, not that she'd ever imagined herself in a situation like this. Apart from an adrenaline rush of quick thinking in his stark, dark, mirrored bathroom, she hadn't the heart—or stomach—to play the heroine.

"Hmmm. Here's a mystery," His Imperial Highness said in a transparent attempt to distract her from her overwhelming woes. "Martia-Djulia is not at the banquet, either. I'll track her down."

While her tears seeped between her spread fingers, Djinni watched his high-speed virtual tour of the Palace with a vague notion of assessing how good his security systems were. They were very good. Keeping her secret would be impossible. Escape wouldn't be easy. She'd need help.

She tried to memorize the Palace layout. Because she'd been bagged and hooded to protect her from radiation, she hadn't seen much coming in, but Stars! the Palace was vast and mostly subterranean. The four visible pyramids were the tips of an iceberg.

"So that's what my sister is doing," he commented.

A big bed. A fast-moving couple. The big male, on top, hadn't bothered to remove Princess Martia-Djulia's red underwear. Presumably, the camera was behind a mirrored ceiling.

"Martia-Djulia expects me to make him marry her."

It was such a startling leap of logic that Djinni couldn't help asking, "How do you know that?"

His Imperial Voyeuristic Highness grinned.

"Because she's recording this, just as my father suggested. While you were splashing water and perfume all over my bathroom, I watched footage of Martia-Djulia and my father discussing ways of trapping a mate for her. I wonder who my potential brother-in-law is? Do we have a sound track? Ah! How very indiscreet."

"What—are—we—missing?" The male. Between grunts.

"My brother—reciting love poetry!"

"Tarrant-Arragon? Poetry? I'm sorry I missed—that." He stopped mid-thrust. Obviously, he couldn't fornicate and think at the same time. *"I thought it was a regular Virgins' Ball."*

"One might say that the festivities included an irregular virgin's balling. Oooh, Commander Jason! Don't stop."

"Carnality! My vicious bay of a sister had no right to speak about you like that." Tarrant-Arragon shut down the computer. "I've no idea who told her that we can't time Star Forces maneuvers by you, but since she's incapable of giving anyone the rut-rage at all, she's a fine one to talk."

The Princess had called him "Commander Jason"! Djinni

squeezed her eyes shut behind trembling hands. That grunting boor was her J-J. And not hers at all. *That* was the husband she might have been saddled with.

Her heart broke. It was the last straw. Only a straw, that people talked about her like that. Only a straw, but on top of everything else.

From the one-sidedness of the chastity clause that applied only to her, she'd inferred that J-J liked a lot of sex. Why should she be surprised to see him in bed with the enemy?

To hell with all males! She'd never waste another guilty thought on her betrothal contract, or on J-J. But to see it, to hear it, to be betrayed like this . . . Straws hurt.

"I wonder what became of the mystery girl from his wedding permit? No matter. He can't have her after this impertinence."

So he knew that J-J was betrothed. And he made light of it. The arrogant, insensitive oaf!

"I shouldn't mind having Commander Jason in the family, but I wouldn't wish my sister on my best friend. Who would have thought it? My wedding day, and Jason gets lucky."

His Imperial Highness chuckled. His long fingers lifted her hair from her neck. Djinni felt his breath, his lips. She froze.

"Speaking of getting lucky, my love, I should very much like to consummate our marriage. Would you—? No. Ah! Bad idea."

Would he try to change her mind? Djinni gritted her teeth. Her stomach churned again. When she thought back over some of the things Tarrant-Arragon had let slip, she understood how she had been used and would be used.

He'd crossed galaxies to appropriate her sight unseen. By his own admission, he'd checked her blood to make sure. Then he'd set out to make her love him. He'd almost succeeded.

The tragedy was, His Imperial Highness didn't love her. Oh, he pretended convincingly, but he wanted her for the same reason J-J did. Her genes. She was prime breeding stock. That was all.

No, it wasn't all. No one had ever told her about the risk these bloody males were all willing to take—that her second pregnancy might kill her. She'd never forgive them. Any of them.

Hot, angry tears ran undiverted down her face.

There was no point in running away from Tarrant-Arragon, only to be taken by J-J. After what she'd seen, she had no desire to marry J-J either, even if that were still possible.

"The Worlds have marveled long enough at my supposed nuptial excesses. Take your hands from your eyes." His voice penetrated her thoughts, and Djinni realized that the stroking and touching around her neck hadn't just been seductive play. While her face was covered and her mind elsewhere, he'd given her a much more magnificent, black sapphire–like necklace.

He'd also put on another robe, and replaced his Rings on his long, wicked fingers.

Djinni had heard of those rings. The saber-tooth-tiger skull of the Death Ring was a symbol of his right to take or spare lives at his pleasure. The unformed chunk that represented dark matter was the Ring of Gravity. Most dangerous of all was the cunningly faceted blue-crystal of the Fire-Stone on his forefinger.

She shuddered.

"If we're not going to make love, we ought to join our guests. Do you want to use the bathroom again?" He was all heart, all practicality. "If not, I'll dress you, shall I?"

Djinni hadn't noticed the black ball gown draped over the one huge black chair until he shook it out with the going-about rustle and snap of a racing spinnaker.

Since she didn't want him to discover what she'd done in his bathroom, Djinni nodded meekly. Pretending to have a headache, she shielded her telltale eyes with one hand and submitted to being dressed, and to his misguided sympathy.

"My poor darling, it isn't fair, is it? You have so much to deal with, all at the most vulnerable time of your erratic cycle."

Her "erratic cycle" indeed! Djinni seethed. She could tell him . . . But she wasn't going to.

"Don't be nervous. As my Imperial Princess Consort, you

can do no wrong. . . ." He narrowed his eyes. Maybe something in her face gave him pause. He knew her too well.

"Hmmm. My love, I should warn you that I am the ultimate legal authority in the Empire. If, ah, anyone were to challenge the validity of our marriage, I would try the case personally. Of course, I'd rule in my own favor."

He said "anyone," but he meant her.

Perhaps she'd do exactly what he was warning her not to do. It was the one thing that seemed to worry him.

Chapter Nineteen

The most powerful, viscerally terrifying male in existence wanted her. Had high-handedly taken her. How did she dare to defy him? She must be a little bit mad.

Sitting on the steps of the throne-stage, Djinni took stock. The banquet was like a sprawling Roman orgy in a pentagonal Colosseum, minus sex and furniture.

"The aphrodisiacs aren't a good idea for you," Tarrant-Arragon said, dividing a tray of finger food into what she should and should not eat. "Take your time. I must circulate. No one will bother you." He indicated a sunken area like an orchestra pit around the twin throne-stages, where Imperial tigers prowled.

Djinni toyed with her fork-spoon, and waited until Tarrant-Arragon had circulated as far from her side as he'd be if he were at third base and she were behind the dugout.

White pawn's move. Djinni stood.

"I want a divorce."

Not knowing the High Court word for "divorce," she spoke in English. It would be enough if one White Knight understood her and reported back to her father. She hoped for more.

In a sudden hush, heads turned. Rustling females mouthed *What-did-she-say?* to uniformed warriors. Farther-off guests climbed the terraces until their heads were level with the tops of the double avenues of living trees that flanked four grand entrances and divided the raised seating into five sections.

Black's move.

"Editors. Delete!" Tarrant-Arragon thundered. The noble groundlings around him backed hastily out of his way.

The Black Prince trained his narrowed gaze on her and stalked toward her. Djinni felt his fury like a sudden pelting of hail followed by the lightning shock of Djinn-craft. Her knees wobbled. She braced herself and refused to sit or faint, despite what she knew and he didn't.

Why? Djinni willed someone to ask. Beyond speech, she looked for an ally. A boyish figure in white struggled to move against the retreating tide of lords and young ladies. Djinni's heart pounded with hope.

Black vaulted onto the throne-stage. His lips formed a hard, thin line. Danger smoldered in his eyes.

"Have you any idea what you're doing?" he demanded in a harsh whisper, though he must have known she could not answer. He released her from the grip of Djinn-craft, only to take her by the back of the neck and force her to lift her mouth. Staring at her lips, he swore softly at her. "Ah, damn you, darling."

Djinni wondered what he'd eaten and drunk, since he seemed to be aroused to the point of incoherence.

"My sore love, it will get better." This stage whisper was in High Court for all his guests to hear. "Maybe the sixth time. And trust me, the sixth time is imminent."

Excitement swirled around the great room.

"But first—" He turned her to face the audience, and held her against the front of his hard body. "Ka'Nych!"

Something white and badly stained unfurled from a balcony high above the banqueting hall. Ka'Nych rode a majestic cherry-picker up to the same level as the exhibit. "Confirm what that is."

"This is Your Imperial Highnesses' wedding sheet,"

Ka'Nych said. "Fresh shows of 'exuberance' prove that Your Highness is the only male whom Her Highness has ever known."

Male guests whooped and thumped their thighs. Djinni wanted to cry out that the bloody "exuberance" wasn't hers, but no sound came.

"What else?" Tarrant-Arragon proceeded. He glanced down at her with savage appraisal, then away again.

"Your Highnesses' mating has been thoroughly consummated." As he spoke, the gynecologist shone a light beam on five areas of the sheet. "Five times. Her Highness is understandably shocked."

"Understandably," Tarrant-Arragon repeated.

Events took on the slow inevitability of a well-rehearsed courtroom performance. Tarrant-Arragon had ruthlessly discredited her testimony and destroyed her as a witness.

Would the humiliations never end? And whose blood was it? The first time he'd had white sheets on the bed, she tore them up to make a rope ladder. The only other time, she fought him off and gave him a nosebleed.

He must have saved this sheet from that occasion. They must have frozen it and applied his silvery "exuberance" later. Oh, the pig! How many people were involved in this gross deception?

"Checkmate," he whispered. He'd won, and he knew it.

Hostile judge, hostile jury. No one would believe her, even if she could summon the words. Everyone gloried in this "proof" of their Prince's sexual ferocity.

No one had taken her side. Djinni threw a glance of mute appeal to the White Knight who'd almost come forward, but who was staring up at the sheet in fury and revulsion.

Their eyes met. She felt a vibration of sexual envy, and of virulent hatred coming from the White Knight. Her brother— no, her disguised *sister* Knight wanted her dead and bloody and buried under priapic old men . . . also dead.

Something was very wrong with that Knight.

Djinni swayed in shock. Being hated was one blow too many. It was too much. She couldn't cope. . . .

"I've got to get you away before you drive us all crazy," Tarrant-Arragon gritted against the top of her head, then turned to the other throne-stage, where the Emperor was scratching the base of a tiger's raised tail. "You must excuse us, Sir. I'm overcome with lecherous urgency."

"So it's like that," the Emperor said. He waved a dismissal. "I thought so. Go. Take her away before we all are similarly overcome. Well away."

Like what? Through her haze of depression, Djinni felt the Emperor's contemplatively predatory gaze like two fingertips probing her body. Behind her, Tarrant-Arragon's breath was heavy in her hair.

All the world was thinking of sex with her. Violent, perverted, deadly sex. . . . The Imperial males' arousal made no sense. It wasn't—couldn't possibly be—her setting them off.

Oh, Stars! She had to get away. But how? She might throw Tarrant-Arragon over her hip, break free and jump . . . but their throne-stage had begun its ascent. What good would it do her to fall among enemies and tigers?

Djinni closed her eyes, took a deep, shuddering breath. She still had her secret. Enraged as he was, he wouldn't dare hurt her . . . if she told him.

Foiled, Bronty stared after the royal newlyweds as the throne-scape ascended to the Imperial suites above.

She'd been so close. She'd have been near enough to touch him if the lightning-eyed witch hadn't ruined everything. She might yet have got to him if not for his sudden exit.

Roaring approval, guards and guests alike craned their necks, hoping their virile Prince might not wait until he was out of sight. Looking up like everyone else, Bronty backed to an exit, past the guards, then turned and dashed into the nearest rest room.

She fought back tears of frustration as she unbuckled her swordbelt and clattered her weapon onto the counter. She tugged her tabard over her head and tore off the supposedly Djinn-scented camisole. It was now soaked with her perspiration. Bronty crammed it into the nearest receptacle and let the slipstream suck it away.

"We ought to sex it," someone said.

Bronty half turned. Martia-Djulia's evil spawn, Prince Henquist and Prince Thor-quentin lounged in the doorway, staring lustfully at her nude torso. The Dragon had hinted at this.

If there was any justice, they'd be fighting over their mother while the scandalized worlds looked on. Instead, the sex-crazed Commander had beaten them to her, and Tarrant-Arragon was having at his flashy new wife for the sixth time since first dawn.

"Those look like unripe breasts to me." Thor-quentin circled closer. "But I think we need to feel them—and taste them—just to be sure."

"Then we should investigate what's between its legs." The bigger Henquist leered lopsidedly and put his hand over the flat of her Saurian sword. "I'll bet Grandfather will let us have fun with it, since we caught it legally, with its uniform off."

Thor-quentin advanced. Bronty retreated until the wall was cold on her bare shoulders and closed her eyes in dread.

"I'll talk," she whispered. "Don't hurt me."

She'd gladly betray the Saurian Dragon, but the princes' cruel laughter told her that they would do as they pleased with her. No matter what she told them, they intended to gang-rape and sexually torture her for as long as it amused them.

The door swished.

"Out!" Henquist said. "Get out, you quivering An'Koori!"

There was silence, broken only by the intake-hiss of the air system. Bronty opened her eyes, and lifted them all the way up a green and silver uniform resplendent with an An'Koori Commander's insignia to dark, color-slashed, emotionless eyes.

"I'm a White Knight," she pleaded. "Save me."

Very slowly the Commander brought up his hand to his broad chest and snapped a fastener shut. The gesture was one of deliberate, raw intimidation, made doubly effective by the fresh bruises on his knuckles.

Bronty recognized him by those ugly grazes. He had savagely attacked 'Rhett and left her without protection, while he'd gone off like a barbarian and ruined her plans for the princess.

"Get dressed, White Knight," he said, and while Bronty obeyed, he turned to the princes. "Your Highnesses, you don't want to interfere with your uncle's guests."

The air prickled with tension, but the princes backed away.

"Come," the Commander ordered, holding out his hands.

Bronty had no choice. Nervously, she put her hands in the sex maniac's, never expecting to receive the Saurian handshake.

"I'm Tyrannosaurus." He hissed the code name of the greatest Saurian Knight of recent memory. "We've got to find 'Rhett."

Ark Imperial (The "Brig")

Grievous felt he owed it to the little miss to make her mysterious ex-boyfriend see reason. So he popped down to the brig, armed with good intentions and a bottle of An'Koori wine.

"Now, you're not to worry, J-J." Grievous came straight to the point, and was taken aback to find himself being eyed with cool hostility. "You don't mind if I call you J-J, do you, Sir?"

"Not at all, but my name is 'Rhett."

"Hah! You don't like being called J-J. Can't say I blame you," Grievous humored him. "All right, then, 'Rhett, I've come to set you straight about Their Imperial Highnesses. Drink?"

The resentful prisoner shrugged.

Grievous did the honors. "Tarrant-Arragon adores her. You'll hear chaps say he beats her. Not true. Now, she drew his cork once, but that's another story. She got most of her bruises falling over. Had a spot of trouble with the Tigron gravity, she did, and with her weak heart—"

"What weak heart?" 'Rhett swirled his wine and held it up to the light. As deliberately offensive as a taxman, he examined his drink for dregs—or drugs.

"Hers. The first time he tried to have his way, er, well, he

didn't. He thought she was going to die of fright." Grievous
cut a long story diplomatically short.

"My Djinni doesn't have a weak heart, Grievous."

"No?" He hadn't come to argue, so Grievous switched to a
more political rationale. "Look at it this way. We'd all be better
off if Tarrant-Arragon has his happily-ever-after with the girl
he loves. Yes, he loves her. I'll bet your Saurian sword to my
Swiss army knife, he'll use Djinni's weak heart as an excuse for
all manner of humane reforms which aren't consistent with
what he'd call his 'usefully vile reputation.'"

"You interest me, Grievous." 'Rhett sipped his drink, and
Grievous felt honored. "Do you expect me to believe that The
Terror of the Dodecahedrons has been changed by love?"

"Nah, a man only changes as far as he wants to, but from
what I've heard, he's mellowed mightily since he got his hands
on her."

Grievous raised a silent toast to that. 'Rhett did likewise, and
Grievous found himself warming up to the prisoner.

"My point is, she's his, and he's going to keep her. He's like
a big cat with velvety paws. There's wicked-sharp claws
sheathed beneath his soft-touch surface."

"Is that a threat?" 'Rhett lifted an eyebrow, just so. Tarrant-
Arragon to a T. The off-the-wall idea of 'Rhett somehow being The Great Djinn's kin started to take hold.

"It's a threat to galactic peace if the chap she calls J-J doesn't
let sleeping tigers lie. I warn you, my boss hasn't got the hang
of offering incentives. He's pretty subtle at making threats, but
he makes an incentive sound like it's a bribe."

"Which, of course, it is," 'Rhett remarked dryly.

"I daresay. However, I'm told his kind used to kill off their
rivals, so they didn't have to get bribing down to a fine art, nor
apologizing. He doesn't do that, either."

"So if I don't accept his generosity I'll be killed?"

"No, Sir," Grievous assured 'Rhett hastily. "He wouldn't do
anything nasty that the little miss might find out about."

"That leaves a large loophole," 'Rhett drawled. "I might fall
through it to my death."

Honeymoon Flight—Over the Royal Desert

"What the Carnality were you *thinking?*" His Imperial Highness's angry words ricocheted in Djinni's mind. It was the only thing he'd said since leaving the banquet.

Djinni was glad of his silence. She needed to think. In the terror and confusion of the past hours, she'd acted on instinct and adrenaline. Most of her actions had been wholly selfish and highly irresponsible.

Stars help her, she paid close attention as he snapped the canopy shut, said "Tarrant-Arragon" and something unrecognizable, chopped his right hand into a contoured, reverse-J-shaped cradle, and waggled it twice. She was crazy to think she could steal his starfighter, let alone fly it. No doubt it responded only to his voice and to his hand.

An A-shaped wall slid away. Djinni saw cross-hatchings of midafternoon light, heard and felt a whoosh of power, and was slammed by g-forces. Then a roller-coaster plunge kept her too busy trying not to be sick to notice anything for quite some time.

When she felt it was safe to peer down, she watched their Thorcraft's V-shaped shadow race low over an unevenly baked and painted desert, distorting on structures that looked like massive termite mounds, stampeding herds of dog-sized deer, and causing basking lizards to nod. So this was the "Royal" side of Tigron.

What "the Carnality" had she been thinking, anyway? She'd wanted to throw Tarrant-Arragon? She was pregnant. Pregnant! Oh Stars, oh joy, she was pregnant.

Djinni closed her eyes, raised her face like a sun worshiper, and let the idea sink in and glow.

What kind of mother took such insane risks? The father might be the nastiest monster the Communicating Worlds had ever seen, but their baby was innocent. Her first duty was to protect her baby from its father.

Djinni felt a change in air pressure, an elevator sensation in her insides. Fine! If he wanted to fly in circles, let him. She would not say a word about his stupid Top Gun daredevilry, nor about the cold air-intake blasting their faces.

Through closed eyelids, she became aware of a change in the light, then a soft triple bump, a settling. The air cut off.

They'd landed. Tarrant-Arragon spoke. Not to her. He was shutting down and securing the Thorcraft, she assumed.

Djinni opened her eyes and blinked in disbelief.

If she could believe her eyes, Tarrant-Arragon had made a vertical landing inside a sort of blowhole. She stared up at the silver circle of sky. She was going mad! Therefore, she saw no reason to cooperate when Tarrant-Arragon opened the canopy, threw off his harnesses, then stood, straddled her, and unbuckled her.

"Did you *want* me to rape you in front of all the Worlds?" he erupted, giving her little incentive to leave the cramped confines of her seat.

She had no choice. He thrust his hands under her shoulders and lifted her at arm's length—like an incontinent puppy—then swung her out onto the sloped wing. He followed. In a swift, fluid movement he was on top of her, trapping her body on the wing.

"Something close to rape is what the law requires. Is that what I should have done?"

"I didn't think you'd do it." Djinni looked him in the eye and did not tell him the reason she didn't think he'd do it.

The little mate didn't think he'd do it! Hope flared like a painter missile across the icy blackness of space.

"Then you don't know me very well," Tarrant-Arragon retorted, yearning for her to contradict him. "You've told me more than enough about myself and the atrocities my kind commit. Great swirling nebulae, girl, when you demanded a divorce, did it never occur to you that I might kill everyone who understood you?"

He paused, giving her every opportunity to blurt out a word in his defense, or some admission of trust or of lingering love.

She bit her lip.

"A divorce!" His anger rose as he thought how the happiest day of his life might have gone terribly wrong because of Djinni's on-and-off hormones, and because of Martia-Djulia's spite in putting aphrodisiacs on the menu. "Never. Over my dead body! Over my father's. Do you realize that if anything happened to me, you'd have to get past the Emperor? And Django? And my nephews—who might gang up and share you?"

He lowered his weight onto her, masking a shudder in a display of sexual aggression, though he had no intention of taking her on the stealth-built swing wing of his Thorcraft. Not unless she gave him some encouragement.

Now, more than ever, he had something to prove to his distrustful little mate and to himself.

The Great Originator be thanked, her faint and terror-tainted scent had vanished. He could take his time and be glad that his prompt action at the banquet had shocked her out of her rageousness. Nevertheless, he gave her neck an experimental caress with his open mouth.

"By all the Lechers! I'm not the nicest Djinn that ever there was," he murmured hopefully.

"No," the perverse little mate agreed. "But you've always been . . . civilized about one thing. . . ."

"Ah, yes." One of her favorite tactics. Perhaps she'd be more receptive after she'd freshened up. He got off her and helped her down the ramped wing to the ground.

"This way. I'll give you the tour, shall I?" He smiled as he took her arm above the elbow and led her into the cave complex. "We're in the hollow core of an extinct volcano. Imagine a range of rock volcanoes as bent old men, thumped on their ridged backs by meteoric impacts, coughing up their magma plugs."

"I wouldn't have thought it possible," she murmured, trailing a finger over a paint-splatter shape in the dark glass-stone surface. "How can there be caves?"

"You think like an Earthling, darling," he teased, delighted by her interest in his world. "No matter how heavy the world and how dense the rock, caves are always possible if the interior is rubblized. You've seen how cratered Tigron is—"

"Why did you say *rock* volcanoes?" she asked, but from the sudden tension in her arm, he knew she'd heard the water ahead.

"Tigron also has ice volcanoes, metal volcanoes, and invisible volcanoes of magnetic force. Here's the bathroom." He showed her into a translucent-walled cavern.

"Glass-stone. We quarried beyond, but it was too flawed—" He noticed her urgent expression. "Bathe in the upper pool. See the overflow?" He pointed to the uneven end of the broken-saucer-shaped pool, then lower to where water tumbled into a narrow chute, which he'd modified by explosives, before churning against rock and vanishing underground. "Do the necessary downstream. I'll be nearby, rigging up our bed," he said, and left her to it.

"The more things change, the more they stay the same," Djinni quoted bitterly to herself, remembering other times Tigger had "rigged the bed" while she loitered in bathrooms.

She managed, then washed her hands in the whiskey-colored water of the upper pool, and dried them on the front of her wet-hemmed ball gown.

"Ah, but this is different, isn't it? Quite primitive," she commented with Helispetorial sarcasm on her surroundings. "What 'the Carnality' is he thinking of . . . ?"

Mindful that sound tended to carry in caves, Djinni continued her analysis in silence. At least this plumbing wasn't rigged, unlike his toilet at the Palace, which was bilingual and programmed for pregnancy testing, until she deprogrammed it with a blunt instrument.

The all-powerful, all-knowing Tarrant-Arragon didn't know he was going to be a father. He wasn't going to find out. She knew he liked to count things. He'd probably put a fetal monitor on her so he could count his son's heartbeats, and then it would be impossible to leave him.

★ ★ ★

"Grievous, report. Did you arrest J-J?" Tarrant-Arragon commanded from the shaggy shade of a black, spike-fronded shrub that was part cactus, part tree.

"Well, I think so, Sir," Grievous's voice hissed out of the forearm communicator.

"Carnality!" Tarrant-Arragon swore. "What's he like?"

"Quite good-looking, if you go for the elegantly lethal, épée-fighting type. About your height. Hair's blue-black like yours, Sir. Lookswise, he could be your sickly younger brother. Except, he's got mean, green eyes. Talk about looking daggers at a man. When we stepped into Xirxex's welcome party on the Ark Imperial, he looked at me in such a way—it felt like cold claws in my guts, Sir."

A cold sensation gripped Tarrant-Arragon's own guts. High in the ochre-streaked sky, a carrion bird altered course. Below, Djinni shielded her eyes against the harsh light.

"Hard-damn, what's she doing? She has no idea of the danger. I'm going after her. Message ends."

Chapter Twenty

Either the plant moved or Djinni was more dizzy than she'd realized. Not just the geology of Tarrant-Arragon's world was different and intriguing, the plants were too.

Things popped and cracked, groaned, rustled and hissed. Some but not all sounds Djinni attributed to teeming desert wildlife. Gray and red sand seethed underfoot, as if each grain were an ant. Her high heels sank in.

She swayed in the midafternoon sunlight and wondered whether it was her imagination, or whether it truly grew hotter with every breath. The "Body Imperial" hung heavy overhead, scab brown with mackerel-sky streaks and twenty times as large as she remembered Earth's sun looking. The small sun was a white daisy with pink-tipped petals.

In the hazy heat, sharp and fuzzy-edged shadows and serrated dark plants melted together like a choppy sea of gorse. Easter Island heads of monster cacti heaved upward from thick bases, with blunt charcoal features instead of Saguaro arms.

Slowly, to avoid overbalancing in the heavy gravity, Djinni bent toward a gleaming, lover's-knot-shaped fruit the color of a Granny Smith apple. *Odd that a thicket of cactus should produce such fruit,* she thought.

"Stop! Stand back." She heard Tarrant-Arragon shout, turned her head just as a swarm of big burrs sprayed at her, and he hit her. Whack! Heavy hitter, heavy world . . . He swatted her across the face and held her head to his chest like a football.

Pinned in darkness, Djinni felt his free hand rip at her waistline. Was he going to strip her and beat her?

"They go for the eyes. Anywhere wet," he panted, wrenching off her skirts down the front. "They burrow . . . for veins, arteries. Go through soft tissue in minutes."

His words registered. The burrs were the problem. He'd got to her just in time. Releasing her, he slung the burr-heavy fabric aside. "Lucky you wet your dress," he grunted.

Djinni looked down instinctively, and looked again. Black on black, there was a strange puckering. . . . Something was on him.

"Your arm!" she gasped. Two burrs were in his quilted, black kimono-like sleeve, an eye-width apart. As she stared in shock, one of them sank deeper.

"Spit," he said in a voice she'd heard only once before. His mouth worked. "They go where it's wettest. Spit."

She spat. Papery spines telescoped, turning lychee burrs into medieval maces. He spat air. Sweat beaded on his forehead.

"Get them off you. Oh my God. Can't you knock them off?" Djinni spat again, but her mouth was almost dry with horror.

"Can't risk leaving spines in. Come." He grabbed her hand and they ran. Djinni didn't question, didn't think, until they splashed headlong into the upper pool.

Tarrant-Arragon was afraid of something!

Bemused, Djinni watched him ease up his saturated sleeve—away from the forearm communicator that had probably saved his life—as gingerly as a blood donor peeling Elastoplast from a hairy arm, until the evil spikes lifted from his flesh and the dislodged burrs bobbed away like sea mines.

"I want to go home," Djinni said, breaking the awkward silence. Her complaint was so ridiculous, Tarrant-Arragon ought to have known she was trying to be funny, but he looked terribly stern.

"I should have warned you," Tarrant-Arragon conceded, which was as close as he was going to come to an apology. "I assumed you'd avoid me by taking a long bath. How far did you expect to get in this heat and gravity? Seriously, my love, promise me—"

"I can't be serious. I just spat all over your arm." A wild giggle bubbled from the little mate's lips, reminding him how young and fragile she was. "And you saved my sight. How can I be as angry with you as I should be?"

She lifted that stubborn chin of hers. "I wasn't running away. I wanted something green and crunchy, to settle my stomach after the rich banquet food."

"Then green and crunchy you shall have, my love," Tarrant-Arragon said, delighted to be able to assert his natural, loving dominance over her without further argument. He got up and held out a hand to her.

His heart ached with love and tenderness at the feminine way she put her hand in his, and looked down to shake her streaming skirts where the missing panel exposed a wide strip of white petticoat clinging between long, shapely legs.

Perhaps misunderstanding his interest, she curtsied. "I look like one of King Henry VIII's queens. Stars!"

In the lurch of a heartbeat, the purple mischief left her eyes, and she clapped her free hand over her mouth. Their fragile flirtation was over, and he didn't know why.

"Explain. If you're going to compare, do it aloud."

Frustration made him speak harshly. Tarrant-Arragon had no interest in human history, but he recalled a movie portraying marriage to the vicious and syphilitic Henry as a death sentence. It was very much the way Djinni was reacting to him.

The poor little mate gasped in terror. He posed a simpler question. "You said 'one' of his queens. How many did he have?"

"S–s–six."

"Consecutively?" Determined to force the issue, whatever it was, he aimed a low blow. "Unlike your Saurian Dragon?"

"The Saurian Dragon only had *three* wives, and he loved them all. He never divorced or beheaded any of them." She tried to twist her hand free. Tarrant-Arragon held on.

Her absurdly loyal defense of the Dragon provoked him into sneering, "He 'loved' them to death. They all died young, and in his bed. Whereas I—"

"Whereas *you* ripped apart your first fiancée and dismembered her lover, too." She hurled an accusation no one had ever dared to make to his face.

"Alleged lover," he snapped. "Her infidelity was never proven. Unlike Saurian Knights, I don't presume someone is guilty without giving them a fair hearing. I didn't kill—or mutilate—either of them, you little bigot."

She turned as red as sunset. Her hands flew to her cheeks. Oh, yes, she was aghast to be accused of hypocrisy and prejudice, the very flaws she hated most in others.

"I'm so sorry," she whispered. "I never thought . . ."

"To question your sources?" he finished her apology for her, and took advantage of her confusion to slip a forgiving arm around her. "Ah, Djinni, why must you believe every scabrous lie that the Saurian Dragon invents about me?"

"He's not a liar," she insisted, but without her usual fire and conviction.

"Is he not?" Tarrant-Arragon purred, well pleased with the damage he'd done the Dragon that day. "Someone is."

Asgaard—Stronghold of the Saurian Dragon

"I declare a conflict of interest," the Saurian Dragon announced as the wedding sound track faded.

Every Saurian headmask turned from the viewing wall where they had just watched the celebrations. Wearily, Prince Ala'Aster-Djalet stood up and removed his ceremonial headmask.

"I am Ala'Aster-Djalet, runt-twin son of Helispeta and Djevoron-Vitan. I am full-Djinn. Djinni-vera is my daughter. Which is how I came to be in a position to appropriate her underwear."

His voice was hypnotic. No one pointed out the impropriety of the free worlds' intergalactic policy being directed by a Great Djinn with a personal claim to usurp his cousin's Tiger throne if the Saurians overthrew Djerrold Vulcan V and Tarrant-Arragon.

"Apart from the Imperial Princesses, my daughter is the last female Djinn of reproductive age. It was her copulin-scented underwear which failed to distract our enemy, presumably because he had already fixated on Djinni-vera herself during his first rut-rage with her."

"Can we annul this marriage?" the Recorder asked, focusing on the immediate crisis.

"Not without Djinni-vera. This wedding will not bring sympathizers to our side, because there is no evidence that she did not consent—unless Djinni-vera herself impeaches him. To do that, she must escape or be rescued."

"Other Imperial brides have escaped!" An unusually subdued O-Garr offered faint hope to an outraged father.

"You refer to the Empresses Helispeta and Tarragonia-Marietta. Neither escaped in time for the marriage to be annulled," Ala'Aster-Djalet replied heavily.

"Helispeta was Djohn-Kronos's second Empress. The succession had already been secured with the birth of Djerrold Vulcan, before Djohn-Kronos tricked Helispeta into his bed. He couldn't prevent Helispeta from running away with my father because half his Star Forces defected to the Saurians with them.

"Tarragonia-Marietta bore Tarrant-Arragon, and—of course—his sisters, before she left Djerrold Vulcan. She had our help, and Djerrold Vulcan was unable to pursue her owing to a regrettable incident with, ah, poison."

Ala'Aster-Djalet smiled wryly.

"My new son-in-law is more efficient. If he suspects that

we hope to rescue Djinni-vera, he'll keep her in Imperial Restraints, or worse. If she is to have any chance at all, we must convince him that we disown the girl and she has nowhere to go.

"If you agree, please signify your acceptance in the usual manner." The thunder of table-thumping approval filled the Planetarium chamber as Saurians drove their assent knives into the voting slots. There was no debate, just palpable relief that the Saurian Dragon hadn't demanded war.

Tigron Desert Hideaway

"Allow me to protect you," His Imperial Highness said with seductive chivalry, ripping off his trailing, wet sleeves. He draped one like a hood over Djinni's hair, and did the same for himself before leading her back out into the sunlight.

Only a consummate player like Tarrant-Arragon could turn Samurai-stylish fighting robes into a long muscle shirt and pretend he was being altruistic.

"Our 'Body Imperial' can make the heat of the day six percent hotter on the Royal side. It also makes our side more volcanic, especially during the daily eclipses," he explained.

"I declare a truce. At least while we eat," Tarrant-Arragon announced, and set about catering.

Watching him, Djinni had a hard time remembering he was The Terror of the Dodecahedrons as he squatted, gently steaming in the sun and using his Fire-Stone Ring to burn papery spines off burrlike cactus pods retrieved from the torn part of her dress. Once he'd peeled off their black outsides, they looked like kiwi fruit.

He held a cactus out to her. "The ultimate revenge. Eat your enemy." From the gleam in his eye, she knew he was parodying another scurrilous myth she'd recently believed about him.

"I want to work this out," he said. "Let's talk. We both know that I'm the only possible mate for you, don't we? Or do you know something I don't?"

Djinni ate her first cactus using both hands to hide her smile. Tarrant-Arragon's idea of a truce didn't stop him from questioning her, but, he was far from being the deadly interrogator of Helispeta's cautionary tales. Rather, his questions told her how much he did not know, which Djinni found reassuring.

"You don't know that you're self-centered, manipulative, and condescending. Who'd dare to say so?" she said cheekily.

"Obviously only you, my love," he flirted. "I love your honesty, also your intelligence and your gentleness. And I'd love to discuss the source of your misconceptions about me."

"I'll bet you would!"

He might not know everything, but Djinni gave him some credit: He knew what he was doing. Every move, every *thought* was a calculated, cynical play. If his mind-shields were down, it was because he wanted her to read his loving thoughts. He'd tricked her with thought-lies in the past. Never again! Djinni didn't trust him in the least.

"You loved me when you didn't know my identity. I haven't changed," Tarrant-Arragon said, handing her two more cacti. "How can you not see through the lies and propaganda?"

Tarrant-Arragon hoped Djinni didn't understand his gentle interrogation technique. He was trying to undermine her prejudices by asking the occasional barbed question that he wanted the fair-minded little mate to think about.

"It was lucky for you that I did believe the stories."

"Why is that?" he asked, somewhat bemused by her reasoning but thrilled by her choice of past tense.

"If not for your reputation, I'd have guessed who you are," she said, calmly crunching her fourth cactus. He was counting, but was too experienced to comment. A prisoner who enjoys her food unintentionally demonstrates her will to adapt and survive.

"There were times when I almost hoped you would guess. Every time you began a sentence with my name, my heart kicked me."

She didn't respond. He didn't care. Every time he gave her a cactus, he moved closer. He'd got his arm around her again, and she was pretending that she hadn't noticed it. He kept talking. "I've often wondered how you recognized the rut-rage, and why you didn't guess who I was when I had the rut-rage."

"Grandmama Helispeta described her experiences with the rut-rage. She had a much worse time than I had with you. I don't think your grandfather or my great-uncle ever . . ." She blushed.

Tarrant-Arragon grinned. He wanted her to think about his sexual prowess and generosity.

"I thought you might be a bit of a bastard. It never crossed my mind that you were a full-blooded Great Djinn. Grandmama told me the scandals about your wicked appetites, Tarrant-Arragon. Terrible, depraved things," she said in an awed voice.

"I know, my love," he purred. He watched her through half-closed eyes and gave her something else to think about. "And they can't all have been true, can they?"

Trojan Horse

"I was sent to prevent the marriage," Bronty claimed. "But I had unreliable backup and defective equipment. If I'd had this gun, I could have killed him. And her."

Jason took his Desert Eagle from Bronty's clutching hands and put it away with the rest of his collection.

The secret Saurians had returned to Jason's suite, having toured the Trojan Horse and the quarters recently vacated by Stegosaurus, which would now be Bronty's. Already, Jason was worried about Bronty.

"There's nothing we can do about it now," Jason said philosophically. "Tarrant-Arragon will breed, and it'll be more complicated to organize an orderly and bloodless overthrow."

"Shall we put a name to the upstart witch and drink to her poor reproductive health?" Horn't suggested, refilling goblets for Jason, Bronty, and himself. "What was her name, Bronty?"

"It's Djinni-something. I've got it: Djinni-vera. Quite a pretentious mouthful. Jason, are you all right?"

Jason felt sick. "Where's the footage? Djinni is my missing fiancée. The bitch! I'd like to kill them both." He took a wild swig of his cactus brew. "How could she do it?"

"Hmmm. Isn't this the girl who kicked him and tried to run away from him at Eurydyce?" Horn't buzzed.

"Maybe she wasn't willing." Bronty conceded. "He has the technology to fake a bride's consent—that's what the Saurian Dragon told me when he thought Tarrant-Arragon might try to marry me."

Jason and Horn't stared at Bronty. She took the cake for irrational leaps in logic.

"Well?" she continued. "All the Worlds and their sister-moons now know the Imperial Household has taken over a secluded resort in the polar mountains. Doesn't it make you wonder why Tarrant-Arragon chose it for his honeymoon?"

"Zzzing odd choice. Though there are two schools of thought about the effect of cold weather on virility."

"Males! Don't you ever think of anything else?" Bronty said. "Think about the target he must present on an icy skyline."

"It's a bitter irony," Jason fumed. "My war-star is making sure Tarrant-Arragon can sleep easy in his bed with my girl. Doesn't that take top honors for adding insult to injury!"

"Yes. But you said you wanted to kill them. We're ideally placed to do it," Bronty persisted. "You just said this war-star is guarding the honeymoon resort. Earlier you said you can go anywhere and do anything without the An'Koori on the Bridge being any the wiser. Couldn't you send a remote-controlled destruct-craft to kill them?"

Jason was shocked that Bronty and Horn't had taken his wrathful words at face value. Cultural dissonance was a pain in the arse. Now he'd have to find a way to back off from murder without losing face.

"The Saurian Dragon would never forgive me for killing her," Jason said. "I probably wouldn't forgive myself." It was a sobering thought. Literally.

"We can't kill her, people. She's too important. Come to think of it, we ought to take him alive, too."

The others were looking at him oddly. Jason rationalized a gentler course of action. "It would be almost as easy to rescue her and take him hostage, and we'd stand a better chance of getting out of Imperial space without Tarrant-Arragon's Warstar Leaders blasting us to particles."

"True," Horn't agreed grudgingly. "Our Trojan Horse couldn't withstand a hit from the Ark Imperial. Slayt and his colleagues wouldn't think twice about killing our An'Koori crew along with us if they knew we'd killed His Imperial Highness."

"It's settled." Jason put on his most decisive tone. "We'll never have such a perfect opportunity. There's even a slim chance she's not yet pregnant. We rescue Djinni at dawn."

Tigron Desert—South of the Polar Dawn

J-J's roar of outrage ricocheted off the snowy ridges of Djinni's dream. She knew, without knowing how she knew, that the voice was J-J's. Her dreaming mind could not make sense of where J-J was, or why he was raging outside some kind of winter palace.

What had polar dawns and ice volcanoes to do with anything? Was this a psychic experience? A sexual metaphor? Or something that came with pregnancy, like food cravings and "morning" sickness at any and all hours of the day?

"Where is she? Why aren't they here?" J-J howled.

How typical of J-J. In the wrong place, at the wrong time, again and again and again.

"Oh, J-J!" Djinni cried out between remorse and exasperation. Somewhere, in the wrong hemisphere, J-J had tried to rescue her, she was sure of it. He'd risked his life, his cover, and the work of thirteen years for her. The least she could do was keep quiet.

Carnality, she still dreams of J-J. Slackness damn him. Tarrant-Arragon's chest burned with savage envy. It was too soon to talk to her about J-J. He wasn't ready to reveal that J-J was a prisoner on the Ark Imperial.

Fully dressed, he lay with his beloved bride in a warrior's hammock any other girl would love to be tumbled in, slung from the Thorcraft's missile cradles.

"Are you awake, my love? What are you thinking?" he asked.

"Same as you," she retorted drowsily.

Had she read his mind this time? His heart lurched, but he brazened it out.

"Then tell me what you think about having negotiated the end of an interstellar war."

"When did I do that?" Wide awake now, she shifted onto her side. He was sure she hadn't been thinking about their written agreement any more than he had. "Are you talking about your promise never to attack another Saurian?"

"Yes, little peacemaker."

"Oh." She was thinking about it. The blood sang in his veins. His mind played lightning chess with the possibilities. It might not be necessary to tell her he'd had J-J arrested.

"I'll honor our bargain, unless—of course—they attack me first. I reserved the right of self-defense."

Djinni's loose hair tickled his face as she tilted her head in the darkness. "In exchange for peace, I'd have to live with you and love you."

"Very true."

"I'm not sure if I can. What you did was unforgivable."

Forgive me, he wished in the long, dark silence. He did not say it. She did not take orders, he did not offer apologies.

"Even if I could forgive you, how do I know you'd keep your word? Knowing you, as soon as you've consummated this so-called marriage, you'll go back on your promise."

"Ah!" He understood. But he had what Grievous would call "an ace in the hole." J-J was back on the negotiating table. "Would a meaningful gesture of good faith convince you, my love?"

Lights flashed on his forearm communicator.

"What?" Tarrant-Arragon snarled.

"Sir, the good news is, a certain party who shall remain nameless didn't do it."

"Grievous, it is our wedding night," Tarrant-Arragon said, warning Grievous that Djinni was listening. "My bride may not mind the interruption, but I am not pleased. What was it that the 'certain party' did not do?"

"Assassinate you, Sir. We've had word from War-star Leader Reivven. The honeymoon resort was attacked by Reman marauders at its dawn, Sir."

Tarrant-Arragon felt Djinni become very still and tense.

"You see, my love, we were supposed to be at a polar resort," he explained. "There were elaborate security arrangements made for our safety—including an orbiting An'Koori war-star to protect us from aerial attack. Grievous, tell me exactly what happened."

Grievous told him.

They were keeping something from her, Djinni realized. Grievous had always seemed forthright. Now his coy references to a "certain party" made her suspicious.

What did they not want her to know? They couldn't realize that J-J was Commander Jason, or they would not think it impossible that he was responsible for the attack.

What she didn't understand was how J-J could carry out an attack from his An'Koori war-star without Reivven's knowledge, or why having failed in his mission, he would report the "Reman" attack and then pursue these imaginary Remans.

"We're returning to the Palace, Grievous. Message ends," Tarrant-Arragon said, and rolled out of his high-tech hammock.

"What about our agreement?" Djinni demanded.

"What about it?"

"Damn you, I knew you wouldn't keep your word," she lashed out. "There's no point trying to love you, is there?"

Chapter Twenty-one

The honeymoon was over before it had even begun. Tarrant-Arragon stormed into his suite, carrying his furious little mate to hide the torn state of her dress from Palace eyes.

Why did she think he'd broken his word? It made no sense, unless J-J was somehow invoved with the Remans. The idea that she might still care for J-J maddened him.

These slack damn Reman marauders had snatched away his happiness. His careful progress had unraveled. His credibility was in tatters, and he couldn't retrieve it by telling her that J-J could not have attacked the official honeymoon resort, because J-J was a prisoner aboard the Ark Imperial.

She wouldn't look at him. She wouldn't speak. Carnality, how could he bear this unsensical estrangement? He wouldn't!

"I don't know where you got the idea that I've reneged on our agreement." Swallowing his pride, he spoke through gritted teeth. "You heard Grievous as well as I did. The perpetrators escaped in Reman starfighters. What makes you think Saurian Knights were involved?"

"Put me down, please."

He put her down. On his bed. She scrambled off as if he'd dropped her in a bed of hot coals.

"Djinni, I can't overlook an assassination attempt, even a failed one. Surely you can understand that?"

"Excuse me." She stalked into his bathroom. He let her go.

Tarrant-Arragon flung himself on the bed, flicked aside his flag, and scowled at the array of Message Waiting and Intruder Warning lights blinking on his screens.

First things first. Using his communicator, he checked on the irrational little mate. He'd never seen her so angry. Catlike, she vented her feelings by doing her business in his shower. On the other hand, her behavior was not dangerous.

Tarrant-Arragon shook his head. It made him crazy that she had to witness his necessary ruthlessness just when he'd begun to win back her good opinion. He badly wanted to love and reassure her, but he also had a crisis to deal with and an armada to call up. He brought his equerry onto the screen.

"Well?"

"Your Imperial Highness, the Saurian Dragon wishes to speak with you. We are trying to track, my Lord, but he is hologramming via multiple relays out of a moving base."

That meant it would be a one-way communication, but Djinni didn't need to know that. Tarrant-Arragon saw his chance to correct at least one misstep.

"Activate my projection field. Keep trying to get a fix. Record this." Tarrant-Arragon sprang off the end of the bed and stepped onto the pentagonal pattern on the carpet.

Even if the Dragon couldn't see or hear him raise the subject of peace talks, Djinni would. Moreover, why else would the Dragon be seeking an audience if not to claim or disclaim responsibility for the "assassination" attempt? Either way, Djinni would be disabused of any vain hope she might be cherishing that J-J had tried to rescue her.

Pleased with his strategy, Tarrant-Arragon folded his arms. "Put him through."

The projection was of poor quality, but gradually the tornado of glitter resolved into a majestic figure. Tarrant-Arragon was intensely interested. He'd never seen the Saurian Dragon before, and had not known whether his enemy was a two-legged anthropoid type or some less efficient life-form.

What he saw was a tall male wearing a long red robe over pale yellow thoracic body armor and long, slashed nether-robes. The headmask was distinctive and hid everything but the Saurian Dragon's extraordinary salted-fire blue eyes.

Tarrant-Arragon inclined his head slightly, as one warrior would to his respected, but defeated, foe.

"My respects, Saurian Dragon," he began solely for Djinni's benefit. "I have sought a peace conference, and thank you—"

"Hear me, cradle-raider! We curse Djinni-vera. We strip her of her Knighthood. We disown her and drink to her death in miscarriage. She is less than nothing to us!"

In a vicious hiss of static, the image dissolved and faded.

The Dragon never mentioned the assassination attempt. Of all the self-indulgent stupidity! Tarrant-Arragon stared into fizzled space unseeingly. To risk so much for a meaningless outburst . . .

A gasping sob. Djinni was on the far side of the projection field, white-faced, both hands over her mouth, looking shattered.

"Oh, my love, I had no idea the Dragon was such a fool. I'm sorry you heard that. It was unjust," he said, his voice hoarse with sympathy. "But it's war, beloved, nothing personal."

"Of course it's personal," Djinni retorted, too distressed to realize what she'd implied until too late. She turned away to face the A-shaped, black-gold-tinted window wall.

"Perhaps you're right. Let's take it very personally. Your death in miscarriage is a terrible curse—on me as well as on you, or would be . . ." He came up behind her and placed comforting hands on her bowed shoulders. "Ah, don't cry."

His skilled fingers massaged her neck. She stilled.

"Little love, does this outburst change your mind about whether Saurian Knights attacked us? If the Dragon wishes death in miscarriage upon you, do you think he is more or less likely to have sent assassins to kill us on our honeymoon?"

Djinni opened her mouth and shut it again. She saw where Tarrant-Arragon was going. There was no way the Dragon would come out of this prosecutorial line of questioning looking good.

"I'd like to know what the Saurian Dragon was thinking when he knighted you."

"I can't testify about his state of mind," Djinni shot back a line borrowed from an old courtroom drama.

His reflection grinned appreciatively. "Then tell me why you think he'd welcome a Djinn into his organization. I take it the Saurian Dragon knows that you're part-Djinn?"

Djinni didn't dare to reply.

"Knowing you, I'm sure he knows. You're too honorable for your own good, my dear. If he hadn't known, you'd have told him. So it makes no sense to strip you of your Knighthood when in time it might be used to convince superstitious fools that you—as my widow, perhaps—fulfill the prophecies about a Saurian Royal Djinn."

"It's not like that," she whispered.

"No? Well, I can think of one other possibility. I've always wondered why the Dragon left you so vulnerable. You know the chess term 'a poisoned pawn,' don't you?"

Djinni was outraged at the idea.

"You can't think the Dragon wanted you to abduct me!"

"How else do we make sense of his insane reaction just now? If he knows you are Djinn, does he know you're rutrageous?" His soothing hands cupped her throat from behind. "Might he be furious that you didn't give us all the rut-rage at our wedding?"

"The Saurian Dragon isn't capable of such infamy."

"Isn't he? Suppose I'd killed all my male relatives, all the heads of state, and all the War-star Leaders. The Empire would have been leaderless. The Communicating Worlds would have been—justifiably—up in arms. Who would have stepped in?"

J-J! Was that why he'd been there? Djinni saw her eyes widen involuntarily. Tarrant-Arragon was watching. He knew she knew something. A hurtful counterattack was her only defense.

"That was not the Dragon's plan. I know him well enough to know that much."

"How well do you know him? Think about it. Don't you know that even charismatic people lie?"

"I know *you* do," she gasped, and preempted further discussion by deliberately bursting into tears.

He'd missed something. For some reason, his gentle, adorably predictable darling had become highly unpredictable. The Dragon had cursed her, and she'd turned on *him*.

There was a third dynamic at work. Djinni knew something he didn't. He intended to find out what it was.

She'd said something she thought she shouldn't have at least twice. Maybe more. A small twist of her lips and the pulse in her neck betrayed her whenever she lied.

He hadn't checked her heartbeat in front of her, not wanting her to know about the state-of-the-art surveillance necklace that gave him her heart rate and recorded and transmitted everything she said. Now it was time to put it all together.

He heard the intruder long before he reached the doorway of his office—the scrabble of long nails on a command pad. Martia-Djulia was watching his recording of her activity with Jason.

"An irregular virgin's balling? Princess, do you always make coarse puns to strangers?"

"In future, Martia-Djulia, you will speak of my Princess Consort with respect," Tarrant-Arragon growled.

His sister screeched, and spun guiltily around. She did not have the presence of mind to turn off the footage.

"Also, you will stay out of my quarters."

"You don't understand." Martia-Djulia wrung her hands.

"Don't I? You and Father discussed your plan to trap an impulsive lover into becoming your mate. In my office. Unhappily for you, Jason is my friend. I will not be your cat's-paw."

To his disgust, Martia-Djulia burst into tears. He looked

away. On footage, she and Jason were talking about the existence of Jason's adoring, missing fiancée. Sentimental rot.

"Oh, Tiger, do you think Jason would have stayed if I'd acted virginal and reluctant?" she sobbed.

"Slack damn!" Tarrant-Arragon swore. "You're asking me?"

"I've never felt so appreciated, so feminine, as I felt with him. Don't look at me like that. Don't you males talk about . . . ?"

"I never discuss my preferences, or my private perversions."

"Oh, I have to know . . ." Martia-Djulia's myopic blue eyes overflowed again. "Can a forced mate be enthusiastic in bed?"

This, of course, was the question burning in his own heart.

"I said, I'm not prepared to discuss my sex life," he snapped. "In general terms, I might point out that unwillingness in a female is not insurmountable. With male anatomy, unless Jason is a Djinn—and I'll kill him if he is—his unwillingness could be a slack damn hydraulic problem for you."

"I want him to be happy." Martia-Djulia clasped her hands over her bosom, as if she thought her heart might leap out of her chest at the thought of Jason. "Do you think he'd be happy with me if I force him to be my mate?"

"No," Tarrant-Arragon said with brutal honesty.

"Do you think there's a chance he'll find his missing bride, discover that he doesn't want her, and come back to me?"

Tarrant-Arragon considered. "That depends how good she is in bed, how good he thought you were, why she went missing, and whether he is broad-minded. Your chances would be somewhat better if he were part-Djinn and if they'd been your pheromones scenting up the palace on my wedding day. It wasn't you, was it?"

"No." She snuffled. "But my chances wouldn't be better. You just said you'd kill him if he were Djinn."

"So I did," he agreed urbanely.

"Jason must never know that I filmed him, or that I meant to force him to marry me." Her voice shook.

"I won't tell him. Turn away." As soon as Martia-Djulia obeyed, he entered his private erase code. "All gone," he said.

The monitor showed the footage as a comet tail being sucked into a black hole. "That was everything we recorded on Jason since the festivities began. If you like, none of it ever happened—unless he compounded his insolence by getting you pregnant."

Which, of course, was supposed to be as laughable an idea as Jason being Djinn. Martia-Djulia didn't laugh.

"Thank you, Tiger. I think." Martia-Djulia fell to her knees and kissed his Ring hand. "I'm sorry for the things I said about Djinni. In future, I'll try to be nice."

"If I'd known a hard docking would make you so amiable—" Tarrant-Arragon started to tease her, then reconsidered. "Ah, I should have kept the footage and used it. Don't cry. If Jason doesn't come back to you, there may be more like him on his home-world. When I've dealt with my would-be assassins, I'll make serious inquiries about Jason's origins."

An'Koori Bridge, Commander Jason's War-Star

"Prince Tarrant-Arragon wouldn't atomize a World like Rema to avenge an attack on a tiny Djinndom resort?" the An'Koori War-star Leader Reivven said with a vicarious shudder. "Would he?"

"Why not?" Jason said, feeling savagely masochistic. "The Great Tiger isn't looking for a Djinn virgin anymore, is he?"

It was Commander Jason's third day in pursuit of his own decoys, and he regretted the open use of Reman Shrike starfighters. They should have been disguised. Jason groaned inwardly.

He was appalled to think of what he'd started. Moreover, his conscience about the fate of Rema wasn't the only reason he was wretchedly ashamed of himself.

"I hear the Imperial Ambassador and his household pointedly left the planet," Horn't said, rolling one of his chameleon eyes toward the Message decoder.

Jason glanced across the Bridge to the engineering station

where Horn't was six-handedly going about the official business that unsuspecting, draft-dodging An'Koori paid him to do. Despite the serious topic, Horn't was grinning. Jason knew why. Feya's influence on the infatuated War-star Leader was laughable. Not only had Reivven installed her in her own cabin, but he'd turned into an incorrigible gossip in an effort to become interesting.

Feya was doing a good job of distracting the horny An'Koori both on and off the Bridge. So far, Jason had switched reality and virtual reality onto the Bridge screens with impunity.

"I have it on good authority, the bride was very reluctant," Reivven chortled. The Imperial love-life was a hot topic, thanks to Feya, who knew someone who'd met the bride when she was the love-slave. "All the more fun for Tarrant-Arragon! No wonder he's furious that his honeymoon was interrupted."

Jason blushed under his tan. He'd been titillated by the stories that the Prince's love-slave had been drugged, beaten, and chained to the Imperial bed and he'd embellished the scandals in the retelling. He'd considered only the effect of a heavy-duty sex life on Tarrant-Arragon's reputation.

Now he knew the hapless girl was Djinni, he felt doubly responsible for her. His blood throbbed painfully, even in his eyelids, as he thought of the abuse she'd suffered. If his alibi and cover held, he was still going to rescue the poor damaged kid.

Jason winced at another secret worry. He'd heard Bronty complaining about "that ineffective camisole." He was deeply humiliated by his suspicion that the Dragon's scent-trap had caused the wrong Great Djinn—himself—to behave disgracefully.

And he was angry. Too angry to attempt to speak to the old fool Dragon, even if he could under the heightened security.

Only time, he supposed, would tell whether he'd fixated on Djinni's scent, which Bronty had planted on Martia-Djulia, or on Martia-Djulia's generous body.

This confusion could ruin his life. There was a solution, but it was insupportably immoral. If he were already the Emperor, he could get away with it, but he couldn't marry both his cousins and expect the Saurians to support his claim to be a plausible reforming Emperor.

Ark Imperial—Officers' Gym

Tarrant-Arragon's masculine frustrations needed an outlet, perhaps in violence. He went down to the gym looking for a fight.

He folded his arms across his chest, leaned against a rack of fighting staves, and silently watched the elegantly lethal White Knight, who refused to admit that he was J-J, fencing against a light beam.

"Why did you attend my wedding in disguise?"

Disappointingly, his rival continued to slash airborne dust particles. His Saurian insolence reminded Tarrant-Arragon of the way Djinni had treated him when they first met.

"You had a perfectly good invitation, issued to you . . ." Tarrant-Arragon consulted a list on his forearm communicator, deliberately flexing his biceps in the process, "in the name of, ah, 'Rhett. Is 'Rhett an alias, like J-J?"

"'Rhett is an abbreviation. My initial apostrophe implies as much," the White Knight answered.

"Have my people treated you well?" Tarrant-Arragon bared his teeth in a polished predator smile.

"I have been courteously refused my rights, and my diplomatic status has been ignored. Otherwise, I've not been abused."

"An interesting choice of words." Tarrant-Arragon stared pointedly at his rival's jaw, still purplish from the fight that Grievous had mentioned.

He felt a twinge of regret that the surveillance footage had somehow been erased. If he couldn't find an excuse to blacken this smooth bastard's eyes, he'd have enjoyed watching someone else beat the backbone out of him.

"You know your rights?" Tarrant-Arragon called up further

data on his prisoner. "Hmmm. I see you do. You're the ambassadorial Knight for the Eurydycean Dodecahedron. My *mother* speaks well of you."

Touché. The White Knight blinked but made a rapid recovery.

"*All* females speak well of me." The prisoner shrugged. "I was told that Djinni-vera is a prisoner on the Ark Imperial. I demand to see her."

"You have no rights regarding her," Tarrant-Arragon snarled, infuriated by the sexual innuendo about his mother. As he glared at 'Rhett, he noticed that his rival was young for his high and very honorable rank. Nearer Djinni's age, slackness damn him.

"As her brother Knight, I do." Apart from the croak in his voice, the Knight showed no emotion.

Instead it was he, Tarrant-Arragon, who was wild with jealousy. He could taste the black bitterness of it, like thick liquid lava rising in his throat.

"I have taken Djinni. She is mine. I love her passion—ah, very much." He half said "passionately" on purpose and pretended to correct himself to underscore his meaning. He knew he was behaving badly. So was the so-called 'Rhett aka J-J, and too cowardly to admit it.

Tarrant-Arragon called up Djinni's lifesigns on his forearm communicator and watched the dance of her heartbeat on the monitor. The thought of her calmed him.

He felt 'Rhett's eyes on him and glanced at the mirror wall, seeing them side by side for the first time. He studied the younger—damn—male's dark curly hair, defiant posture, and seven-foot stature. At that moment, 'Rhett raised an eyebrow. It brought to mind something Grievous had said and that Djinni had unconsciously let slip.

Grievous was right. They could be brothers, or first cousins. The time had come to confront Djinni about J-J.

"Djinni, you once said you want babies—" Tarrant-Arragon let his casually unfastened robe fall open as he moved up the bed toward her on all fours.

The nervous little mate was up to her old tricks with prickly sewing projects in bed. She pulled a threaded needle on him. Avoiding being stabbed, he touched her bare forearm. "Who else could give you babies? Can J-J?"

Her face gave him his answer. Since the night she'd run away from him, he'd been careful not to mention J-J to her except when she was asleep. As he'd intended, she thought he'd forgotten all about J-J. Now she knew he hadn't.

"Who is J-J? *What* is J-J? And what is he to you?"

"I vowed never to tell." She tried to shake her head and her whole body shuddered, but she continued to do whatever it was she was doing to one of her black dresses.

"Then I will tell you what I suspect, and you may choose whether or not to set the record straight. J-J is either your brother or your cousin, a Djinn and a Saurian Knight. He's the reason you were terrified of sex until I took you in hand."

His tone carried a deliberate undercurrent of menace that implied endless vengeful possibilities left unsaid but which Tarrant-Arragon might consider.

In the silence, he heard her needle pierce the fabric twice. Then the little mate rolled her sewing into a ball and put it aside in a gesture of surrender.

"He never touched me. I haven't seen him for over thirteen years, though we were betrothed seventeen years ago. I owe him my loyalty. Is there some way I can save him?"

"Not if you'd rather be with him."

Instead of taking what she unwillingly offered, Tarrant-Arragon flung himself onto his stomach beside her. Disconsolately, he opened a computer file and stabbed at his keypad. *Ah, slack damn,* he thought, *why did I say that? I don't want her to pretend to love me.*

Djinni read his thoughts and, despite everything, she felt sorry for him. "For your information, Tarrant-Arragon, I haven't decided whom I'd rather be with."

"Slack damn!" he retorted, but he wrapped an arm around her waist and drew her close. "You're a soothing little presence when you're not driving me crazy. So you haven't decided, hmmm?"

"That's an An'Koori program." She nodded at what was on the bedhead screen-wall instead of answering an impossibly open-ended question. "Why are you so interested in them?"

"I audit the auditors. The An'Koori are the most corrupt of all the worlds I rule. Look at this. Lax inventory control, sloppy record-keeping, evasion of the draft—"

"Demilitarize them, then. They shouldn't be a war power. As I told J-J, they ought to be shepherds."

"Shepherds?" He lifted his eyebrows, then rolled onto his back and hauled her on top of him. "On watery An'Koor?"

"I wouldn't want an An'Koori at my back in a fight, would you?" Djinni made her case as seriously as possible. "Besides, they'd enjoy herding sheep around. You know how manly and bold they feel when they are bullying female creatures."

"Is that why you thought I was an An'Koori?" He chuckled. "It's an interesting idea. I'll consider it." Then she felt his fingers twine in her hair and a note of jealousy crept into his voice. "So you and J-J discussed how you'd carve up my Empire?"

"We call it 'setting the world to rights,' Your Highness. In a free society, everyone does it all the time. Wise world leaders welcome better ideas."

"Such as turning the An'Koori into shepherds?" he teased. "Suppose I did. Who would I put in charge? J-J?"

"Oh!" Djinni was appalled that she'd mentioned J-J and An'Koor in the same breath.

"Djinni, I don't know how to tell you this, but I have your J-J."

"Oh, Stars! Why? What did he do?"

"Nothing serious. Don't be alarmed, my love. The night before our wedding, two White Knights and a Star Forces officer got into a fight over my sister. There was a discrepancy during some name-calling, which is how Grievous knew that J-J was using a false name and felt justified in making the arrest."

"You mean J-J has an alibi for the assassination attempt?" she squeaked.

"The best—unless he masterminded the attack from the Ark Imperial's dungeons."

"So you'll let him go?"

Instead of answering, he turned them onto their sides and curled his body around her like a spoon. "Mmmm," he purred. "Maybe. When I've figured out how to win your love fairly. Unless, of course, J-J happens to be a Great Djinn."

Djinni swallowed hard. "I want to see him."

"Mmmm. I was afraid of that," Tarrant-Arragon said.

Chapter Twenty-two

"Your Imperial Highness, last time we met, you said your mother speaks of me—" The prisoner froze.

Tarrant-Arragon wasn't surprised that 'Rhett had asked. It had been something of a bombshell. The implications were that Tarrant-Arragon knew where his fugitive mother was, had allowed her to continue her subversive work, and spoke with her about other Saurian Knights. It was enough to make even the Saurian Dragon break into a cold sweat.

However, this was not what had silenced 'Rhett.

"Oh, Stars!" Djinni whispered beside him. "I thought—"

Watching jealously, Tarrant-Arragon observed a warning look from 'Rhett and a slight shake of his head. Djinni's eyes widened and she nodded, as if in answer to an unspoken question.

"I'm all right," she said. "And you?"

'Rhett smiled and turned his attention back to his host. "Sir, I was about to ask—are you and your mother on speaking terms?"

"Indeed we are. However, I knew I was taking a risk when I took Djinni to see her."

Tarrant-Arragon was pleased to see that 'Rhett looked shocked. Djinni's reaction was more animated.

"You did?" Realization dawned, and his beloved punched an Imperial biceps. "The fortune-teller *was* your mother? 'Rhett, his mother read my runes—rigged—and told me it was my destiny to go with this villain. Tarrant-Arragon, you *devil*! Did she know who I was?"

"No, my love. She just wanted me to settle down with a nice girl." He took possession of her fist, delighted with the byplay he'd provoked. "I've known for gestates that my mother works for your Saurian Dragon. Saurian spies—most recently Stegosaurus—vanish once they get into her vicinity. I haven't worked out how. I've never cracked her communication codes either, but then, I haven't tried because I don't want to catch her."

"You don't?" 'Rhett frowned. "Why? Is she a double agent?"

"Not as far as I know," Tarrant-Arragon said, enjoying himself. "My father has vindictive tendencies. He can't do much about it without my help, and I refuse to be an accomplice to matricide. One day, with Djinni's help, I might attempt to reconcile my parents."

"Do you think about that?" 'Rhett choked. "How very romantic of you!"

Tarrant-Arragon swung Djinni's hand gently. This meeting was a test for all three of them, and they were acquitting themselves astonishingly well.

"I'm not the only romantic, 'Rhett. Djinni seems to believe she can rehabilitate me and put a stop to my, ah, tyrannical excesses. Don't you, my love?"

'Rhett's expression was priceless. He blinked, and dropped his guard.

"I have inferred that we are cousins, 'Rhett." Tarrant-Arragon inclined his head, as one warrior to another. "What is your real name?"

"Djarrhett," 'Rhett rasped.

Tarrant-Arragon nodded. The first J of J-J. *Jaera is for a "J" pronunciation, however it's spelled,* Djinni had once said. "Simple J or royal Dj?"

"The latter."

Djinni's hand trembled in his. Tarrant-Arragon intertwined his fingers with hers.

"You're a Djinn and a Saurian Knight, 'Rhett? You could easily unseat the present Saurian Dragon. Do you think he has considered what a threat you could be to him?"

"The Dragon is aware of the possibilities."

Djinni looked up. A grin was exchanged as if 'Rhett and Djinni were sharing a joke. Tarrant-Arragon grinned, too. He was learning a lot. "Ah, while we're on the subject of Djinn powers, 'Rhett, I'm curious about the extent of yours. Djinni tells me that you never touched her."

"You might say that I am not fully Djinn." 'Rhett took his meaning. "I caught an Earthling infection as a boy. I lost my VNO, saturniid, and my tonsils."

"Almost a sensory eunuch?" Tarrant-Arragon chuckled with relief. 'Rhett was no threat. His rageless status justified a breach with tradition. "Then you're safe to have around. We can do business. There's something I want to show you."

He reached into a sleeve pocket as he spoke. "My Djinni has requested my written undertaking that I'll never attack another Saurian. I'd be interested in the opinion of a ranking Knight."

Watching Djinni, he passed 'Rhett the handwritten paper, torn from Djinni's legal pad, and was pleased to see her eyes widen.

"Yes, my love, I not only signed it but had it witnessed by War-star Leader Slayt of the Ark Imperial, and by Grievous."

'Rhett was smiling, perhaps at the incongruous splendor of the Imperial seal on this humble document or perhaps at something Djinni had drawn in the ruled margin. Tarrant-Arragon saw no significance in a crude outline of a heart-shape with a smiley face. 'Rhett seemed fascinated by the childish doodle and traced a finger over it. He glanced at Djinni.

"Well? Would this document constitute a peace initiative?"

"It would." 'Rhett nodded. "If it were ratified."

"Ratification is the issue." Tarrant-Arragon held out his free hand, and 'Rhett returned the paper. "I was hoping to prevail upon the Dragon to sign it. At present it seems unlikely. A complication has arisen. . . ." Djinni tugged her hand free. "What, again, my love? Go on, then."

He smiled as Djinni made her way to the officers' showers. 'Rhett raised an inquiring eyebrow.

"This, ah, frequency is psychosomatic. I've always had an unsettling effect on warriors. Djinni stands up to me very well. My poor little Tigress, she's had a hard time. The vomiting is new; she started it when she found out who I am. She also sleeps a lot and whispers to herself. If she doesn't settle soon, I'll send for Ka'Nych. I'll give her a bit longer to get over the latest upset. The Dragon has cursed and disowned her."

"Poor Djinni," 'Rhett said. No question, he cared about her. "Supposing she 'lives with and loves' you, what will you do?"

"About peace? I shall follow the ancient principle of divide and rule. I'll make peace with any Saurians who are reasonable. Yourself, for instance. I'd like to find you a replacement bride and a modest kingdom of no strategic value. I was considering An'Koor. Djinni believes that we should deprive An'Koor of its war-power status."

"You asked her?" 'Rhett threw him a narrowed look.

"She told me." Tarrant-Arragon sighed. "She is not afraid to tell me things which I do not necessarily enjoy hearing. To be honest, 'Rhett, I've too many responsibilities: private, public, judicial, military, and royal. I find it hard to delegate, especially when experience has taught me not to trust anyone. One of my deepest regrets is that I don't have brothers. I could use a cousin. If the vice-regency of An'Koor doesn't appeal to you, would you accept a position as one of my equerries?"

"Either occupation would damage my Knightly credibility." 'Rhett grinned. "And would be a conflict of interest."

"Only if my peace initiatives fail."

Djinni reappeared. It was an opportunity to demonstrate

that she was no prisoner. "My love, I'm going to show 'Rhett the Bridge. Will you come? Or meet me later?"

"Later." She smiled. "Now I'm here, I think I'll exercise."

Tarrant-Arragon gave her a husbandly kiss on the cheek and moved on, doing his best to ignore the beseeching look she gave his rival.

"Ah, 'Rhett, perhaps you've heard that there was an attempted assassination? Officially, I'm blaming Rema. We're proceeding unhurriedly to avenge ourselves, and waiting for the Saurians to do something about the injustice."

"You don't think that a softer image . . . ?" 'Rhett thought he was making a helpful suggestion.

"I do not," Tarrant-Arragon replied forcefully. "You cannot imagine how convenient it is to quell the rebel quadrants by merely raising an eyebrow instead of having to commit gory atrocities and sacrifice productive lives."

'Rhett had almost grown used to being startled. Tarrant-Arragon was making an obvious effort to be pleasant, but much of what he revealed about himself had been corroborated independently by Grievous. Then there was the way Djinni looked at Tarrant-Arragon when she thought no one was watching.

'Rhett scratched his eyebrow and wondered whether this civilized Tarrant-Arragon was Djinni's doing, or whether the Communicating Worlds had always been much mistaken about "The Terror of the Dodecahedrons."

"Tiger on the Bridge!" a duty officer announced the presence of His Imperial Highness.

"As you were," Tarrant-Arragon responded.

'Rhett watched closely, tried to read lips as The Great Tiger toured the Bridge, and noted the professional manner in which an incoming message for Tarrant-Arragon was handed to him.

"I think this might be a chance to show Djinni how merciful I can be," Tarrant-Arragon commented when he rejoined 'Rhett.

"Do you need to do that?" 'Rhett said carefully.

"Every chance I get. She wouldn't believe me if I told her

I'm not quite the monster she thinks I am. She needs proof."
Tarrant-Arragon tapped the message against his upper lip.
"This is an invitation to visit War-star Leader Reivven's war-
star, to dine, and to hear the voluntary confession of one of the
assassins who attacked our honeymoon resort."

"Will you go?" 'Rhett kept his voice neutral.

"The trip is unnecessary, but it might be fun. Besides, I want
Djinni to meet a friend of mine. I'd like to see if she can defeat
Jason at chess."

"That should be interesting," 'Rhett said, sorry that he
couldn't be a fly on the wall. There'd be fireworks tonight, he
was sure. Djinni was playing a deep game. As was he.

Djinni glanced apprehensively at her mate. He almost always
flew silently, but halfway to their dinner host's war-star, he'd
started to swear.

Though she had no idea why 'Rhett was playing the impostor, the real J-J was still a threat to her happiness and to
Tarrant-Arragon's life. But, given his present dangerous mood,
she'd be courting disaster for herself and even more so for
'Rhett if she informed Tarrant-Arragon that J-J was still at
large and might try again.

"Another damn zzzing mercenary!" Tarrant-Arragon parodied the unmistakably foreign accents of the Approach Con-
troller as he maneuvered into an open docking collar. "Are
there any An'Koori in the An'Koori Star Forces?"

Having docked and cut the power, he turned to unfasten her
harnesses and patted her twined fingers.

"Don't worry, little mate. I'll be civilized. I won't spoil our
evening. You're about to meet my best friend, Jason." He
turned his attention to his own belts.

No one had told her they were going to dine on Commander Jason's war-star. Now it was impossible to warn him that
they might be walking into a trap without seeming like a
traitress.

Go ahead! her intuition told her. With a sudden spurt of energy, she threw open the canopy and scrambled out.

"Wait!" he barked.

She did not wait. She had to assess the danger. Prevent it.

She didn't recognize the White Knight a hundred paces away in the shadow of a docked starfighter, but she felt the disturbed psychic vibrations of a fanatic. The thin Knight's weapon seemed out of place in a highly advanced world. It was a Desert Eagle Magnum—a human killer's weapon.

No time to wonder How? Or Why? Faced with such an accurate weapon, Djinni had no doubt the target was Tarrant-Arragon's head.

Time slowed. It was like watching a film frame by frame on an ancient slide projector. She saw the barrel arcing stiffly in the assassin's fully extended, two-handed grip.

She felt her mate's anger, like a vortex sucking at the edges of her concentration as he stormed after her.

"No-o-o-o, Bronty!" a male voice howled.

The shooter squeezed the trigger. Djinni visualized a .357 Magnum bullet moving at 1,250 feet per second—too fast for a warning to be understood. Too fast for Djinn-craft to stop it, even if she knew how. So she did the only thing she could.

Apart from the powerful blow that knocked her arm backward, Djinni hardly felt the bullet hit her hand. Then, as the crack of a shot reverberated around the bay, Djinni felt her knees buckle, and the first messages of pain exploded in her brain. Through a blackening haze, she heard shouts. Tarrant-Arragon snapped an order.

"Damn! She's fainted again. Take her! I'll deal with the assassin."

Djinni felt herself being thrust into strong hands. Through the waterfall roar of pain that filled her head and fogged her hearing, Djinni heard her name murmured. Someone lifted her. She thought she heard other orders, the escape-blast of four or five starfighters, and then her world went dark.

On the Ark Imperial the lights went out.

"Bugger me! Did we do that?" Grievous leapt out of bed in the pitch darkness. "Rats, love. Did I blow something?"

The lovely, talented, and very well-traveled Feya giggled as if she thought he was being witty. Grievous ignored her, and by the fading gray-light of a shut-down screen, he scrabbled to remove her alien porn view-disc from the computer outlet.

"Garn-darn it! Nothing for it. I'd better go and confess." He fumbled for his key-ring torch. "You'd better come with me. My Tigron war-star shipmates are going to want to know where you got this dirty video."

Set, and recharge blast shields. Tarrant-Arragon made sure his Thorcraft was adequately defended before he did anything else. Complacency was not one of his weaknesses, even when he was on a simple hunt-and-kill foray. He didn't anticipate much difficulty with the assassin's starfighter, but there was always the possibility that the entire botched exercise had been the lure to lead him into an ambush.

"Tarrant-Arragon to Ark Imperial." He might as well log in. There was no point in forgoing an advantage when one had one, even though he didn't want Slayt to send out wingmen. In deep space it was dangerous to have too many attackers for a single target. He could do without having to dodge friendly fire.

"Ark Imperial? Slayt?" he snarled, his fury mounting over his war-star's silence. The space-waves were static soup. He was on his own. No matter.

He rechecked the systems he'd checked outward-bound, before he risked Djinni in the small fighter. For an instant, he allowed himself to worry about her. His frightened, fragile mate. Something was wrong with her. She was fainting too often. She'd have to see Ka'Nych. That decided, he focused on the hunt.

He checked his rear sweep. No, he wasn't being followed. He locked his automatic pursuit systems on the fleeing assassin and set the controls at smart-closing speed to be sure the enemy couldn't suddenly drop his foils, brake, and force the pursuing Thorcraft to overshoot. He'd had enough of being shot at.

"Slayt. Grievous. Respond." He tried his forearm communicator. This time, someone was replying. From the broken syllables Tarrant-Arragon inferred that one of the Ark Imperial's systems had been frazzled by some kind of computer virus.

The damage had been contained. Outriders were on their way to other war-stars to tow in umbilicals for supplementary power. Tarrant-Arragon's War-star Leaders were competent.

A quick check showed that he was not making up space on the assassin. Normal calculations didn't apply. Apparently, the enemy craft had been enhanced.

Tarrant-Arragon took the star-drive out of auto and selected maximum manual thrust, calculating that this was going to be a longer chase than he'd anticipated. He swore. He ought to have delegated. And he was worried about having left Djinni—even with his best friend.

"Damn! She's forced our hand. . . . Send three remotes and one volunteer after him. . . ."

Through a fog of pain, Djinni tried to make sense of the chaos of shouts around her.

"Aren't you going, Jason?" She thought she recognized the buzzing voice as the one Tarrant-Arragon had mocked.

"This is the prize." Someone put a gentle hand on her belly. Someone was a lot more savvy than Tarrant-Arragon.

She was being held down by unfamiliar arms, on what seemed to be a hastily cleared map-table. She protested. The people either didn't understand her or purposely ignored her. So she screamed.

One of the uniformed males clutched his ears and swore vehemently. Other people yelled in dismay as fused atoms of silicon and sodium vibrated and danced apart, causing glass-type substances to shatter in delicate instruments.

"Shut her up!" someone shouted in An'Koori.

At the same moment, the male with sensitive ears bent over her. His personal force was enough to intimidate anyone—except someone accustomed to Tarrant-Arragon's tempers.

"Djinni-vera," he roared in English. "For pity's sake, kid.

Don't you know me?" He was holding her down, one strong hand pinning each of her arms, and he radiated exasperation.

J-J! Djinni looked up into a handsome face that was stronger, leaner, and more virile than she remembered, and made menacing by the diagonal scar running from the bridge of the nose to the widest point of his jaw. His eyes were all wrong. Djinni tried to focus her pain-dazed eyes.

"No, Djetthro-Jason. I don't know you. I don't want to know you. Don't touch me. What have you done to your eyes?"

"Ssshhh. Colored contacts, darling. Don't announce it. And try to call me Jason, just Jason. That's my cover name. We don't want to confuse people, even if they are on our side."

"I haven't decided whose side I'm on. And don't you dare kill him."

"That wasn't the plan, believe me. I wanted to talk."

"I wanted you to talk, too."

"Jason, she needs surgery!" someone said urgently.

"Crazy females!" a droning voice muttered in An'Koori. "I can't believe she tried to catch the bullet."

"What is all the fuss, little Dragon?" J-J said, ignoring the other voices. "You've got to let the doctor see your hand, kid."

"No drugs," Djinni said. "Don't touch me. I'm pregnant."

"I guessed you would be by now. Do you want to be pregnant?"

"How dare you ask!" Djinni was surprised at her own maternal savagery even as she hissed at him.

"Woah." He sounded startled. "I wasn't . . . I didn't mean . . . Pregnancy-friendly care," J-J snapped to someone. "Make sure you irrigate that wound well. What's that?"

"It's a saline drip, Commander. She needs blood, but we don't have her type."

"Give her some of mine," he ordered, and started to roll up his jumpsuit sleeve the old-fashioned way.

"No, thank you," Djinni whispered. "If it's a girl, I don't want her to have your hormones."

The medical team was regrouping about her like vultures.

"How far along are you?" J-J asked.

"Six or seven weeks. What difference does it make?"

"None, I suppose. If she's a girl, we could pretend she's mine. If it's a boy, the decision is more complicated."

"Jason! Orders. Are we trying to kill him?" someone said.

"No!" Djinni shouted as loudly as she could.

"Look, kiddo, this isn't the way I wanted it, but Bronty's started a war. I don't see what choice we have. Now, you'll have to excuse me. I'll come to you when the situation is under control. Okay?" Suddenly, J-J kissed her forehead. "Be good, brat. Patch her up, Doc, then put her on my bed."

"Are we trying to kill him?" someone repeated.

Djinni didn't hear what J-J said.

Chapter Twenty-three

Tarrant-Arragon had decided that he did not wish to kill the assassin. Yet.

Since the Ark Imperial was now back up to full operational performance, he relayed the assassin's course, ordered another war-star to intercept, and fired off a heat-seeking, painter missile to tag the quarry.

He turned back while he still had more than enough power to rendezvous with the Ark Imperial. As he maneuvered, he reconfigured his blast shields and recharged his weapons systems.

Grimly, he wondered why War-star Leader Reivven seemed to have no knowledge of the royal visit to his war-star, nor of Djinni's whereabouts. After this, the An'Koori would definitely forfeit their war-power status. An'Koor would get the toughest, meanest, military governor he could find. He might take the job himself.

He sensed the first Shrike before it was a blip on his zone screen. He cut his engines and glided on his inertia, waiting, invisible, and alert.

Four blips appeared. Two appeared to be in a scouting mode, and the other two sped toward him. Tarrant-Arragon observed, and waited to confirm that they were legitimate prey.

". . . kill him?" The question crackled out of the static.

Confirmation enough.

Tarrant-Arragon announced his presence with one shot, then powered away, avoiding the explosion debris. He circled into position below the second Shrike.

Sweeping in, Tarrant-Arragon locked on fired straight between its tail fins, and pulled out steeply in a vertical loop, not waiting to see the fireball. From the shock waves, he knew he'd scored. Two down, two to go.

"This is a devil of a coil."

Gingerly, Jason sat on the sleeping couch beside Djinni, being careful not to jostle her injured hand. He set down a tray of fruits and nuts and ran a medic's wand over her, ostensibly looking for shrapnel.

The crystals around her neck crackled. A thought pinged on the edge of his mind. There was something he ought to remember.

"I suppose Tarrant-Arragon gave you this? Do you feel like taking it off?"

"Yes. No," Djinni said. "I've better uses for my one good hand." She munched nuts and watched him, with eyes the color of oysters and mother-of-pearl, like the late-autumn sunrises he remembered on Earth.

"You know, Djinni, it wasn't my plan to murder him in front of you. You don't know Bronty, do you?"

Djinni glared. "It's not very honorable to pin all the blame on Bronty, even if she was the shooter. It was one of your guns."

"I mean, you girls are both Knights. I've known girls . . ." His thoughts were firing on all cylinders now.

"You don't say." She was hurt and angry, and deliberately taking everything the wrong way.

His trouble was a conflict of learned Earthling taboos and genetic imperatives. He should have kidnapped Djinni when she was a needy infant, in the manner of young male macaque apes, and groomed her to be his ideal mate. There hadn't been a mother to interfere, and Helispeta's supervision had been as predictable as the sweep of a lawn irrigation system.

"Girls share clothes and stuff." Not that he honestly thought that Djinni had knowingly supplied a loose cannon like Bronty with inflammatory underwear.

"And also your bed."

"Would you like to share my bed?" He grinned, happy to be distracted from the grimness of their situation.

"With whom?"

"Me."

"You and who else? With every female you've ever had unprotected sex with? No, thank you."

"Don't you think I have a right?"

"No, I don't! You threw away all your moral rights when you wrote a *one-sided* chastity clause into our betrothal contract."

Djinni was furious with him for telling his aides to put her on his bed, because every time he came to visit her everyone probably assumed that he got into it with her. He hadn't yet done so, but eventually he would need to sleep.

"Damn it, I've waited pretty much all your life—for you."

"No, you haven't," she fired back, disgusted by his hypocrisy. "I don't believe you've been celibate. In fact, I heard you have orgies." She was sorely tempted to say more—about Martia-Djulia, for instance—but he'd never been privileged to see film of himself having sex at fast-forward speed, and she wasn't about to tell him how ridiculous he'd looked.

He strode to a drinks bar and helped himself to a clear liquid that smelled as potent as tequila. He looked askance at her. She declined the unspoken offer with a quick headshake.

"Are you reading my mind, kiddo?" J-J asked abruptly.

"Your mind is too confused to read," she said, unwilling to admit that she knew what he was thinking.

"Damn right it's confused! I'm confused."

"It's simple. I can't love you. I love him."

Aboard the Ark Imperial all bets were off. From the Bridge to the condensation bilges, everyone hoped that His Imperial

Highness and Her Imperial Highness had merely had a misunderstanding—or so Grievous alleged. The Earthling also had the impudence to report that his shipmates were saying that the Terror of the Dodecahedrons patently needed to be loved.

"Next, Grievous, you'll dare to say I have a broken heart," Tarrant-Arragon snarled. A full Watch after he'd stormed back, alone, his temper was still the blackest ever seen. He knew it, and he didn't care to hide it.

He stood on the Bridge, waiting for the traitor to negotiate. The An'Koori war-star had not responded to demands that the Princess Consort be returned. He was furious with Djinni. Now he'd had time to replay events in his mind, it was painfully obvious that she'd been part of the plot. Why else would she have tried to run away as soon as they docked? Why else had she waved, if not as a signal to the assassin?

He'd no one to blame for his loss but himself. And Djinni.

Tarrant-Arragon noticed that the pounding in his chest had lessened. Sensation was returning to his extremities. He realized he was rubbing the side of his right hand against his thigh. His scowl deepened as he became aware of a dull ache.

"Word is, Sir, her hand is in much worse shape."

"What are you talking about?" Tarrant-Arragon glared at Grievous.

"They're saying that the little miss tried to catch the bullet. Of course, Sir, that's an impossible feat."

"Who says she tried?"

"The charming young ladies of the Imperial Escort Service, Sir. They have their own little bush telegraph. They all check in with each other between tricks, Sir. They're saying she saved your life."

"She saved my life?" His heart kicked him. Slack damn laxwit! he swore silently at himself. "I thought she'd betrayed me. She's hurt, you say?"

"Yes, Sir."

"Damn! If anything happens to her . . ." He'd think of vengeance later. Now was the time for cold efficiency. "My suite's systems are separate. They'd better not have been affected by the damn computer virus. We ought to be able to pick up her vital signs and hear what she's saying on the necklace-track.

"Grievous, get the prisoner. 'Rhett, J-J, I don't care what he wants to call himself. If he cooperates, we'll be civilized. If he won't help, I don't care what we have to do to him. I want my Djinni. And I want the traitors identified and taken. Alive."

"He can't be that good in bed. Can he?" Tarrant-Arragon's amplifiers kicked in mid-conversation at a most unfortunate moment.

"Carnality, what is he doing?" Tarrant-Arragon raged. He'd heard a groan and suspected the worst.

"He's better," a faint, pain-filled voice whispered. *"I can't begin to tell you."*

"That's my Djinni," Tarrant-Arragon said unnecessarily.

"Didn't you wonder about me?" a voice like Commander Jason's said.

"After I'd been to bed with him, I never gave you another thought—except to practice how I'd ask you to release me from our betrothal contract."

"Cruel brat."

'Rhett didn't seem to appreciate his own peril. He chuckled. Tarrant-Arragon shot him a swift interrogatory glare.

"I don't think J-J expected her to be a scolding, liberated little vixen," 'Rhett explained with a disrespectful grin.

"I'd say she's doing it on purpose so—" Grievous's jaw dropped. "You called him J-J, sir. I thought *you* were—"

Tarrant-Arragon was glad that Grievous took up the mistaken-identity issue. He'd lost enough face without drawing attention to his own embarrassing assumption that Djarrhett Raven Perseus Pendragon Roland Djames was J-J. He held up a hand for silence.

"Quiet," he ordered. "I want to hear what they're saying."

"Even Princess Martia-Djulia has a sweeter disposition."

"Marry her, then! You don't want me, J-J."

"You've turned my little sis into a monster," 'Rhett mourned.

"Your sister?" Tarrant-Arragon glared at him. "Exactly what degree of brother have I acquired in you, 'Rhett: A brother-in-law? Half-brother-in-law? Or a brother-Knight-in-law?"

"Your Highness, I'm her elder half-brother," 'Rhett replied.

"Same sire, different mothers, I presume?" Tarrant-Arragon tapped his lip. "Do you consider yourself the head of her family? Do you have the theoretical right to cede her to me? Should I be politic in what I say to you?" He grinned. "I always wished for a brother. . . ."

"You don't have to flatter me." 'Rhett smiled back. "J-J is the head, but many Saurians would listen to me if I argued in your favor."

"How is J-J head of the family? . . . Ah, yes. He's my father's half-brother's son, isn't he? Djinni told me about that in her sleep. My grandfather gave her grandmother a son." Tarrant-Arragon eyed his half-brother-in-law. "Was it you or J-J who taught her to go for the saturniid?"

"Did she hit you?" 'Rhett's jade eyes lit up with gold sparkles of amusement. "Well, it couldn't have been J-J. He hasn't been near her since she was five. He was too busy infiltrating your An'Koori Star Forces." He examined his hands as if they had suddenly become objects of immense interest.

"I suppose she must have seen me give the twins bloody noses." 'Rhett glanced up challengingly.

"Twins too? In-ter-est-ing," Tarrant-Arragon drawled to let 'Rhett know that his slip—if it had been a slip—hadn't gone unnoticed.

"Twins. My stepbrothers. When Djinni was eleven, she had her first scent-time. They noticed, being full-Djinn. Luckily, she could climb like a cat. After that, we had to be separated."

"I had begun to suspect that there were more of us. I take it my friend Jason is a Great Djinn. He had the slack damn balls to break my sister's heart. And now he thinks he's going to steal my Djinni." He was lashing himself into a rage when he realized that Djinni was asking for trouble.

"I'm not the adoring child-bride of your fantasies. I didn't choose the frilly knickers and short, puff-sleeved frocks I wore when I was a baby, and you still remember me that way!"

"Not bad, Djinni. You're right. I can't see you wearing clouds of see-through white stuff and flowery perfume, waiting for me in bed."

J-J sounded as though he might be casting admiring eyes over Djinni.

"I never thought you'd grow up to be a firebrand and call me an idiot. Nevertheless, I could get used to you, kiddo."

"Damn him!" Tarrant-Arragon swore. "If he touches her . . ."

"If you're responsible for his death, it'll complicate your attempts to make peace, and it'll upset Djinni," 'Rhett warned.

"How practical of you," Tarrant-Arragon sneered. "I have a practical difficulty, too. I can't set a precedent of forgiving people who try to kill me, even if they are relatives. He must know that. We have to assume he's not suicidal. Therefore, we've got a standoff—or, in chess parlance, a Zugzwang. One of us has to do something, but whoever makes the first move risks everything."

"Well, Sirs," Grievous spoke up. "This is quite a conundrum, isn't it? Quite a puzzle." He scratched his unshaven chin noisily, and used the natural pause to assess whether the two Great Djinn were open to a suggestion from the ranks. "Now, I'm a simple man, and I know which side I'm on."

"Do enlighten us, Grievous," Tarrant-Arragon drawled. "I've often wondered."

"Why, hers, Sir," Grievous said without hesitation. "Aren't we all?" He was encouraged to see similar rueful smiles, and decided it was safe to continue. "What does the little miss want, Sirs, although she mightn't've out and out said it?"

"I think we can safely take it, she does not want J-J," 'Rhett answered with a boyish grin at Tarrant-Arragon.

Grievous took the liberty of winking at 'Rhett.

"Quite so, Sir. You might say she prefers the lesser of two evils, or the Greater of two devils. I daresay J-J is a prince too?"

"Greatness doesn't motivate her, Grievous," Tarrant-Arragon growled, and the icy blackness of space in his eyes might chill a man to his bones.

"I stand corrected, Sir. Excuse me, Sirs, if my humble wits go a-begging in the company of two Great Djinn princes."

"Ah, Grievous, it may seem churlish of me to point out—" Tarrant-Arragon began.

"Strictly speaking," 'Rhett broke in, "I'm not a Prince. You see, Grievous, my grandmother the Empress Helispeta couldn't divorce the Emperor Djohn-Kronos, so my father was illegitimate."

"Who knows it, Sir? I'm sure we males don't care about such niceties—especially when they don't give us an advantage over the other side. As we stand, nobody knows who's who. Or who's on whose side. It's enough, I'd think, to confuse an Armada."

Grievous thought a modicum of calculated confusion on his part might clarify matters in the Princes' minds. As a rule of thumb, it was always safer if the Commander-in-Chief was the first to formulate a risky plan.

"So, Sirs, what do we know that they don't? Of course, you, Prince Djarrhett, are a bit of a wild card, because no one outside this suite knows which side you're on. That's one."

He held up one finger and half-raised another.

"From what we've heard on the necklace," 'Rhett obliged, "J-J hasn't revealed his identity to his fellow Saurians."

"That's right, Sir. Which means—?"

"They don't know that he's entitled to call himself Prince Djetthro-Jason," 'Rhett filled in, frowning.

"That brings me to the Royal Saurian Djinn business. A little bird told me a lot of her friends believe quite fanatically in this mythical Saurian savior-figure. Now, is it just a faradiddle, made up by the Saurian Dragon? Do we care?" Grievous asked slyly, nodding at 'Rhett. "It seems to me, Sirs, that the title is up for grabs. My guess is, most of the local undercover Saurians will fall in behind whoever claims it first."

"Grievous, perhaps you'd be good enough to fetch Prince Djarrhett's Saurian sword," Tarrant-Arragon said with a twisted smile. "My Earthling, you're suggesting a daring gamble."

Grievous snapped to attention.

"Daring never fails, Sir. In the British S.A.S. we had a proud motto, Sir, and we lived by it: *Who Dares Wins.*"

Chapter Twenty-four

"Of course you've got to take 'Rhett in." Djinni sat bolt upright on J-J's sleeping couch, shocked that he would hesitate. "You can't ignore an S.O.S. 'Rhett's in trouble. Even if he weren't my brother and your cousin, he's a brother-Knight, and you swore to help any and all White Knights who request aid."

"I don't like it," J-J grumbled. "I don't see how he could have escaped from the Ark Imperial. And you haven't told me what he was doing there in the first place."

"He was arrested at the Wedding Ball for being in disguise. It was probably your fault he was caught. You hit him," Djinni retorted. "Tarrant-Arragon's people thought he was you. Did you get into a fight with him over Princess Martia-Djulia? You did, didn't you? So you owe him. I don't know how he escaped, but I did it myself once."

"I suppose he took advantage of the virus black-over," J-J conceded. "Okay, kiddo. I'll tell Horn't to let 'Rhett aboard."

Horn't swiveled his eyes at the two males who ought to be archenemies, but who stood shoulder to shoulder in his receiving bay, looking like brothers in arms and defenders of an unheard-of armistice. Both exuded confidence. He recognized the ambassador-Knight 'Rhett, and he knew Prince Tarrant-Arragon by sight.

With them was a third male who spoke surveillance-English and who acted as an irreverent herald. "On my right, the Imperial Tiger, Prince Tarrant-Arragon," the herald announced. "On my left, the Royal Saurian Djinn, Prince Djarrhett. Their invincible Highnesses command loyal Saurians and loyal Star Forces warriors alike to surrender Commander Jason and the Princess Consort."

"Prince Djarrhett?" Horn't gaped at the seven-foot-tall White Knight and noticed for the first time his striking physical resemblance to Prince Tarrant-Arragon. "The Royal Saurian Djinn?"

"I can't understand why you think Tarrant-Arragon is remotely lovable." J-J took a long swig directly from his bottle. "It's an obscene idea. You sure he hasn't brainwashed you? Abduction syndrome or some such thing? Your brain must've shrunk from being dominated for too long."

"You're talking utter rot!" Djinni said, glaring at him. "Of course, it doesn't help that you're drunk."

"What a little dragon you've grown up to be!" he said. "Kid, I deplore your taste, but if you insist on loving Tarrant-Arragon, then I warn you, I won't ever try to save you from him again. That's assuming I survive and have another chance."

"Good. Because I didn't ask to be saved, and now you can give me back." It was a brave bluster. Even before he replied, she knew she was being unrealistic.

"Don't be so sure, darling. Matters have gone too far to simply give you back."

The quarrel between the beloved little mate and J-J could be heard by everyone on the secret stairway between the Trojan Horse and "Commander Jason's" state-suite.

"No, I'm not going to surrender. I can't give you up, kiddo. Here's why not. Tarrant-Arragon wouldn't dare come here to fetch you. He'd

fear another trap. And if I send you to him, there's nothing to stop him from destroying my war-star and all my crew."

Tarrant-Arragon turned to see whether the others on the stairs appreciated the joke. 'Rhett raised an eyebrow; Grievous had a hand over his mouth; Horn't's horny mandibles were spread in a broad grin. Tarrant-Arragon drew on everything he'd learned since finding Djinni and winked at Gil, the most nervous and junior of the Saurians.

Gil responded with a Star Forces sign: the two-fingered Lower-Eyelid Pull. Tarrant-Arragon knew the sign had two meanings: either admiration for someone else's cunning, or scorn for someone's ignorance. He assumed Gil intended it as a compliment.

He gave silent thanks to the Great Originator that the Saurian Dragon had conditioned loyal Saurians to obey a "Royal Saurian Djinn." Even Horn't accepted "Prince" Djar-rhett as their savior and liberator.

"You're wrong about him." It sounded as though Djinni was trying a different strategy. *"Why don't you open communications and try to negotiate?"*

"Machismo. Neither of us wants to be heard backing down in a public negotiation."

Tarrant-Arragon caught himself nodding. He knew how J-J felt.

"May I speak with him, then?" Djinni pleaded.

"No. I'm not going to hide behind your skirts, sweetheart."

Time to go in, Tarrant-Arragon decided.

"Damn right you're not, you traitor!" he roared as he kicked open the wardrobe doors and rushed to Djinni's bedside.

The sight of her made his heart thunder with rage. His precious little mate! There were dark circles around her eyes, and her skin was pale. One white-knuckled little fist was clenched; the other was lost in a ball of bandages.

He heard J-J swear and ignored him. Djinni's lovely eyes widened in silver alarm, her lips parted, and out of the corner of his eye he saw movement.

J-J lunged for a mirrored door. There was the scrape of

metal. Tarrant-Arragon drew in his breath sharply as he realized he couldn't use his rings in the confined space and would not use them in front of Djinni. Ever. Which left him unarmed.

'Rhett's steel hissed from its scabbard and clashed on J-J's. Sparks cascaded over all the reflective surfaces in the spartan room as the crossed Saurian swords hung in the air. For a moment long as death, the balance of power rested with 'Rhett.

"You can't fight in here, Sirs. Not with those great long swords," the ever-practical Grievous said, sidling between the swordsmen and Djinni's sickbed, and motioning for Horn't and Gil to follow him. "No, Sirs. There's no room."

"What, J-J, is the point? There's nothing to fight over," 'Rhett panted. Perspiration made slick spikes of his raven-wing hair. His light-worlder's body visibly shook with the effort of forcing the heavier Djinn's sword up and keeping it there.

"What about democracy? Reform. The end of oppression . . . ," J-J demanded, his fierce gaze challenging, and perhaps attempting to be-djinn, the Saurians who had switched sides. "All those things we Saurians are supposed to stand for."

"Stop it, both of you. Stop it, J-J," Djinni cried, white-lipped and struggling to get up. "Damn you, you bloody Djinn!" At which even J-J looked at her.

"You're not to use Djinn-craft when there are innocents in the room. And you're not going to fight Tarrant-Arragon over the right to rule the Empire. You know it's too late to change that." She used both hands to thrust herself off the couch and onto her feet, gave an agonized little gasp, and swayed.

Tarrant-Arragon caught his brave little mate around the waist before she could fall. Across the room, J-J took a half-step toward them. Djinni held up her hurt hand as if to halt him.

"Don't do anything silly, J-J," she scolded, seeming unaware that her hand had started to bleed through her bandages. "Even if you manage to murder my husband, my baby is going to be the next Emperor, not you."

"Enough, little Tigress," Tarrant-Arragon ordered softly. He swept her up in his arms, crosswise so she could brace her injured arm against his chest.

He ignored J-J and spoke over her head. "I want my surgeons to look at her. I'm taking her to the Ark Imperial. You others may follow. Gil, create electronic confusion. I don't want any of our departures to be detected. 'Rhett, I leave you in charge."

"But what about J-J?" Djinni protested. Even as he carried her down the secret stairs, she squirmed in his arms for a last look at the traitor.

"Later, love." Although his heart burned to see her in pain, he shut his mind to what he wanted to do to J-J. "We'll decide later. Not now."

" 'Rhett," Djinni whispered to her dawn visitor while Tarrant-Arragon conferred with Ka'Nych and his colleagues at the Imperial suite's outer door. "Has Tarrant-Arragon said what he's going to do with J-J?"

"Not yet. Right now, his only concern is you, sis," 'Rhett said soothingly. "I gather they operated successfully. How do you feel?"

"Tired." Djinni stretched out in the conversation pit. "It wasn't easy to get a night's sleep with three doctors watching and whispering over me, and my overprotective husband pressing my acupressure points so I wouldn't feel the pain in my hand. But it doesn't hurt now."

"Tarrant-Arragon told me you'll have full use of your hand again, and the baby is doing splendidly." Her brother smiled teasingly. "You certainly have a dramatic way of breaking news to him, don't you?"

She chuckled, "You mean when I said, 'My baby's going to be the next Emperor'? I couldn't see his face when I said that. Did he look surprised? He's pleased, isn't he? I think he'll be a good father, don't you? What do you think of him?"

"Yes. Stunned, actually. Of course. Yes." 'Rhett laughed. "Ambassadors never say what they think, but I'd say he adores you. You've done well. By the way, Djinni, you haven't told

him that our father is the Saurian Dragon, have you? When—
and how—do you intend to tell him?"

"When he makes peace, not before." She noticed that 'Rhett
looked relieved, but was too tired to wonder why. She nodded
across the room at Tarrant-Arragon. "He thinks I'm asking you
for permission to love him."

"Do you need my permission, sis?"

"No." She smiled mischievously. "You approve anyway.
What changed your mind about him?"

'Rhett leaned closer and whispered, "His mother. Or rather,
his kindness to her. A male who is good to his mother is almost
invariably good mate material."

Djinni nodded sleepily. "Good answer. Now tell me what
happened on the An'Koori war-star after Tarrant-Arragon
took me away."

"We decided to stage a dogfight. The traitor 'Commander
Jason' had to die."

"Oh Stars, no! You mean you killed J-J? How could you?"
She struggled to sit up.

'Rhett put his hand on her chest and forced her back down.

"We killed off 'Jason,' dummy, not J-J," 'Rhett answered
with brotherly scorn. "We got rid of the traitor by blowing up
the last of Gil's remote-controlled starfighters. Empty. As far as
the Star Forces are concerned, Jason was killed trying to escape."

"Then where is he really?"

"J-J is large as life and very uncomfortable in my old quarters—which Grievous calls 'the brig.' He's furious with me,
and spoiling for a fight."

"He seems to want to fight everyone." Djinni shook her
head. "You don't think it could have something to do with
Martia-Djulia, do you? He hit you—of all people. He went to
bed with her—"

Suddenly, she had a strong impression that 'Rhett knew
everything she knew about J-J and Martia-Djulia and more.
She looked questioningly at him. He shrugged noncommittally.

"I couldn't say. However, there's going to be a showdown."

★ ★ ★

"You're not going to fight, are you?" Djinni protested as, stiff-legged with aggression, Tarrant-Arragon carried her toward the rolled fighting mats. She looked around for someone to back her up and noticed the ominous players stationed about the Officers' Gymnasium.

J-J was stripped to the waist and looked spectacularly, bare-chestedly male. His star-bronzed skin shimmered with a rich mix of adrenaline and testosterone. Like sunbeams thrusting through summer clouds, his tawny aura was streaked with darker tones. He looked as invincible as the god he thought he was.

'Rhett stood guard, sword drawn, making small Zorro-like slashes in the charged air with every casual flick of his supple sword fighter's wrist.

Grievous was holding two long fighting staves upright, like posts on each side of his body. He looked for all the world like a squire holding the lances at a medieval jousting tournament.

It was first Watch, the Star Forces equivalent of dawn. The Great Djinn were going to fight a duel! Would it be to the death? She frowned again at the long weapons. They looked lethal and crude, but in fact they were simple, elegant instruments, and her husband was very good with them. What if J-J was better?

Djinni glanced at the trophies of deadly arms on the walls, to which her Saurian sword and J-J's had been added.

What if J-J fought dirty and cheated?

"Why must you fight? I don't want you to fight," she whispered, as Tarrant-Arragon deposited her gently on her rolled-mat grandstand.

"Why not?" Tarrant-Arragon said silkily. With slow, deliberate menace he began to remove his robes and drape them over her legs, not so subtly marking his territory.

"It's not fair to blame J-J for what happened," she said in a low voice so the others wouldn't hear. "I don't think he knew what he was doing. I think Martia-Djulia gave him the rut-rage. Don't tell me it's impossible just because you never noticed her that way."

"Hush, my love. Sit quietly, and guard my things," he said, all soft-spoken male chauvinism, then he looked at J-J and raised his voice. "Djetthro-Jason deserves a thrashing, and I think it would re-establish a proper perspective if I gave him one."

A thrashing?

Across the gym J-J's fists clenched and his jaw tightened. His scar lit up like a jag of lightning as he reddened with rage and seemed to grow bigger.

Tarrant-Arragon calmly took off his communicator.

"My life, my Rings, my heart, I trust them all in my Djinni's hands." He took off his Rings, slipped them into her good hand, and folded her fingers into a fist. Then he gestured to the staves that Grievous held. "Choose your weapon, cousin."

"You want to fight with those? They're just sticks," J-J jeered.

"Ah, but they have many of the properties of blade-weapons. They simply hurt more and do less damage, which is perfect for a thrashing," Tarrant-Arragon flashed J-J a very nasty, daggers-drawn smile. "Choose, you!"

J-J twisted his upper lip in an exaggerated sneer, curled his fingers around one of the six-foot-long staves, and suggestively moved his hand slowly up and down the thick shaft.

He was not going to take a thrashing lying down.

"Wait," Djinni interrupted in a fair imitation of Grandmama Helispeta. "Djetthro-Jason, if you insist on fighting, you must remove your contact lenses. They don't serve any purpose now that everyone knows who you are."

J-J removed them. Then to her dismay he swaggered toward her, giving her a full frontal close-up of the bulge in the front of his short, kiltlike underwear. He liked to fight! He thought he was fighting over her. Oh, Stars, he was enjoying himself.

"I trust my eyes, my identity, and my life to her," he said, imitating Tarrant-Arragon, and he dropped the startlingly colored lenses in her lap. Then he sauntered into the center of the room and took up his en garde position.

"Now you're almost unrecognizable as the traitor," Tarrant-Arragon growled. "Well, Djetthro-*Jason*." He stressed the name his treacherous friend had used. "Djinni doesn't want vengeance. I do. You may beg my pardon, and I might spare you for her sake. I may not kill you anyway—if I can think of something worse for you."

"Hah! Don't hold back on my account. I'll do you all the injury I can!" J-J snarled while he gave his long, notched pole an experimental swing. He lunged at Tarrant-Arragon's throat. Tarrant-Arragon leaned slightly to one side, hardly seeming to exert himself. Recovering his balance, J-J thrust forward with his left hand. His right hand leveraged the weapon to swing a wicked upthrust aimed at Tarrant-Arragon's crotch.

Djinni held her breath. Again Tarrant-Arragon evaded the blow. He laughed. "Ah! Only the most vestigial chivalry?"

He stepped back into his en garde stance, holding his staff across his body at a five-past-seven angle, his hands dividing the staff into equal thirds. His left arm was bent at hip level; his right arm was held on a line with his chin. He waited.

Fight if you must, Djinni willed him, not understanding why Tarrant-Arragon seemed to be on the defensive. *You're bigger, in better shape— Win, and get it over.*

Then she began to understand. Tarrant-Arragon fought like he played chess. He was patient. It cost him little effort to block and parry. He took ground gradually and held it. It reminded her of the way he had wooed and won her. As she watched, the memories flooded back.

Oh, yes, J-J. That's good. Posture. Slash. Wear yourself out, she directed her thoughts at J-J. *You fight like you make love. Wham, bam. No finesse.*

Certainly, seventeen years of lifting heavy-worlder women off their feet with the upthrusting force of his . . . lust . . . had given him powerful buttocks to rival Tarrant-Arragon's.

You animals! she thought, blushing because she'd noticed their male display as they wanted her to. Still they fought.

When J-J was off balance, recovering from the momentum of blows that missed, Tarrant-Arragon closed in. Their weapons click-clacked. Tarrant-Arragon locked sticks, then pushed and twisted in a circular motion. He caught J-J's weapon-tip and used his superior wrist power to wrest it from his rival.

End it! Djinni wished.

The staff clattered across the floor. J-J clutched air, and Tarrant-Arragon rapped him across the upper thighs.

"It stings, doesn't it?" Tarrant-Arragon said pleasantly. "If we'd fought with blades, J-J, you would now be gelded."

Knowing Tarrant-Arragon, Djinni had to assume that this blatant inaccuracy was an effective insult, because anyone could see that J-J's stiffly elevated parts weren't near his thighs.

"Which would, ah, grieve my sister." Tarrant-Arragon twirled his fighting stick aside and jerked his head toward J-J's staff. "I haven't finished with you. Get it!"

J-J pounced on it and launched without finesse into the attack, scything his stick in vicious, rhythmic sweeps.

Don't take such risks, my love. What would I do if J-J won? Djinni thought, glancing to the door, where 'Rhett stood guard. 'Rhett was a pragmatist. If J-J killed Tarrant-Arragon, 'Rhett would revert to Plan A. After all, J-J was the legitimate next-in-line. Two Great Djinn could take the Ark Imperial, and having it, they'd control the Empire and her.

On an impulse she slipped her fingers inside Tarrant-Arragon's heavy rings. The Death Ring gave her the right to kill. The Fire Stone gave her the means . . . at least to bluff long enough to stop them from murdering each other.

As if he too had made a decision, Tarrant-Arragon suddenly powered an underarm lunge, battering-ram-style, like throwing a punch. It caught J-J in the solar plexus, winding and crumpling him to the ground.

It's over! Djinni sighed deeply. *Surely you've made your point, Tarrant-Arragon.*

Still, he circled, prodding J-J. "Beg for mercy," he taunted. "I've thought of the worst doom in all the Communicating Worlds. You'll wish you were dead. You'll curse the day you crossed me."

Swift as a snake strike, J-J snatched up his weapon and swung it in a low arc of bone-shattering velocity, but Tarrant-

Arragon jumped over it with a laughed, "Hard damn, you're predictable!"

J-J rose, charged, and feinted to one side with his staff. He aimed a kick at Tarrant-Arragon's head. Tarrant-Arragon side-stepped. J-J recovered and threw a second kick, which seemed to take Tarrant-Arragon by surprise and to land hard on Tarrant-Arragon's powerful right biceps.

Tarrant-Arragon dropped his staff. His arm seemed paralyzed. J-J pressed his advantage. He rushed, his stick leveled like a lance.

"No!" Djinni screamed.

Tarrant-Arragon caught the oncoming weapon with his left hand, wrenching it high and off to the side. Simultaneously, he fisted his right hand, which moments before had seemed useless, and brought a devastating uppercut onto J-J's unprotected jaw.

J-J dropped heavily to the floor and stayed there.

"Please stop now," Djinni cried. "Please, have mercy."

Tarrant-Arragon looked toward her. His nostrils flared, his chest rose as he took a deep breath. Then he sauntered over to her and smiled triumphantly.

"You want him reprieved, my love? Very well." Nonchalantly, he snapped on his forearm communicator and requested the presence of surgeons. He patted her thigh and touched the contact lenses.

He narrowed his eyes for an instant, took them between his thumb and forefinger, and crushed them to powder. He raised an eyebrow, dusted off his hands, and turned to J-J.

"Now for the fate worse than death. Djetthro-Jason, my sister thinks she needs a mate. A big one. I think you might satisfy her. So I'm going to give you to Martia-Djulia on, ah, a trial basis. If you please her, she can have you for her mate. Perhaps you can keep each other out of my way in future."

"But I . . . ," J-J blurted out.

"Understand this, Djetthro-Jason, I am not interested in your objections. You have been checked by force, and you will be mated—by force if necessary. Take him away, 'Rhett."

Tarrant-Arragon turned his back. Only Djinni saw him smile.

"He doesn't know?" Djetthro-Jason whispered incredulously. "He has no idea that I want to marry his sister, has he? He thinks he's got me, but as far as I'm concerned, marrying Martia-Djulia isn't a punishment at all."

"How could he know?" 'Rhett put an arm around his shoulder to help him away. Sometimes, when 'Rhett spoke with exaggerated sweetness, he sounded just like his father. As with the Saurian Dragon, it made Djetthro-Jason wonder whether he'd been conned.

He turned to stare suspiciously at the Imperial couple, as if Tarrant-Arragon's broad back might give him an answer.

"If I were you, coz, I wouldn't question your luck," 'Rhett croaked. "Act like the rabbit in Djinni's stories—the one who begged the fox not to throw him into the briar patch. Make sure you complain a lot. But not now, okay? Don't talk. For one thing, your jaw may be broken, and your slurred speech makes you sound revoltingly drunk."

Djetthro-Jason fingered his damaged jaw in resentful silence.

"For another, you are now Prince Djetthro-Jason. You have to pretend you've never met Martia-Djulia. She must never find out that you were once Commander Jason. So if there are any distinguishing marks on your body that she might recognize, you'd better let the cosmetic surgeons take care of them at the same time as they remove your facial scar."

"What the Carnality . . . ?" Djetthro-Jason growled, then remembered where, when, and under what circumstances he'd flattened 'Rhett, and how he'd all but announced what he was going to do to Martia-Djulia. Obviously, 'Rhett knew. He changed tack.

"Listen to you. You sound like an equerry. And look at them!" Djetthro-Jason mumbled disgustedly, tossing his head at Tarrant-Arragon and Djinni. "He's stolen Djinni's heart, he's secured the succession, he's even turned you to his side."

"It seems to me it might be he who's been converted. Give

Djinni credit for a bloodless coup," 'Rhett pointed out with a politician's chuckle. "Who cares if it's really my little sister who fulfills our father's prophecy about a Royal Saurian Djinn? The aim was that the next Emperor would be enlightened and reforming. Would it be a disaster if the description fits Tarrant-Arragon?"

Djinni felt her heart begin to thud as Tarrant-Arragon folded his long limbs until his eyes were level with hers as she sat. Crouching at her feet was as close as the Great Tiger came to going down on one knee. He rested his forearm across her thighs.

He seemed fascinated by her left hand, took it, and uncurled her fingers. First he played with the Fire Stone, sliding it up and down her forefinger in erotic body mimicry that made her catch her breath.

"Do you trust me, beloved?" His voice was hoarse.

He repossessed his Ring, put it on, retook her hand, and gently nibbled her bare finger. His smoky gaze held hers.

"I am beginning to entrust myself to your care . . . ," she replied, telling the truth but not the whole truth. Of course, he wasn't entirely trustworthy, and probably never would be.

However, he had lived down his appalling reputation. He had shown mercy to a rival, and he was keeping his promise to make peace. It was her turn to honor a bargain.

"I can honestly say that I trust myself with you."

"That's good, my Tigress," he purred. He seemed satisfied with her answer, and his caress slid to the finger that guarded his Gravity Ring. "Little love of my life, do you think you might be ready to admit that you love me?"

"Oh, dear. Yes, Tigger, I'm afraid I do. I love you."

"Good girl!" he breathed, and closed his eyes briefly, whether with relief, or bliss, or to hide an inappropriate flare of triumph, Djinni didn't know. "Such a grudging admission, my dear," he teased, rough voiced. "Like sex, it gets easier after the first time. And like lovemaking, I shall require and demand I-Love-Yous several times a day from now on."

The signet Death Ring hung on her curled little finger. He tried it for size on each of her fingers before pressing it as far as it would go on the third finger of her left hand.

"Do you know why I punished him the way I did?" His expression was full of yearning to be understood—and loved.

"How else could face be saved?" Djinni replied softly, but she let her smile undermine the pragmatism of her words.

"If I had done things differently with you, right from the start, my beloved, do you think there's a chance that you would have chosen to marry me?"

Djinni took his anxious face between her palms and nuzzled his forehead with hers. She was silent for a moment, while she considered how to answer such an impossible question honestly.

Then her lips spoke caresses into his ears. In full knowledge of the irrevocable meanings, she repeated the words of the Imperial Wedding Ceremony—words that he had taught her were a love poem. Which, of course, is exactly what they were.